**Adam joined her in the kitchen a few minutes later. She was preparing a salad on the counter next to the farmhouse sink. She was going to make grilled chicken breasts and spicy brown rice, too.**

Adam came up and hugged her from behind. "Thank you for keeping all my stuff," he said next to her ear.

His body's warmth and the tender tone of his voice made her all gooey inside. She also appreciated his kind words. She'd been so anxious about how he would react to a new space. The apartment they had been living in before he left had been his own. It was hard giving up something you were used to, even if you logically knew you couldn't hold on to it. Adam probably knew that she couldn't continue to live in his apartment with him missing. But she couldn't guess what a visceral reaction he would have to the reality of his place being gone.

She put down the lettuce she'd been tearing into chunks, and in the circle of his embrace, she turned and faced him. Looking into his eyes, she said, "There were some decisions I had to make without you. But I made them all with you in mind."

**Janice Sims** is the author of over forty titles ranging from romance to romantic suspense to speculative fiction. She won two Romance in Color awards: an Award of Excellence for her novel *For Keeps* and the Novella of the Year Award for her short story *The Keys to My Heart*. She won an Emma Award for Favorite Heroine for her novel *Desert Heat*. She has been nominated for a Career Achievement Award twice by *RT Book Reviews*. Her novel *Temptation's Song* was nominated for Best Kimani Romance Series in 2010. Her novel *Safe in My Arms*, the second novel in the Gaines Sisters series, won the 2014 RT Reviewers' Choice Award for Kimani Romance. She was the 2016 recipient of the Francis Ray Lifetime Literary Award from B.R.A.B., Building Relationships Around Books. She lives in Central Florida with her family.

### Books by Janice Sims

### Harlequin Kimani Romance

*A Little Holiday Temptation*
*Escape with Me*
*This Winter Night*
*Safe in My Arms*
*Thief of My Heart*
*Unconditionally*
*Cherish My Heart*
*His Christmas Gift*

Visit the Author Profile page
at Harlequin.com for more titles.

# JANICE SIMS
## and
# PAMELA YAYE

*His Christmas Gift &*
*Decadent Holiday Pleasures*

**HARLEQUIN**® KIMANI™ ROMANCE

ISBN-13: 978-1-335-47097-3

His Christmas Gift & Decadent Holiday Pleasures

Copyright © 2019 by Harlequin Books S.A.

His Christmas Gift
Copyright © 2019 by Janice Sims

Decadent Holiday Pleasures
Copyright © 2019 by Pamela Sadadi

Recycling programs for this product may not exist in your area.

Printed in U.S.A.

www.Harlequin.com

# CONTENTS

Writers get their inspiration
from all kinds of places. This book is dedicated
to my dear, sweet mother, Lillie Jean, and her
mother, my feisty grandma Ester Jean, both of whom
reminded me of Adam's mother in this book,
Ramona Kingsley-Braithwaite, who was fiercely
protective of her family and one of the most honest,
funny characters I've ever put in a book.

## Acknowledgments

Thanks to senior executive editor Glenda Howard,
line editor Rachel Burkot and the rest of the staff
at Harlequin who make sure the book you're reading
is an enjoyable experience for you. Also, I have to
thank my husband, Curt, for his support.
I couldn't do this without him.

# HIS CHRISTMAS GIFT

Janice Sims

Dear Reader,

When I dreamed up the idea of newlyweds Adam, physicist, and Alia, marketing manager, being separated because he'd been kidnapped while working on a government project in the Middle East, I had no idea what a challenge writing such a story would be. But that's how it is when I write a book. I'll come up with the idea and let the story unfold. I had my research cut out for me, and a lot of late nights ahead of me, and ended up with a twisty, suspenseful, humorous and passionate story.

I enjoyed every minute of writing Adam and Alia's story. I hope you enjoy reading it. Let me, and other readers, know how you felt about their story by posting your feelings online. My next book will be about Alia's brother, Brock, and his lady love, Macy Harris. Look up my page on Facebook for updates and feel free to email me at Jani569432@aol.com, or, if you're not online, write to PO Box 811, Mascotte, Florida, 34753.

Blessings,

*Janice Sims*

# Chapter 1

October in New York City. The day was cold, gray and blustery, but in her Harlem loft, Alia Joie Youngblood-Braithwaite was warm and toasty. She lit a candle at the makeshift shrine to her husband, Adam, on the fireplace's mantel. She hadn't thought of it as a shrine in the beginning, only as a way to sort out her feelings about Adam's kidnapping over two years ago. At that time, it had been a photo of him in a frame. A photo she'd talk to and sometimes scream at when her emotions got out of control. Now there were several framed photos of her and Adam at various stages of their relationship, fresh flowers and candles in decorative candleholders. The longer Adam was gone, the more it felt like a permanent shrine to his memory.

Lots of things had changed after Adam had gone

missing. She'd moved out of their old apartment and purchased the building she was living in now. She'd had it fully renovated, taken the top floor for herself and rented the other apartments on the remaining four floors, to artists mostly. There was an elderly couple on the fourth floor who were not in the artistic community but had needed an affordable, safe place to live in the neighborhood. Alia was able to provide that place because she was fortunate enough to come from an independently wealthy family. Her family owned Youngblood Media, a company with interests in television, publishing and the internet. Alia was the company's marketing director. These days she worked her own hours, many of them away from the office, and devoted a large amount of time to her artistic endeavors. She was a talented painter and was working on a series of paintings that were scheduled to be shown at a Manhattan art gallery a month from now.

Tonight her girlfriends were taking her out to celebrate her birthday, which had been a few days ago. Before she left to meet them, she wanted to get in one more therapy session with Adam's shrine.

Alia was a tall, attractive woman with warm dark-chocolate skin and golden-brown eyes. She wore jeans that fit her shapely body as if they'd been designed specifically for her and a red cashmere square-necked sweater. On her feet were black leather boots. Her natural dark brown hair was in glossy braids that fell to the middle of her back.

She paced the hardwood floor as she poured her heart out to Adam's photo. "Two years! You said you'd be back before I missed you! But where are you? Still missing! I know I shouldn't be angry at you, but I am. I'm angry because you're too trusting. You're a big man with a big heart, and it never occurred to you to say no when the military came calling. Maybe you were flattered that they knew about your research, which was supposedly being kept secret. Did it ever occur to you that if the government wants to find out something, they have ways of finding it out? I'm so mad, I don't know what to do!

"Now here I am, alone, getting ready to reveal my heart, my soul, to the world in the form of my paintings, and you're not here to share it with me. I don't care if I sound selfish to the universe. You should be here holding my hand. Holding me!"

And with that, she burst into tears, grabbed one of Adam's photos off the mantel and hugged it to her chest. Taking a deep breath, she held the frame away from her and peered at his face. When the photo had been taken, he'd had a full beard, dreadlocks down to his waist and a devastatingly beautiful smile. His milk-chocolate-brown eyes sparkled. He had a square-jawed face underneath that full beard. His skin was reddish brown with golden undertones. An island boy from the Bahamas, he loved the sun, and his skin tone changed from season to season. She could almost hear his voice, a mix of standard English with a proper British accent, to Bahamian English when he lapsed into the way he had spoken when he was growing up in Nassau. He was a big man, at six foot four, and through hard work had built up muscles that rivaled professional athletes' toned bodies.

But it was his vibrancy that had won her heart. He

had a zest for living that spoke to her soul. Just being around him made her feel more alive.

Did she miss him? With all her heart!

Alia put Adam's photo back on the mantel and sighed sadly. That was enough wallowing in misery for one day. The fact was, she didn't know whether her husband was dead or alive. She'd paid a detective to try to find him, with no results except for the warning from the government to stay out of it. The official rationale was that the people who were holding Adam might do something drastic and violent if they found out civilians were trying to stick their noses in their business. The government assured her they were in negotiations with Adam's captors. They would eventually get him set free. She had to be patient. What was more, she and her family had to make sure nothing about Adam's situation was leaked to the media.

In other words, for over two years, Alia had been helpless to do anything to alleviate her husband's suffering. And she knew he had to be suffering. Knowing Adam, he was doing everything in his power to get back home to her. Her rants in front of his shrine were not an indication that she had lost faith in him. They were simply a way to get her frustrations out. She loved him, and would always love him.

Sylvia's, the soul food restaurant that was a Harlem landmark, was alive with the sound of its patrons enjoying themselves: silverware on fine china, glasses clinking, voices buzzing like bees and tinkling laughter. Alia looked around the table at the lit-up faces of her dearest girlfriends: Macy Harris, her best friend, a security company owner; Diana Winters, a lawyer; and June Stratton, a surgeon. She'd known Macy since childhood and Diana and June since college.

June, a redhead with light green eyes, raised her glass of white wine. "To Alia," she said brightly. "Thirty-three today, but you look twenty-three. I don't know how you do it, girl. But keep doing what you're doing because it's working for you!"

The other women raised their glasses and laughed. Macy, a petite beauty with caramel-colored skin and dark brown eyes, clinked her glass's rim with Alia's. "Unless, of course, you've made a Dorian Gray–type pact with the devil and have a portrait of yourself in an attic somewhere that's aging while you stay young. In which case, I say, repent at once so that your soul won't burn in hell!"

"Ignore the preacher's daughter," Diana advised Alia. She turned sober eyes on Alia. "Seriously, though, how are you holding up? No news about Adam?"

Alia took a deep breath. She'd been wondering when the subject of Adam's absence would come up. Her friends were well-meaning, but she'd grown tired of discussing it. All they knew was that he'd gone missing two years ago. A sad occurrence, but one that happened to many people every year. Her friends weren't privy to what was really going on. Only her family was aware Adam and his colleagues had been kidnapped.

"Nothing at all," she said softly, eyes downcast because she didn't want her friends to see she was fighting back tears. Macy, who was sitting beside her, reached over and gently squeezed her hand. Emotions under control, Alia smiled and glanced up at her friends, who were looking at her with sympathetic expressions in their eyes.

"I'd much rather talk about your upcoming wedding, June," she said.

June grinned. "Two doctors getting married is a logistics nightmare. We can't decide when to get married, where to get married. Our schedules are booked up. I suggested we just elope and forget about an elaborate wedding. Maybe go to the courthouse and get it over with. But my guy says his Italian mother would kill him, literally!" She laughed. "I've met her. I don't think he's exaggerating." Everyone laughed at that.

"It's the marriage that counts, not the party," Macy said. "You and Tony love each other and have for a long time. Do what you two want to do and don't worry about anyone else."

"I don't agree," Diana said. "You only get married once, hopefully, and it should be celebrated. Memories should be made. I don't mean go broke getting married, but have a party for friends and family. They should be there on your special day."

"I didn't know you were so sentimental," Macy countered. "You treat men like playthings. You haven't been in a committed relationship in years."

Diana rolled her eyes. "That doesn't mean I don't eventually want to get married and have children. It means I'm still not finished having fun."

"The trouble with people who think like you do is when you get married, you look at it as something boring. You're having fun now. What will you have when you have a husband? Will he satisfy the fun girl in

you? Or will you lose interest in a matter of months?"
Macy asked.

Diana frowned at Macy, and Alia wondered if this
was going to turn into another slugfest between the two
of them. Diana was very opinionated and liked thinking of herself as a truly liberated woman who behaved
like a man when it came to relationships. That is, she
juggled men, used them and tossed them aside when
she'd had enough of them. Macy, a preacher's daughter, believed love was sacred and hearts were not to be
played with.

"Girls…" June, who acted as mediator when Macy
and Diana got into arguments, cautioned. "We're here
to celebrate Alia's birthday, remember? Not to discuss
the merits of breaking or not breaking men's hearts."

"Your problem," Diana said to Macy, ignoring June,
"is you're still looking for Prince Charming, that perfect man who was born only for you. Listen up—he
doesn't exist. He's a fictionalized character created by
greeting card companies, rom-com movie producers
and romance writers to satisfy their customers. You've
never fallen in love or lust with anyone!"

Alia was well aware that Diana's assertion that Macy
had never been in love was untrue. Macy was in love
with Alia's brother, Brock. But that was a secret she'd
shared only with Adam, and he wasn't going to tell
anyone.

Macy only smiled. Alia hoped that smile meant
Macy's temper was held securely in check, because
Macy could be dangerous when provoked. She owned
a security firm for a reason. A third degree black belt
in karate, she'd joined the Marines right out of high

school and earned the rank of gunnery sergeant by the time she was twenty-five. She'd served in Iraq and Afghanistan. She could probably kill Diana with her little finger. Diana knew all of this, yet she seemed to get a kick out of sparring with Macy. Alia didn't believe Macy was a killer. But still...

"Girl, you were born to be a lawyer. That tongue of yours can be vicious when you want it to be, and your heart as cold as ice," Macy said. "But I know you're hurting and that's why you lash out at people who love you. And I do love you, even though you like to draw my blood at every opportunity." She continued to look Diana in the eyes, her smile never wavering.

Diana sighed heavily. "Your daddy did a number on your brain. You actually do turn the other cheek."

"I'm no saint," Macy said. "I'll probably beat the hell out of my sparring partner at the gym tomorrow. But just so you know, Diana, I'm the one who controls how violent I get. So don't think you're going to provoke me into whipping your behind, because it's not going to happen."

Alia was amazed by the look of relief on Diana's face. Was that what Diana was trying to do? Goad Macy into physically attacking her? That made her wonder just how psychologically damaged Diana was inside. Who had hurt her? Diana had never spoken about it. She had said she became a lawyer because she wanted to help abused women. Could she have been an abused woman in the past?

"Are we done?" Alia asked hopefully. "No more hurting each other with cutting words." She saw their waiter across the room and called for him. "We'd like to order dessert!"

Her friends started to protest, but she insisted. "You'll just have to work out a bit more tomorrow," she said. "But you've stressed me out so much that I need dessert tonight. So shut up and order something decadent."

Her friends' protests promptly ended when they saw the array of goodies on the dessert tray as the waiter wheeled the cart next to their table.

After the waiter had served them and left, they dug in.

"A bit more running won't kill me," Macy said as she spooned a piece of strawberry cheesecake into her mouth.

"I'm sure Tony will be happy to help me work off the extra calories," said June teasingly, a naughty expression in her eyes as she tasted a piece of pecan pie.

"I'm not going to pretend," Diana said as she tucked into her apple pie. "I'm just going to enjoy this and not care about the extra calories. Do you think men care if they enjoy a huge piece of pie after dinner? They don't give it a second thought. We've got to chill out, ladies."

Alia smiled as she enjoyed her red velvet cake. It had been a wonderful birthday dinner. She could always count on her girlfriends to entertain, enlighten and generally keep it real.

Because of their friendship, it would be a little easier facing another lonely night without Adam.

"Ninety-eight, ninety-nine…one hundred!" Adam Braithwaite breathed as he finished doing his push-ups. He got to his feet and walked slowly around the eight-by-eight-foot room he'd been kept in since they'd brought him to this facility. He wasn't exactly sure of his location, but he guessed it was somewhere in Abu Dhabi, the capital of the United Arab Emirates. After his capture—however long ago that had been—the van he'd been tossed inside of hadn't driven far enough to leave the country, in his estimation. Before his capture, he and his colleagues had been living in Dubai, the UAE's biggest city, working on a government project.

As he walked in a circle in his room, his heartbeat returning to normal after his exertions, he wondered what day it was. His captors hadn't provided him with a calendar, or anything to keep track of time passing. They had taken his watch, which he wouldn't have cared about, except that it had been given to him by his wife, Alia Joie. They'd also, of course, taken his cell phone.

When he and his team were taken from the lab they'd been working in, those among them who had resisted, including himself, had been roughed up, but since that day they had not been physically abused as far as he knew. He saw his colleagues about once a week when their captors allowed them to have a meal together in a communal dining room in the facility, and he hadn't noticed any bruises on them. While they ate, they were free to converse. All of his team were still in relatively good health when he saw them: Arjun Sharma, a particle physicist, Calvin Hobbes, a quantum physicist, and Maritza Aguilar, a theoretical physicist like himself.

They had all lost some weight, which he attributed to the fact that their captors were not giving them enough to eat to maintain their body weights. Adam had been told by his primary inquisitor that if he began talking, they would increase his rations. Once or twice, Adam had been tempted, but was too obstinate to comply. He was glad to note his colleagues were, as well. When they'd first been allowed to eat together once a week, Adam was afraid that each time he walked into the communal dining area, he would find a colleague missing until the number dwindled down to just him. Their captors hadn't threatened them with death if they didn't cooperate, but Adam still feared violence. However, that hadn't happened yet, for which he was grateful.

Adam had no idea how long he'd been held prisoner at the facility. After some time, he'd begun to make scratches each day on the wall next to his bed, but he knew the amount of scratches didn't come close to the actual number of days he'd been here. He counted 563 scratches on the wall. That amounted to a little over a year and a half. To him, the time away from Alia Joie felt like it had been much longer.

Keeping Alia Joie foremost in his mind was what gave him the strength to keep going. Being held against his will was eating away at his sanity. The silence was sometimes unbearable. He was a big, happy, gregarious guy who relished life. No four walls could contain his spirit. Yet he had been bound by four walls for what felt like forever. His captors might not physically abuse him, but they certainly were mentally abusing him. What's more, he wasn't allowed to read or have paper and pen to write down his thoughts or mathematical equations, which he had a habit of doing for relaxation. There was no relaxation in here.

The doorknob jiggled and he knew someone was about to enter his room. He'd observed the face of every man who brought him his meals. Four different men were apparently assigned to his care and feeding. They brought him meals, changes of clothing, soap, towels, toothpaste and toothbrushes when the need arose, and about three times a week they escorted him to the office of his inquisitor, who questioned him about the work he and his colleagues were doing for the US military.

The man entering his room today had a familiar face. Adam didn't know his name. He didn't know any of their names. He'd named this particular man simply Number Three. Number Three was an Arab of average weight and height wearing a green military uniform and black combat boots. He had wavy black hair and a mustache and beard. Adam noticed beards were common, as all four of the men he saw on a regular basis wore them. He had his own full black beard now, while he used to have dreadlocks down his back. He'd held out as long as he could, but had recently asked to have his locks cut off because he was unable to wash his hair often enough and didn't have access to the essential oils required to keep his hair healthy. Now he was bald headed with a full beard and mustache.

At six foot four, he towered over the Arab. The man peered up at him, and Adam waited with interest for what would come out of his mouth. He was so bored in here that the variety of options intrigued him. Would he go see his inquisitor or go see his colleagues? It was obvious the man hadn't come to bring him a meal because there was no tray in his hands.

In halting English, the man said, "You will have a meal in the dining room. Follow me."

"I'll put on my boots," Adam said, and went and sat down on the bed while he did that.

Adam was dressed in his usual attire of a khaki shirt and slacks—no belt—and black combat boots. Whoever ran the facility had a very basic dress code. Except for Maritza, who had been supplied with apparel appropriate for an Arab female, all of his colleagues wore the same thing.

In the dining room, Adam was relieved to see that the whole gang was there. The air was redolent with the heavy spices cooks in that part of the world used when they prepared meals using a combination of vegetables and meats like lamb, beef, chicken and sometimes camel. Adam hoped it wasn't camel today. There was never any pork because Dubai was a Muslim area.

Maritza, a petite brown-skinned woman with coal-black hair and soft brown eyes, smiled when she saw him coming. Adam thought that of all of them, this time had been the hardest to endure for her. Maritza was the mother of a small child. Her husband, Raul, was taking care of little Mariana while she was here. The rest of the team didn't have children. But all of them had loved ones who were missing them as much as they missed them.

He sat down at the table, and for the next few minutes they clasped hands tightly. Adam remembered that before they had been kidnapped, they had rarely been demonstrative with each other. They were scientists, after all. They were friends, too, but their caring was expressed by doing good work together. Now, though, they were not embarrassed to hug or clasp each other's hands with affection. They were survivors, and it did their hearts good to see that they were all still here from one week to another.

"You look good with a bald head," Maritza told him, smiling.

"He looks like a genie," Calvin joked. Calvin was British, with pale skin and gray eyes. He vaguely reminded Adam of British actor Colin Firth, but younger and fitter. Calvin was a devoted runner.

"Leave him alone. He looks like Will Smith in *Suicide Squad*," Arjun, an Indian American with warm brown skin and deep-set brown eyes, chimed in. Arjun was the youngest among them at twenty-five. He'd been a math prodigy before turning his focus on physics. Adam believed he was also the smartest among them, although Arjun was too kind and modest a fellow to own up to it.

Adam chuckled. "I'm happy to see you all are well, too," he said in his British Bahamian accent. He dug into the meat stew on his plate. It was sitting on a pile of white rice, and there was a bottle of water beside it. After chewing and swallowing, he said, "My guess is lamb."

They played a game of "guess the mystery meat" every time they were together. Maritza smiled. "My family kills a goat every year and Mama makes a stew out of it that tastes just like this. I'm going with goat."

"Don't be ridiculous," Calvin said. "This is camel. I saw some hair in mine. I'm positive it was camel's hair."

"You're going to make me gag," said Arjun. "My

money's on beef. Which I really shouldn't be eating, anyway. It's a good thing I have no appetite."

They laughed. Adam said, "You win."

After their laughter had died down, they started speculating, as they usually did, on when and how they were going to be rescued. Being in enemy territory, though, they kept these conversations low-key and at a soft volume.

"I had a dream last night," Maritza told them in a whisper, her brown eyes animated. "We're going to be rescued soon, and the military is going to do it in the middle of the night with commandos everywhere! It's going to be like an action movie on steroids."

"I hope it's soon," Calvin said in equally low tones. "I know Beverly is probably dating someone else by now. She doesn't strike me as someone who'll wait until the end of time like Alia." He tossed a meaningful glance in Adam's direction.

Adam's heartbeat quickened at the mention of Alia Joie. He missed her so much it was a physical ache in his heart. What was she doing right now? He knew there was an eight-hour time difference between here and New York City. When it was midnight in NYC, it was eight in the morning here. When she was going to bed, he was rising. He supposed it was only fitting that they were living opposite lives now. But when he got home, everything would be in sync again. What they had was meant to last forever. He fervently believed she would never give up on him. Somewhere, she was out there thinking of him and praying for his return, as he was here, praying to be returned to her.

# *Chapter 2*

In her studio in the loft, Alia signed her name on the last painting in her *Women of Strength* series and stood back to give the painting another once-over with the critical eye of an art lover. Or so she hoped. She'd like to be able to let go of her ego long enough to judge her work honestly.

She loved ballet, and had taken lessons until she was fourteen, when her instructor advised her that due to her height and curvy build, ballet wasn't a suitable career for her. Therefore, she had chosen Sierra Leonean American ballerina Michaela DePrince as the subject of her final painting in the twenty-one-painting series about strong, inspirational women from myriad walks of life such as Harriet Tubman, Toni Morrison, Aretha Franklin and Ruth Bader Ginsburg. She'd painted Michaela, midleap, in a beautiful pale pink tutu. To Alia, Ms. DePrince was the personification of grace under pressure. Her life had not been easy, yet she made all of her performances look effortless.

Her cell phone rang and she grabbed it off a table next to one of the floor-to-ceiling windows in the studio. Bright November sunshine illuminated the sizable area on the eastern side of her loft. Glancing at the display on the cell phone, she said, "Hi, Mom. How're you and Dad?"

Debra Youngblood laughed softly. "I was calling to see how *you're* doing. Two days before the showing. Are you nervous?"

Alia thought for a moment. "No, I'm not nervous, exactly. I'm in more of a state of expectation than nervousness. I feel like something monumental is going to happen soon, but I don't know why. Maybe I'm an eternal optimist, even though it feels like the universe is conspiring to turn me into a pessimist.

"And lately, I'm having conversations with God in my head, wondering why he's allowing my life to go this way. I'm wondering if I'm the new Job and he's putting me through trials to toughen me up for something even worse than what I'm already going through. Then again, I sometimes feel guilty for complaining about my life. I'm not sick with an incurable disease or anything. I'm not poor and destitute. The only thing wrong with my life is my husband is missing and I don't know whether I'll ever see him again. I should be grateful for all I have."

Debra laughed. "Nah, honey, you have a legitimate reason to feel put-upon. Come on, you lost the only man you ever loved! God can take your complaints. He's strong that way. If it makes you feel better, keep talking to him.

"On a more practical note," her mother continued, "what are you doing for dinner tonight? Your father is making his special chili and I'm baking those cinnamon rolls you like to go with it."

Alia smiled, remembering the mouthwatering aromas that filled the house when her parents made spicy chili and homemade cinnamon rolls. The treats had really hit the spot during the winter months.

"We invited your brothers and Petra, too," Debra said. "Seven o'clock good for you?"

"I'll be there," Alia said. "Wait, is Brock bringing anyone? I may not be in the right frame of mind to meet one of his ladies."

Her mother laughed. "No. Brock is being very secretive about whom he's dating. When I asked if he was bringing anyone, he said, 'I'm not ready to introduce her to you all just yet.'"

"This is getting interesting," Alia said. "He's rarely without female companionship. He's never been secretive before, though."

"Personally, I'm glad he's slowing down. It's time for him to stop fooling around and choose someone who will be his match in every way. There are a lot of good women out there who can keep him on the straight and narrow," Debra said.

Alia didn't say it, but she knew her friend Macy would gladly take the job. Macy, with her strength and generous heart, would be good for Brock. But Alia wouldn't wish Brock, with his current behavior of loving and leaving them, on anyone.

"Chance found love," she said, instead. "There's hope for Brock."

"There's always hope," her mother agreed, sounding optimistic. "See you later, sweetheart."

"Bye, Mom," Alia said, smiling.

After she hung up, she went back to considering the Michaela DePrince painting, observing it from all angles, squinting, her nose wrinkling as a sign of displeasure. It was no use. She wasn't a good judge of her work. She always felt she could have done a better job, never satisfied. She supposed it was best not to rest on one's laurels but to always be trying to improve.

Adam was startled from a sound sleep when he felt a hand cover his mouth. Sitting up in bed, he elbowed his assailant in the jaw as hard as he could. "What the hell…" a man cried indignantly, and grabbed him, pinning his arms at his sides. "Steady, Dr. Braithwaite, I'm here to get you out of this place."

When Adam had calmed down, the man who'd awakened him briefly shone the beam of a flashlight in his own face, showing Adam the visage of Number Three. "I'm American," he said, his Arabian accent totally gone. "Took us a while to infiltrate this group, but tonight's the night we move. Come with me."

Adam didn't have to be told twice. He quickly pulled on clothes and shoes. After he was dressed, the two of them stealthily traversed the dimly lit corridor— it looked to Adam like the facility's emergency lights were on—until they came to a door several doors down from Adam's room. Number Three opened the door and told Adam, "You were the last one. You'll find your friends in there. I want you all to remain here, no matter what happens. I'll come back for you. Understood?"

"What if you don't return?" Adam asked softly. He was peering into the darkened room and could make out three figures huddled together, but not much else.

"Good point," said Number Three. "If I don't come back, then you'll know we failed. But at least you'll know we tried." He had the grim-faced expression of a soldier determined to carry out his mission. He grinned suddenly. "Either way, you'll have a story to tell. Lock the door behind me." Then he was gone.

Adam walked farther into the room and was immediately hugged by Maritza. "Thank God, they got you," she breathed.

Adam could feel her body trembling. "Yeah, me, too," he said as he held her. "Arjun, Calvin, you two all right?"

"Still accounted for," Calvin said.

"Here, but not enjoying this one bit," Arjun said. "I hate the dark."

"They obviously cut the power to the building to disorientate the enemy," Adam said.

"Well, it's definitely disorientating me," Calvin said. "And I never used to be afraid of the dark."

A moment later, they heard gunfire in the distance. "Maybe we ought to get on the floor," Adam suggested. "Just in case bullets start flying."

"Yeah," said Maritza. "Good idea."

They lay down beside one another. Adam's night vision was improving somewhat. He could now make out the shapes of the furnishings in the room, which was apparently used as an office. It had a wide desk, some filing cabinets along the wall and a couple of armless chairs in front of the desk. The floor they were lying on felt like it was made of stone.

"When you got into physics, did you ever think you'd be in a Middle Eastern country with the US military trying to rescue you from terrorists?" Calvin asked.

"When I got into physics," Arjun said, "I never thought I'd get a girlfriend, let alone be involved in something this crazy!"

The others laughed nervously.

"May I suggest we hold hands and pray?" Maritza, who was a devout Catholic in spite of being a scientist, said. They did as she suggested and she started them off with a prayer. "Dear God, thank you for bringing us this far in our captivity. Now, if you'd be so generous as to get us all the way back home, we'd really appreciate it. I promise to go to church more often and stop sleeping in on Sunday mornings."

"You know I don't share your religious beliefs..." Arjun said.

Suddenly another hail of gunfire could be heard in the distance, the sound lasting longer than the former volley of bullets.

"However," Arjun continued, after the gunfire had subsided, "I'm willing to believe in your God tonight if he'll get us out of this."

"There's only one God," Adam said. "We just call Him or Her by different names. So, call on whomever you wish."

"I'm an atheist," Calvin said. "I believe we choose

our own destiny. I'm choosing to come out of this alive. I'm willing it with all my might."

"Good," Arjun said. "Then we agree that we're all scared witless and are praying to whomever to get our butts out of this unscathed."

"Agreed," said Adam.

"Agreed," said Calvin.

"I most definitely agree," said Maritza.

"Women are much more articulate than men," Arjun joked. "She had to use four words to your one."

They all quaked with fear when the sound of gunfire started getting closer to their location. Then there was a blast. Adam suspected a hand grenade. He felt the force of the explosion through the stone floor. His eyes were squeezed shut in case the subsequent tremors sent debris flying through the air. There were two more blasts, then silence.

The door to the room was thrown open, and Number Three yelled, "Everybody up and out of here! We're moving, and we're moving fast."

The four scientists got up and followed Number Three down a darkened corridor that now had debris from collapsed walls dotting it. Emergency lights were flashing red. There was smoke in the air, and the scientists coughed and covered their noses with their sleeves. Adam saw other American soldiers in full gear, rifles held at the ready. He saw the facility's personnel on the floor, either wounded or dead. But his group was moving so fast, he didn't get a close look at much of anything. Soon they were outside and being bundled into a military vehicle. The four of them sat in the middle seat of the vehicle. There were two soldiers in the front, one of them the driver, and two in the rear seat, rifles aimed outside from lowered windows. There was a vehicle in front of them and another behind them. He could barely think with all the noise of gunfire, soldiers yelling to each other and an alarm that no one had bothered to disable.

The convoy began moving, and Adam noticed all of the vehicle's windows were now rolled up. He suspected the windows were bullet resistant. He tried his best to see his location. Where had he and his colleagues been held all this time? He gazed up at the building as the vehicle he was in sped away from it. It looked like an office building. Nothing special.

Minutes later, as the vehicle kept moving and the driver got on an expressway, he realized that they were in Abu Dhabi, about an hour-and-a-half drive from Dubai. He recognized this area. He'd driven this very expressway. He and Arjun used to take long drives to explore and acquaint themselves with the cities of the United Arab Emirates.

Arjun, too, had recognized where they were. "We're in Abu Dhabi," he said, his tone filled with wonder. "I guess whoever paid them to kidnap us didn't give them a big travel allowance."

"I don't care where we are," Adam said, "as long as we're on American soil soon."

"Agreed," Maritza said with conviction.

Alia looked at herself in the full-length mirror, twirling around so that the soft fabric of the African-inspired print dress fell caressingly down her legs. Her mom stood nearby, watching her with a smile on her lips. "Your grandmother would be so proud," she said.

Debra Youngblood, a petite, golden-brown-skinned woman in her early fifties, wore an off-white pant-suit with a pearl choker as her only jewelry, except for her wedding band and engagement ring. Alia admired her mother's simple but always fashionable manner of dressing. She tried her best to emulate her mother in that respect.

She smiled at her mother in the mirror's reflection. "I miss Grandpa Nero and Grandma Angelique so much."

"I do, too," said her mother. "They were more like my parents than my in-laws. When they found out my parents were gone, they really tried to make me feel like family. And they were." She carried on in a reverent tone as Alia went to the closet to pick a pair of shoes to wear to the gallery showing tonight.

Alia loved hearing about Nero and Angelique Youngblood, the parents of her father, James. They were gone now. But Nero, who was a writer, had started a newspaper in Harlem in the thirties. From that humble beginning, the family's company had grown to the mammoth company it was today. Nero, her parents liked to tell their children, was a man of taste and refinement. He'd known many women in his day, but had waited until he was forty to meet and marry the one woman for him: thirty-year-old Angelique. Angelique was an independent woman who didn't care that her family was beginning to fear she'd never get married since she was an old maid at the ancient age of thirty.

At any rate, Nero and Angelique must have been

destined to be, because their marriage lasted fifty-five years before Nero passed away in his sleep, and Angelique followed eight years later, also in her sleep.

"What I learned from your grandparents," her mother was saying as Alia slipped into a pair of brown leather boots, the shade matching designs in her dress, "is that a marriage is a journey. No one stays the same. We're not the same people we were when we were newlyweds. We're not the same people we were when we started having children. Each of you children brought something rich and wonderful to our lives when you were born. That's what you have to remember, Alia. When two people fall in love and decide they want to spend the rest of their lives together, they have to each be willing to let the other grow and change. Your father and I are willing to go with the flow. I hope the same for you and Chance and Brock, that you will live your lives with someone who will support your growth as a human being. That's happiness."

Alia went and kissed her mother on the cheek. "That's what Adam and I were working on before he disappeared."

"And you'll continue to work on it when he returns," Debra said reassuringly.

Alia looked deep into her mother's eyes. "I love you for still believing that's possible, Mom. Some days I have to convince myself."

Debra patted her arm. "Don't give up on him."

"Never," Alia promised.

The gallery where Alia's paintings were being shown was in Manhattan and exhibited contemporary art. It had been founded in Paris, she was told, and the owners opened a branch in New York City five years later and also had a branch in Zurich. The gallery's curator, Armand Simone, a short, bald gentleman in a black suit and black-framed glasses, welcomed her and her parents, and immediately began introducing her to some of the gallery's patrons. After an hour or so of this, Alia said she would like a few quiet moments before he introduced her from the podium, as he'd told her he would do later. She wanted to get what she wanted to say straight in her head before appearing before the more than two hundred art lovers who'd shown up.

She was in Armand's office in the back of the gallery with her parents when her cell phone rang, and she glanced down at the display. It simply read, US Government. Alia wondered who from the government would be phoning her. When the government contacted her, it was usually by mail. It seemed an archaic way of keeping her informed about Adam's status, but that was how they liked to do it.

"Hello?" she answered.

The person on the other end didn't say anything at first. However, she could hear someone breathing. He cleared his throat. "Alia Joie?" the voice said, sounding hoarse. "I can't believe I'm hearing your voice." He sounded as if he were fighting back tears.

Alia had been standing, pacing the room as she went over the speech she'd prepared for tonight. Now, however, her legs felt so weak she had to quickly sit down on one of the spindly mauve-upholstered chairs that looked like pieces of artwork in the curator's office.

Heart beating fast, she took a deep breath. "Adam? Oh, my God, is this really you?"

Upon hearing her say Adam's name, her parents both took tentative steps closer to her, their faces wearing astonished expressions. They were silent as she continued to listen.

The deep voice chuckled, and Alia fairly melted. That sounded like Adam's laugh. Rich and lusty, so full of mirth and joy. "You need proof besides the sound of my voice?" he asked. "Your birthday is September 27. We met at a charity event where I spoke and you asked me to have a coffee with you afterward. We were married ten months later in Nassau because you wanted to make sure all of my family could attend the ceremony. My mother loves you for that. I love you for so many more reasons."

Alia burst into tears. "Are you safe?" It had occurred to her that even though he was calling, apparently from some government office, maybe he wasn't entirely safe yet. She thought that as soon as he was back on American soil, the government should have informed her.

"I'm safe," he assured her. "We were rescued two days ago in Abu Dhabi. At least I think it was two days ago. Time has a way of getting away from me lately. But I'm in the US, at the Pentagon. We were all rescued. Maritza, Calvin and Arjun and I are being debriefed here at the Pentagon. I'm told we're going to be able to come home soon. I can't say any more over the phone."

"I'm coming to you," Alia told him, her mind made up. Her husband was back in the United States. Nothing, and no one, was going to keep them apart any longer if she could help it.

"I don't know when I'll be released," he said again.

"I'm coming," Alia said emphatically. "I'm at a gallery in Manhattan right now. They're showing my work tonight, babe. My first show."

Adam chuckled again, sounding delighted that she was realizing her dream. "I'm so proud of you," he breathed. "So proud. You don't know how many times I imagined you in your studio, painting. But then, I imagined you in so many scenarios while we were apart. I'm relieved that you didn't give up your art. It's an important part of you. I prayed for you every night, that you'd grow stronger and even that you'd have the strength to go on if I never found my way back to you."

"Adam, I never gave up," she told him. "Somehow, I knew we would find our way back to each other. I knew it in my gut."

"I never gave up, either," he said with a sigh. "I've changed, though, babe. I've lost weight and had to cut my dreads off for sanitary reasons."

"Oh, no, not your dreads. You loved your dreads," she moaned sympathetically. A beloved image of him, his dreadlocks falling down his back while they were walking hand in hand on a beach in the Bahamas, came to mind.

"I'm bald now," he warned her. "I still have a beard and mustache, though. What about you?"

"I'm the same," she said softly. "My 'fro is in braids now and they're down my back."

"You stayed natural," he said, sounding pleased. She knew he loved her natural hair. He used to wash it and oil her scalp. The feeling was so sensuous that they would often make love afterward.

"God, I've missed you so much," she said with a sigh.

"I've missed you, too, my Joie," he said huskily.

Alia almost started bawling when he said that, because he always called her Alia Joie, not just Alia. He said she was his joy and you couldn't leave out the Joie when you said her name. She encompassed everything he believed brought him happiness. She was so glad he considered her his joy.

"I want you to go out there and be your brilliant self, babe," he said. "Here's the number where you can reach me. My cell phone got confiscated at the beginning of this nightmare."

After Alia had written down the number he recited, she took a deep, cleansing breath, steeling herself for the inevitable. "I can't let you go," she told him, sniffling. She was afraid to say goodbye. What if this was only a dream, and once she disconnected with him, she'd wake up and never experience this sublime feeling of relief and happiness again?

"I'm back," he told her. "I'll never leave you again. It's okay to hang up. I'll see you soon. I swear it."

Her mother and father were looking at her with concern mirrored on their faces. Because she didn't want to cause them any more distress, she bravely said, "Okay, but I'll see you as soon as I can. Tomorrow. I love you!"

"I love you, babe. With all my heart," he said softly.

"Goodbye," she said, her voice breaking.

"Ah, babe, don't cry. I wish I could hold you. You know I can't stand it when you cry."

She laughed suddenly. "No, you never could. I'm going to stop this foolishness right now. I'll call you tonight so we can talk each other to sleep."

"It's a date," he said.

Hanging up on him was the hardest thing she'd ever done.

# *Chapter 3*

"Not even our spouses?" Maritza asked incredulously. Adam and the other three scientists were being debriefed by Colonel Edward Butler in a small conference room at the Pentagon after their return to the States. Colonel Butler had just informed them that they were not to tell anyone that they'd succeeded at inventing technology capable of disabling enemy missiles aimed at American troops.

"Not even your spouses," Colonel Butler, a tough man with iron gray hair and eyes to match, reiterated firmly. "We will make a statement to the press when permission comes down from the top. At the moment, it's wise to forgo any publicity about the project due to national security concerns."

This bit of news was disappointing to Adam because

Alia Joie hadn't wanted him to take the assignment in the first place. Now he had to return home appearing to be an abject failure.

Apparently, Maritza was also disappointed with the government's decision to keep a lid on their success, because she narrowed her eyes at Colonel Butler and said in an icy tone, "Because of the government, I didn't get to see my child take her first steps. My husband didn't want me to accept the assignment, and now I have to go back home without having accomplished what we set out to do?"

"Please, Dr. Aguilar," Colonel Butler implored her, "try to understand."

"Oh, I understand," Maritza said angrily. "You asked us to improve upon your technology. You already had the means to defuse some missiles, but we managed to invent technology that allows you to defuse every sort of missile. That's good news!"

"Indeed, it is," agreed Colonel Butler. "I hope you realize that what you just said is the reason you were kidnapped. You created technology that defuses every kind of missile, and someone wanted to steal that technology. Until we feel secure in the knowledge that it won't be stolen, we're keeping quiet about its existence."

Adam reached over and clasped Maritza's hand. "Don't cause yourself any further distress, Maritza." He looked Colonel Butler dead in the eyes. "We know how the government operates. We've had over two years to learn that lesson. They do things in their own time. And then they say their decisions serve the greater good. But I can't see how letting us rot in Abu Dhabi for two years was for the greater good."

A muscle jumped in Colonel Butler's face, and Adam knew he'd struck a nerve. "Are you saying we didn't do everything in our power to rescue you and your colleagues, Dr. Braithwaite?"

"I'm saying Agent Number Three, at least that's what I call him, was in that facility for over a year before you all decided it was time to bust us out. What happened? You needed more time to gather intelligence so you waited over a year after you'd infiltrated the facility to initiate a rescue? That's what it sounds like to me."

"Me, too," Maritza put in, her eyes fiery with defiance.

"Sounds fishy to me," Arjun commented dryly.

"I'm not saying anything," Calvin said, his British accent rife with sarcasm. "I'm not a naturalized citizen yet, and I'm hoping my ordeal helps me to become one soon. I want to stay in this country."

Colonel Butler laughed shortly. "None of you have even a basic knowledge of military strategy. You're scientists. I assure you, we got you out when we were reasonably sure we could do it without one of you getting killed in the process. I don't know what sort of secretive practices you're trying to assign to the government, but we are human, too, and we didn't want you to suffer. I'm a prisoner of war myself. I know how it is to be separated from your loved ones."

Adam felt bad at hearing this, but no less bitter. "I'm sorry you had to experience that, Colonel, but I'm sure you understand why we feel this way. I'd only been married a couple months when I took the assignment. Maritza had a six-month-old little girl. Calvin and Arjun were in love."

"Um, not with each other," Arjun clarified. "At any rate, the object of my affection is probably married with a child by now. She didn't answer her phone when I tried to call her earlier, when we were allowed to call friends and family."

"Oh, Arjun, I'm sorry," Maritza said. "Maybe she changed her number. It's not necessarily because she doesn't want to talk to you."

Colonel Butler looked kind of lost for words with all these emotions coming to the surface. His brows furrowed in either sympathy or confusion; Adam wasn't sure which. "Your lives were disrupted. You're afraid the people you cared about may not feel the same about you when you return home," he said. "Believe me, I understand that, too. Military families live with uncertainty all the time. But strong families stay intact. We just have to have faith that those who love us will continue to love us."

Adam's anger had subsided. The colonel spoke the truth. The past couldn't be changed. He had to look to the future. "All right," he said. "So we go home looking like we failed at our assignment. I suppose it won't be as bad as still being locked up."

"At least we can get Netflix," Arjun said. He looked intently at Colonel Butler. "Netflix still exists, right?"

Colonel Butler smiled. "Yes, Dr. Sharma, we still have Netflix."

Arjun breathed a huge sigh of relief. "Thank goodness."

Adam smiled. Arjun, in his own inimitable way,

reminded him that it was the little things in life that delighted you and made you feel glad to be alive. Of course, he also remembered that he was going to talk to Alia Joie again tonight. That thought put an even broader smile on his face.

"They're getting the plane ready, and we're leaving as soon as we get the call," Alia told Adam that night. She was lying in bed at the loft. It was well after midnight by then, and they'd been talking for at least two hours.

The showing at the gallery had been a success. She'd sold quite a few paintings and had been approached by private individuals for commissions to paint their portraits in the future. But she'd made no promises and said she would let them know when she was ready for that step in her career. The gallery's curator was happy to take down the potential clients' contact information.

After she'd told her family about Adam, they'd gone into action on her behalf. Her parents, brothers and her brother Chance's girlfriend, Petra, were all set to accompany her to Arlington, Virginia, and the Pentagon. Chance had made the travel arrangements, and a car would pick her up to take her to the airport as soon as the plane was ready.

"You should be resting," Adam said with concern.

"I'm too excited to sleep," said Alia. "I'll sleep after I've seen you."

"I'm not going anywhere," he tried to reassure her. Alia was lying in their king-size bed wearing her pajamas. She looked at his side of the bed, a spot that had been empty for too long. His not being there hadn't turned her into a bed hog. She still slept on her side of the bed.

"You keep saying that," she said softly. "But I'm not going to be satisfied until I have you in bed beside me, where you belong."

Adam laughed. "All right, then. Tell me more of what I've missed."

"Mmm, let's see." Alia paused, then told him about the latest happenings in politics and entertainment.

Adam laughed delightedly after she finished telling him about the new superhero movie. "I can't wait to see it."

Alia giggled. She felt high with happiness. She was actually talking with her husband over the phone. She'd asked him earlier if he could use a phone with video capability, but he'd said he wanted to wait until they were face-to-face. He didn't want his first glance of her after more than two years to be on a phone or laptop. He said when he saw her, he wanted to be able to hold her—that it would tear him up inside to see her and not be able to touch her. She'd understood because she felt the same way. She ached to be in his arms again.

"I told you I moved from the apartment in Manhattan," Alia continued. "Because I wanted to be closer to Mom and Dad, and I also wanted to be in the neighborhood where Grandpa Nero and Grandma Angelique used to live. But there's more, sweetie. The building has tenants. There are eight apartments and they're rented to fellow artists, except for one elderly couple, the Johnsons, who are the nicest people."

"I'm sure I'll like them all," Adam said. "You know, coming from the Bahamas, I don't mind a lot of people around. Where I'm from, everyone knows everyone else. And it wasn't unusual to have fifteen or more neighbors who'd combined their resources, around a table eating a meal together."

"I'm glad you're open to the idea," Alia said. "I doubt we'll be having them over for dinner on a regular basis. I just wanted to prepare you for the fact that we won't be the only people in the building."

"Ramona would be thrilled with the arrangement," Adam told her. Alia smiled at the mention of his mother. She didn't know why Adam always referred to his mother by her first name when talking about her. He called her Momma when they were together. It was a reminder of the fact that there were still things about him she didn't know. They had, technically, been newlyweds when he'd left.

"I often wondered why you call your mother Ramona when you're talking about her to someone. But, to her face, you call her Momma," Alia said.

He laughed shortly. "Because Ramona is a character. She's too big a personality to simply call her Momma. Her spirit is a thing with no bounds. Like you, Alia Joie. When I think of you, it's never without the happiness that you bring to me. I don't know. I guess I'm weird that way."

"Well, I can't wait to have my weird guy back in my arms," Alia told him, then yawned.

Clearly Adam heard her, because he said, "It's time for you to go to sleep, baby girl."

When she started to protest, he cut her off. "None of that, now. We'll see each other tomorrow. I hope you like my new look. I got on a scale today. I'm down forty pounds."

Alia felt tears welling up. She tried her best not to sniff because Adam would know his comment had made her cry. She took a deep breath and let it out slowly. Those villains had withheld food from Adam. What other sort of mental and physical forms of torture had they used? "I love you," she told him, her voice without a quaver that might betray her state of mind. "Mom and I will fatten you up in no time."

Adam laughed. "You two do like to cook together. But neither of you can bake like I can."

"Those are fighting words," Alia joked. "You're going to have to put your baked goods where my mouth is, mister!"

Still laughing, Adam said, "Christmas is coming up. You'd better get the tins ready, because I'll be baking and you'll be filling the tins for friends and relatives."

"Can't wait!" Alia said contentedly.

"Then let's say good-night as if we've said it to each other every night of our lives," Adam said softly.

Alia knew he was trying to make saying goodbye easier on her, and she accepted his gift of understanding. "Good night, sweetie."

"Good night, my love," he answered.

Alia wept after hanging up. She didn't know whether she was crying from relief that tomorrow she was going to see Adam again, or if it was simply a way of releasing stress. Or both. But once she was cried out, she felt better, and she actually slept until near dawn, when her phone rang with news that the plane was ready.

\* \* \*

The Gulfstream extended-range jet landed at Dulles International Airport in Loudoun, Virginia, early the next morning. Dressed in coats, scarves and boots for the cold weather, they got into a black SUV whose driver took them to Arlington, Virginia, where the Pentagon was located.

Alia was tense. She could feel the tension in the air in the SUV as everyone was lost in their own thoughts. Her brother Chance sat up front with the driver. She, her parents, her brother Brock, and Chance's lady love, Dr. Petra Gaines, took up the other two rows of seating in the large SUV. She was sitting between Petra and her mother. Chance had just asked her if she might want to stop at a luxury hotel and get some rest before going on to the Pentagon. But she couldn't think of resting before seeing Adam. She was glad her brother knew her so well and put up no protest whatsoever when she'd stated her preference for going straight to the Pentagon.

After that exchange, once again the tension in the SUV was so thick she could feel it. Then Brock's stomach growled loudly. Everyone in the SUV heard it.

"What?" Brock cried in his defense. "I haven't eaten anything substantial in hours."

"You ate snacks on the plane with the rest of us," their mother said.

"Airplane snacks don't qualify as food," Brock replied.

"You've just got a tapeworm," their mother insisted.

Brock sniffed the air and looked suspiciously down at their mother's voluminous bag on her lap. "What do you have in that bag, Mom?"

Alia also sniffed the air. "I smell cinnamon," she said, siding with her brother. She was a little hungry herself. Stress always made her crave something to chew on, which was a habit she worked against because she didn't want to become dependent on comfort food to quell her emotions.

Their mom laughed, then went into her bag and pulled out a huge zippered bag of homemade oatmeal cookies. Alia recognized them at once as one of Adam's favorite recipes. He put not only raisins in the mix but shredded coconut, walnuts and chocolate chips. Her mother deposited the bag in her lap. "When I couldn't sleep, I made Adam's favorite cookies."

Alia smiled at her mother. "You're so sweet for thinking of him. Thank you!"

"Oh, baby, we love him, too," her mother said.

Alia heard Brock clear his throat and guessed what was coming next. Brock, a tall, handsome man who was over thirty and formerly a person with total self-control, looked at that bag like a five-year-old with a cookie craving. "May I have one of those?" he asked.

Alia laughed and passed the bag to Petra. "Why not?" she said. "I think we could all use a cookie right about now."

Petra opened the bag and passed it around, and for the next few minutes, all you could hear in the SUV was the sound of seven adults, including the driver, devouring homemade oatmeal cookies.

The tension was broken by baked goods. Under the circumstances, Alia thought Adam would have thought that quite funny.

About forty minutes later, the SUV was on the

grounds of the Pentagon, and a few minutes after that, they were being escorted into Colonel Edward Butler's office. Chairs were brought to accommodate all of them, after which the colonel solemnly regarded them and began, first of all apologizing for how long it had taken the government to bring Adam home.

Alia couldn't have been less interested in their apology and tried to contain her irritation. She simply wanted to see Adam. She sat silently, however, while he had his say and then forewarned them not to look surprised when they saw Adam because his appearance had changed substantially since they'd last set eyes on him.

Alia was prepared for this because Adam had already told her his physical appearance might come as a shock to her. She felt she was prepared for anything.

Finally the colonel said, "So, if you're ready, I'll take you to Dr. Braithwaite."

*Boy, the Pentagon is big*, Alia thought as she and her party walked down the vast corridor with Colonel Butler. The wide-block stone floors were white and looked like they were cleaned every day. The sound of their heels and the faint murmur of people's voice in adjacent corridors and in offices they passed were the only noise. Alia got more anxious with each door they passed. She kept thinking this was where the colonel would stop. But they kept walking.

The colonel finally stopped at a door and indicated with a nod in its direction that they were at their destination. He knocked politely on the door before opening it and strolling inside, saying, "Dr. Braithwaite, your family is here to take you home."

He turned then and walked away, leaving them to their privacy. Alia walked in first, closely followed by her party.

It was a large room, and her initial glimpse of Adam was from about ten feet away. He was standing quite still, his body turned toward her. She kept moving closer to him. She noticed that everyone else had halted just inside the room. But she couldn't have stopped walking toward Adam if her life had depended on it.

He was thinner. He was wearing a short-sleeve blue T-shirt and gray sweatpants with a pair of black athletic shoes. Formerly his body type had been like that of a professional football player in perfect form. He had been 250 pounds of muscle when he'd left. He still looked like an athlete, but now he had the body type of a basketball player, lanky and muscular. Except it was his eyes that she was looking at. As if by silent consensus, they were moving slowly toward each other. His face crinkled in a smile. A small, tentative smile that tugged at her heart. It was as if he were afraid she might not like what she saw. Her smile grew broader, and tears formed in her eyes. Not like what she saw? That was ludicrous! He was beautiful! His head was bald as a cue ball and looked as smooth as a baby's bottom.

It was with relief that she threw herself into his arms at last, and whispered, "Adam, my Adam, I thought I'd lost you forever!"

"Alia Joie!" he cried, and then they were kissing each other's faces and she was in his arms, and they were hugging so tightly she felt she could meld with him if it were humanly possible.

They drew back momentarily to peer into each other's

eyes. Their grins encompassed their whole faces now. Alia stared into his milk-chocolate-colored eyes. Eyes she'd fallen in love with over a cup of coffee three years ago when, on a whim, she'd asked him to join her for a cup. It had been a case of smitten at first sight. He'd just given a speech at an awards ceremony her family's company was sponsoring. She hadn't organized the ceremony, so she hadn't known who the speakers would be before she got there. She'd heard of the brilliant Bahamian physicist whose out-of-this-world ideas were the talk of the scientific community and had earned him notoriety in the mainstream world, as well. He was charismatic and articulate, from humble beginnings, and was an inspiration to a lot of people. She'd seen him on a late-night talk show once, promoting one of his books. She'd thought he was good-looking and charming then. But when she'd seen him in person, she'd been blown away by his presence. She thought she would be a fool if she ignored the opportunity to get to know him better, so she'd worked up the nerve to ask him for a coffee. Ten months later, they were married.

Now, after a prolonged separation due to circumstances neither of them had any control over, they were finally back together.

"You're everything to me," she breathed, smiling up at him.

"You're more beautiful than I remembered," was his response. "I must have done something right in my former life!"

She giggled and hugged him again.

Then the others descended on them, and everyone was crying, including her father and brothers and her soon-to-be sister-in-law, Petra, whom she already loved like a sister.

She hoped their enthusiasm wasn't overwhelming Adam. She didn't know how he was feeling inside. How he was coping with all this hoopla. The Adam she used to know was a gregarious person who loved being around people. But after being mostly isolated for months and months, as he'd told her over the phone, this might be sensory overload for him. So, after only a few minutes of hugs and exclamations, Alia put her arm through Adam's and respectfully suggested they be given a few minutes in private. Her loved ones promptly left the room to wait outside.

Alone with Adam, she looked into his eyes. "Just tell me what you need, and I'll make it happen."

Adam smiled ruefully. "I just want to sleep in my own bed with you, babe. I feel so tired."

She nodded. He did look tired. The weight loss made his cheekbones very prominent and his jawline more angular. There were dark circles under his eyes. So he obviously hadn't been sleeping well. Most of all, though, his eyes were guarded, as if he feared sharing what he was truly feeling deep inside. She had never before seen that reflected in their depths.

She took his hand. "Let's go home."

# Chapter 4

Adam brushed his teeth three times before he was satisfied that every surface was clean and particle free. Realistically, he knew why he was doing it. His tendency toward obsessive-compulsive disorder was rearing its familiar old head. He had suffered from this when he was a teenager but had, in essence, talked himself out of it. Symptoms hadn't manifested themselves in years. Yes, he sometimes found himself being overly organized, but it was nothing compared to counting everything and having to check multiple times whether he'd turned off the stove or electrical appliances that might start a fire before leaving his apartment.

Now, knowing Alia Joie was on the way, he'd stood at the bathroom sink and brushed his teeth three times, gazing in the mirror, inspecting his perfectly white teeth again and again.

He found himself worrying that his breath might offend her when they hugged hello or when they kissed. The kiss had to be perfect. The kiss had to be solid proof that the man holding her was the same one who'd left her. So he had to make sure his breath would be minty fresh when their lips touched.

After obsessing about his breath, he took a long, hot shower and dressed in the clothes they'd brought him. He didn't waste time worrying that they weren't the brand he usually wore. He was just grateful they fit. They were fine. He was fine. Or so he tried to convince himself.

Where was this insecurity coming from? Maybe it was because he hadn't seen so much as a photograph of Alia Joie since his kidnapping. He thought he'd remembered everything about her. He'd had her image firmly etched in his mind. Or was his mind lying to him? He knew one thing for sure: when they were together, he'd always thought he'd married up. She was clearly out of his league. How had he convinced himself he was good enough for her?

It wasn't that she carried herself like a rich spoiled brat. Alia Joie was so down-to-earth you wouldn't know she'd been born into a wealthy family. She was warm and generous, and she was at home anywhere. She had friends from all walks of life. No, she had never made him feel like he was beneath her. That feeling was due to his own upbringing—simply the consequence of being born poor. He knew the lack of money didn't mean your circumstances were never going to change for the better. His parents had inculcated in him the notion that a person could become anything he wanted to be, as long as he worked hard enough.

Still, when he'd first come to the United States on scholarship to MIT, he'd met other students who did believe they were better than he was. They showed it by excluding him from certain activities, by complaining that they couldn't understand him when he spoke. He spoke perfect English now, but then, he'd had a thick Bahamian accent. He hadn't lost his lilt; he simply didn't let it out in academic settings. Only with friends and family.

In many ways, he was a self-made man. It had taken him years to build up his confidence. Had his incarceration torn down some of the walls he'd erected around his psyche? He was not the type to go around quoting self-affirmations. His insecurities were unfounded, and he knew it. That didn't make the feelings go away, though. He had to concentrate in order to block them.

When the colonel opened the door and called, "Dr. Braithwaite, your family is here to take you home," he'd frozen in his tracks, fear suddenly gripping his insides. He realized, when he saw Alia Joie's face, that he had not remembered her with precise accuracy. The woman before him was exquisite. She was tall and shapely with the body of a dancer, lithe and athletic looking. Her nose, eyes, ears, chin and mouth were perfectly formed, and he couldn't imagine them being any other way. Her crown, in all its glory, was long and obviously healthy and strong, as any African queen deserved. He couldn't wait to run his hands through it.

His Alia Joie had been pretty, too. Beautiful, even.

What was causing the altered perception of her outward appearance? He wasn't sure. This was, indeed, the woman he'd married.

When she spoke, he calmed down a bit. He was positive the voice was Alia Joie's. But then, they'd spoken on the phone since he'd gotten back.

He hoped she couldn't read the confusion in his gaze when they stood there looking into each other's eyes. Her eyes were cinnamon colored. His memory agreed with that, at least. Her skin was dark chocolate with reddish undertones. Beautiful skin. And when she began kissing his face, he felt how soft her skin was, and exhaled with relief.

She smelled wonderful, like some tropical fruit, papaya or mango. He said something stupid like, "You're more beautiful than I remembered. I must have been good in my former life." What the hell did that mean? Would she think he had lost his mind in Abu Dhabi, talking about another life?

Finally she'd asked what she could do for him, and he'd said, "I just want to sleep in my own bed with you, babe. I feel so tired."

Truer words were never spoken. He was tired, and his brain needed rest. As they were walking to the door to join the others, who were waiting in the hallway, she asked, "Do you need to get your things?"

"I already have everything I need," he'd said.

They checked into a hotel to rest in comfort while the plane was being readied for the return flight to New York City. Alone in their hotel room, Alia lay in Adam's arms in bed with the lights dimmed, dressed except for their shoes, as both of them tried to sleep. However, neither of them were able to. She had the crazy idea that if she slept he wouldn't be here when she woke up. For the last hour or so, she'd been smiling so much her cheeks ached.

"I don't know what to tell you," Adam said when she'd asked him to tell her everything. She'd regretted asking because maybe he wasn't ready to revisit the horrors of what he'd been through. "I don't want to give you nightmares."

"Tell me what you're comfortable saying," she told him, snuggling closer to him. She loved the feel of his beard on her face. "I don't want to rush you."

Her body was reacting to his nearness. No sex for over two years was taking its toll on her. But, just as she didn't want to rush him into revealing everything he'd been through for the past two years, she also didn't want to be demanding when it came to sexual intimacy. That had to come naturally. It was unreasonable to assume they'd fall back into their former routine of honeymoon sex. That was how it had been between them. They were learning each other, exploring what brought each other pleasure. She was tingling just thinking about their lovemaking.

She tilted her chin up, gazing into his eyes. "Or don't say anything—just hold me."

"I can tell you that they didn't physically torture us," he offered. "When we were snatched, we did get knocked around until we cooperated, but after that there were no beatings. They withheld food if we wouldn't talk to them, though. And none of us would tell them what they wanted to hear. We all lost weight."

"They didn't get any information out of you," Alia said.

"They didn't get anything out of any of us," Adam said softly. "Whenever I was questioned they would threaten me with the fact that they were waiting on orders from the higher-ups—whether or not they had permission to go ahead and kill us, or continue to try to get the information they needed out of us."

"You were mentally tortured, then," Alia surmised.

"And they kept us isolated," he said, nodding slightly. "When we first got to the facility, we were alone in a room for several months. Then, once a week, they started letting us see each other."

"Those bastards! They knew isolating you would be worse than keeping you together."

He nodded slowly. "I started talking to myself."

"Oh, baby," she sympathized.

He looked deeply into her eyes. "God knew what he was doing when he made Adam a companion. Man isn't made to live alone."

Alia silently cried, thinking of him alone in that room, not knowing if he'd get out alive. "I hope they're punished for what they did to you and Arjun and Maritza and Calvin!"

"Honey, they've already been punished," Adam assured her. "I'm not certain, but I don't think many of them survived the night we were rescued."

"I mean the higher-ups," Alia clarified.

A guarded look came into Adam's eyes. "I can't say what the government is going to do about them. If anything. I can't even talk about the outcome of the work we were doing in Abu Dhabi. The government will tell the public about it in their own time. And that's all we can say about it. So I'm sorry if you're disappointed that I've come back home empty-handed. We've lost two years of time we could have been together because I chose to go to Abu Dhabi. I…"

Alia put her hand over his mouth. "Stop! Stop saying those horrible things. I never blamed you for going over there. You're a man with a big heart, Adam. I never thought for a moment that you wouldn't go. You were just trying to help save the lives of countless military men and women. I'm proud of you! Yes, it's true, I didn't want you to go, but that was because I'm selfish where you're concerned. I love you and I didn't want to be without you. We had been married less than a year, and I didn't want to share you with the world. But I know now that sometimes I'm going to have to share you. I want you to be whomever you want to be. I don't want to dictate your actions. Marriages don't last when spouses try to control one another, and I want to grow old with you. Just like my grandparents, parents and your parents."

"I'm just afraid I'm not the man you married anymore," Adam said.

"Kiss me," Alia ordered as she met his eyes.

He seemed hesitant to do it. He looked into her eyes for a long moment, then lowered his gaze to her mouth. She moistened her lips, trying to fight back more tears because it appeared that her husband was afraid to kiss her. She didn't dare initiate it because if he turned his face, preventing it, she would be devastated.

After what seemed a long time to her, he pressed his mouth to hers, and she closed her eyes. But his lips were immobile, like he was just learning how to kiss and was waiting for her to teach him. Then he ground out, "Oh, God, I've missed you," and on his exhale, the kiss transformed into something rife with longing. It was slow and tender, and sweet, and so sensual that her nipples got hard and she got wet between her legs in a matter of seconds.

He climbed on top of her and she opened her legs to welcome him inside of her, but they were only assuming the position, because they were still clothed. The kiss deepened and they moaned with pleasure, grinding on each other, her feminine center throbbing and his erection growing harder by the second.

Then he stopped kissing her, looked down at her and said, "It's too soon."

With that, he got out of the bed and went into the adjacent bathroom. The next thing she heard was the sound of the shower water turning on.

Alia sat up in bed, breathing hard, wondering if she'd pushed him too far out of her own need for intimacy. She got up and walked over to the window to peer at downtown Arlington. It was a Saturday, but the business district was bustling with activity. *Life goes on,* she thought cynically, *even when you think yours is standing still.*

That was the attitude that had gotten her through her separation from Adam. The knowledge that even if your life felt like it was falling apart around you, the world kept on spinning, and you had to keep going, too. There were times when she had felt like just lying down and dying. But she didn't. Her family wouldn't let her give up. However, the burden had been on her. They couldn't have prevented her from doing something drastic if she'd chosen to do it.

Somehow she'd found the strength to pray for Adam's release every day. To go to work. To maintain her relationships with friends and family. To care whether or not she ate right and exercised. Even the basic things were hard to do. Depression was just one tub of ice cream away. She kept working on herself. Shoring up her strength because, by God, the women and men she'd grown up with didn't just give up. They fought. They endured. They got off their butts and made a difference in the world.

She smiled at her reflection in the glass of the window she was looking out of. Adam needed time, that was all. He needed time to adjust to life. She didn't selfishly want the old Adam back, because she knew that wasn't a reasonable thing to wish for. She simply wanted an intact Adam who remembered the strength inside of him, and remembered where he came from, and what kind of people he came from.

There was no way her Adam was going to let the people who'd imprisoned him win by virtue of his collapse. No way!

When he came out of the bathroom, having showered for the second time that day, Adam felt not cleansed but somehow more in control of his emotions. Alia Joie was sitting at the little round table near the window, a chessboard on the table. She'd put the pieces on the board and smiled at him when he entered the room. "Do you feel up to a game?" she asked innocently enough.

Tension drained out of his body when he saw she was not going to react to his abandoning her on the bed a few minutes ago. He knew, however, that Alia Joie was a shark when it came to chess, and she'd eat you alive if you gave her the chance. She wasn't fooling him with that demure smile on her beautiful face. She was depending on his inability to decline a challenge.

He sat down across from her. She rolled her shoulders, a sure sign that the game was on and she meant to beat him and then dance on his grave.

"You and your dad still have your weekly game on Sundays?" he asked.

"It's tradition," she said.

"Who won the most games while I was away?" he asked as he made his first move. Her eyes were keenly watching the board although her right index finger was moving up and down his arm in a sensual manner. She grasped his hand and squeezed it reassuringly, then released it.

It was to let him know she understood why he'd had to leave her so abruptly and take a cold shower. It told him that she was patient and she loved him and was going to see this through with him, no matter how long it took. That was why she'd brought out the chessboard. Chess was a game of strategy. It was also a game you didn't rush through. You had to be able to outthink your opponent. You had to be able to anticipate his next move in order to ensure the safety of your pieces on the board.

Of course, what her motives could be were all assumptions on his part, but he'd be willing to bet he was right.

"Oh, he still beats me most of the time," she admitted, elbow on the table and her chin resting in her hand. "He's played the game a lot longer than I have. Plus, he's sneaky."

Adam laughed. "Your dad's not sneaky."

"Sure, he is," she said, laughing with delight. "He tricked me into going to business school. I was all set to go to art school, but he wanted me to learn the business instead. You can have a head for business and a heart for art, he said. But the business couldn't wait. I was the eldest. I had a responsibility. He didn't go in for that 'a son will take over the business after me' routine. He wanted me to be as competent as a man. We'd been playing chess for a long time, and sometimes I would beat him. I thought I was good enough to accept his challenge when he said if I could beat him in a game, he wouldn't protest any more about my wanting to go to art school instead of business school. You know what happened?"

Adam looked down at the board. She had him in checkmate already. "Something like what just happened here?" he said, grinning. "He beat you and you went to business school."

"Yes, my love," Alia Joie said, her eyes sparkling with joy. "And I didn't regret it. I didn't neglect my artistic side, though. I went to art school for a while and found out the classroom didn't suit me, so I'm basically self-taught like Gauguin, van Gogh, who studied only briefly, and Grandma Moses. I have the best of both worlds. I'm good at business and art. Want to play another game?"

Adam started positioning the pieces on his side of the board.

"Two out of three?"

"If we have time before the plane's ready," she said nonchalantly.

"Oh, the way you play, I'm sure we will," he said.

She just smiled sweetly at him and trounced him in two more games.

By the time they boarded the plane that evening, he was looking forward to getting home and resuming his marriage with this intriguing woman. He just wished that he could get over the anxiety he felt at making love to her. It had been so overpowering earlier that he'd had to run away from her and jump into a cold shower.

It wasn't that he didn't want to have sex with her. The thought of not pleasing her was the problem. And he couldn't recall ever doubting his ability to please her before.

# Chapter 5

"It used to be a hotel," Alia Joie said softly as the two of them stood in front of the building he would soon be calling home. A hired car, which was gone now, had brought them from the airport. Adam gazed up at the five-story building. It was an elegant-looking creamy-white stone building. As they approached it, he saw a golden plaque around three inches high and eighteen inches long that read: The Village.

"Grandpa and I used to walk past this place and he'd tell me stories about it. He said it was one of the best hotels in Harlem when he was young. I don't know if you've ever heard of *The Green Book*, being born in the Bahamas, but back before black people in America had civil rights, traveling around the country without getting caught in areas where they weren't welcome required planning. Victor Green, who was a postman here in Harlem, started making a list of places where a black traveler could find shelter. This hotel was on that list. A lot of black celebrities stayed here when they were in town—Ella Fitzgerald, Cab Calloway, Louis Armstrong, Sammy Davis Jr., Lena Horne…although Grandpa was quick to add that Ms. Horne was a home-town girl and had relatives nearby. Yet, she still liked to luxuriate in a room in this very building when it was a hotel.

"I named it the Village because of the old saying—it takes a village to raise a child, and this is where I want us to raise our children. In this village of Harlem, where Mom and Dad are just down the street."

They walked up the steps, and the doorman called, "Mrs. Braithwaite, welcome home from your trip!"

Alia Joie smiled at the elderly gentleman and said, "Mr. Stewart, I'd like you to meet my husband, Dr. Adam Braithwaite."

Adam could tell by the surprised expression on the man's face that he'd had no idea the purpose of Alia Joie's trip had been to bring home her long-lost hus-band. It was apparent, though, that Mr. Stewart was well aware of his existence.

Mr. Stewart, a tall, slender African American in his sixties with snow-white hair and mustache, removed his forest green hat, which matched his forest green uni-form. "Well, I'll be! Dr. Braithwaite, welcome home, sir!" He offered his hand, and when Adam reached out to him, he clasped Adam's hand in a firm grip. His brown eyes danced. "This is wonderful news, just wonderful!" He glanced at Alia Joie, who was beaming. "Mrs. Braithwaite, I've never seen you look happier. God bless you. God bless you both!"

"Thank you, Mr. Stewart," Adam said with a smile. "It's a pleasure to meet you."

"The pleasure's all mine, Dr. Braithwaite. Now, you two young people get on in here. I'm sure the others are going to be happy to see you, too!"

And with a tip of his hat, he ushered them into the lobby of the immaculately maintained building and returned to his post.

"This is beautiful," Adam said, his voice echoing off the walls of the high-ceilinged lobby. If he had to guess, he would say that the floors were Italian marble. As they walked into the lobby, to their right was a wall of mailboxes for the tenants. To their left was a sitting area with two comfortable leather couches and a modern glass coffee table between them.

As they walked farther into the lobby, he also noticed stairs on the left, which looked brand-new. They were made of a light-colored wood, varnished and covered in dark green short-nap carpeting.

Alia Joie must have noticed him looking at the stairs because she said, "We have an elevator, too. It's the latest in modern conveyances." She grinned. "Anyway, this building used to be like a boutique hotel back in the day. I had it converted into an eight-apartment building by removing non-load-bearing walls between the rooms. The apartments have either two or three bedrooms, an open-concept living room and kitchen, two full baths, a half bath and washer dryer hookups. And each has its own balcony. They're very nice spaces.

You and I have the top floor to ourselves, but the tenants are allowed to use the rooftop amenities."

"Which are?" Adam asked, curious.

She was beaming again. "Oh, baby, the rooftop is like paradise. The entire place is tiled in indoor and outdoor flooring. There's a terrace with outdoor furnishings, chairs, couches, chaise longues, coffee tables and end tables. In one corner is an outdoor kitchen complete with a barbecue pit, fridge and a pizza oven. Oh, yeah, a bar, too." She gestured toward the elevator. "Why am I describing it? Let's go up and you can see it for yourself."

Adam followed her inside the elevator, which was larger than he'd expected for the size of the building. "Kudos on the elevator not bringing on my claustrophobia," he joked as Alia Joie pressed the rooftop button.

"I hate tiny elevators," she said as the conveyance began moving upward. "I was lucky the hotel already had an elevator system, so the engineers didn't need to carve out a space for one. But everything about this baby is ultramodern. I didn't want to be bothered with it breaking down anytime soon. Most of our tenants are young and healthy, but we do have the elderly couple I mentioned who might not be able to manage the stairs for long, and we have an artist who uses a wheelchair. The building is wheelchair accessible, and I had the workmen make a few adjustments, like the heights of the cabinets and countertops in the bathroom and kitchen and a wheelchair-accessible bathroom, to make his apartment more comfortable for him."

Adam was not surprised by any of these revelations. Before he'd left, Alia Joie had talked about buying a building and renovating it. He hadn't realized she was serious about it, though. He thought it had been a pipe dream, a bucket list item.

He looked down into her upturned, smiling face. "I'm really proud of you."

She wrapped her arms around his waist and momentarily laid her head on his chest. "Thank you, babe."

The elevator stopped and the doors slid open to let them out onto the rooftop. It was getting dark, and the solar lamps strategically positioned around the large space were lighting up. They stepped onto the terrace and it looked, to Adam, like an upscale resort's pool area, minus the pool. "A pool would have been expensive to put up here, huh?" he joked.

Alia Joie laughed. "Yes, you know me too well. I asked about putting one in, but the architect said he wouldn't advise it. The building is sound, and he could have used metal instead of concrete, but the weight of the water alone made it inadvisable. We do have a hot tub, though." She pointed to the far left corner. "At any rate, we don't need a pool. There's a YMCA not too far from here if you want to get some swimming in."

Adam chuckled. "It's wintertime, anyway."

They strolled around the huge area. Adam saw that Alia Joie had sectioned off the rooftop into specific spots with different functions. The area next to the outdoor kitchen had tables with umbrellas, enough to seat about twenty people. There was also a section with eight chaise lounges where people could sunbathe if they wanted to, or just relax and read a good book.

Live plants in decorative planters dotted the entire rooftop, and the railing surrounding the whole thing was extra tall and reinforced in case someone got careless and lost their footing.

"You thought of everything," he complimented her. "Even safety measures for when someone gets tipsy and forgets they're on a roof."

"The city has safety codes for rooftops," she said sensibly.

He smiled to himself. That was his Alia Joie. She was meticulous to a fault. "How long have you been living here?"

"Only about a year." She looked down, the positive energy he'd formerly sensed coming off her dwindling. "I had to stay busy while you were gone," she said softly. "If I didn't stay busy, I felt I'd go crazy worrying. So, in addition to work and painting, I needed a big project to focus on and this was it. And I needed something to take me out of myself. To care for someone besides myself. So I put ads out in the neighborhood inviting artists to put in applications for the apartments. I wanted people who were truly trying to make a living as an artist, be it painters, actors, dancers, writers. I ended up with some really good people, babe."

"How did you meet the elderly couple you told me about?" he asked.

"Mom introduced them to me. They go to her church and they've been struggling financially since Mr. Johnson had a stroke and lost his job. They're the cutest couple. Mrs. Johnson was a teacher for over forty years. Mr. Johnson worked as a postman until he got sick. They gave him grief over his disability and their combined income didn't cover all the bills. So I welcomed them here. They're the soul of this building. You'll see."

Adam smiled at the prospect. He reached over and gently touched her cheek. "Now, let's take a look at our place."

When they got to the loft, Alia told Adam breezily to look around. She had to go freshen up. She did this not because she actually needed to use the bathroom, but because she wanted him to explore his new space on his own. When she'd moved in, she had chosen the furniture, the unique decorative touches, everything with him in mind. He was an electronics geek, so she'd made sure the electronics in the place were top-of-the-line, from the TV to the sound system to the alarm system.

She hadn't thrown away any of his belongings. His office was set up with all of his computer equipment, his textbooks and the books he read for pleasure. He was a comics fan, and his collection was just as he'd left it. He was also a video game enthusiast, and that collection was intact, as well.

She disappeared for about twenty minutes. Longer, and he would have gotten suspicious. She found him in the gym, cycling on his Peloton bike. He smiled at her when she walked in. "Hey," he said cheerfully, white teeth flashing in his bearded face. "You won't believe how much I missed this thing."

She laughed, delighted he was smiling. She glanced down at her watch. "Have fun. It's dinnertime. I'm going to see what I can put together for a quick meal."

Adam joined her in the kitchen a few minutes later. She was making a salad on the counter next to the farmhouse sink. She was going to prepare grilled chicken breasts and spicy brown rice, too.

Adam came up and hugged her from behind. "Thank you for keeping all my stuff," he said next to her ear.

His body's warmth and the tender tone of his voice made her gooey inside. She also appreciated his kind words. She'd been so anxious about how he would react to a new space. After the wedding, she'd moved in with him. Now, they would make this place their home. It was hard giving up something you were used to, even if you logically knew you couldn't hold on to it. Adam probably knew that she couldn't continue to live in his apartment with him missing. But she couldn't guess at whatever visceral reaction he would have to the reality of his place being gone.

She put down the lettuce she'd been tearing into chunks, and in the circle of his embrace, she turned and faced him. Looking into his eyes, she said, "There were some decisions I had to make without you. But I made them all with you in mind."

"I know," he said, and kissed her forehead. "I had a lot of time to think while I was locked up, and I thought about your moving. I thought about so many things. I wondered how long it would take before you had to give up on me."

"I'd never give up on you!"

"I know that," he said softly, his arms tightening around her. "What I meant was, how long it'd be before you had to move on or risk coming apart. It's hard waiting on someone to come back to you when you're not even sure they're coming back. The government wasn't telling you anything. It was kind of like I was a prisoner of war. I once read a study about men who were thought dead and turned up years later. Their

wives were with other men by then. Or the men suffered from post-traumatic stress disorder, and it was
impossible for their wives to live with them."

"But some of the couples stayed together, right?"
Alia asked hopefully.

"Yes, but they had to work hard at it. It required a
lot of love and patience on both the soldier's part and
his wife's."

Alia could see the pain in his gaze. He wasn't just
talking about some study he'd read in the past. He was
talking about them. He was telling her it was going to
take time for him to feel normal again. To feel whole.

"I hear you," she said.

His eyes grew misty as he continued looking deeply
into hers. "And I would understand if you got lonely
and turned to someone else for comfort, Alia Joie. I
know it was hard not knowing what was going on. Not
knowing anything. I know you suffered."

The expression in his eyes was almost pleading. As
if on one hand, he really didn't want to hear her answer,
and on the other, it was imperative that he know. Had
she been unfaithful to him while he was gone?

Alia took a deep breath. Honestly, the question upset
her and gave her a sick feeling in the pit of her stomach. Unfaithful to him? It had never occurred to her
to cheat on him while he was being held captive, perhaps being tortured on a daily basis. What kind of
woman would she be to even contemplate such a thing?
A monster, that's what kind. She didn't want to cause
him any more distress, though, so she said in as calm
a manner as she could muster, "Adam, I'd rather jump
off the Brooklyn Bridge than cheat on you. I'm a one-

man woman. When I married you, it was until death do us part. And I meant it!"

She felt his body relax and saw the sadness disappear from the depths of his eyes. The mist cleared from them, too, and he smiled weakly. "I'm sorry, but I had to know."

"What about you?" she asked quietly. "Did you find comfort in someone else's arms while you were gone?"

He laughed shortly. "Babe, I was locked up. The only people I saw were our captors and Calvin, Maritza and Arjun."

"I mean before you were captured," Alia said.

"I love you, Alia Joie. I would never cheat on you," he stated emphatically.

"That's exactly how I feel about you," she told him. "And just for the record, I would not be understanding about it as you said you would be about my cheating on you. I would be furious! I wouldn't care if I'd been on a desert island for ten years and came back to you. I would expect you to have been faithful to me, Adam Braithwaite!"

Adam chuckled. "Ten years, babe?"

"Twenty, if it came to that. I'm yours for life. Not just for a decade. Forever! Do I make myself clear?"

"Yes," he said, still chuckling.

"Good," she said, standing on tiptoe to kiss him high on the cheek, where his face was beardless. "Now, make yourself useful and get the gas grill on that machine over there that I call a stove ready for the chicken." She gestured to the stove, a stainless steel double range replete with all the cooking capabilities any chef would covet. Her husband, who loved to cook and also got a kick out of new appliances, was going to have fun getting acquainted with that monster. It'd taken her a while to learn all of its functions. He went to do her bidding, sorry now, she was sure, for bringing up the subject of infidelity in their marriage.

She smiled when his back was turned. That would teach him to get her riled up. She walked a tightrope where her responses to him were concerned. She had to be patient and kind and understanding. She also had to be truthful when he asked something as important as that. Yes, there had been men who had tried to seduce her while he was gone. She had never put herself in a position to be seduced, though. One man had been a business acquaintance the company was making a deal with. He'd found her attractive and made it clear he wanted to get to know her. But she'd gotten him straight in no time. And, once, she'd been traveling, and the man sitting next to her on the plane had flirted outrageously and asked her if she would have dinner with him after they touched down in London. She'd shown him her engagement ring and wedding band, which he had obviously chosen to ignore. She'd declined his offer firmly.

Yes, she'd ached for the touch of a man some nights when she couldn't sleep and memories of making love to Adam ran on a loop in her brain. Cold showers helped in those instances. Or she'd get up, put on her dance togs and pointe shoes and go through her ballet routines until she couldn't dance anymore. Most of the time, though, she simply immersed herself in work, either for Youngblood Media or her painting. They were distractions that worked for the time being. None of that kept her from missing Adam, though, or praying fervently for his safe return.

Now that she had him back, she wanted to relive those hot lovemaking sessions they used to share. But his reaction at the hotel had put a big question mark on whether or not her wish was going to come true anytime soon. He was going through something. Something he had to figure out on his own, obviously. Because he was not confiding in her the way he used to. They used to be able to talk about anything. Now he was behaving like her father's generation of men: like he was an island unto himself. They lived by credos like *A man doesn't show emotions. A man takes care of his own business. A man doesn't show weakness.* Her mother had once told her that it had taken her father years to let go of the behavior he'd been taught by his father. She hoped it wouldn't take years for Adam to open up to her.

After Adam had gotten the grill prepared for the chicken, he turned to her and asked, "Do you suppose I have time to watch *Black Panther* before dinner?"

She laughed. "No, that movie's over two hours long. We'll just eat in front of the TV tonight. Go on, enjoy yourself. I can handle dinner-cooking duties."

He grinned and loped into the adjacent great room where the wide-screen TV and other electronics were. She watched him go, her heart aflutter due to his presence. It was taking her a while to convince herself this wasn't a dream. Adam was physically here. He looked a bit different. Ganglier because of his weight loss. He appeared taller, somehow. Maybe because with the forty pounds gone, his center of gravity had changed.

His body shape used to look a bit like Dwayne Johnson's. Now he had more of a LeBron James body type. Still yummy, as far as she was concerned, although she sensed his confidence wasn't what it used to be. He didn't appear to believe in his rugged sensuality the way he formerly had. He was a man who was well aware of his attractiveness to the opposite sex and didn't mind ribbing her about salivating over him. And she honestly didn't mind admitting that was the case. She enjoyed their saucy love life. He loved it when she seduced him, too. Their love affair was full of fun, passion and fire.

She sighed as she turned her attention back to preparing dinner. *Lord, give me strength and patience*, she silently pleaded.

# *Chapter 6*

His first night back home, after dinner and watching *Black Panther* twice, Adam bit the bullet and went to take a shower. Alia Joie had taken one earlier while he was watching the movie for the second time. He was sure she was wondering if he was purposely putting off going to bed, what with his behavior at the hotel room in Arlington. That was part of it. But he'd also enjoyed the movie and wanted to see it again. He had to admit to himself, as well, that sleeping all night with Alia Joie might prove problematic. He hadn't worked out yet in his mind why he'd had a panic attack after he'd gotten an erection and was preparing to make love to her in the hotel.

He'd dreamed about making love to her countless times while he was gone. Now that he had her within his grasp, he was having doubts. He had no trouble getting a hard-on. It was psychological, not physical. He was terrified he would get naked with her, get her all worked up, then at the penultimate moment, his penis would shrivel and he'd be worthless to her. Worthless, with a withered pecker. Why was his self-esteem at its lowest point in his life? That was what he had to figure out.

He finished showering, stepped out of the stall, selected a thick, white towel from the rack adjacent and began drying himself off in the large bathroom. He could hear Alia Joie in the master bedroom talking on her cell phone and wondered who she was talking to at nearly midnight. Her mother, probably. The two of them sometimes chatted several times a day. Debra was more than likely wondering how he was doing. His mother-in-law was a lovely woman. She reminded him of Ramona, except Ramona didn't censure anything she had to say. Debra showed tact. Ramona just let you have it with both barrels.

He strode into the bedroom wearing only a towel wrapped around his lower half, and Alia Joie smiled at him, gestured to her phone and mouthed, *Chance*.

Ah, he was wrong. Chance and Alia Joie were very close, and now that Chance was in love, he was sure the two of them had plenty to talk about. Adam liked both her brothers and wished Brock, too, would find someone to love. But Brock was a playboy, and he doubted he'd settle down anytime soon.

He rummaged in the dresser drawers until he found a pair of his pajamas. He smiled when he saw Alia Joie had bought him new sets of pajamas that hadn't even been taken out of their packages, but had not gotten rid of his old comfortable ones. He selected a black-and-white-striped pair of the old ones and noticed, once he had them on, that he had to pull the drawstring tighter; otherwise, they felt great. He dropped onto the bed like he used to, causing Alia Joie to bounce on it. She shook a fist at him for his naughtiness and exclaimed, "She said yes! I'm so happy for you. She's great. She's perfect for you. Hurry up and get married."

Adam watched as Alia Joie's face scrunched up in a huge grin. "Van Cleef & Arpels is where Dad buys jewelry for Mom!" she said. "Mmm-hmm. Don't make me cry. Good night, baby brother. I love you."

She ended the call, placed the phone on its charger and turned to face him. "Chance proposed to Petra."

He was busy propping himself up on the headboard, shoving pillows behind his back until he was satisfied. "That's great. How long have they known each other?"

"Around six months," Alia Joie answered, her eyes animated. Then she went on to tell him the fantastical-sounding tale of Petra Gaines being someone akin to Tarzan in the Congo and how she was single-handedly saving the chimpanzees in Equatorial Africa and that their network was going to premiere a television show about her life in a matter of weeks.

"Boy," he said, after she paused to catch her breath. "I've missed a lot while I've been gone."

Alia Joie laughed, turned off the lamp on her side of the bed and snuggled up to him. "What are you going to do about getting a new phone? You going to go to a store or order one online?"

He shrugged. "Having been without one for so long,

I don't even miss it. But I suppose I'll get online tomorrow and order one."

She was looking at him with a smile curling her luscious lips, and her cinnamon-colored eyes left no question in his mind that she was delighted to have him sharing her bed tonight. He reached over and switched off the light on his side of the bed, and they lay in each other's arms in the dark except for the faint illumination of the streetlights through the window blinds.

She yawned. "It's been some day. Welcome home, sweetie."

"Thank you, my joy," he said. Her head was on his chest and he enjoyed the feel of her soft braids as he tenderly ran his fingers through them. She smelled so good and her body, with its feminine curves, reminded him that he did, indeed, still possess the normal reactions a real man had when presented with sexual stimuli. His manhood would soon be making a tent in his pajama bottoms. He lay motionless with his arm around her until he heard her steady inhalations and exhalations, denoting sleep.

Then he sighed deeply with relief.

*This is just the first night,* he told himself. *I'm going to get over this. Whatever this is.*

December came in like a roaring lion, or so that was how Alia felt when she was outside trying to walk against the blistering cold winds tearing around corners on New York City streets. She'd gone back to work about a week after Adam's return. Youngblood Media required their marketing department to be in full gear whether her head was in the game or not. Plus, she thought it best that Adam have the opportunity for some time away from her constant mothering. She was so glad to have him back that she was spoiling him. And both her mother and mother-in-law had warned her against doing that. *He ain't no baby*, was Ramona's retort when she'd spoken to her over the phone, her Bahamian accent thick. *You're not doing him any favors by coddlin' him, child.* Her mother was in agreement. *Love him,* she'd said, *but don't do everything for him. You never waited on him hand and foot before. I know you're happy to have him back, and that's why you're doing it, but give it a rest!*

All Alia knew was that she hated leaving him every morning to go to work. She left early, and he was usually still asleep when she kissed him goodbye. He would awaken, smile at her and murmur, "Have a good day, sweetheart."

She'd hear his quiet breathing, proof that he'd already fallen back to sleep, only a few seconds afterward as she walked through the loft to the front door.

When she returned home, he would always greet her at the door with a kiss, and she'd smell wonderful aromas coming from the kitchen.

It was domestic bliss, actually. All except for sexual intimacy. They slept in each other's arms, but she'd been reluctant to force the issue of sex with him. She wasn't going to go there after he'd bolted for the bathroom that time in Arlington. She told herself he needed to be the one to initiate sex. She wished he would talk to her about it, though. They were in sexual limbo, and she didn't know what to do about it.

She got home from work one evening in early December and found Adam putting up Christmas decorations. They'd talked about decorating the loft, but neither had suggested a time to do it. So she was happy that he'd taken the initiative and decided to just do it. A few feet from the front door, mistletoe with a red ribbon tied around it hung upside down. He was up on a ladder putting an angel atop an eight-foot-tall Christmas tree when she entered the loft.

"Hey, babe," he said cheerfully. Finished with his task, he climbed down and started walking toward her. She set her shoulder bag and briefcase on the foyer table and admired him, which was something she did all the time now. He was letting his hair grow back, and it was coming along nicely. Soon, she knew, he would begin twisting it to train it to grow in separate spirals in hopes of growing his dreadlocks out again. His beard was thick and beautifully shaped. He kept it oiled, and it was shiny and soft to the touch.

Alia inhaled the sexy, male scent of him. She offered him her lips to kiss, which he did with gusto. Afterward, she smiled and said, "Hello, sweetie. The place looks festive. Does this mean you have the Christmas spirit?"

He smiled as he cocked his head to the side, thinking. "To be honest, I'm hoping this will give me the Christmas spirit. You know I was always as wild as a child about Christmas, but I just don't have that feeling right now."

"Well, you've been through a lot," she sympathized. "I didn't celebrate much while you were gone. It just didn't feel right without you. But I'm looking forward to it this year. We've got something to celebrate."

They walked to the great room together and sat down on the couch in the leather seating group. She turned toward him. "Tell me about your day," she said expectantly.

"They want me to come back to work," he said, not sounding enthusiastic about the prospect.

"The others are ready to get back to work, too?" she asked.

She hadn't heard how Arjun and Calvin and Maritza were doing after getting back home, and she was curious.

"They're scientists," Adam said dryly. "All they know is work." He laughed shortly. "I do have good news about them, though. Turns out Arjun's girlfriend really loved him and was hoping for his return, and they're engaged. Calvin's girlfriend wasn't as faithful and got engaged while he was gone. He claims he didn't take it hard, though. He's giving his little black book a workout, and I fear he might turn into a player just to prove he's attractive to the opposite sex. Best news of all, Maritza's family is doing great. Raul turned into a good father after she left. He had to learn how to care for Mariana on his own and did a fine job. Maritza's having fun getting to know her daughter, whom Raul didn't let forget her."

Alia smiled with satisfaction. "I'm glad to hear that. Poor Calvin, though. I wish his girlfriend had waited for him."

She sat back on the couch. "So, are you thinking of going back to work?"

He nodded. "I think it's for the best. Maybe it'll

help me get rid of some quirks I need to get out of my system."

"Like?" she asked gently, hoping he was finally going to open up to her.

He averted his gaze, a sure sign to Alia that she was going to hear something she wouldn't like. But he surprised her by saying, "I know you've noticed the lack of sex in our relationship, Alia Joie." He looked her straight in the eyes.

She didn't look away. "I figured you'd talk to me about it when you were ready to."

"I've never had a problem making love to you before," he said. "I don't know why this is happening to me, to us."

"Nothing about this is routine," she said reasonably. "You were never kidnapped before, either. Maybe you should talk to a professional about it."

"You know how I feel about therapists," he said, his tone bordering on belligerent. "I don't want anyone messing with my head. I've already had my head messed with enough over the past two years!"

Then she thought of something he'd mentioned when he'd first gotten home. "You said you read a study about returning servicemen and their relationships with their wives after being prisoners of war. Did any of them have problems with making love to their wives after their experience?"

In his beautiful eyes, she could see the wheels turning in that analytical mind of his. He cleared his throat, then frowned. "Yes, I do recall reading that some of the men felt emasculated by being held against their will.

As if their manhood, or power, had been taken away from them. And they felt weak and helpless."

"What did they do about it?" she asked softly.

His expression didn't look promising. "There were a lot of divorces. Some men turned violent out of frustration and beat their wives. The wives felt they had to leave them to survive. It was a depressing study. Now I wish I hadn't read it."

Alia placed a reassuring hand on his leg. "That couldn't be all the study talked about. Being starved also has an effect on the libido, you know. There had to be other reasons for the men's lack of sexual drive."

He brightened. "You're right. There were men who said their sexual urges returned after they got healthier."

"The key is not to panic," Alia offered. "We'll take this slowly. I won't try to seduce you, so you can relax around me and not worry about my trying to force you to perform. If you want me to wear a granny nightgown to bed, I will."

Adam chuckled. "Oh, no, not the granny nightgown!" He continued more seriously, "No, babe. Come to bed just as you are, and I'll concentrate on getting back to my former good health." He regarded her with a look of admiration. "And I promise I'll consider talking to a professional. I'm a scientist. I shouldn't have antiquated notions about having my head shrunk."

"Deal," she said.

He got up then, reached for her hand and pulled her off the couch. "Come on, I made Ramona's fried snapper and peas and rice."

"Mmm," Alia said. "Did you make any johnnycake to go with it?"

"You know I did," he said happily. "Did you know that there's a store just down the street that caters to Bahamians?"

"Of course," Alia said with a laugh. "I've been there lots of times."

In the kitchen, Adam took the fried fish, crispy and golden and lying on a platter, out of the oven, where Alia figured he'd put it to keep it warm. On the stove, the peas and rice were simmering in a Dutch oven. And the corn bread sat on the stove top.

"I should wash up," Alia said after seeing that dinner was ready. She turned to walk over to the sink to wash her hands, but Adam had other plans, and stopped her and pulled her into his arms. "I've been wanting to kiss you properly for a long time," he said. Then he bent his head and pressed his mouth to hers in a soft kiss. Taken by surprise, she was tense and stiff in his arms, but relaxed in an instant and sighed, her breath mingling with his.

That exchange of breath warmed her up considerably and ignited a sweet feeling of desire that was waiting below the surface of her emotions. It had been so hard to turn off the passion she felt for him. Now she was free to express it, and she felt her body let go of the negative, petty demons that were always berating her, taunting her that maybe Adam wasn't interested in making love to her anymore. Maybe she wasn't attractive to him anymore. Maybe, maybe, maybe. She was sick of maybes.

He moaned with pleasure, and she could tell that his

body was responding to hers. His muscles were even
closer to the skin than before, when he'd carried an
extra forty pounds. She felt them as he held her close.
His arm muscles were hard as rocks. His thigh muscles,
pressed against hers, were corded.

Her body was singing with joy. From her head—which
was a little dizzy, if she was being totally honest—to her
toes, she rightfully exulted in this moment. This was the
kiss she'd been waiting for. It left her weak and breath-
less after they came up for air, and, boy, did it answer
one question she'd been asking herself. Was her husband
still attracted to her? Yes! Her husband still wanted her.
He just had to find his way back to her.

Throughout dinner, they gazed into each other's eyes
like lovesick idiots, smiling and feeding each other. It
was nauseating behavior that she would have derided
her friends for displaying. And they would have kid-
ded her about it, too. She didn't care.

"I'm beginning to get into the Christmas spirit," he
told her with a sexy smile. "Want to go skating tomorrow night?"

Tomorrow was Friday, and Alia usually left the office early on Fridays unless something pressing came
up. She nodded, feeling shy suddenly, like they were
going on their first date.

"Good," Adam said. "I'll meet you at 30 Rock.
Around five? We'll go to dinner afterward."

"It's a date!" she said.

She climbed into bed that night and went into Adam's
arms, confident that they were making progress now.
He kissed her gently on the mouth and murmured, "I
love you."

"I love you," she returned. "Sweet dreams."

He gave her a quizzical look but didn't say anything else. He just reached over and switched off the lamp on his nightstand. She'd already turned hers off. She settled with a sigh in his arms. This not talking about things was getting to her. He was withholding information, and now, because she didn't want to upset him, she was forced to keep quiet about subjects she would much rather have out in the open.

The fact was that he'd been having violent nightmares since he'd returned. He talked in his sleep. No, he shouted in his sleep, as though he were being pursued by demons. After the first time it had happened, she'd done some research online and found out that some people in REM sleep can kick, grab the people sleeping with them and jump out of bed, all while in rapid eye movement sleep. But so far all he'd done was yell in his sleep and toss and turn.

She was tired. It had been a strenuous day at work, and this constant worrying about Adam's state of mind was exhausting. She closed her eyes and soon was sleeping soundly.

The next thing she knew, she felt a sharp pain on her right shoulder. She awoke in the dark and felt Adam turning from side to side next to her as if he was fending off an attack. Not bothering to turn on a light, she clambered off the bed on her side and stood at the foot of the bed, watching his hulking figure moving about. He was shouting, "No, no, no!" over and over again.

She rubbed her shoulder. Should she wake him? She wasn't sure what to do. She'd heard that you shouldn't awaken people when they were in the throes of a nightmare. Before she could make up her mind, he quit fighting whomever he was tussling with in his dream, and all was quiet. Within seconds, he was sleeping peacefully.

She got back into bed. It was a while before she could fall back to sleep, but when she did there were no more disturbances.

Adam felt momentarily overwhelmed when confronted with the statue of Prometheus and the towering Rockefeller Center Christmas tree, to say nothing of the sixty-six-story Rockefeller Plaza that towered above the famous skating rink. He'd been on the lookout for Alia Joie the past twenty minutes. He was finally rewarded when he saw her hurrying toward him. She wore a tan overcoat with a sweater peeking out at the collar, casual slacks and boots, and was carrying a tote with her skates undoubtedly inside. He held a bag with his skates, as well.

His heartbeat sped up at the sight of her. His desire for her felt like a painful ache that he knew wouldn't go away until he could fully claim her. It felt as though he had to woo his wife all over again. As if something within him was dictating his actions, tormenting him, so that when he finally overcame this obstacle that stood between him and Alia Joie, he would appreciate her more. He would know how lucky he was to have her in his life again.

They kissed briefly. She was smiling, her eyes alight with happiness. He wanted so much to be the person who put that light in her eyes.

They paid the fee, and soon they were skating while

holding hands. Neither of them had forgotten their routines. They were perfect partners, both athletic and graceful in their movements. She was his equal when it came to athleticism. She'd started ballet at six and had studied it into her teens. To him, she was beautiful to watch while in motion.

After a good workout on the ice, they went for coffee while they decided where to go for dinner. Sitting across from each other in the coffee shop, he thought he saw a bruise on Alia Joie when her sweater's shoulder lowered a bit as she took off her coat. He frowned as he regarded her with concern. "Babe, what's that dark mark on your shoulder?"

Alia Joie smiled. "It's nothing."

"It looks like a bruise," he insisted. "Did you run into a door? Did someone grab you?"

He was becoming agitated. He couldn't stand it if someone had put his hands on her. He knew he was making her uncomfortable because she refused to meet his gaze. "Alia Joie, tell me how you got that bruise on your shoulder," he demanded.

She huffed in frustration. He knew that sound all too well. She didn't want to tell him what he was trying to pull out of her.

He gave her a determined look. "Talk to me."

Looking him in the eyes, she said, "All right. The fact is, you've been having nightmares. You thrash about in your sleep. You're a big man, and sometimes it can be dangerous to sleep next to you. Last night, you hit me in the spot where I have a bruise. You were dreaming. You weren't in control. I debated whether or not to mention it."

He couldn't have been more shocked. Yes, he knew about the nightmares, but he had no idea he was moving around in bed while he was having them. He felt like a heel. He felt like a wife beater, even though he knew he'd acted against his will and would never in his waking moments hurt her.

He had to fight back tears. "Oh, God, baby, I'm so sorry. You know I would never put my hands on you in my right mind."

They held hands across the tiny round table in the coffee shop. She smiled through her tears. "I know you wouldn't. Maybe I should have said something last night. But I was afraid it would be a setback for you. I didn't want you to heap on more self-recriminations. You already blame yourself for things you had no control over. It was a nightmare, which is a manifestation of your daytime worries. *We're* going to be fine."

Adam was busy berating himself. His foremost thought was, *If I'd been man enough to confess my fears to her, to admit my weaknesses, this would never have happened.*

He brought her hand to his mouth and kissed the palm. "This crazy code of silence between us ends here. We talk about everything from now on. I promised myself I would never hurt you, and I've hurt you. I'm making an appointment with a therapist as soon as possible."

## Chapter 7

True to his word, Adam began having sessions with Dr. Jared Klein. In the beginning, Dr. Klein suggested they meet twice a week for an hour in his office. Adam was taken aback during the first session when Dr. Klein asked him why he'd chosen him as his therapist.

Adam was sitting across from the therapist in his fashionable Manhattan office, which was decorated in soothing, muted colors, the air cool and not stuffy as some offices were in winter. Adam shrugged, knowing that his mind wasn't focusing because of panic. Instead of concentrating on the doctor and what he was saying, he was thinking about the room.

Dr. Klein, who was a tall, lanky man in his late thirties with thick and curly dark brown hair and a beard, must have thought Adam appeared confused because he smiled at him and said, "I apologize, Adam. I always ask that question just to break the ice. And to determine if you, like a lot of my male patients, chose me solely because I'm male and you think talking to a male might be easier for you. Which would be perfectly fine. I just want to find out where you're coming from."

Adam laughed nervously. "Look, Dr. Klein, I'm here because I've been having nightmares since coming back home after I was held captive for two years in the Middle East. I can't discuss any of that, by the way. I'm here for personal reasons. I thought I could handle my problems by myself, but after hitting my wife in my sleep a few nights ago, I realize I need help. Can you help me?"

Dr. Klein leaned toward him, a look of concern on his face. "I'll do my best. Without giving me any details about your ordeal, tell me the extent of the abuses you suffered. I do need to know that in order to figure out how to aid your recovery."

For the next half hour or so, Adam recounted his experience for the psychiatrist, speaking of his kidnapping, how he and his colleagues had been treated at the facility and his isolation, which he thought had been the most difficult part.

"And what are the nightmares about?" Dr. Klein asked when he was finished. The doctor waited patiently while Adam gathered his thoughts. His nightmares were numerous and varied. "Sometimes I'm in pitch-black darkness. It feels like it's hard to breathe and I can sense someone's in the room with me, but they're silent. In one dream I could feel the exhalation of someone's breath on my neck. I woke up then in a cold sweat.

"In other dreams I'm fighting off my attackers. But I never win. I'm always held down, my hands tied behind my back, my head covered with a black hood. The common theme is helplessness."

"Helpless," Dr. Klein commented. "Like you felt when you were kidnapped."

Adam nodded.

Dr. Klein leaned back in his chair, watching Adam intently. "I like to learn as much about my patients before my first appointment with them, Adam. The more I know, the more I can get a feel for how you might think, based on my years of education and experience treating patients. To be honest with you, I'd already heard of you and your wife. You're both pretty well-known in the city."

Adam had been expecting this. It was one of the reasons he had not wanted to seek out a therapist. Could a therapist be completely discreet and nonjudgmental of someone they had heard about, maybe had even admired? He wasn't referring to himself. Alia Joie was known for her charitable work in the city. They'd met at a charity event. Her family contributed to several charities, and there was a lot of publicity surrounding those endeavors. He was a minor celebrity compared to her.

So he was surprised when Dr. Klein said, "I've read all your books. You're a brilliant man. You make physics accessible to the masses. I loved it when you admitted that you'd taken up ice-skating because your physics idol, Michio Kaku, loves ice-skating." He paused, a smile causing crinkles to appear around his eyes. "I'm telling you all this to be completely transparent. Many celebrities have therapists and trust the fact that we are sworn not to disclose anything we discuss. I wanted you to make up your mind about whether or not you want to go forward from here. When a patient has gone through what you have, I know it's hard to trust anyone for a while. But if we're going to make progress, we must let down our guards and trust one another. Can you do that, Adam?"

Adam shifted uncomfortably in his chair. He was grateful for the doctor's honesty, but a bit uncertain about what his next move should be. He was here because he wanted to be able to make love to his wife again. And he wasn't sure why he feared trying to. If this professional had answers, then he needed to hear them.

"Well, I can't stay in the state I'm in," he told Dr. Klein. "So I'm going to trust you."

He thought the doctor looked relieved at that statement. Dr. Klein sat back in his leather office chair and regarded Adam with an inquisitive expression. "Good. Then tell me what it is that you think is at the center of your feeling helpless. Don't answer right away. I know you're an accomplished person, and feeling helpless isn't something you've experienced before now. Am I right?"

Adam wanted to exclaim, *Damn right!* But held his dry humor in check. This was serious business. "No, I can't ever recall feeling helpless about anything. Even when I was a poor kid growing up, I never felt as if I had no control. I was aware that my future depended on my behavior. By behaving a certain way, I created positive outcomes."

Dr. Klein chuckled. "You were behaving like a scientist even back then."

Adam smiled. "Yes, I suppose so. But now I'm crippled by my own thoughts, Doctor. Physically, I'm fine. I was a little malnourished when I got back to the States, but since then my body has healed. But I still can't make love to my wife. My body wants to, but my mind isn't cooperating."

"Your wife is a very beautiful woman," Dr. Klein said matter-of-factly. Adam was a little irked by his observation. Of course Alia Joie was beautiful. What did that have to do with anything?

"The problem is not with Alia Joie," he said, looking Dr. Klein in the eyes. "She's practically perfect. I'm not saying that to give you the idea that she's so perfect I no longer feel I'm worthy of her or anything like that."

"She comes from a very rich family," Dr. Klein put in. "You've never felt, like some men, that a woman shouldn't earn more money than her husband?"

"No, why should I feel that way? We both knew what we were getting into when we got married. I knew I would never earn billions. I don't even covet such riches. Alia Joie and I love and respect each other for who we are. I want her to reach for the stars. And she supports me in every way possible."

Dr. Klein smiled. "Go on, you're doing very well. You don't feel emasculated by her level of wealth, then?"

"Emasculated? Believe me, Doctor, I had no trouble making love to my wife before my experience in the

Middle East. None whatsoever!" Adam almost shouted, half rising out of his chair.

He settled back into his chair and sighed. "Sorry about that," he apologized. "I'm just frustrated."

Dr. Klein smiled benignly. "Adam, you're displaying symptoms of PTSD. I talk to a lot of returning soldiers who complain of not being able to make love to their wives. It's not because they don't love their wives. It's because psychologically they believe they were rendered weak and helpless by their experiences. They came back feeling as though their manhood had been taken from them."

He took a deep breath and continued, "You say you never had a problem making love to Alia Joie before your incarceration in the Middle East. Adam, do you think being powerless to do anything against your captors might have something to do with feeling helpless now?"

The timer went off, and Dr. Klein said, "Think about it until we meet again on Thursday."

Adam almost laughed. He felt they were actually getting somewhere, and it was time to quit for the day. This was yet another reason he hadn't wanted to talk to a therapist. When you started making progress, you were obliged to vacate the premises. Dr. Klein undoubtedly had another patient waiting to see him.

Adam rose, feeling emotionally drained. He and Dr. Klein shook hands and he left. He would make up his mind later whether or not he'd return for a second session. He still didn't like the idea of spilling his guts to a total stranger.

He could hear Ramona in his head saying, *Why you*

*wanna pay good money for somebody to listen to your
problems when you've got me or your wife or your
brothers-in-law or father-in-law to listen to them?*

In this case, he had to admit it was better to talk to a
professional. He couldn't very well talk to his father-in-
law or his brothers-in-law about not being able to make
love to Alia Joie. There was no one in his life he felt
comfortable talking to about such a sensitive subject.

Alia was standing in front of the mirror in the master bedroom putting in her earrings. She could hear
Adam singing in the shower. Lately he'd been in a good
mood. He was singing more now like he used to. He
loved old-school soul music and was singing an Otis
Redding song, "These Arms of Mine." He had a solid
baritone with enough soul in it to curl her toes. That
song reminded her of a particularly erotic lovemaking
session they'd shared in their old apartment.

A warm, sexy feeling came over her at the memory, and she let it run its course, which ended with her
body shivering a little. She smiled at her reflection in
the mirror. Her hair was no longer in braids, but in a
naturally curly halo around her face, the length falling
to the middle of her back. She was wearing bold gold
hoop earrings with a circumference of two inches, a
short black dress with long sleeves that clung to her
figure and black sandals. She'd kept her makeup to a
minimum. After moisturizing, she applied a little mascara and red matte lipstick. Her skin was glowing. She
knew it was because she was happy and looking forward to the Christmas party here in the loft tonight.

For weeks, her friends had been wondering when

they could get together with Adam. They wanted to see for themselves that he was okay. It was understandable because Adam was well liked among their friends. He genuinely cared about them, and they had missed him and been praying for his safe return right alongside her.

Plus, since Adam had started seeing Dr. Klein, with whom he'd had six sessions now, his nightmares had decreased. He was back at work and enjoying the camaraderie of his work family. Things were starting to feel…normal again. Although she hated putting that label on their life together. What was normal, anyway? Every couple had their own way of meshing. She didn't want to focus on what they used to have, but what they could have in the future.

As for making love, that hadn't happened yet although Adam was not stingy with hugs or kisses. They still slept together, and there hadn't been another violent incident. And early in the mornings, she often felt his erection on her backside as they spooned in bed. That was reassuring to her. That and his habit of nuzzling her neck while he was holding her and breathing in her essence.

When they were dating, she'd found it peculiar that he would always take huge whiffs of her and exhale, a smile on his face, and say, "Ah, your scent gives me life!" No other man she'd ever dated had done that. Or perhaps she'd never noticed another man doing it. Adam, with his zest for living and his unadulterated honesty, let her know exactly how he felt about her. That was something she missed—his bold sensuality.

Adam came out of the bathroom with a towel wrapped around his waist and gathered her in his arms from behind. He kissed the side of her neck. Alia looked at their reflection in the mirror. They looked like a couple very much in love.

"It's going to be crazy," he whispered in her ear. "Your friends, my scientist pals, your family, the tenants, all mingling together."

She smiled. "I can't wait."


Adam was glad they'd decided to have the party catered buffet-style with a bartender mixing drinks. He and Alia Joie were free to entertain their guests and catch up on their lives. The loft was tastefully decorated for Christmas. The eight-foot-tall Christmas tree was lit up with multicolored lights, and poinsettias were placed around the large space where he imagined couples would gather in small groups chatting and enjoying the food and drinks.

Guests started arriving around seven; the first was Macy, Alia Joie's best friend since childhood. He opened the door and she immediately gave him a warm hug. He'd always liked Macy. She was solid, a true friend who, Alia Joie told him, had never let her down. He hugged her back, then, setting her away from him, peered into the hallway as if he were looking for someone. "What, no date?" he asked.

She grimaced and playfully punched him on the arm. The woman boxed for fun and was in great shape, so that tap had hurt, something he tried not to let show on his face. "Don't you start," she warned him. "No, I'm not dating anyone at the moment. My parents tried to fix me up, but I'm not in the market for anyone who has to be foisted on me by my parents." She grinned up at him. "Welcome back! You had us worried there for a moment, or two years to be exact."

She walked farther into the loft, looking around. "This place looks like Martha Stewart got soused on eggnog and had her way with it."

Adam chuckled. "I'm going to take that as a compliment."

"As it was meant to be," Macy assured him.

Alia Joie walked into the room then, and the women squealed with delight at seeing each other again. He knew they hadn't gotten together in about a month, but really?

The doorbell rang and he went to answer it. Outside stood Calvin and his date, a beautiful blonde with cool gray eyes. He guessed she was a model because lately Calvin had been going through models as frequently as he changed shirts.

Calvin was six feet, the model an inch or two taller. "Adam," Calvin said as he stepped across the threshold, pulling his date after him, "this is Nadia."

She greeted him in Russian. He knew a little Russian and reciprocated, which earned him a huge smile. She gave him a lascivious once-over. Calvin noticed and rolled his eyes in exasperation. "Another one bites the dust," he said to Adam in a low voice as he and Nadia headed over to the bar to order drinks. Nadia apparently didn't know much English. Poor Calvin was having no lasting luck with women. They were attracted to him because he was a sought-after scientist, he was good-looking and personable, and he had been born into an extremely rich family.

Adam didn't have time to ponder Calvin's love life

further, because the doorbell was ringing again. This time, Maritza and Raul were on the other side of it. Before he could usher them inside, he glanced down the hallway and spied Arjun and his fiancée, Madhuri. Arjun had told him her name meant charming, and, indeed, she was the epitome of charm. Long, silky black hair, parted in the middle, fell to her waist. She was wearing a beautiful peach-colored sari, and Arjun wore a festive suit consisting of black slacks, a deep purple velvet jacket and a crisp white shirt, and the latest Air Jordans. They were a handsome couple.

"Welcome," Adam said enthusiastically to both couples.

"The place is gorgeous," Maritza said, her dark eyes sparkling with excitement. Adam noticed her husband, Raul, had his arm about her waist, holding her close. He appeared happy, too, and it did Adam's heart good to recognize such contentment in the couple.

"Thanks," he said. "How's Mariana? Is she thrilled that it's almost Christmas?"

Raul laughed. "You'd be surprised by how much a toddler knows about Christmas. She's convinced she's going to stay up and catch Santa coming down the chimney. We don't even have a chimney. I don't know where she learned that fairy tale."

"From your mother," Maritza said, smiling at her husband. She regarded Adam. "Raul's mother is visiting us from Florida, and she reads Mariana a different Christmas story in Spanish every night."

"That's good," said Arjun as he helped Madhuri off with her coat and she returned the favor. "My family didn't celebrate Christmas, but there are Christians in India, and I had a friend whose house I would visit and get stuffed with all sorts of sweets. The women in the family would get together in the kitchen and cook and gossip all weekend. I loved to eavesdrop on their conversations."

"That's why he's so sensitive today," Madhuri said sweetly, and gave him a kiss on the cheek.

While Arjun was blushing, Alia Joie and Macy walked up, and hugs were shared all around. Then the doorbell rang again, and Adam was off to answer it. This went on for about another half hour as Alia Joie's family and the building's residents arrived. His brother-in-law, Brock, showed up alone, which surprised Adam, but he didn't joke with him about being solo as he'd done with Macy. The two men hugged hello. He could see the concern for him in Brock's eyes. Like Chance, Brock was very protective of his sister and rightfully worried that her husband might not be all there. The thought made Adam cringe inwardly. Still, he felt he and Alia Joie were making progress.

Brock jokingly said, "I see you've been eating well. You're filling out, bro."

Adam replied, "Between your mother's cooking, and Alia Joie's, I have no chance of not gaining weight. But I've got a handle on it. I don't think I'm going to aim for my former weight. I like being a bit lighter."

"I heard that!" said Brock, who was fit but boasted a big appetite. "Where's the buffet?"

Adam pointed in the general direction of the food, and his brother-in-law went to see what was on tonight's menu.

Alia Joie's friend Diana arrived last with a handsome man on her arm, as she invariably did, Adam remembered. Although Diana was one to put on airs sometimes, tonight she greeted him with warmth, introduced him to her date and went to join the others.

Soon the loft was full of folks standing around or sitting while engaged in lively communion. Drinks flowed, and delicious food was eaten with gusto.

Adam soaked up the love and camaraderie. He'd assumed he would feel claustrophobic with a full house and a bit uncomfortable around strangers, as most of the building's residents were to him. But he felt at ease and was enjoying himself.

He was happy to hear his friends' and in-laws' stories and catch up with their lives. Chance and Petra shared how Chance had proposed. Alia Joie's friend June and her fiancé, Tony, recounted their own proposal story.

After that, Alia Joie's dad, James, joked, "Back in the day, we used to have to ask the parents' permission to marry the daughter, before we even asked the woman we loved. You two didn't do that? Just curious."

Tony and Chance confirmed that neither had asked the parents' permission before proposing. "Well, did you get down on one knee?" asked Jefferson Zachariah Johnson, or J.Z. as he was known among the other tenants, a grin on his always cheerful face. Adam had met him numerous times in the building, and J.Z. had never failed to tell him that the apartment he shared with his wife, Emma, was directly below Adam and Alia Joie's place. And then he'd mention that he never heard any noise from their loft. This behavior puzzled Adam, but he'd never asked J.Z. to explain himself.

"I did." Chance answered J.Z.'s question.

"In the middle of the restaurant just like in *Moonstruck*," Petra supplied with a meaningful look at Chance. "He was so cute."

Adam could have sworn Chance blushed, something he'd never seen him do. Suddenly he was jealous of all these people in love and expressing love. Their happiness emphasized the lack of the expression of physical love in his and Alia Joie's marriage. He glanced at her, sitting between her parents on the couch. She looked up and their eyes met across the room. She inhaled, her chest heaving, and reached up to tuck a tendril of hair behind her ear, and that movement seemed like the most sensual act he'd witnessed in ages. God, he loved her so much. She deserved to be cherished. She deserved all the love in the world.

"I didn't get down on one knee," Tony said, smiling into June's eyes. "We'd just completed a heart surgery together and after we scrubbed up, I turned, looked in my jacket hanging on a nearby hook, got the ring and said, 'Would you marry me and take me away from this stressful life?'"

June laughed. "And I said yes, I'll marry you, but since we're both doctors I don't think we're going to get away from the stress. But the times we have away from this place will be full of love and laughter."

"That'll work!" Debra, Alia Joie's mother, exclaimed.

"Amen," her husband, James, agreed wholeheartedly. He smiled at his wife. "Unfortunately, my darling Debbie's parents had both passed away when I proposed to her. But I did the traditional knee thing."

"And I made him get up in a hurry," Debra said. "He proposed to me in Central Park in the middle of December and it was freezing."

"You warmed me up nicely once we got home," James said with a naughty expression in his eyes.

"Daddy!" Alia Joie exclaimed, aghast at his behavior. "Your children are listening."

"How do you think you got here?" Debra asked, laughing.

And so it went as the guests shared stories about their lives, getting to know each other in some cases and renewing friendships in others.

Later, when the mood was quieter and the guests had broken into smaller groups, Adam went to the bar to get his first drink of the night.

As he stood in front of the bar, waiting for the bartender to make him a whiskey on the rocks, The Temptations' Christmas album was on the sound system, and they were singing "Silent Night." He watched Alia Joie standing near the fireplace, drink in hand, her head thrown back in a fit of laughter. Her father had probably told one of his ribald jokes. She looked sexy as hell in that dress, her curves delectable. He could imagine those long legs wrapped around him in the throes of passion, his hands full of her firm, round ass.

"Here you are, Dr. Braithwaite," said the young African American man, gesturing to the drink he'd placed in front of him. Adam jerked back to attention, inwardly chiding himself for lusting after his wife, when he should rightfully be demonstrating his desires instead of imagining them.

He thanked the bartender and had turned, with the

intention of joining Alia Joie across the room, when someone grabbed him by the arm.

"Adam, a word?"

# Chapter 8

"Oh, Mr. Johnson," Adam said, turning to face his seventysomething-year-old neighbor. He wasn't surprised to see him. J.Z. was a talkative man who often waylaid him in the building while he was trying to go outside, on the sidewalk when he was going for a run or in the elevator when he was taking groceries up to the loft. Mr. Johnson always had a story to tell him about his wife and how long the two of them had lived in this neighborhood, and about his many years as a postman. Oh, the stories he could tell him about the people who had lived on this street before he and Alia Joie moved here. They were great stories. But Adam often didn't have time to listen to his drawn-out tales. He hoped he didn't appear disinterested to Mr. Johnson when he hurried off each and every time. He respected his elders.

He smiled at Mr. Johnson now. "I hope you and Mrs. Johnson are enjoying yourselves."

Mr. Johnson, around five-ten and stocky with a full head of curly gray hair, which he wore neatly trimmed, smiled at him. Adam imagined he was one of those gentlemen who went to a barber on a weekly basis, just to keep looking sharp.

Mr. Johnson nodded. "We sure are. Em's as happy as a lark." His gaze wandered across the room and rested on an attractive, golden-brown-skinned woman in her sixties. It seemed to Adam that like many women of her generation, she was comfortable in her skin and had style and panache. She was well put together from head to toe. From the look of admiration on Mr. Johnson's face, he agreed with Adam's assessment of his wife.

Mr. Johnson returned his attention to Adam. "I'd like a word with you in private, if I may."

Adam hadn't seen that one coming. What on earth could Mr. Johnson want to discuss with him in private? In the middle of a party? And why did whatever it was seem so urgent to him?

"Of course. We'll step into the gym." The gym was about thirty feet away from the area where the party was in full swing. That distance should get them out of earshot of the others.

Once in the gym, Mr. Johnson took a moment to admire the room and the various means of torture within it. Or so Adam got that impression when Mr. Johnson said, "The leaders of the Inquisition probably would have loved to have some of this equipment in their day!"

Adam laughed because Mr. Johnson was referring to an elliptical, on which he routinely did cardio workouts. Some days, that machine indeed felt like a torture device to him.

"You look in pretty good shape," he complimented Mr. Johnson. "What do you do to keep fit?"

"Young man," J.Z. said, "I'm seventy-two years old. Walking up and down the stairs in this building is quite enough. Em and I enjoy a stroll together in the mornings. She's much spryer than I am."

He squinted up at Adam. "Now, the reason I wanted to speak with you is that I've noticed something about you and Alia, and it's concerning to me."

He let that comment hang in the air as if waiting for Adam to decipher what he was referring to. When Adam gave him a confused look, he continued. "There's no noise coming from up here at night, if you get my drift." Again he peered at Adam as if he might be the densest human being on earth instead of a successful physicist.

Adam finally gave up and said, "I have no idea what you're talking about." Adam wondered if Mr. Johnson was on meds and if he'd been keeping up with his doses.

"From what I understand," Mr. Johnson said, sounding a bit exasperated, "you've been gone for a long time. You've been back over a month now, and you and Alia are as quiet as mice up here. I hear the other young couple who live in the apartment next to ours all the time, but you two? Nothing!"

It finally dawned on Adam what Mr. Johnson was alluding to: he and Alia Joie weren't making the bedsprings talk, as he'd heard his father say on occasion.

What business did this man have asking about their love life?

His irritation must have shown on his face because Mr. Johnson held up his hands in surrender and said, "Now, don't get all offended. I might not be explaining myself to your satisfaction yet, but bear with me."

Mr. Johnson went and sat down on a weightlifting bench. Adam, holding his anger in check for this invasion of his privacy, leaned against the wall and waited for the older man to explain himself.

"I noticed how you were looking at Alia a few minutes ago," J.Z. began. "Like you're a man dying in the desert and she is the water that can save you. Like a lovesick puppy. Like a—"

"I think I know where you're going," Adam interrupted him. "You saw me looking at Alia Joie as if I want her. Well, you're right. She's my wife and I love her. I'll always want her."

"Nah, I saw more than that in the way you were looking at Alia," J.Z. said. "You looked like a kid with his nose pressed against the window of a candy store. But he doesn't have any money in his pocket. You looked like you wanted her, but you couldn't have her."

Adam started to deny it and then thought better of it. It had been his experience that when your elders wanted to tell you something, it was best to let them talk. So he kept quiet.

J.Z. took a deep breath. "When I was a young man, I was drafted and sent to Vietnam. Em and I were engaged and she promised to wait for me. That wait, which was supposed to last a couple of years, lasted four because several of my buddies and I were captured by the Vietcong. We were beaten and starved, treated like animals. I don't know what your experience was like, but any time someone holds you against your will it's no walk in the park. After we were rescued and I came back home, I couldn't go through with marrying Em. I didn't feel worthy. I felt like dirt. I believed that she would've been better off without me. I wished I'd died instead of come home to a life I had no idea how to live anymore. But Em felt differently. She was just happy I'd come back home alive. She'd faithfully written me every week, even though my letters were few and far between. It's not easy writing during a war.

"Em and I eventually got past my initial problems. I got healthier. My mind felt more settled. I remembered how much I loved her, even though she never forgot how much she loved me. We set the wedding date, got married and on our honeymoon night, I was like a limp noodle." He paused. "We're both men here and I don't think we should be embarrassed to talk about the facts of life."

Adam, who was riveted by his tale by now, nodded.

"You see, I believed that everything was just fine and once Em and I got married, we'd live happily ever after. I thought the war was over for me. Back then we didn't know anything about the effects war has on survivors. I mean, they talked about something called shell shock and that just meant the soldier had mental problems, but nobody defined those problems or how to solve them. We'd never heard of post-traumatic stress disorder. So here I was with a new bride who, believe me, was expecting me to perform my husbandly duties, and I didn't know why I couldn't. I was looking at Em the way you were looking at Alia. I wanted her so badly!"

"So how did you solve the problem?" Adam asked, stunned that J.Z. had hit on his problem so astutely. It showed that you shouldn't judge a person based on your first perception of him. Listening to an ex-postman's tale appeared to be positively affecting him more than six sessions with Dr. Klein had.

J.Z. carried on in a serious vein, his tone low and reverent.

"I was lost and, back then, it never occurred to me to seek help from a mental health professional. I was going to have to solve my own problems. Em was an innocent. She held tight to her virginity, and there was no intimacy before marriage. She expected to have a normal, healthy sex life now. And I was disappointing her."

Adam could relate to that. He felt he was disappointing Alia Joie, too. This story was beginning to resonate more and more with him.

J.Z. continued, "I'm an old man now, Adam, and I've given this some thought. Men are taught from birth that their power, their manhood, lies in their penises. Think about it. If you believe in the Bible, you know that Adam was created first and given the task of naming all the animals. Eve was created specifically as a helpmate for Adam. Men were given physical strength. My point is, by virtue of his penis, the male has enjoyed certain privileges. Men ruled the world for a long time and they ruled it because they took it by force, using sheer physical strength. From the beginning, men have been taught that their manhood is attached to their penises. That's the starting point of their identity. Our psyches are so attached to our penises, a woman who has a sharp tongue can make it wither with words. In essence, we believe our manhood depends on our penises functioning properly. So is it any wonder that when I went to Vietnam, where my freedom, my power, was taken from me, my manhood was, too? But I'm telling you now, Adam. Your power is not in your penis." He stabbed at his forehead with a finger. "Your power is in your brain, and you tell it what to do. You do. Not anyone or anything else. If you want Alia, you will satisfy her. And that's the end of my speech."

J.Z. sighed and looked at Adam with brows raised, as if wondering if anything he'd said had made sense to him.

Adam pushed away from the wall he'd been leaning on and ran his hand over his head, thinking. J.Z. might not be as eloquent as some college professors he'd heard speak over the years, but yes, he made a whole lot of sense.

No one was stopping him from making love to Alia Joie except himself. This was his body, damn it. Those bastards who had kept him from her for over two years were not going to win. His experience hadn't defined him. He was his own man.

He smiled at J.Z. "How could you have known what I've been going through?"

J.Z. smiled back at him. "Because I've been there. We're from different generations, but I know what a man who's been stripped of his self-esteem looks like. I've seen one looking back at me in the mirror more than once in my lifetime."

On impulse, Adam hugged the older man. Then he

held him at arm's length, still smiling. He felt elated. He felt as though, in his mind, he'd broken down a barrier that had been hampering his normal way of thinking. He felt more clearheaded than he'd felt in months. He grabbed J.Z.'s hand and shook it.

J.Z. grinned. "Good luck, Adam."

"Thank you," Adam said, still shaking his hand. "I don't know if what you said has cured something inside my head or not, but I appreciate your willingness to talk to me, even though you don't know me well."

J.Z. laughed at that. "Alia talked to me and Em about you all the time."

This didn't come as a surprise to Adam, but Alia Joie hadn't mentioned how close she was to the Johnsons. However, he remembered she'd told him when she'd given him a tour of the building that he'd soon realize that J.Z. and Emma Johnson were the soul of this building.

As they turned to leave the gym and rejoin the party, Adam asked, "What did she tell you about me?"

"She said you were the most intelligent, and also the most humble, person she'd ever met," J.Z. answered without hesitation.

"That sounds like something Alia Joie would say," Adam told him. "However, in the great scheme of things, I'm not that smart. And if not for my ego, I might not have waited this long to realize how lucky I am to have her."

"You're really lucky," J.Z. agreed with him. "If Em and I had ever had a daughter, I would want her to be just like Alia—generous, brilliant, hardworking and let's not forget beautiful. I could go on." He winked at Adam. "If I didn't have Em and I was thirty years younger, you'd have some competition."

Adam laughed. "I bet I would."

When they returned to the party, Emma Johnson made a beeline for them. She gave J.Z. a stern look. "I looked around and couldn't find you anywhere. You haven't been doing what I expressly asked you not to do, have you?"

J.Z. must have looked guilty to her. She grabbed him by an ear and J.Z. cried, "Em, take care you don't pull my ear off!"

Adam could tell they'd had this conversation before because Emma Johnson was livid. She didn't forget her manners, however. She peered up at him. "Adam, I hope my husband hasn't been putting his nose in your business. Honestly, he means well…"

Adam smiled at the lovely lady and said, "On the contrary, Mrs. Johnson…"

"Call me Em, sweetie," she cooed. She still had a firm hold on her husband's ear.

"On the contrary, Em, J.Z. has been very helpful to me. He's a wise man and I'm grateful for his advice."

Emma's face brightened. She let go of J.Z.'s ear. Tears appeared in her eyes as she turned a proud gaze on her husband. J.Z. took the opportunity to bestow a sweet kiss on her silken cheek and whisper, "I told you so. No harm, no foul."

She hugged him. "Just behave yourself for the rest of the evening," Adam heard her say. She smiled at Adam over her shoulder.

Adam suppressed a laugh at the triumphant expression on J.Z.'s face as his wife dragged him off, probably to chastise him for going against her wishes.

The party broke up around two in the morning. Before the guests departed, Alia and Adam presented their guests with tins of homemade Christmas cookies that had been made by Adam and wrapped up by her. Thankfully, guests had been respectful of their home, and except for clearing off the buffet table, there wasn't much cleaning to do afterward, so Alia took Adam by the hand and led him to their bedroom. Being around loved ones and friends had given her a feeling of contentment.

Also, the looks Adam had been giving her all night made her feel desirable. He'd always made her feel desirable, but there had been something extra in the way he'd been watching her tonight. His gaze on her caused her core to heat up with intense sexual desire. She didn't know if she could lie next to him tonight without wanting more than a cuddle from him.

He was fairly devouring her with his eyes right now. Her nipples hardened as his gaze went from her eyes to her mouth to her cleavage.

If she didn't love him so much, she'd be angry with him. He knew exactly what he did to her when he looked at her like that. It wasn't fair! He continued to make her burn beneath her skin by purposely letting his gaze roam over her sex-starved body, and then, when they went to bed, he would sleep like a baby beside her while she'd lie awake wishing he was making love to her.

In the bedroom, she undressed, all the while talking

to him as he also undressed. She kept her eyes averted, not wanting to see his pecs or his abs, that perfectly shaped butt or those long muscular legs. Any naked skin. She'd wait until he put on his pajamas, and then she'd look.

The way Adam had been regarding her reminded her of how Brock had been looking at Macy earlier. "I don't know what's going on in Brock's head," she said as she stepped out of her dress, which she'd unzipped and bent to pick up off the floor where it had fallen around her ankles. "If I didn't know better I'd think he'd fallen in lust with Macy."

This must have gotten Adam's attention because he strode out of the walk-in closet where he'd been hanging his clothes up and exclaimed, "Really? Wouldn't that make Macy happy? You've been saying she has a thing for Brock."

Alia was still refusing to look at him so she didn't notice he was nude until he hugged her from behind and she felt the outline of his body against hers.

More specifically, she felt his erection on her backside.

She immediately panicked. What was this? Was it an experiment he wanted to conduct to see if his therapy sessions were working, and he'd neglected to warn her that it was coming?

She was terrified the experiment would fail and he'd suffer a setback, and they'd have to start again at the beginning of this…whatever this was they were going through.

Her mind was trying to figure out what he was up to, but her body was ready for action. He appeared ready, too. His penis felt very hard. She resisted the impulse to reach back and grab it. "Um, is that what I think it is?"

"What do you think it is?" he asked huskily.

She was afraid to say.

It wasn't as if he hadn't gotten an erection since he'd been back. There had been numerous times he'd woken up with a stiff penis. But he'd quickly cover it. She believed he knew that seeing him with a hard penis, with no benefit in it for her, made her feel neglected.

Now, though, he was hard and he was pressing himself against her. What was a woman to do? She was weak with desire. He pressed harder against her. The decision was made.

Wearing only her panties, bra and heels, she turned and faced him. Her eyes met his. "I think it's my husband, come to fulfill every sexual fantasy I ever had."

He smiled seductively. "Every last one."

And then he kissed her.

# *Chapter 9*

Alia Joie's lips were soft, her breath clean and warm and tasting slightly of the white wine she'd drunk earlier. She closed her eyes and he felt the flutter of her eyelashes on his face. As he kissed her, his tongue dancing with hers, he marveled at the confidence building within him. The fear was gone. He didn't even worry that his excitement was going to get the better of him and he'd come before entering her. *He* was directing his actions, not his fear. It was as if his former skill as a lover had switched on in his head.

His hands remembered the shape of her, the little dips and curves and planes of her body. He loved the soft exclamations of delight issuing from her kiss-swollen lips.

Their bodies still touching, he reached up and pulled

down one bra strap, and she took care of the other side. He was accustomed to getting her out of her lingerie in record time, and he hadn't lost his touch. She was braless and pantyless in seconds.

He hadn't been pressed against her completely naked body in such a long time he had to take a moment to relish the sensation. Her nipples were hard and he was distracted by them. In fact, he was so excited, wanting all of her at once, that he almost didn't know where to start.

Then he remembered something that might derail his plans for tonight, and softly said, "We haven't discussed birth control since I've been back."

She hadn't been on the pill when he'd left. They had been using condoms until they decided they wanted to have children.

She smiled up at him. "The condoms you left in the nightstand are still there."

"You don't think they're too old?"

"They'll do in a pinch," she said breathlessly. "Unless you want to make love without them. After our time apart, I've decided I definitely want to have children."

He breathed a sigh of relief. "I was hoping you'd say that."

She gyrated against him. Her hands grabbed his backside and squeezed. She was still wearing her heels and kicked them off. Three inches shorter now, she raised one leg and wrapped it around one of his. Now their pelvises were so close all he had to do was gently push her against the wall behind them and impale her. Which he did. It was a good thing the wall was well built because once his penis connected with her vagina, the pressure they put on that poor wall would have caused a weaker structure to come crashing down.

She was hot and tight and his member had never been hungrier for her. He'd spent sleepless nights in his tiny room at the facility, wondering if he'd ever be inside his bride again. Cursing himself for ever leaving her.

Alia Joie clung to him, her beautiful brown body glistening now with a thin layer of perspiration, which only made her more delectable. She threw her head back in ecstasy and he redoubled his efforts. She felt so good. His muscles ached with righteous exertion. He was glad he worked out so hard. It gave him the strength to give his woman what she needed, what she had been needing and he hadn't been giving her. That thought made him kind of giddy with power. He didn't care if his penis turned out to be a cruel dictator and abused its power. It was working now and that was all that mattered.

He gave her all he had, and when he met her eyes, and saw she was totally engaged and eager for more, he gave it to her. He was sweating trying to hold back the orgasm of all orgasms. Her enjoyment was the important thing here. When she let out a protracted moan that sounded like a release that had been a long time coming, he howled as he came inside of Alia Joie. Yes, the wolf had to put in an appearance tonight.

Then Alia Joie screamed, too. He'd been fooled by her reaction. She hadn't come yet. He attributed it to the length of time they'd been apart. That was okay; they'd get back in sync soon. He observed her as she climaxed. Her breasts were heaving, her skin moist and glowing, and her nipples reminded him of dark berries. As she came down, he couldn't resist licking them. She quivered in his arms, looked into his eyes and smiled at him. "Shower together, then round two in bed?"

He grinned. "You're a greedy woman. I like that."

They spent several minutes soaping and stroking each other's bodies with sponges in the huge shower. Alia Joie wore a shower cap to keep her hair from getting wet, but the rest of her body was his to revel in. She really was more beautiful than he'd remembered. He'd told her that when they'd met again at the Pentagon, but now he knew he hadn't been exaggerating. How could he have denied himself this pleasure for so long?

Her flawless dark-chocolate-brown skin with red undertones looked so healthy and vibrant. Her body was soft in the right places, and firm and muscular in others, all of it consisting of feminine curves. He'd never been attracted to bony bodies; he liked having someone he could hold on to. Alia Joie had a body built for love. She gave as good as she got and she had stamina, for which he was grateful.

She was looking at him like he was something good to eat. She flashed him some teeth, her lips red and heart-shaped. "Your eyes have that swagger back that I recognized in them the night we met."

He bent and gently kissed her high on the cheek. "Oh, yeah? Are you saying I was conceited, arrogant and maybe even cocksure?"

"All of the above," she teased him. "But I could see that underneath your overconfidence you were a sweet human being."

"Did you really?" he asked. "Or were you willing to go out with me and hope for the best? As I recall, you were the one who asked me out."

She laughed softly. "I knew you'd never get up the nerve to ask *me*. You were confident, but you didn't want to risk rejection. Like with some men I've known in the past, my family's money incapacitated you."

They'd had this discussion before. He'd confessed that her position had intimidated him. He knew her family was worth billions and wondered what an heiress would want with him.

"What any woman would want from a man," she'd told him. "To love and cherish her."

So now, he gazed lovingly into her eyes and said, "I've always liked a challenge."

"So have I," she replied saucily, and stood on tiptoe to kiss him.

Alia felt like doing a pirouette right in the middle of her bedroom when her husband carried her from the bathroom after their shower and set her down at the foot of the bed. But she thought it wise not to act like a crazy woman the first night Adam had made love to her in over two years. She didn't want to scare him. All sorts of questions she wanted to ask him about his miraculous recovery were bouncing around in her head. Those, also, would have to wait. Nothing was going to get in the way of some more of his good loving.

"You sit there while I get a few things," he said, his eyes raking over her naked body.

She sat down on the bed and crossed her legs, watching him as he walked over to the tall chest of drawers.

In one of the drawers, she stored essential body oils that she used to keep her skin, hair and nails healthy. There were also oils that Adam liked to use on her when they were making love.

She held her breath, anticipating his opening that drawer. When he did, she let out the breath and sighed. Yes, she was in for a treat. He opened the drawer and pretended he needed a moment to select just the right essential oil that would help him work his magic.

In the meantime, she enjoyed the view. Damn, the man was fine. He moved with grace and power. Reddish-brown skin, the play of muscles underneath, that six-pack and V spot just below his waist, kind of pointing to his manhood. He was well endowed, but she didn't care about that as long as he knew how to use what God had given him. And he did. He'd always known how to please her. What had happened to him in Abu Dhabi to make him forget that?

"Aha," Adam said triumphantly, holding up a small brown bottle. "Argan oil infused with lavender." He twisted the cap off and lifted the dropper out of the bottle, appreciatively sniffing the fragrant oil. Putting the dropper back into the bottle and turning to regard her as he walked slowly toward her, he said, "Moroccan women have been enticing men with this beauty enhancer for thousands of years, and it still works today."

Alia feigned ignorance. "Thousands of years, Professor?"

"I'll have you know, wife, that the Moroccans have been using argan oil since ancient times. It's recorded in history books."

Alia sighed languidly. Her egghead husband *would*

know the history of argan oil. She played along. "Pray tell, Professor."

He came and gently pushed her down on the bed, gesturing for her to lie back and relax. Smiling, she complied, secretly looking forward to his next move.

He took his time pouring some of the oil into the palm of his left hand, recapping it with his right and setting the bottle on the adjacent nightstand, then rubbing his palms together. "It's recorded in the history books that in 1510 African explorer Leo Africanus— you've heard of him, right?"

"Yes," Alia acknowledged.

"When he was traveling in Morocco he was introduced to argan oil. Later, the oil was brought to Europe, where only rich people could afford to use it. But today, my beauty, even the lowliest of the low can use this incredible rejuvenating oil."

Alia laughed softly. He did have a way with words. When he began rubbing the oil on her thigh and down her leg, she had to admit he was also a talented masseur.

He indicated he wanted her on her stomach, and she rolled over. She felt drops of oil falling onto her back, following the length of her spine. Then he straddled her and began massaging the oil into her shoulders and back, down to her buttocks. It felt so relaxing, having his hands on her, that she didn't dare close her eyes because she would have drifted off into a satisfied slumber. Not wanting to do that, her eyes flew open out of panic, and she saw the time on the clock on the nightstand. It was after three in the morning. She hadn't realized it was that late. "You don't think when we shouted earlier, we disturbed any of the neighbors, do you?" she asked.

Adam chuckled. "I wouldn't worry about that if I were you."

At the base of her spine, she felt his penis growing hard again. "No," she said. "I have more pressing things to think about right now."

He laughed. "Indeed, you do." And with that he got off her, rolled her onto her back, spread her legs and positioned himself between them. Their eyes met and held. In his she saw his love for her. It was indomitable in its purity. God, she'd missed that look. She hadn't known until now how much.

With her legs spread like this, she felt vulnerable yet strong. In this position, she was at her weakest. However, the assurance of his affections, knowing that he was hers and she was his, made her feel powerful. He took his manhood in his hand and placed the tip at the entrance of her feminine center. He felt warm and extremely hard. Her vagina moistened even more. She was so excited. He pushed into her and she welcomed him, her vaginal walls contracting and loosening. He pushed farther inside and she gasped. It was so sensory laden. She thrust upward, moving him deeper inside. He pulled out, the length of him growing cooler on the outside, and when he penetrated her again, she could feel the coolness, which stimulated her, causing her nipples to harden.

To Alia, this was a ballet on the sheets. She relished the feel, the grace, the sheer miracle that was two human bodies giving and receiving pleasure. Adam was looking deeply into her eyes, his communicating his love for her. Hers were misty, she was sure, because she felt very emotional. She was so grateful they had finally arrived at this level of trust. He was coming back to her, body and soul.

Their hands were clasped tightly when the orgasm hit her. She squeezed his hands tightly within her own and cried out, "I love you so much!"

He groaned with his own release and she felt his seed flowing into her. She knew they had made a baby. Was it wishful thinking? No, there was no doubt in her mind. One sexual encounter and she was pregnant. Her body was ripe for it. The waiting had been agonizing. She'd wished, so many times when he was away, that he had left her with a child before he'd gone off to the Middle East. A child would have made the waiting more tolerable. But she hadn't even had that to console her.

She felt his body relax. He'd let go after his orgasm, but he hadn't collapsed on top of her. He bent his head and gently kissed her, making it a sensual interlude that capped off their lovemaking nicely. He met her gaze after that and said, "I will never leave you again."

She threw her arms around his neck and clung to him. "I'm going to hold you to that promise. Especially since I think we just made little Adam."

He grinned, seemingly delighted with the notion. "You think so?"

"Yes, I do."

He lay beside her and pulled her against him, spooning her. "I hope it's true. It's time we had an addition to the family."

They remained there for a few silent moments, then

Alia had to know. "How did you know you were ready tonight?"

She listened raptly as he described his state of mind for the past few weeks. He told her his sessions with Dr. Klein had been helpful. He had begun to realize that the reason he felt unable to make love to her was because when he was taken against his will, he'd felt emasculated and, unfortunately, many men equate feeling less masculine with being unable to get an erection. Dr. Klein had not said outright that some men felt their penises were the seat of their power, but Adam believed that's how he subconsciously felt. Then he'd had an enlightening conversation with J. Z. Johnson.

"Mr. Johnson!" she exclaimed. "What would possess him to even broach a subject like that with you?"

"I was as surprised as you are," he said as they lay in the dark, the room quiet, streetlights giving the room its only illumination.

He went on to relate Mr. Johnson's experiences in Vietnam and his struggle to return to normal when he got home. She said, "Theirs is a wonderful love story. They told me some of this before. I've even seen pictures of them from that time."

He continued with how Mr. Johnson's tale had mirrored his own, ending with, "It was something about his willingness to embarrass himself just to help me that got to me, I guess. That, and when he said that self-affirmation crap about my brain belonging to me and I could tell it what to do... That made sense to the scientist in me. That if there is nothing physically wrong with me—and there isn't—then what's wrong is in my belief system. I believed they'd taken something from me, so I was rendered helpless. But if I can refuse to let them win by keeping me from doing something I want to, then I'm the one in control once more."

"You talked yourself out of it," she said happily.

He chuckled. "It was a combination of everything, really. But, yes, I suppose I did."

She laughed, too. "You know what we should call Mr. Johnson from now on, don't you?"

"What?" he asked.

"The sex guru," she said. He shook the bed laughing.

When he'd finished laughing, something suddenly occurred to Alia. "Wait," she cried. "Earlier when I asked you if you thought we might have disturbed the neighbors with the noise we were making, you laughed. That was because you were thinking Mr. Johnson was probably listening to us!"

That only made him chuckle harder. "Yes, and I hope he was entertained."

"Honestly," she scoffed. "This building is too well built. There's no way he can hear us making love up here. He's just pulling your leg!"

"Are you sure about that?" Adam asked skeptically.

Alia didn't want to argue the point. She was too happy. She snuggled closer to him.

Seeing she was going to let the subject drop, her husband yawned, kissed the top of her head and said, "Merry Christmas, my love."

She beamed at him. "You're the best Christmas gift I've ever had."

"Ditto," he said.

She lay awake awhile thinking about the possibility of being overheard while making love, though. She didn't know how she felt about their elderly neighbors hearing them, but decided the Johnsons had lived a long time and knew more about love than she'd ever learn.

She slept after that.

# Chapter 10

About two weeks after Christmas, Adam and his team were in their lab at Bristol Institute of Technology, a private college in New York City with emphasis on the sciences and practical applications of technology, when they heard the news. Besides teaching at the institute, they worked in scientific research and development, their individual strengths enhancing one another's. Earlier, they had discovered a way to interfere with a missile's signal, thereby rendering it ineffective. Now they were back to another project they'd been working on: the problem of time. In some instances the flow of time is an absolute; in others the flow of time depends on the curvature of space-time and the space-time trajectory of the person doing the observing. Therefore, some scientists believed humans create time. Adam and his team were trying to prove that conjecture with mathematical equations.

They had a unique manner of working. Each scientist had his or her own space that they might spend time in entirely alone all day working on equations, as Adam did on a huge blackboard that rose up twelve feet in the high-ceilinged room. But even though they worked alone, they shared data and ideas throughout the day. They pooled their knowledge to come up with answers to the conundrums of the universe. Or that was how Adam thought of their methods, anyway.

It was around two in the afternoon when each scientist heard a musical tune like the repetitive ringing of bells coming from their laptops. Being techies, they were attuned to a variety of sounds coming from their electronics and rarely ignored them.

They didn't this time, either, and discovered a group message from Colonel Edward Butler. The scientists grabbed their laptops and gathered at the huge center table in the lab, looking at each other with curious expressions.

Adam pondered the situation. *What does the government want with us now?*

They set their laptops down and in unison opened the message from Colonel Butler. It was a video from the colonel. His face appeared on the screen, his hair in a buzz cut now, but still steel gray. He didn't smile in his greeting, so Adam assumed he had something serious to tell them.

"Dr. Braithwaite, Dr. Sharma, Dr. Aguilar and Dr. Hobbes, I'm making this video to give you an update on your case, and a fair warning about coming events.

We were under the impression that you had been kidnapped by extremists, an offshoot of a Muslim terrorist group. We have since found out that the person responsible for your incarceration is a private businessman who own a munitions company. Yes, a weapons warlord who was afraid your invention was going to put him out of business, so he decided you had to be stopped. I'm sorry, we can't disclose his name at this time. Rest assured, he's in custody and won't be causing you any more trouble. However, you are in for a media storm because now that we have figured out who was behind your kidnapping and your invention is safe from being stolen, I've been told the president is going to make a statement concerning your invention and will, as a gesture of thanks, give you a medal at the White House for your hard work."

Adam almost cursed. A medal? He could see by the stunned expressions on his colleagues' faces that they too were underwhelmed by this information.

Adam couldn't protest to a recorded message, however, which was probably why Colonel Butler had decided to deliver it in that manner, so he kept his caustic comments to himself.

Colonel Butler continued to speak. "Travel arrangements will be made for you and a plus-one. Details will be messengered to your residences in a matter of hours. I certainly hope you're adjusting well to your lives, and that you and your loved ones are in good health. I look forward to seeing you soon."

The message ended, and Adam and the others stood around the meeting table looking at each other with shocked expressions on their faces.

"We can't *not* show up," Maritza said reasonably. "It will look as if we're not loyal Americans."

"Colonel Butler didn't say anything about their disclosing that we were held prisoner for two years," Adam pointed out. "Maybe revealing that would be embarrassing for the government. This is some publicity stunt to make the president look good. You know he's going to take credit for the invention. He's going to say he handpicked us. Personally, I don't want to look like some kind of political flunky."

"On the other hand," Calvin said, "money will be pouring in to the institute, we'll be rock stars, and since we're the inventors, we'll make more money than we've ever seen in our lives. To say nothing of the publicity. Late-night talk shows, morning shows and women, women, women!"

Maritza laughed. "I thought you were swearing off women for a while."

"If my public wants me, I'm there," said Calvin with a smile. He regarded Arjun, who hadn't said a word. "Don't you agree?"

"This reeks of manipulation," Arjun said. "I'm with Adam. We need to define the parameters of this thing before we agree to do anything. What's really in it for us? I missed out on two years with my family and Madhuri, and I'm not happy about that. Our families went through hell worrying about us, and the government wants to sweep what happened to us under the rug? That's not right."

Adam nodded. "Yeah, I'm not going to dance like a trained monkey for the government. I want assurances that we're going to be treated with dignity and respect."

Maritza pursed her lips, thinking. She sighed. "Okay. My family is also going through changes because of my absence. So what do we demand?"

"We tell them we're not coming to the White House for a photo opportunity unless the American people are told what happened to us as a result of our taking the job that produced the new technology the government's so excited about. We've done our part, now they need to do theirs," Adam said vehemently.

"What if we do that and they get pissed off and I'm denied citizenship?" Calvin worried.

"Calvin, you've contributed positively to the American economy," Adam told him. "You've proven that you're an asset to this country. They're not going to deny you citizenship. I went to school here on scholarship, wrote a couple of books that were popular, and applied for citizenship and was granted it. Your qualifications are as good as mine. Go ahead and apply and stop talking about it."

Calvin laughed. "All right, already!"

"I think that makes sense," Maritza said. Adam assumed she was referring to his suggestion on how they should proceed.

"Yes," said Arjun. "Then we're agreed?" His gaze was on Calvin.

Calvin's head was bobbing up and down although he didn't say anything. The others stared at him.

"Okay, okay," he finally answered. "When do we phone Colonel Butler to give him our verdict?"

"Now's as good a time as any," Adam said. He took out his cell phone, which he had programmed with important numbers, one of which was Colonel Butler's.

He was using the video feature, and since Colonel Butler's phone was likewise equipped, the four of them gathered around Adam's phone and saw Colonel Butler's face in real time.

"I thought I'd hear from you soon," Colonel Butler said. "I take it the president's plans didn't sit well with you all."

"That's an understatement," Adam said. Then he asked, point-blank, "How is our kidnapping going to be handled, Colonel? There was no mention of it in your message."

Colonel Butler cleared his throat nervously and squinted at their image on his phone. "The president has chosen to handle that at a later date."

"Why?" Adam asked.

"Because the warlord is lawyering up and threatening to sue the US for false arrest."

"I thought you had him dead to rights," Arjun put in.

"All evidence points to him," Colonel Butler allowed. "We have testimony from men who worked at the facility and named his right-hand man as their contact between the warlord and them. They took their orders from him. The warlord is claiming his right-hand man acted on his own."

"So why does the president want to trot us out and make a big spectacle of the new technology when nothing's settled yet?" Adam asked. "It's political, isn't it? The president is getting grief from all sides and he needs a big win. We're not idiots, Colonel Butler. If our discovery goes mainstream, this could mean thousands of future American soldiers' lives will be saved."

"We're talking the Nobel Peace Prize," Arjun said.

"Because this could change how wars are fought. As well as the Nobel Prize in Physics, because of making an outstanding contribution to mankind." He looked at his colleagues. "Hey, I'm thinking big."

Adam laughed shortly and turned his attention back to Colonel Butler. "What we're trying to say, Colonel, is we want no part of this publicity stunt until the president agrees to tell the American people about our kidnapping, the length of time we were held and why the government took so long to rescue us. And we're not budging on this."

Colonel Butler let out a long sigh. Then he smiled. "Good man. I'll relay the message and get back to you. It's been my pleasure to speak with you all again."

"It's been ours, too, Colonel," Adam told him with a smile.

After Adam ended the call, he regarded his fellow scientists. "It appears the colonel is sympathetic to our cause. Now, we wait."

When Adam got home that evening, just as he was about to put his foot on the bottom stair and start climbing, he heard behind him, "Long time, no see!"

Immediately recognizing the jovial voice of J.Z., Adam smiled and turned around to face him. J.Z. pulled his hood down as he strode into the lobby. He was carrying a cloth carryall, which Adam figured he used for groceries.

It was true—he hadn't seen J.Z. since the night of the Christmas party. He'd been very busy, and it wasn't as if he were going to seek the man out and give him a report on whether or not his pep talk had worked or failed to inspire him. Still, he was genuinely glad to see him.

"J.Z.," he exclaimed. "How are you? And how is the lovely Em?"

J.Z.'s brown eyes danced merrily and a slow smile curled his lips. "Fine, fine, thanks, Adam. How are you and Alia doing?"

"Great," Adam said. "We couldn't be better."

"I'll say," J.Z. readily agreed. "Em and I are so happy for you. We expect invitations to the party, too."

Adam resisted the urge to laugh uproariously. J.Z. truly was a character. He reminded him of his father, who could crack you up with just his observations of human behavior. "What party?" he asked, even though he knew what was coming.

"Why, the party where you two will make the announcement that you're expecting a baby," J.Z. said, not cracking a smile. It was as if he thought his prediction was written in stone, he was so sure of it.

Adam did laugh then. When he had control of himself again, he wiped a tear from the corner of his right eye and said, "I hope we didn't disturb you and Em too much the night of the party."

"Em and I got out the champagne and drank a toast to you."

"Thank you, J.Z., or should I call you the sex guru? Courtesy of Alia Joie."

J.Z. dissolved in a fit of laughter. "That's a good one. Em's going to get a kick out of it when I tell her." He shook his head at the notion. "Well, see you, young man. God bless you and Alia."

"You and Em, as well," Adam returned before continuing up the stairs as J.Z. walked toward the elevator.

Alia was in the kitchen preparing dinner when she heard Adam come through the door. Putting down the knife she'd been using to chop hot peppers to go in the stir-fried chicken and vegetables, she hurried in his direction.

Adam grinned when he saw her. Her heart did a flip-flop. She never got tired of the sexy way he looked at her lately, like he couldn't get enough of her. It felt like they were newly in love. She thought of this period in their life as a second honeymoon.

He'd shed his coat and hung it in the closet before she got to the foyer.

He picked her up and she wrapped her legs around him, her short dress's hem rising practically to her waist. They kissed hungrily. After all, it had been hours since they'd seen each other. Much too long.

Afterward, she slid down his hard body until her feet hit the foyer floor, and she smiled up at him. "How was your day, sweetie?"

His eyes alight with humor, he said, "Eventful." He gave her a quick buss on the forehead and, as was their habit, they went to the kitchen and continued cooking dinner together.

He was washing up at the sink as he began telling her about his day. She took in his physical form while he talked. Since he'd been home, he'd regained around fifteen pounds of muscle. His energy level was back up to his liking, and he'd told her he felt comfortable at his new weight. She would love him either way, but was glad he was happy with himself. The thing she'd worried most about was his self-esteem. It scared her when he wasn't sure of himself. She was so used to his being confident. That confidence was back. She could feel it coming off him. Or were those pheromones? Whatever it was, she was drawn to it. He had on a dark gray long-sleeved cotton shirt, open at the collar, a pair of jeans that fit his athletic body perfectly and his favorite pair of Nikes. He dressed for comfort, not sex appeal, although with a body like his, he didn't need to put in much of an effort. He was always sexy.

She realized she'd been daydreaming and snapped back to attention when he said something about going to the White House.

"They want us to come to Washington, DC, and do the patriotic thing while they ignore what we've been through. Do you think that's fair?"

"Back up," Alia told him, meeting his gaze. She turned the gas down on the stove where she'd been putting strips of skinless chicken breasts into the olive oil in the wok. "They want you all to come to the White House to get a medal for your work? What do you mean? You all succeeded? I thought part of your trauma was the fact that you hadn't succeeded."

"We were told to keep quiet until they determined who was trying to steal the plans," he said. "I was sworn to secrecy. You know how the government can be."

"Details," Alia demanded. "What was the secret mission? I don't even know what you all were working on."

"A way to defuse missiles directed at military personnel," he said. "We figured out how to direct a signal that makes the missile's payload ineffective. No explosion on impact."

"What? That's amazing. That's science fiction material!"

"Science fiction," Adam said, smiling, "is now science fact."

She went and hugged him. "Congratulations, babe." Looking up at him with quiet reverence, she said, "I'm so proud of you."

Adam blushed. She kissed his chin. "So they're trying to hide the fact that you all were kidnapped, huh?"

"Obviously that part doesn't look good for our president's administration. We were kidnapped under the previous one. Seems to me if the president wanted to make himself look good, he would have sent someone to rescue us as soon as possible."

"Don't worry about it," Alia told him. "You married into a family that owns a network. Say the word, and what you've been through will be broadcast all over the world."

Adam grinned. "I have no doubt you'd do that for me, my darling wife, but I'm not the only one affected by this. Maritza, Arjun and Calvin also have private lives they'd like to keep private. I can't do anything rash like embarrass the government. I'd rather negotiate than make threats."

Alia calmed down. "Yes, you're right. Whatever you decide to do, I'm there for you."

He squeezed her tightly against his broad chest. "Thanks, I appreciate that."

They went back to their cooking. "Oh," Adam

added, smiling, "I ran into J.Z. in the lobby." He went on to tell her about the exchange, and she laughed until tears started falling. She was about to wipe her eyes with a finger but remembered that she'd been chopping hot peppers and thought better of it. She grabbed a paper towel instead and dabbed at her eyes. "That man is a riot," she said. "I bet he's kept Miss Em entertained over the years." She washed her hands at the sink.

"You know he has," Adam said. "She probably never knows what's going to come out of his mouth next."

"There's something to be said for spontaneity," Alia said, her eyes raking over him with lascivious intent.

Adam must have also been thinking about seduction since he'd gotten home from work because he reached over and turned the stove off, picked her up and tossed her onto his shoulder, fireman-style, and began walking in the direction of their bedroom. "What about dinner?" Alia cried, giggling.

"It'll keep. I won't," was her husband's response.

"Shower?" she ventured.

"You smell fine to me."

She laughed harder. "We've made love practically every night since the Christmas party. What if I just wanted to cuddle?"

"We can cuddle when we're old and white-haired."

In the bedroom, all she had to do was hold her arms out at her sides. He undressed her, then himself. And since they had dispensed with the condoms, everything else followed its natural course.

She was underneath him on the bed in no time, wearing nothing but a pair of diamond stud earrings and a smile. He was hard and hot and determined. He entered her slowly so as to not hurt her. She was wet and ready for him by the time he began pressing against her entrance, though, and she gave a little thrust upward to let him know. After that movement, he delved deeper inside, pulling out and pushing in until he'd worked her up into a pulsating frenzy of sexual tension. She loved this part, when her climax felt so close yet so far away. Sweet torture. It made her body tremble. And judging by the manner in which his eyes were intently gazing into hers, he knew it. He knew it, and it gave him pleasure to make her delight last as long as possible.

He gathered her close to him with his strong arms. They were so close not even air could get between them.

"You feel so good," he breathed.

She clung to him, her arms and legs wrapped around his body while he pumped into her. Then she grasped his firm buttocks and held on. She felt closer to the edge, at the precipice, about to free-fall. It hit her harder and quicker than she'd anticipated. Her inner thigh muscles felt weak with the release. Her feminine center throbbed with it, a delicious flutter that spread out to the rest of her. Like a prayer of thanks, she uttered, "Oh, God."

Her husband smiled down at her. "Amen."

## Chapter 11

"We should have let her know we were coming," Alia whispered as she and Adam climbed out of the taxi in a busy tourist section of Nassau, the capital of the Bahamas. It was a beautiful day. The temperature felt like it was in the high seventies, the sun bright, the sky a cloudless baby blue. In order to surprise her, they'd come straight from the airport to the street where Adam's mother's gift shop was located.

The trip had been Alia's idea. Adam had been back from the Middle East for over three months now, and he hadn't seen his folks. When she'd pointed that out to him, he'd looked surprised, as if it had never occurred to him that his family might want to see him. She chalked it up to his being an absentminded professor. He and his team, he told her, were getting close to a breakthrough in their research. His mind was consumed with work.

Also, there had been no word from the government concerning their negotiations with the president. The president was being stubborn. Adam and his team were being stubborn. Alia didn't know how the situation was going to be resolved, but she was willing to bet the announcement of the new missile-defusing technology was something the president wasn't going to sit on for much longer. That was quite the coup for him, and she didn't believe he was going to let an opportunity to shine in the public's eye like that slip through his fingers.

After she and Adam got out of the taxi a few stores down from his mother's shop, they stood on the sidewalk, holding their carry-on bags, sunglasses on, a necessity in the bright sunshine of the Bahamas. Alia marveled at how colorful Nassau was every time she was here. She loved the pastel colors of the buildings, the palm trees, fronds flowing with the sea breezes, the painted horse-drawn carriages and, best of all, the police directing traffic in their sharp British-style uniforms. All sorts of people were on the street coming in and out of shops, restaurants and bakeries that catered to tourists. She inhaled the aroma of freshly baked bread as she and Adam began walking toward his mother's gift shop. Her stomach growled in response to the enticing odor. Adam looked down at her. "We'd better get you something to eat soon."

Alia didn't say it, but she thought, *Yeah, we're a little hungry.* She put her hand on her stomach. She hadn't taken any pregnancy tests, but she felt certain there was a little person growing in there.

Adam reached over and pulled her close to his side. "Come on, let's go see what Ramona's up to."

Ramona's shop was busy with tourists riffling through the racks of sundresses, straw hats, costume jewelry, sandals, anything a visitor might need in order to enjoy their stay in Nassau. Ramona had island music playing softly in the background. Alia's gaze swept back and forth, trying to locate her mother-in-law among many other brown-skinned women. She'd noticed that a lot of African American women loved coming to Nassau. It was a very short trip from Miami, and cruise ships were regularly bringing people here.

Suddenly, someone let out a shrill scream. Alia knew, then, that Ramona had spotted her son. He was the tallest person in the shop. "Ay, yee! God has blessed me today. Here is my baby from America!"

Ramona Kingsley-Braithwaite, a short, stout, medium-brown-skinned woman, dressed in a purple sundress with matching sandals and cowrie shells shot throughout her braided hair, leaped into her son's arms. Adam picked her up in a bear hug. He had tears in his eyes, Alia noticed. As for Ramona, she was too busy laughing to cry. After he set her down, she cried, "Let me look at you!" She took a step back to get a better view. Around them, tourists had stopped to observe mother and son and to show their support with loud clapping and whoops. The whoops, Alia suspected, were for their appreciation of the son's good looks. She noticed the interested stares and winning smiles of the women and the frowns and suspicious glances of the men aimed at their companions.

She had to smile at that. And she stood at a respectful distance as Ramona inspected her son from head to toe.

"They didn't hurt you, did they?" she asked, her voice combative, as though she'd kill whoever might have laid a hand on her son.

"No, Momma," Adam gently told her. "I'm fine."

Ramona threw herself in his arms again, and that was when she burst into tears. "I never prayed so hard in my life. Thank God you're safe and sound."

Then Ramona noticed Alia and gestured with a beckoning hand for her to come over. Alia went and hugged her. Ramona squeezed her with such force Alia feared she might crack a rib. "Hello, daughter. I see you've been taking care of my son, and I thank you," she said, her Bahamian accent sounding especially lyrical to Alia. She peered closely at Alia's face, then she looked her straight in the eyes and said, "You're pregnant."

Alia was too emotional to say anything. She began to cry, leaving Adam with two tearful women to console.

Adam didn't know how Ramona had pulled it off, but it seemed every relative he had in the Bahamas was at his parents' house that night, along with half the neighborhood. It was a good thing his parents had a big backyard because the partyers were a rowdy group that needed the space. Aaron, his kid brother, was lead singer in a band that provided the entertainment. They weren't bad. Adam didn't know exactly what kind of music they were playing, but he guessed it was influenced by ska, reggae and calypso, elements many musicians from the islands borrowed from.

Aaron was nineteen and finished with secondary school, with no idea what he wanted to do with his life. Adam was standing with his sister, Regina, who was in her midtwenties and mere months away from becoming a physician, and her husband, Peter, ten years her senior and a tall, muscular guy with dark skin and a shaved head who looked every inch a construction worker. He owned a construction business and was a native Bahamian, too.

Regina was tall, attractive and fit, with similar skin color to Adam's reddish brown, and natural hair that she wore in a short afro. She grinned at Adam. "Please, don't encourage him," she said of their kid brother's musical aspirations.

"What?" Adam asked nonchalantly, as if he didn't know what she meant.

"I can see you're enjoying the music. You're almost dancing," she accused lightly. "Making it in the music business is a lot harder than becoming a doctor or a lawyer. Aaron's smart. He needs to do something that's going to make him financially independent. Something that'll give him the means to have a wife and family."

Adam smiled at her. "Seems like I've heard that before. Good thing I didn't listen or I'd never have gone to America and met Alia Joie. I would have gone as far as I could at college and married an island girl, a wonderful person I'm sure, and had a few children by now. Why can't Aaron follow his heart? He has that luxury now. Momma and Dad already have the success story in you and me. They can afford to give Aaron a little slack."

"Still the dreamer," Regina said, smiling warmly. He knew that was one of the things she loved about him. The two of them might not see eye to eye on certain subjects, but that didn't stop them from truly loving each other.

Regina was a pragmatist who liked having an orderly life. She hadn't even balked at her father fixing her up with Peter. Their father, Adam II, was a master carpenter, as was his father, Adam I, before him. Adam II had met Peter when he'd been hired to construct built-in shelves in several of the houses Peter's company was building there on New Providence Island. Adam II had invited Peter to dinner at his house and made sure Regina would be there. Regina and Peter were instantly attracted to each other and were married about a year later. It didn't matter that Regina was in medical school and needed to keep her mind on her studies. She was a multitasker from way back.

"Yeah, I know," Regina said now. "In some ways I don't think you and I had much of a childhood. Let Aaron enjoy himself a little longer. The baby of the family usually gets spoiled, anyway."

When she said the word *baby*, Adam thought of Alia Joie and looked around for her. He didn't see her in the backyard. Knowing her, she was in the kitchen stealing recipes. She told him she'd learned how to prepare Bahamian dishes by watching what Ramona and his grandmother Violet put in the dishes they prepared.

"Go dance while you're still young," he told Regina

and Peter. "I'm going to find Alia Joie before Momma tells her what sex the child she's carrying is going to be."

Regina laughed. "Tell Alia if she wants a doctor's opinion, I'd be glad to examine her."

Adam laughed at that. "Great, now I have the island witch who predicts pregnancies and a legitimate doctor offering free advice. Thanks, but Alia Joie and I will wait until she starts having morning sickness and go buy a pregnancy test at a drugstore. Then if it's positive, we'll make an appointment with a doctor who isn't my little sister."

"No offense taken," Regina said, smiling. "Curiosity is eating me up, though. This would be Momma and Dad's first grandchild. I'm anxious to be an auntie."

"You'll be the third person in the family, right after Momma and Dad, to find out, I promise," Adam said, and bent to kiss his sister's forehead like he used to do.

She smiled up at him. "Welcome home, Adam."

"Yes," Peter said, offering Adam a manly hand to shake.

Adam shook his brother-in-law's hand. "Thank you both. It's good to be home."

He hurried away after that to find Alia Joie. He had some things to discuss with her, like the fact that she hadn't mentioned she thought she might be pregnant to him. The reaction she'd had when his superstitious mother had pronounced she was pregnant in front of thirty or more tourists had surprised him. They hadn't had one moment alone since then to talk about it.

In the kitchen, the noise level was almost as high as in the backyard. His mother, his grandmother and several aunties, both by blood and not, were gossiping, dancing about and singing, while they cooked up delicious-smelling island cuisine.

If he didn't know better, he would think he'd interrupted a secret society's ceremony to induct a member into motherhood. Alia Joie was in the middle of it all, standing beside his grandmother Violet at a huge wooden block cutting board as his grandma Violet instructed her on the proper way to get the conch meat out of a conch shell.

He felt proud and fearful at once. Alia Joie was game to learn a new skill, but he knew a conch shell could be sharp and he didn't want her to cut herself. He breathed easier when he saw his grandmother, an old hand at separating the snail's shell from the snail itself, demonstrate the safe way to get up in there and remove the meat. Violet, a still-handsome woman in her seventies, had thick salt-and-pepper hair that was naturally wavy and that she wore upswept from her slightly wrinkled but beautifully flushed face. The flush, he guessed, was due to the effort to get the snail loose from its shell.

Grandma Violet calmly split the snail in half and handed a steel mallet to Alia Joie. She must have told her to tenderize the snail meat with it because Alia Joie began pounding the snail meat, and his grandmother encouraged her to put her back into it. He smiled as his determined wife pounded with added vigor.

He walked up to them as Alia Joie was pounding. "Can I help?" he asked. Alia Joie glanced up at him and smiled. She looked like she was having fun.

His grandmother waved him off. "No," she said, her brown eyes twinkling with mischief. "But you can come and give your grandmother a kiss on the cheek."

He did as he was told.

He kissed Alia Joie's cheek, too. "Stealing recipes?" he whispered when he got close to her ear.

"Shh…" she cautioned him. She obviously didn't want to get caught.

"No men allowed," Ramona called from across the room.

"You taught me how to cook," Adam said in his defense.

"That's because when you got out on your own, I didn't want you to starve to death," Ramona returned. She was in her element, queen of the kitchen with her cohorts surrounding her. "And since you're giving out kisses, come over here and give me one."

He wound up kissing every female in the kitchen on the cheek. He beat a hasty retreat after that, figuring he'd be better off, and perhaps safer—one of the aunties had surreptitiously pinched him on the butt—with the revelers in the backyard.

That night as Alia and Adam lay in bed, face-to-face, in his parents' guest room, Alia whispered, "I love it here. Your mom and your grandma had me laughing like crazy. They are two of the dearest women I know."

"They're bossy and opinionated," he countered, grinning. "In a sweet way."

She laughed softly. "And Aaron! I didn't know he was so talented. He sounds like one of my favorite singers, Leon Bridges. You know him—I played his CD, *Coming Home*, for you. You loved the song 'River' on it."

Adam sang a few lines from the song.

"That's it," she said, smiling with satisfaction. She loved to hear him sing. His soulful baritone made her heart melt and her libido catch fire. "But don't sing now. You know what your singing does to me, and we're in your parents' house."

"They're on the other end," he said. "They won't hear us."

"I don't care," Alia said. "We're not making love in this house. Call me a prude if you want to."

"You're already pregnant, according to Ramona," he teased. She could see his flash of white teeth in the darkness so she knew he was having fun at her expense. She wasn't about to let him goad her into having sex in his parents' house, though.

"What if I told you I think she's right?" Alia asked, hoping her comment would shock him silent.

"I'm a scientist. I'd say show me evidence," he said smartly.

"It's early yet," Alia said. "My breasts are a little tender, but other than that, I don't have any symptoms. I'm eagerly waiting for nausea and mood swings."

"I don't think anyone would be eagerly awaiting feeling nauseous. Although you cried today," he pointed out. "Wouldn't that be under the definition of 'mood swing'?"

"I guess," Alia said. "I'm new at this."

"If you thought you were pregnant, why didn't you mention your suspicion to me?"

"Because I wanted to be sure before I got your hopes up. I'll make an appointment with my doctor when we get home. I didn't want to disappoint you. If I found out I was wrong, only I would have been let down."

"You don't need to protect me, Alia Joie. I thought we said we'd have no more secrets."

"Is that such a big secret from you?" she asked curiously.

"No," he admitted. "It's just that we were apart for so long, and now I want to share everything with you."

She got closer to him in the dark until her forehead came in contact with his chin. She tilted her head up and planted a kiss on his jaw. "I'm sorry if you feel I left you out. It wasn't my intention."

He wrapped his arms around her and squeezed her tightly against his chest. "Are you sure you don't want to make love? Your voice, in the dark, is turning me on."

"We'll be that much more ready for love when we get back home."

"We could go to a hotel," he suggested, his mouth on her neck, his lips soft and warm. Her whole body was tingling, but she held on to her resolve.

"Adam Braithwaite the third, stop trying to seduce me. And that's probably the only time I'm going to ask you to do that."

He laughed quietly. "Do you know how many times I lay in my little hard bed at the facility wishing I was in this exact position with you?"

"Now you're hitting below the belt."

"Whatever it takes," he said lightly.

She huffed exasperatedly and turned her back on him. But that move only made it worse. Within seconds she could feel his member hardening.

"Have you no shame?" she asked, laughter evident in her voice.

"None," her horny husband replied, his hands on her breasts.

"If your parents hear us—and you know your mother will let us know—I am going to be so embarrassed."

"Why?" Adam asked reasonably. "Ramona already thinks you're expecting. She knows what has to be done to get you in that state."

Quietly they took off their nightclothes, and equally quietly they began to make love in the missionary position. The bed squeaked, but not too loudly, Alia hoped. She closed her eyes, letting the tension at the thought of getting caught slide off her. Adam took it slowly, his penis hardening even more with each strong thrust inside of her. Her vaginal walls contracted and relaxed around his hard shaft, the results so deliciously satiating that she found herself sighing out loud. Just soft inhalations and exhalations, she told herself. You would have to have ears like a bat to hear them.

"Oh, baby," Adam crooned. His hands traveled the length of her body, inciting little fires of desire everywhere. It was bad enough that the feel of his muscular body rubbing against her soft curves was already driving her crazy, but he had to add further stimulation.

On top of that, he began to softly sing "Beyond," one of her favorite Leon Bridges songs.

It spoke of a man finally finding the perfect woman for him, and he's afraid to commit, but he has to admit to himself that he'd be a fool if he didn't, because she might be his everything and beyond his imaginings.

"You are diabolical," she told him. "You know I love that song."

"I aim to please," Adam said. He hummed as he continued to ply her with all the sensual pleasure she could take. She arched her back, accepting it, coming to the conclusion that while they most definitely shouldn't be doing this in his parents' house, what they didn't know wouldn't hurt them. She was at her peak, and she could tell by his breathing that Adam was, too. Now, if they could just contain their enthusiasm through their climaxes, all would be well.

She came with a prolonged sigh, kind of like the sound of air gushing out of a tire, only with a much lower volume, she thought with a little giggle. Adam also managed not to holler.

They would have gotten away with it if, within seconds of their release, the bed hadn't collapsed with a loud noise.

They sat in the dark room, stunned for a moment, not daring to move, hoping that the sound hadn't carried. But a couple minutes later, Ramona and Adam II came running, knocking on their door.

"Children," cried Adam II anxiously. "Are you all right?"

Ramona was laughing uproariously. "Don't you recognize that sound?" she asked. "You and I have broken a bed or two in our time."

"We're fine! I'll buy you another bed, Momma," Adam yelled through the door.

"You sure will!" Ramona yelled back.

In the bedroom, Alia and Adam were climbing out of the wreck of the antique wooden bed frame. Adam switched on the lamp on the bedside table. "I should have known this old bed couldn't take a beating. This probably belonged to Ramona's grandmother," he groused.

"You might have mentioned that to me!" Alia said, laughing.

"We're gonna leave you kids to it!" Ramona yelled from the other side of the door.

"Okay, good night!" Alia yelled back. "We're sorry for disturbing you."

"Look, there's room to put the mattress over there." Adam indicated the corner of the room near the double doors that opened onto a patio.

They carried the mattress with the sheets still on it over to that corner, and after Adam turned the lamp back off, they settled down on it. "I can't believe I let you talk me into that," Alia said as she lay in the crook of Adam's arm.

"We weren't doing a whole lot of talking," said her incorrigible husband.

Alia thumped him on his forehead. "You know the whole family's going to know about this by tomorrow."

"Oh, Ramona's on the phone right now, waking up Grandma Violet," Adam informed her.

"No!" Alia cried, horrified by the thought.

"I'm afraid so," Adam said. "There are no secrets in the Braithwaite family."

# *Chapter 12*

A month after Adam and his team had made their demands, Colonel Butler phoned Adam to tell him that the president had assented and said that he would acknowledge what they had gone through, extolling their virtues and officially apologizing for their lengthy imprisonment in Abu Dhabi, before presenting them with the Presidential Medal of Freedom, which was given to civilians as recognition for their contributions to the security or national interests of the United States and to world peace.

"I'll be phoning your colleagues as soon as I get off the phone with you," Colonel Butler said. "I'd like to congratulate you for standing up for us. I somehow feel as though you're representing those of us who didn't get a hero's welcome when we got back home."

Adam, who was standing in the kitchen with Alia Joie, where they'd been preparing dinner when the colonel had phoned, didn't know what to say. He felt unworthy of the recognition when he thought of what soldiers must have endured while in the service of their country. "Please, Colonel," he said. "What we experienced pales in comparison to things our enlisted military personnel have gone through. But I thank you for saying it."

The colonel cleared his throat, and when he spoke again it sounded as if he was holding back emotions. "As before, a packet with details of the event will be messengered to your residences in a matter of hours. I hope your lovely wife will be with you. My wife and I will be attending the ceremony and I look forward to seeing her again."

Adam looked up at Alia Joie, a smile crinkling the corners of his eyes. "I'm sure she'd like that."

"Good evening, Dr. Braithwaite."

"Good evening, Colonel Butler."

Alia Joie gazed at him expectantly after he ended the call. "Well?" she asked, cinnamon-colored eyes widening.

"They're going to admit what happened to us," Adam told her, grinning.

Alia Joie, jumping up and down, hopped over to him and threw her arms around his neck. "Oh, my God, I knew he would cave eventually. I'm sure he wants to start manufacturing the device."

"Honey, that's already being done," Adam said. "It's been tested and retested. By the time the president makes his announcement, the device will be ready to be added to the military's equipment for actively combating air targets from the ground."

"Wow," Alia Joie said, and made the sign of her mind being blown with the subsequent whoosh sound that accompanied it.

Adam hugged her and said, "I'm glad that's settled. What I was looking forward to talking about tonight was your visit to the doctor today. You insisted on telling me face-to-face when I phoned you for an update. Then when I got home you wanted to dive right into making dinner. I'm done waiting. Let's have it. Are you pregnant or not?"

Alia Joie was looking especially delectable today with her hair in an upswept style that displayed her lovely neck and bold earrings, which she had a liking for. Today they were white and had a circumference of at least two and a half inches. She wore a short long-sleeved dress in brown with geometric white shapes on it.

She merely smiled at him, then said, "I have something for you."

He released her and watched her stroll over to a deep drawer next to the farmhouse sink. She withdrew a green box with a bronze ribbon tied around it and a large bow on top. She gave it to him.

Confused, Adam took the gift, carried it over to the huge center island, sat down on one of the stools, gingerly untied the ribbon and opened the lid of the box. Alia Joie joined him at the island, watching every move he made. Inside was a white mug made of thick ceramic that could hold around fourteen ounces. Admittedly, he loved a big cup of coffee, but what did that have to do with whether or not Alia Joie was pregnant?

Alia Joie laughed suddenly. "Talk about an unobservant scientist."

He peered inside the mug. Sure enough, there were words printed at the bottom. It read, Congratulations on Becoming a DILF!

"Okay," he said. "Is that some kind of slang a nerd like me would never get?"

She whispered in his ear, "Dad I'd like to—"

He jumped up from the stool, grabbed her in his arms and spun her around, all the while yelling, "I'm going to be a dad! I'm going to be a dad!"

Alia Joie was laughing, too. "Yes, my love, I'm having your baby. I went to the doctor. We're definitely pregnant."

Adam squeezed her tightly, then thought that perhaps he should be more careful and let up on the pressure. He peered down into her upturned smiling face. "I never knew until this moment how much I wanted to become a father. I mean, I knew I wanted to have children with you because I love you, but I hadn't given much thought to what it means to become a dad." He set her up on a stool. She spread her legs and he moved between them and took her into his arms. He didn't want to let her go, he was so happy. He gently rubbed her cheek with the back of his hand. "I know this is a very natural occurrence. Men and women have been producing children since the beginning of time. It feels special to me, though. Imagine a little being with your beauty, your brains and my sense of humor."

"What about your beauty, your brains and my sense of humor?" Alia Joie joked.

"I'll take that," he said, and bent to kiss her lips. "I'll take it all."

His next thought was Ramona, and he excitedly said, "That Bahamian witch knew what she was talking about. How could she have known you were pregnant?"

Alia Joie laughed. "It was wishful thinking on her part. You know how much she wants a grandchild. She told me I was pregnant when she first saw me in her shop because my skin was so lovely. Her words. She said when I burst out crying after she'd made that comment, she knew I was pregnant. The first thing that changes with a pregnant woman, she says, is that your hormones make you emotional. She'd never known me to cry like that before. So, you see, she's just observant, like her son."

Adam couldn't stop smiling. He kissed the top of her head and said, "I'm going to call her and let her know. I don't have to worry about the rest of the family. She'll make sure they find out."

Alia Joie nodded, climbing off the stool. "Good idea. I'm going to phone Mom and Dad, too." She went into the bedroom, and he picked up his cell phone and pressed the button that would connect him to his parents' home phone in Nassau.

"I love you!" he called after Alia Joie.

She turned and blew him a kiss. "Back at you, Professor."

While the phone rang, he picked up the mug she'd given him and looked at the message inside it again, murmuring, "DILF, indeed. I'm married to a wild woman."

* * *

Alia and Adam, along with his colleagues, were put up at a luxury hotel in Washington, DC, that was within walking distance of the National Mall. This, Adam told her, was a short drive from the White House. Leave it to her husband to know that. Their party was able to check into the hotel the day before the ceremony and do a bit of sightseeing. And after the ceremony the next day, there would be a reception at the White House.

This was their first night in Washington, DC, and the four couples went out to dinner together. The restaurant was Italian. It was very busy, and Alia noticed several famous politicians among the restaurants' patrons. The atmosphere was lively, and looking around the table, Alia felt she and her friends fit right in. The ladies had glammed it up a bit, and the guys were handsome in their suits. Alia was having a good time catching up with Arjun and Madhuri, Maritza and Raul, and Calvin and his new girlfriend, Evie. She found out Evie was short for Evelyn. Evie was British, like Calvin, and she was so far from being a model, the only women Calvin had been dating lately, that Alia held out hope this one might work out. Evie was a research scientist at Bristol Institute of Technology, where the others worked. She told Alia she and Calvin were from Surrey in South East England. Alia asked her about the history of Surrey, which turned into an interesting conversation around the dinner table.

"Well, it's the woodsiest area in England, to begin with," she said shyly. In her early thirties, she had very curly red hair, which grew in abundance. Her skin was fair and her eyes a dark green. Alia thought she was adorable and complemented Calvin's blond handsomeness. "Which is to say it's got lots of woods to explore. A lot of people own property and love working in their gardens. I suppose the most notorious person to ever live in Surrey was Henry VIII, who had a castle there. But as for me, my favorite person to have lived and worked in Surrey is H. G. Wells. He's why I wanted to become a scientist. He made it sound exciting. But as for present-day scientists, I really admire Dr. Maggie Aderin-Pocock."

"I've heard about her. She's a science educator who's been on television in Britain, right?" Maritza asked.

"Right," Evie said, seemingly delighted Maritza had heard of her. "She's inspiring a lot of girls to get into science."

"For me, it was Marie Curie," Maritza put in. "She discovered radium and then died as a result of exposure. I thought she was a hero."

Alia smiled at Maritza. "She was. Because of her, many lives have been saved by having their illnesses properly diagnosed with the use of X-rays."

Maritza beamed at her. Alia was pleased she was able to keep up with the intellectual ramblings of the group, all of whom, except for her and Raul, could legitimately be called doctors. She was an artist and a businesswoman. Her highest degree was a master's in marketing. However, she had been brought up to believe that she should feel at ease in anyone's company.

Calvin said, "For me, it was Einstein. When I was a kid, I read everything about him I could get my hands on."

"And then you became a quantum physicist," Adam ribbed him. He'd said this because though Einstein had inspired Calvin, Calvin hadn't become a theoretical physicist like Einstein.

"Yes, well, quantum physics and theoretical physics are connected," Arjun said. "Which is why we four mesh so splendidly."

Alia thought he and Madhuri made the cutest couple. Madhuri was in medical school, and would one day be a gynecologist.

"Can we please change the subject?" Raul cried. "My brain is about to explode. Does anybody here watch sports?"

Everyone laughed.

"There, you have us," Maritza said, smiling at her husband. "I doubt anyone here could tell you who won the Super Bowl this year."

Arjun whipped out his cell phone and asked it who had won the Super Bowl. Everyone laughed.

Raul laughed. "Arjun, you're nuts, man."

Arjun smiled. "It helps when you're a particle physicist looking for the small pieces that make up the universe and never making any progress. It's maddening."

Sitting beside Adam, Alia reached over and clasped his hand. He responded with a gentle squeeze and a sexy smile directed at her. "Getting tired?" he whispered.

"A little," she whispered back.

That was all her indulgent husband needed to know. He'd been extra protective of her since they found out she was expecting. He rose and announced to their companions, "We're going to say good-night. It's been a pleasure."

"Before you lovebirds run off, I have something to say," Calvin said.

"All right," Adam conceded, sitting back down at the table.

Calvin reached over and took Evie's hand. Evie smiled at him, her lovely green eyes lighting up. Alia wondered if this could be a marriage proposal. Calvin and Evie hadn't actually been dating that long, but she'd heard from Adam that the two had known each other for years. That Surrey connection was just the beginning. They'd attended secondary school in Surrey and had started college at Cambridge at the same time. Old friends turned lovers? She listened with high hopes for them.

"Evie has been a naturalized citizen for a few years now," he began. He took a deep breath, his gaze on Evie's face. "When it got back to the president that I wasn't a citizen, he pulled some strings, and since I already had my green card and five years of continuous residency, all I needed to do was pass an exam and be interviewed. I came through both with flying colors. And a few days ago, I took the oath of citizenship. I'm an American citizen now!"

His friends cheered and made a couple of toasts to him with the remnants of their drinks. However, Calvin wasn't finished. He peered into Evie's eyes. "Evie, darling Evie. You and I have known each other for over twenty years. I think I've loved you since we were both sixteen, but I never got up the nerve to say anything to you. And when we met again here in America, I figured you weren't interested in me in that way. But now that we know we're on the same page, I don't see any reason why we should wait any longer to be together forever."

Tears appeared in Evie's emerald-colored eyes. She remained silent, though, as she waited for Calvin to continue.

"Evie, would you do me the honor of becoming my wife?" Calvin asked as he withdrew from his pocket a gorgeous diamond solitaire.

Evie, hand trembling as she stretched it toward him, cried, "Yes, yes, Calvin, I will! I've been hoping for this so long. And we didn't just meet here again here in America by coincidence. I took a job at the institute because I wanted to be near you. I never thought you'd see me for who I really am—a very patient woman who truly loves you!"

"Oh, Evie, I've been a blind fool!"

Evie was nodding in agreement. "Yes, but now you're my blind fool, and I'll cherish you forever."

They kissed while everyone at the table stood up and loudly applauded them. Seeing the scene unfolding, the rest of the restaurant's patrons followed suit.

Adam beckoned to their waiter. "Champagne all around," he called, indicating their table.

The champagne was brought with alacrity, and the waiter poured it into flutes and served each of them. Adam stood and raised his glass. "A proper toast to the happy couple," he said. "Calvin—it's about damn time. And, Evie, I was rooting for you all along."

Everyone laughed and clinked glasses, tossing back the champagne, all except Alia, who was not drinking alcohol these days. She just smiled warmly, her heart full.

* * *

Later, as she and Adam pulled back the covers on their bed in the hotel room, she said, "I can't believe Calvin has known a woman like Evie for over twenty years and never recognized her worth until recently. Is he dense?"

"Yes, he is," Adam said, laughing. "Some men can be very dumb when it comes to women. He thought having beautiful models on his arm made him a stud. He finally realized that they were using him only for a moment. And for what they could get out of him. He was a part of a transaction. He paid for their time and attention. I'm glad he woke up, because a woman like Evie wasn't going to wait forever."

They got into bed and held each other. Alia sighed contentedly. "Lucky for me, you had Ramona for a mother. And, 'Ramona don't raise no fool'!"

Adam laughed at her attempt at imitating his mother's voice.

He kissed her forehead. "I love you, Alia Joie." He placed his hand on her stomach. "And I love whomever you have baking in there. He or she is going to be a joy to raise, I just know it."

"I hope you still think that when he steals your car and goes on a cross-country trip with his friends," Alia quipped.

Adam, lying behind her, pulled her closer to his chest. "Go to sleep, little Momma. You get testy when you're tired."

The next day, the Presidential Medal of Freedom ceremony started at five. Adam looked for Alia Joie in the audience in the vast East Room of the White House. He strode in with the other recipients to applause as their names were read by a soldier in uniform at the podium. There were six other recipients besides him and his team. He recognized a couple of famous actors, a musician and a retired judge, but didn't recognize the other two people. All of them were seated onstage in a couple rows of upholstered bright blue chairs, which matched the White House decor of mostly blue and gold. After they were seated, the soldier at the podium announced, "Ladies and gentlemen, the president and first lady of the United States!"

The president strode in, his wife following, as "Hail to the Chief" was played by the United States Marine Band. The first lady sat down on a chair in the front row, and the president, wearing a blue suit and a red tie, took the stage and stood behind the podium, which had the presidential seal on it, cocking his head side to side, taking in the recipients, the audience and the prompter in front of him, which he would be reading from shortly.

Adam and his team were in the back row of the recipients' section of the seats onstage. He was nervous. Arjun, Calvin and Maritza also seemed a bit uncomfortable, all of them dressed in their best conservative clothing, but that was to be expected. The ceremony was being televised. His eyes were still roaming the audience, and he finally spotted Alia Joie. She saw him, too, and smiled proudly. He managed a grimace. He would be glad when this was over.

He'd once seen this ceremony on C-SPAN under a

previous presidency. It had been entertaining to watch. He hoped that would be the case today.

Unsmiling, the president began speaking into the microphone. "Good afternoon, everyone. It gives me great pleasure to honor people who have contributed their talent and hard work to making America the great country that it is. You probably already know some of these remarkable people. You've seen their faces at the movies and on television, but there are others here who have quietly served their country, and you might not know them by sight. Men like Albert Charles Wilkinson, who has devoted his life to the education of African American children and has raised enough funds to send over a hundred African American kids to college."

He continued listing the merits and accomplishments of every one of the recipients. When he got to Adam and his team, he finally smiled. "This last group of recipients are a team of scientists who more than two years ago answered the call to serve their nation by inventing a way to defuse deadly missiles aimed at our men and women fighting for your freedom. But while in the midst of accomplishing their mission, they were kidnapped by people who wanted to steal their ideas. No, they were not taken by terrorists, but by a rich munitions company owner who didn't want them to accomplish their mission. That would put him out of business. Unfortunately, this man is an American. Not a very good American. A traitor to his country, and he will be punished for his actions. However, today, I'm here to apologize to the following scientists for not getting them out of Abu Dhabi sooner. No reflection on the men and women of the military, because they were ready and willing to risk their lives to get you all out of harm's way. No, the decision was mine as I tried to please other politicians and avoid embarrassment to the government.

"But the president should act from a moral standpoint, not a political standpoint, and because I didn't act the way I should have, you and your families had to suffer through an extended separation. To say nothing of the horrors you four were subjected to while being held captive. To Dr. Adam Braithwaite, Dr. Maritza Aguilar, Dr. Calvin Hobbes and Dr. Arjun Sharma, my sincere apologies. Your mission began with a heartfelt desire from the nation's leaders to help save lives of military personnel. You achieved your goals, and because of you, thousands of men and women will come back to their families alive and well."

There was thunderous applause. The president looked happy with the reaction and took a moment to bask in the glow of his personal triumph.

After his moment was over, he took a deep breath. "Ladies and gentlemen, may I present the 2019 recipients of the Presidential Medal of Freedom!"

After that, each recipient walked up to the president, where they shook hands with him and turned their backs to him while he put the medal, which was suspended on a blue ribbon, around their necks.

When it was Adam's turn, he walked up and smiled at the president, who smiled back. The president shook his hand and said, "It's my pleasure, Dr. Braithwaite. Thank you for your contributions to the American people."

"Thank you, Mr. President," Adam said respectfully.

Adam could hear Alia Joie in the audience hollering "Yeah!" as the medal was placed around his neck.

Later, at the reception, Arjun summed up the day quite appropriately. "All's well that ends well," he said as they stood in a group sipping drinks and enjoying very nice finger foods. "The president's likability will go up, and we got our acknowledgment. Let's go home and invent something else that's worth a medal."

"What was that about a medal?" Colonel Butler asked as he walked up to their party. He was smiling warmly and was holding hands with a lovely African American woman in her late thirties whom he introduced as his wife, Claudette.

Everyone greeted him and Claudette warmly, after which they all chatted the evening away while interacting with some of the other recipients, who were, understandably, in the best of moods. Adam had gotten his wish, and the day had been enjoyable, after all.

# Chapter 13

Even for someone whose family made its living via the media, there was a bit too much attention focused on them in the next few weeks for Alia's comfort. She was watching a late-night talk show after they'd gotten back home from DC, and the host joked, "Is the president growing a heart? Was that an apology I heard him make to those scientists who were held captive in Abu Dhabi for two years? Could America be gaining a new and improved president? One who genuinely cares about us?"

Alia turned the channel. She and Adam were in the great room, sitting on the sofa, feet up. "Don't they have anything better to do?" she asked.

"That's what they do," Adam said. "Take current events and make them fodder for their comedy. Don't let it get to you. This'll all blow over soon. Too much is happening in the world for their focus on us to last long."

Adam was wrong, though. When he returned to the institute, news vans from the major networks were camped out on campus. He counted himself lucky that they hadn't been able to find his home address. When he tried to cross to the building that housed the lab, four or five reporters hurried toward him, but it was a female reporter who got to him first and shoved a microphone in his face. "Dr. Adam Braithwaite? Jocelyn Meadows. Our viewers want to know what you and your team are working on next. Any more fantastic inventions in your future?"

Adam, who had been looking forward to enjoying the beautiful April day with the first hint of warmth in the air in a very long time, forced a smile and said, "I'm sorry, but we don't talk about our work. Sometimes not even to each other."

The reporter was determined, though. "My sources say that you and your wife, Alia Youngblood-Braithwaite, of the Youngblood Media Youngbloods, are expecting a child! If so, congratulations! I'm sure our viewers wish you the best. They're excited that you and your diverse team are all under forty and are conquering the scientific world. They want to know more about you. Would you like to tell them something they don't already know about you?"

"I can be a son of a bitch when it comes to protecting my family's privacy," Adam said bluntly. "Good day to you."

Frowning, the reporter hastily stepped aside and let him pass. None of the other reporters had the temerity to approach him.

Adam walked rapidly to the front door of the building, opened the door and strode in.

When he got to the lab, Arjun, Calvin and Maritza were already there working in their individual offices. They must have heard him come in because one by one they converged on the center desk in the lab, questioning looks on their faces.

"I see you made it through the blockade," Arjun joked.

Adam set his leather satchel that had his laptop and other essentials in it on the desktop and sat down on one of the four stools around the high center desk. "I was rude, hoping that would scare them off."

Maritza laughed. "You should be so lucky. But, on the upside, I did hear that the president of the institute's phone has been ringing off the hook. He's getting offers of support money from all over the world, according to Tricia, his secretary."

"Good for him," Adam said. "But we have work to do, and it's not getting done when we're being waylaid by cameras getting stuck in our faces."

"True," Arjun said. "But I kind of like all those memes about the president's apology to us. They have him all over the internet apologizing for anything and everything."

Arjun showed Adam a few memes on his phone. Adam couldn't help laughing. "Okay," he admitted, "that's funny. I'm sure the president has tweeted about them."

"Of course he has," said Calvin, laughing, too.

"But the time for fun and games is over," Maritza said, a stern look on her face. "I had an idea about your string theory hypothesis, Arjun."

And they were off and running, sharing ideas about their projects, minds once again focused on work.

Adam smiled with satisfaction. This was why he'd become a scientist.

Alia's belly was expanding, and she'd had some episodes of morning sickness, but nothing debilitating. She was in her fourth month when her sister-in-law, Petra, gave birth to her nephew, Benji, who was named after her father, James, and Petra's father, Alphonse, and grandfather, Benjamin. A lot of names for such a cute little guy. She and Adam volunteered to babysit as often as they were needed, just to be near the adorable guy and to glean some experience taking care of babies.

They were babysitting one Friday night so that Petra and Chance could enjoy a night on the town about three months after Benji's birth, when Benji, who was safely ensconced in a bassinet in their bedroom, started screaming his head off.

They jumped up from their seats in front of the TV in the great room and ran to see what the problem was. Alia had put Benji to bed not half an hour earlier, making sure his diaper was dry, that he was positioned correctly in his bassinet and the blanket covering him wasn't anywhere near his face.

Adam was the first to get to Benji and adeptly picked him up, cradling him in his arms. Benji stopped crying immediately and looked into Adam's bearded face, his brown eyes stretched in curiosity as if Adam's face was the most remarkable thing he'd ever seen. Alia supposed that could be the case, since he'd only been on earth for ninety days.

She'd noticed earlier that Benji's eyes followed Adam even when she was holding him. That could be because Benji wasn't around any other men who had beards. Neither her father nor either of her brothers wore beards.

"Let's take him back with us," she suggested to Adam. "He's wide-awake anyway. God knows my nerves can't take screaming from a baby. I automatically want to comfort him."

"Petra said a little crying's good for him." Adam reminded her of her sister-in-law's theory that babies learned to self-soothe when their parents didn't rush to cuddle them at every sound of discomfort.

"Just a few minutes," Alia said, holding her arms out for Benji. She was becoming addicted to his baby smell and the feel of his reassuring weight against her chest.

"You're going to spoil him," Adam warned.

Alia smiled at her husband. "Who was the first person in here when he started yelling?"

Adam laughed, peering down at Benji's scrunched-up face. Benji gave him some gum action, grinning widely, all of his gums showing. "God did a good job making babies so adorable," he said, carefully transferring Benji to Alia's arms.

Alia held Benji close as they walked back to the great room. "Petra doesn't have to know we couldn't resist cuddling him. We're his auntie and uncle—it's our job to spoil him."

In the great room, they had been watching a movie when Benji had called them. They resumed watching after they'd settled on the comfortable couch. They sat close, Adam's arm draped on the back of the couch.

Benji, breathing evenly and as calm as can be, closed his eyes and was soon sleeping soundly in his aunt's arms. Nothing alarmed him, not the sound of the film through the TV's speakers, nor the cheering from his uncle whenever one of his favorite scenes came on the screen.

They enjoyed the movie, gave Benji his midnight feeding, changed him again and continued to hold him while he slept. Alia was holding him when their doorbell rang at one in the morning.

Panicked because they shouldn't be coddling Benji, they looked at each other with widened eyes. "I'll go put him in his bassinet," Adam said. "Take your time letting Petra and Chance in."

"On it," Alia said, slowly maneuvering Benji into Adam's arms. Once Adam was on the way to their bedroom with Benji, she took a deep breath and went to answer the door.

When she opened the door for Chance and Petra, the couple was kissing. Alia laughed softly. "You two are already working on a brother or sister for Benji, I see," she joked.

Chance and Petra parted, smiling. "What can I say, sis," Chance said. "I'm very much in love with my wife."

He and Petra stepped inside, and Alia closed and locked the door after them.

Petra blushed at her husband's words, but didn't look the least bit embarrassed to have been caught kissing Chance in front of his sister. Alia felt that she and Petra were beyond those sorts of uncomfortable feelings. They had bonded like sisters. And they were both strong women of the world who were fiercely protective of their families. They knew the score.

"Did you have a good time?" Alia asked, walking into the kitchen and hoping they'd follow, which they did.

She went to the fridge and poured herself a small glass of pomegranate juice. "Would you like something to drink before you go?"

"I'm a bit parched," said Petra. "I'll have some of what you're drinking, but just a small amount. We should get home and let you and Adam get some rest. Benji can be a handful."

The three of them stood in the kitchen, Alia in a pair of pants and a comfortable tunic covering her seven-months-along belly, and barefoot. Chance wore one of his tailored suits, and Petra was glamorous in a short white sleeveless flared dress with a wrap that fell beautifully around her legs and cinched her waist, which, Alia noted, was practically back to its pre-pregnancy size. Petra had told her that eight weeks after she'd given birth, she'd started going to her judo classes again. She hadn't started jogging again, instead taking it slowly as she returned to her usual workout routine.

Alia handed Petra a glass of pomegranate juice. "Benji, a handful?" she said, referring to Petra's statement about Benji. "Not at all. We enjoyed taking care of him. He's a good boy."

"He is," Petra said, her eyes going to something on the couch, which could be seen from the kitchen because the entire space was open concept. Alia's gaze followed her sister-in-law's. She grimaced. She and Adam had left Benji's blanket on the couch when they were rushing to put him in his bassinet. The blanket was a multicolored piece of art and had been knitted by his grandmother Debra. Wherever Benji went, the blanket went.

Chance saw what had captured his wife's and sister's attention, and walked over and picked up the blanket. He smiled at Alia. "Adam is just putting Benji in his bassinet, isn't he?"

Caught red-handed, Alia didn't try to deny it. "We enjoyed his baby cuteness for practically the whole five hours you were gone," she confessed unashamedly. "Put me in rehab. I'm hooked on that little guy!"

They heard a wail from the direction of her bedroom, and a few moments later, Adam came into the room cradling Benji. "He didn't want to get back in his bassinet," he said. "I tried to put him down and at first I thought he was going to cooperate, but apparently, he was trying to give me a moment to come to my senses and pick him back up again, and when I didn't, he started protesting, loudly."

All four adults convulsed with laughter. Baby Benji, looking content again, smiled like an angel. Petra went and gathered him in her arms and kissed both chubby cheeks. "You little rascal. What have you been up to? Wrapping these two helpless people around your adorable little finger. Don't you know they can't resist your charms any better than your father and I can?"

Alia laughed. "Then you're not upset that we didn't follow your rules and ignore him when he started bawling?"

"Nah," Petra said, smiling warmly. "My bark is worse than my bite. I'm a sucker for this sweet face, too."

"I knew it," Alia cried.

They all sat down in the great room, and Petra and Chance told them about their evening out. While they were describing where they'd gone dancing after dinner, Petra said, with a side glance at her husband, "You'll never guess who we saw at the club. And I should preface this with, we saw them, but they didn't see us." She was soothingly rubbing Benji's back as he lay on her shoulder, a white cloth protecting her dress. She didn't actually wait for anyone to guess. "Brock, dancing with a woman who looked quite a bit like Macy."

"Macy!" Alia exclaimed. "My Macy?"

"Macy Harris," Chance said, sounding certain of himself.

"I can't believe it," Alia said. "Why would Macy be out with Brock? She hasn't mentioned anything about seeing Brock. This must be about her business. She handles security for us. Maybe Brock was…" Frankly, she couldn't come up with a reasonable explanation why her best friend and her brother would be dancing together at an upscale club in Manhattan on a Friday night. None whatsoever. Macy had told her, for her own sanity, she was avoiding Brock.

"I'm stumped, too," Chance said. "That brother of ours has stooped low in his life, but this is the lowest.

Carrying on with a nice girl like Macy. Why couldn't he stick to women who know his game and don't care when he loves them and moves on? He's going to break Macy's heart."

"Or maybe Macy is going to break his," Petra said. "Macy doesn't strike me as a woman who can be played with. If she's involved with Brock, then she knows exactly what she's doing."

"That's right," Alia said, trying to recover from the shock. "I have faith that Macy won't be one of the women he can just walk away from."

"Yes," Adam agreed. "Macy can handle herself. I just wonder if this is something that's happened recently or if it's been going on under our noses for some time. And if so, why neither of them have mentioned they're seeing each other."

"I'll tell you why," Alia said. She supposed if Macy was secretly seeing Brock, then the cat was out of the bag. However, she still felt like she should take precautions. "But you've all got to be sworn to secrecy."

Petra, Chance and Adam all nodded in agreement, and Alia continued. "About a year ago or so, Macy gave in to temptation and slept with Brock. She's been in love with him since she was in her teens. Afterward, he didn't even call her. It broke her heart. Some months later, though, he went to see her and said he was sorry. He'd acted like a fool. He genuinely had feelings for her and wanted her to give him a second chance, but Macy told him no. She couldn't risk her heart on him again. Since then, she's kind of yearned for him, but figured he was like candy to a diabetic—it tastes good but it's not good for you. Her words. Also, the night of our Christmas party, I wondered why Brock couldn't keep his eyes off her. Now I know why. He obviously hasn't given up on her."

The other three adults in the room sat digesting what Alia had said for a few moments. Then Chance cocked his head to the side in a contemplative pose and said, "Before Petra and I were married, Brock and I had an argument about love. At the time I assumed he'd never been in love, but he told me he had and it was with someone he'd had a one-night stand with and she wouldn't speak to him afterward. That must have been Macy."

"Now I guess she's willing to give him another chance," Adam said. "I hope he doesn't blow it."

"Me, too," Alia said.

Soon after that, Petra and Chance bundled Benji up and they headed home, which wasn't very far since Alia and Adam, Petra and Chance, and Alia and Chance's parents, James and Debra, all lived within a mile of each other in the Harlem neighborhood of Manhattan.

The next few weeks were eventful ones for Adam and Alia Joie. Adam became Alia Joie's chief comforter, as he took it upon himself to make sure she was taken care of. The bigger her belly got, the more difficult it was for her to sleep and move around as easily as she used to. Adam noticed that her center of gravity was slightly off and she sometimes lost her balance, being front heavy, because of her baby bump. He often had a smile on his face, watching her tip this way or that way before she felt confident that gravity wasn't going to work against her.

In Alia Joie's eighth month of pregnancy, Macy conspired with him to plan a surprise baby shower there in the loft. Adam would supply the key to the place, and Macy and their friends would come in and decorate and be ready to yell "Surprise" when Alia Joie got home from the office. Adam, as the uninvited spouse, would make himself scarce for a few hours.

All went off without a hitch, and when Adam got back to the loft that night, Alia Joie was sitting in the great room surrounded by baby gifts galore, wearing a pair of very attractive lounge pajamas—he learned later that there had been a pajama party theme—with her feet up on the coffee table.

She smiled at him as he approached. "You and Macy planned all of this!" she said accusingly. She patted a spot on the couch beside her. "Come here, I'm too tired to move."

He went and kissed her lips sweetly before sitting down. "Looks like you made off like a bandit."

She laughed. "We won't have to buy a thing for Adam IV, or Angelique Ramona."

He frowned. "Have we changed the name again?" What he meant was, his wife had changed the names they'd settled on for Little Girl Braithwaite. She was surprisingly adamant about naming their child Adam IV if it was a boy. "But I like them," he hurriedly added.

"Really?" asked Alia Joie, "Because I'd like to honor my grandmother and your mother, but I don't want to leave Mom out. Maybe we ought to tack Debra on for good measure."

He moved closer and put his arm around her. "I just hope she doesn't come here with Ramona's bossy attitude, and if we're going to name her Angelique, I'd like to call her Lique for short, not Angel. No kid should be burdened with that nickname. We wouldn't expect her to be an angel, just a decent person who loves others."

"You've given this some thought, haven't you?" Alia Joie said with a note of laughter in her voice. "Okay, no Angel."

Suddenly, a look of near panic came over her face, and she reached for the TV remote, which was stuck between the couch's cushions. "Did you see the news tonight?" she asked him anxiously as she flipped the channels on the muted TV until she found CNN.

Adam, who had been playing basketball with Chance and Brock, said, "No, what's going on?"

Alia Joie turned the volume up on the TV. A CNN correspondent was talking about the indictment of a well-known billionaire munitions-company owner who'd been charged with Adam and his team's kidnapping.

Adam watched with interest, but not surprise. The man they were talking about had been in trouble with the law before, but never indicted. His lawyers were too good. Apparently, his lawyers had failed him this time and he was going to jail for a very long time. His money wasn't going to save him. Adam wondered if his colleagues had heard about it, then remembered he'd put his cell phone on silent mode while he was playing basketball with Chance and Brock and had neglected to switch the ringer back on.

He slipped his phone out of his pocket now and saw several messages. He went down the list of callers. Yes, he had calls from all of his team.

Alia Joie sat silently observing him. In moments like this, he really appreciated her calm demeanor. She was his rock.

He hugged her close. "Justice has been done, my love. I can move on now."

His appearance might seem to suggest this news hadn't affected him, but inside he felt enormous relief. Freer than he'd felt in a long time. He had his closure. In fact, with his wife in his arms, with his baby on the way, he thought that if he died now, he would have fulfilled every goal he'd ever had in life and would die happy.

Alia Joie looked deep into his eyes. "Adam Braithwaite, you're too moral a man to say it, so I'll say it for you. I hope he rots in hell for what he did to you and Arjun and Calvin and Maritza."

Adam let out a long sigh and squeezed her a bit. "Thank you, sweetheart."

And as far as he was concerned, that was the end of it.

## Chapter 14

"Dubai! Why does it have to be Dubai?" Alia exclaimed that morning in the scheduling meeting for Youngblood Media's network television winter lineup.

"Because it's becoming a favorite vacation destination of African Americans. And we not only entertain, we inform. We don't want our viewers to go to Dubai without knowing how to comport themselves," Chance said. As CEO, he was sitting at the head of the long conference table. "I'd like to do a comprehensive hour-long special on not only visiting Dubai, but living there. I'm also concerned about safety. Attacks on American citizens are rare, but I did hear about an American teacher who was stabbed to death by a radical woman in the restroom of a shopping mall. The attacker was executed for her crime, but still, we want our viewers to have all the facts."

When Chance had said he wanted to do a television special on Dubai, Alia's first thought had been to wonder how Adam would react to her family's network focusing on the city he'd been working in when he'd been kidnapped. Would it bother him? Or would he not care? He'd said his experiences in Dubai had been wonderful up until they'd been snatched.

She placed her hand on the small of her back. It was a little sore in that spot, and she'd been having cramps throughout the day. She was nine months now, and the baby could come at any time. So why wasn't she at home, relaxing? Because she wasn't sick and she loved her job. She would be taking six months off from work after she gave birth. She had already groomed her second in command, Martin Wilson, to take over for her. Martin, an African American in his late twenties, was sitting beside her in the conference room. Attuned to her moods, he was giving her concerned looks. But then, he'd been doing that ever since her baby bump had started growing bigger. Pregnant women apparently made him nervous. Or maybe he was just being protective.

"Look," said Chance. "I can understand why you're wondering if this is a good idea or not. Talk to the interested party and get back to me."

She was sure most of the employees sitting around the conference table were aware of Adam's experiences in the United Arab Emirates. After the Presidential Medal of Honor ceremony and the subsequent announcement of the indictment of the munitions-company owner, many people were aware. But she and Chance were still reluctant to talk about family business in front of the employees.

"You've done research on the place, and I'm sure your insights would be invaluable to those who'll be traveling there to film the special," Chance added.

He had her there. When Adam had gone missing in Dubai, she'd been motivated to find out as much about the United Arab Emirates as possible. Dubai was a tourist mecca. It offered luxuries that the average traveler rarely saw. Their shopping malls were things of legend. One had a ski slope inside of it. It was like Disney World for adults. However, most people who could afford to leave the city in the summer did because, being in the desert, it got extremely hot. Things didn't start cooling off until October. Also, a lot of the food was imported. Therefore, food was expensive. It was a Muslim country and you had to abide by Muslim laws. You had to dress modestly, there was no liquor, and during Ramadan you couldn't be seen eating in public because adherents to the faith were fasting.

Yes, she could definitely give pointers to whoever would be traveling over there to film the special. She didn't feel right about going ahead with the special without at least telling Adam about it, though. She felt that he probably wouldn't object to their doing it. He would probably say he didn't blame the UAE for what had happened to him within its borders. However, she'd feel better about it if she discussed it with him before things were set in motion.

"All right," she told Chance. "I'll do that tonight."

* * *

Adam was standing in his favorite room, the nursery. The good thing about the loft was that the ceiling was high and the layout wasn't rigid. By moving a few walls, they now had a good-sized nursery right across from their bedroom.

The room had an African jungle theme, with the walls painted a soothing green. Alia Joie had painted a mural on one wall that looked like jungle foliage, and in the lush-looking plants, an elephant poked its trunk through. A black panther, emerald green eyes vivid, was seen in there, too, along with various other African animals. It was fun trying to spot them.

Adam had put together the furnishings, except for the comfy chair, which hadn't needed assembling. It had a handcrafted pillow made by Debra in it, so that Alia Joie's back would be supported while she held the baby.

Lately, every evening when he got home, he found himself going into the nursery to see if there was anything he could do to make it more perfect. He wanted his son or daughter to come home to comfort and safety. He reached up and touched the colorful mobile over the crib and set it in motion. He'd made sure it was secure in case their little one grabbed hold of it and held on. He didn't want it falling on his or her inquisitive head.

He smiled. He kept referring to their baby as he or she because neither he nor Alia Joie had wanted to know the sex of their baby. They wanted to be surprised. Ramona swore that they were having a girl. But then, she was a greedy grandmother, and Adam figured she hoped it would be a girl because he and

Alia Joie would be motivated to try for a boy, as well. They hadn't talked about having more children. However, Adam wanted a large family. That wasn't a topic you discussed with your very pregnant wife, though, when she was concentrating on bringing the one she was pregnant with safely into the world.

He was patient. He'd wait until the arrival of their first before bringing up the possibility of having another. He looked around the room. In addition to the beautiful mural and furnishings, there was a giraffe-shaped wicker basket to hold small toys, and in the crib a cute baby elephant pillow that the baby could cuddle up with when he or she got a bit older. Of course, being a techie, he also had a camera in the room aimed at the crib so that he and Alia Joie could check on the baby using their cell phones from anywhere in the world.

Was he a little paranoid? Yes, expectant fathers usually were.

"I figured you'd be in here," Alia Joie said from the doorway, startling him.

She stood there, wearing a smile and looking healthy and happy, her hand on her big belly. He went and softly kissed her mouth. "Hello, beautiful. How was your day?"

He draped his arm about her shoulders as they turned by silent consensus and walked out of the nursery, heading to the kitchen, where he'd already started dinner. He often made sure to be home before Alia Joie because they'd agreed a long time ago that whoever got home first started preparing dinner. He didn't want that task to fall on her now. He'd wanted her to quit work two months ago, but she was stubborn. He figured she worked hard enough at work and shouldn't have to come home and cook on top of that.

"Oh, it was pretty routine. But I do need to run something by you." She sighed as she waddled—a term that was a bone of contention between them—into the kitchen. She referred to her manner of walking these days as waddling, but he didn't agree. He claimed she was poetry in motion. She'd insisted he not contradict her. She was a woman who knew what poetry in motion looked like. She'd danced ballet in her early years and if she weren't nine months pregnant, she'd still be doing exercises at the bar in the gym that had been put there specifically for her to do her ballet barre workout.

Her hair was in loose braids down her back, the edges laid down as she liked them to be. He smiled at that. It was her opinion that a lot of women who wore braids had their hair fall out because the braids were too tight and they didn't take care of their edges. Women and their hair. But who was he to talk? He was as obsessed about his locks, which were coming along nicely. They were six inches long now, dark brown and healthy looking.

"What do you need to run by me?" he asked, hoping it would be enough to get his mind off his hair.

They sat down on high stools at the center island. Alia Joie looked into his eyes. "Chance wants to do an hour-long special on Dubai because he says more and more African Americans are going there on vacation." She maintained eye contact, seemingly expecting a surprised reaction from him.

However, he felt no particular surge of emotion on hearing her news. He liked Dubai. The people had been welcoming. He'd felt no overt racial prejudice coming from the people while there. In fact, when he'd gotten there he'd been pleased to see so many other visitors with an abundance of melanin in their skin. He had expected nothing but rich white tourists. But there were plenty of people there with black and brown skin.

Showed how closed-minded even he, a scientist, could be on occasion.

He smiled at Alia Joie. He sensed she was worried that he might react negatively to the company's plans to do a special on the place where he'd been living when he'd been snatched and held against his will, but he didn't feel that way. He placed his hand atop hers and dipped his head, peering into her eyes with a gentle smile on his mouth. "Alia Joie, you can stop worrying about me. I'm fully back home now. I don't have nightmares anymore. The mention of Dubai isn't going to send me spiraling into that dark abyss I was in when I got back home." He placed his hand on her belly. "This is all I care about. You, me and our little one. I don't blame the city of Dubai for what happened to me. Sure, we were living there when something bad happened to us, but bad things happen everywhere. The people there are like people all over the world—they just want to live their lives in peace and have a safe place to raise their families. They depend on tourism. If the special gets them more tourists, good for them. At the same time, if the special keeps African Americans safe while visiting, even better."

The look of relief on her face was almost comical. But he didn't laugh because this must be serious if the thought of his having a breakdown at the mention of

Dubai put her under so much obvious stress. He stood and wrapped his arms around her while she sat on the stool. "Listen to me, my beautiful wife. You shouldn't be worrying about anything at this point in your pregnancy. Let it go. You and I are okay. Not just okay, we're splendid."

She looked up at him and smiled. "I'm glad we're splendid because our baby deserves to be born to splendid parents."

She looked down at the floor. Water was spreading beneath the stool she was sitting on. He glanced down, too, and wondered why the floor was wet.

By the time his brain processed the answer to his question, Alia Joie was up and moving toward their bedroom. "My water just broke," she said as calmly as if she'd said the sky was blue. He hurried after her, seeing the wet spot on the back of her dress and trying his best not to panic. They'd planned for this, after all. Her bag was packed. She would now phone her obstetrician. His job was to phone her parents. Her parents would phone her brothers and best friend, Macy. His job was also to be there to do her bidding.

So he trailed behind her to the bedroom, his heart pounding, his mission to do what he was told and stay out of the way otherwise. This was new to him, and he'd just play it by ear.

Alia Joie looked back at him and smiled. "I'm not in pain," she told him. "Don't look so stricken."

*Do I look panicked? Yeah, probably.* "Just tell me what you want me to do," he said.

They were in the bedroom by now, and she was picking up her cell phone. She punched in the doctor's number. The phone was at her ear and she held up a finger. "Ringing. Just grab my bag on the shelf above my winter coats in the closet," she said, and frowned. "A little squeezing of the belly," she explained. "Baby girl or boy has decided to change position."

Adam frowned. That couldn't be good. Baby Braithwaite was probably as impatient as his or her mother.

He went and got the bag, which was heavier than he imagined it ought to be when it contained only a change of clothes for Alia Joie and the baby's outfit for coming home in. Or were there other things in this bag he didn't know about? And why couldn't he stop panicking? Women have been giving birth, according to his biblically minded mother, since Eve gave birth to her firstborn, Cain.

*Concentrate on Alia Joie*, he ordered himself.

He went back into the bedroom carrying her hospital bag. She was talking on the phone. He heard her say, "Yeah, all right, thank you, Doctor. We're heading to the hospital now."

*Now?* Adam thought. *I haven't phoned her parents yet.*

Alia Joie looked up at him. "I'm calling for the car."

They'd arranged with a car service to take them to the hospital and bring them back home.

"I'll phone your parents," he said.

When they answered, James panicked and gave the phone to Debra, who didn't sound perturbed in the least. "I'll let everyone else know, and we'll meet you at the hospital."

He and Alia Joie got off their phones at around the same time and looked at each other across the room.

He suspected he still looked panicked to her, but he couldn't help it. She appeared serene, though, for which he was grateful.

"I'm going to change my clothes," she announced and went into the walk-in closet to do so. He still had the bag in his hand and set it down on the bed.

He knew what he could do while she changed and they waited for their ride to arrive. He'd clean the fluid off the kitchen floor. He was good at cleaning. Cleaning relaxed him. Cleaning would help him focus.

"I'll be in the kitchen," he called to Alia Joie.

"Okay, sweetie," she called back.

He took care of the floor in no time. This done, he headed back to the bedroom, from which Alia Joie was exiting, having put on fresh clothing and thrown her purse on its long strap onto her right shoulder. "I'm ready," she said.

Adam had to look down at himself to see if he was ready. He was fully dressed. He checked his back pants pocket to see if he had his wallet. Check. Cell phone? In the kitchen.

"I'm ready, too," he said. "Let me just grab my cell phone."

The car was waiting at the curb when they got downstairs. As the driver, who already knew where they were heading, pulled into traffic, Adam took a deep breath. "Okay, tell me how you've been feeling today. No contractions? I read that after the water breaks, contractions could already be underway. If you haven't been having any, it can take twelve to twenty-four hours for them to start."

Alia Joie closed her eyes a moment before speaking.

"Actually, I've been having some cramping throughout the day. Nothing alarming. I just shrugged them off and kept working. I didn't call you because I didn't want you to worry. I figured having this baby is going to take its course, no matter what I do. I—we—are just along for the ride."

Adam's brain almost exploded. She'd been having contractions all day, and it hadn't occurred to her to come home early and get off her feet? What was the matter with modern women? First, his sister-in-law had given birth to his nephew in a bookstore, an event his wife had been present for, and now this?

"Alia Joie, when you told me how quickly Petra had Benji, I assumed you would try to be more circumspect about giving birth. I didn't think you'd take from that example that it would be a good idea to ignore your contractions like she did!"

Alia Joie looked at him and broke into hysterical laughter. She could hardly catch her breath, and he supposed that was probably because her huge belly, now, no doubt, in the midst of another contraction, was obscuring her lungs. Crazy woman. He needed Ramona here to talk some sense into her. But then, Ramona would more than likely be on her side and say to let nature take its course, too.

"It's okay, sweetie," she finally said, wiping tears from her face with her fingers. "The doctor says more than likely it'll be hours before I give birth. The key is to get to the hospital. Once there, we'll be in good hands. Try not to worry." As an afterthought, she added, "Oh, call your mom."

Adam did as instructed. It might help him to hear Ramona's voice, however bossy.

She picked up the phone with, "Ay, is it that time? Alia's going to have the baby?" She sounded excited. He heard her turn off either the radio or the TV and yell, "Adam! Your son's on the phone!"

"We're going to the hospital now," Adam told his mother. "We just wanted you to know. I'll call again later."

"Wait a minute," said Ramona. "Put Alia on the phone."

Adam handed his cell phone to Alia Joie, who took the phone and held it to her ear. "Hello, Momma Ramona."

He heard his mother say, "Today, you learn what it means to become a mother, my sweet girl. You already know what it is to be a woman, but this is special. You won't be the same after this. You will know what it means to love someone even more than your own self. You're a strong woman—you can make this transition. And remember, once you have that baby in your arms, you won't mind what's happened just before it got here."

"Momma!" Adam exclaimed, horrified by his mother's words.

He was trying to relax Alia Joie, not terrify her. He tried to take the phone from his wife. But she held on to it.

She smiled at Adam and whispered, "She's right." Then she said to her mother-in-law, "Thank you, Momma Ramona, I'll remember that. Goodbye, I love you!"

"I love you, too, child," Ramona said. To Adam, she said, "Don't panic, and don't faint."

Adam couldn't hold back a chuckle. "Okay, Momma, I won't. Goodbye."

"Goodbye," said Ramona.

His wife smiled at him after he'd hung up. "I adore your mom," she said.

"I know you do," he said, also smiling. "Infuriating women often stick together."

That made her laugh. He supposed being called *infuriating* was a compliment to her. God, he loved this woman.

# Chapter 15

After being in labor for a little over thirteen hours, Alia gave birth to Adam IV, who came into the world weighing eight pounds, fourteen ounces, and measuring twenty-two inches long. Alia took one look at his face and realized Ramona had been right—the misery of the labor and birth receded into the back of her mind, and was replaced by a flood of love so strong she felt overwhelmed with emotion.

Adam was holding him close so she could peer into his face. She smiled up at Adam. He'd been her rock. For one thing, he had been by her side the entire time. He'd refused to leave when she'd told him to take a break and send her mother in. He went and got her mother for her, but he remained there with his steadying presence. She didn't think she could have done it without him. She continued to gaze at Adam IV, marveling at his features. Though they were quite scrunched up like most newborns', you could already see he had his father's nose shape, which was a little on the long side, and his ears, too.

His eyes were closed. They'd remained closed even when he'd been breastfeeding a few minutes after birth. She couldn't wait to see what color they were, whether her cinnamon colored or his father's milk chocolate or somewhere in between. His skin was a coppery brown. Lighter than hers and his father's. The tips of his ears were darker, and she remembered the old wives' tales her folks would tell about African American babies' skin color being lighter when they were born, but if the tips of their ears were of a darker tint, more than likely the rest of their skin would eventually become darker as the months passed.

Suddenly Adam IV opened his eyes and appeared to be looking right at her. She knew newborns didn't focus well at first. But it made her happy to see them open. The color of his eyes was like golden-brown honey.

"Well, look at that," Adam said, chuckling softly. "He's got your eyes."

"He's got your…everything else," Alia said. "I'm glad he's got something from me."

"Let me see him," James said as he came into the room, followed by Debra, Chance, Petra, Brock and Macy. Up until then, she and Adam had been alone with Adam IV. *Adam IV*. They had to think of a nickname for their new son.

Everyone took turns looking over the baby. Permission was given to snap pictures without using the flash, so her family and Macy took out their cell phones to record the occasion. They were good enough not to stay long, though. Alia was tired, and Adam IV went to sleep peacefully in her arms after his father had placed him in them.

Once again alone with their son, Adam bent and gently kissed his sweet head. Then he kissed Alia on the lips. "Thank you for giving me this beautiful child."

She smiled at him. "We did it together."

"You did most of the work," he said.

"And I'm tired, so you'd better take him while I sleep," she warned him with a huge yawn.

Adam took Adam IV into his arms, and that was the last thing she remembered until a nurse came into the room to check on her sometime later. Adam was asleep in a recliner in the hospital room. "Where's my baby?" she asked the nurse.

"He's in the nursery with the rest of the newborns," the young African American nurse said. "We'll bring him to you when it's time for his next feeding."

"Okay," Alia said, glancing over at Adam, who was snoring softly. "I guess I'll sleep until then."

"That's a good idea," the nurse told her. "Get as much sleep as you can. You're going to need your energy the next few…years."

Alia laughed softly. "So true."

Adam took three months off from work to give Alia Joie time to get her strength back. He'd offered to take more, but she'd insisted she wouldn't need him to stay home after three months because she'd have everything organized by then. And, even if she didn't, she'd have three more months off from work to figure it out.

Adam's priority became Alia Joie and A.J., which is what they'd decided to call Adam IV. A.J. let them know he was all too human. He kept them up all times of the night. He demanded attention, and there was no leaving him in a crib when he was wide-awake and interested to see what was going on in the rest of the world.

He was very curious and a fast developer. By three months A.J. was already rolling over, pulling himself into a sitting position in his crib and grasping at the bars. He could hold his head up. And when he looked at you, you knew he was paying close attention to you. To Adam, his rate of growth was uncanny, but he supposed that was because he was a first-time father. Alia Joie told him the doctor had said some babies simply developed faster. His mother, Ramona, had her theory, though. One day he was on the phone with her and she'd told him, "Of course A.J. is growing fast. He's making room for the next one. He wants a sister or a brother, preferably a sister."

"Momma, you're the one who wants another grandchild," Adam called her out. "Stop using A.J. as an excuse to campaign for more grandchildren."

Ramona had laughed. "Doesn't hurt to try."

Adam was a hands-on dad. After A.J. became used to breastfeeding, Adam was able to give A.J. expressed breast milk from a bottle when Alia Joie wanted to rest. He changed him, bathed him and rocked him to sleep. He also started A.J.'s education early by reading to him, letting him listen to different styles of music and singing to him.

Alia Joie encouraged him to sing to A.J. just before putting him to bed at night, and she would leave them alone. Adam knew she invariably stood in the hallway, out of sight, listening. He could sense her presence.

He loved her even more for giving him those precious father-son bonding moments with A.J., who would look him straight in the eyes and grin like crazy. His son's skin was now a uniform reddish brown like his, but his eyes remained the color of cinnamon or dark honey like his mother's. His cheeks were so chubby, Adam often kissed the soft skin there and breathed in his baby scent. A.J.'s hair was dark brown and silky with waves instead of curls. Adam figured it'd get curlier as he got older. He'd seen photos of Alia Joie when she was a baby, and she'd also had wavy dark brown hair.

One night after he'd put A.J. to bed, he and Alia Joie decided to make it a spa night and took a soak in the tub together.

He was washing Alia Joie's back with a sponge, enjoying the relaxing circular motions, looking forward to getting her out of the tub and into bed where they could cuddle, when she said, "Do you know what important date you recently missed?"

He racked his brain, trying to think if he'd missed a landmark holiday or something. Was it her birthday? No, that had been about a month or so ago. Their anniversary? Nope, they'd been married in the summer, and it was now mid-December. Then it occurred to him: in November of last year, he'd phoned her from the Pentagon and told her he was free. How could that have slipped his mind? The anniversary of that date had occurred a month ago. Obviously he'd missed it because he was happy. Those thoughts didn't intrude on his peace of mind anymore.

He continued to move the warm sponge on her shoulders, down her sides, along her spine and her lower back. "A lot can happen in a year."

Her soft laughter was a delight to his ears. "We produced a human being in a year," she said. "Well, God did, but we helped."

While he sat in the tub, he recalled the past year: how he'd been afraid to make love to Alia Joie the first month and a half he was back home. Then his breakthrough, which had been aided by both Dr. Klein and a man-to-man talk with J.Z., who was still a good friend. Now he and Em were like an extra set of grandparents for A.J., whom they adored.

He'd had many successes in the past year. His team had been acknowledged and rewarded for their work on the new technology that was already being used by the military to defuse enemy missiles. And their research on time, although still a work in progress, appeared to be going well. Arjun had been right about the Nobel Peace Prize. They'd been nominated, but had not won.

It had been an honor alone to be nominated. Calvin had been right, too, and their discovery had translated into extra money in their bank accounts. All four scientists were set for life where money was concerned. That didn't mean they'd ever be so satisfied with wealth that they'd neglect their work. Work was still the ultimate rush.

Arjun and Madhuri had gotten married in a traditional Hindu wedding, which Adam and Alia Joie had enjoyed tremendously. Calvin and Evie were waiting until spring to go to Surrey to be married. Alia Joie's friend June and her fiancé, Tony, went to Vegas and got married, then had another ceremony in Tony's family's New Jersey church to appease his angry mother. He and Alia Joie had attended the church wedding.

And last he'd heard, Brock and Macy were still sneaking around with each other and keeping their relationship a secret.

He was brought back from his ruminations when Alia Joie stood up and turned around in the tub. Mesmerized by her wet, lithe brown body, he dropped the sponge and carefully got to his feet, too. He enjoyed the view as he rose, her gorgeous legs and thighs, the dark glistening hair covering her vagina, her belly and her gorgeous breasts, more voluptuous after pregnancy. She was beautiful. She was fuller, lusher, like one of those *Birth of Venus* paintings he'd seen by Botticelli, or was it Bouguereau? He couldn't remember. Art was Alia Joie's thing, not his. His was science, and right now, he was caught up in a chemical reaction of opposites attracting. Her feminine curves were sending out a siren call to him.

He stepped onto the bath rug. Gentleman that he was, he lent her a hand and she emerged gingerly from the tub, her golden-hued gaze sweeping over his hard, masculine form. He grabbed a fluffy towel and began drying her off. She let him. After, she returned the favor.

Neat freak that she was, she hung the towel up to

dry before giving him her undivided attention again. "I have some good news and some bad news," she said as they left the bathroom to enter the master bedroom.

He was aroused already, so he hadn't been listening closely.

"Mmm?" he asked absentmindedly.

Both of them nude, her nipples hard, his member growing harder by the second, he only wanted to feast his eyes on her enticing form.

"The good news is, I feel as if I'm at my sexual peak and I want you more than ever. The bad news is, you're going to have to use condoms until we figure out a better form of birth control because, despite your mother's desire for more grandchildren, I'd like to wait awhile before we have another baby."

His brain fog lifted. That's right. They'd agreed to wait three months after Alia Joie had given birth to A.J. before resuming sex. The waiting was over. He'd been so immersed in fatherhood that he'd put it in the back of his mind. Yes, he'd wanted Alia Joie before now, but he'd seen what she'd gone through to give birth to A.J., and that had been a sight to behold. If men had to give birth, they'd give up sex altogether to avoid it. Women, the wonderful creatures, were much braver, thank God.

"Baby, whatever form of birth control you want to use is all right with me," he said, his gaze back on her body.

Alia Joie smiled. "Your nightstand drawer has a supply of condoms that should last us a while," she said with a coquettish smile. "I'm yours, Professor."

Adam took that as the green light and started the countdown in his head. He sometimes felt obsessive-compulsive because he liked to do things in the same manner. Especially when those steps achieved satisfactory results every time. He'd done it with experiments when he was taking chemistry. Proper steps, expected outcome. He did it with his baking. Right recipe, right temperature of the oven, right amount of time spent in the oven invariably produced good results.

Sex wasn't like that, though. No, they were human beings with brains. Therefore, sex should be relished, the act extended as long as possible for the maximum pleasure of your partner.

So he laid Alia Joie on the bed and began kissing her from her fragrant neck to her lovely breasts to her stomach. He made sure to lick her belly button. She moaned and smiled. He worked his way down to her thighs and went all the way down to her toes, which he also licked. She giggled a little but was able to restrain herself.

Then he got up on his knees, gently encouraged her to spread her legs for him and proceeded to use his tongue to render her absolutely pliant and weak after a climax of a magnitude he'd never witnessed her experience before. Maybe it was true what she'd said, that she was at her sexual peak, because her body trembled and she bit her hand to hold back a scream, probably afraid she'd wake A.J., or give J.Z. something to talk about the next time he ran into him. He'd never felt so proud.

She was panting when he stood up and gathered her in his arms, placing her farther onto the bed because she'd slipped to the edge of it as he'd been pleasuring her. She was putty in his hands. He smiled at her as he walked over to the nightstand and got a condom from the drawer, tore it open and adeptly rolled it onto his engorged penis.

She was hot and tight when he entered her, and she began contracting her vagina around him. Squeezing him, working him up to a sweet frenzy, which was overkill because he didn't need the stimulation. He was already at the point of wanting to explode inside of her. He realized how much he'd missed her. Being inside of her. At this moment, he was so grateful that she hadn't given up on him when he'd been gone. He couldn't imagine what his life would have been like if she'd abandoned him like Calvin's girlfriend had dismissed him.

"I love you so much," he told her. "But I want you to stop doing that because I want to stay inside of you for as long as possible."

She smiled at him and desisted. Under control again, Adam enjoyed moving in and out of her, his penis hot while inside of her, cooling off when it hit the air. She moaned quietly when he went back inside and hit a sweet spot. Her body was glistening with a thin layer of perspiration, her nipples like moist dark cherries that he wanted to taste, but this felt so good he didn't dare change positions right now.

Alia Joie wrapped her legs around him and held on to his hips, her pelvis thrust upward. He could tell she was rapidly approaching another climax and he wanted this one to be memorable, too.

"You're okay?" he asked, this being the first time they'd made love since A.J.'s birth.

She must have guessed he was asking if she could take all of him, because she whispered, "Feels so good.

Deeper." And she thrust upward, encouraging him to let go.

He was so hard, the sides of his penis very sensitive as he pushed. He was in pain as the need to come gained momentum.

Yet he refused to come until Alia Joie reached her second climax. He longed to feel her body convulse beneath him, to feel her tremble in his arms, to know that she could feel the magnitude of his love for her.

Alia Joie suddenly grabbed him by the neck and pulled him close to her. She clung to him and rocked forward. He leaned back with her attached to him, and it was at that moment that he came, and the climax was so powerful that he howled with the release. Alia Joie laughed and covered his mouth with a hand.

They stayed in that position, both of them coming down from a shared climax that he knew had their muscles protesting from the exertion, but their pelvises going through delightful orgasms.

Alia Joie removed her hand from his mouth and grinned at him. "Promise me that when we're old and gray and A.J. and our other kids are long out of the house and living their own lives, that you and I will still be loving each other like this."

Adam chuckled. "Like this," he promised. "But maybe a little slower."

Then he kissed her passionately and thoroughly.

After lying in each other's arms a few minutes and talking and laughing together, they got up, put on their robes and went across the hall to peer at A.J. in his crib. He was sleeping peacefully. Adam looked from A.J. to Alia Joie, whose waist his arm was around as he pulled her close to his side. His life was perfect. It didn't matter if he never discovered the nature of time. It was times like this when it simply didn't matter. That we were allowed to be in the moment, to appreciate it, was what mattered. That, and to give love and receive love.

Three months ago, his son wasn't here. Now he was. That was a miracle in and of itself.

\* \* \* \* \*

## He listened as Rosario spoke, but his gaze strayed to Elise.

It was hard not to lust after her, to imagine himself kissing her. Giovanni slammed the brakes on his thoughts. Mad at himself for fantasizing about the know-it-all chef, he tore his eyes away from her. He didn't want to see Elise at the club every day. Not because he despised her, but because he was scared his desires would get the best of him one day, and he'd cross the line—or worse, jump over it and into her bed.

Worried Rosario would offer Elise the job on the spot, Giovanni realized he had to take control of the interview, and plotted his next move. The Southern beauty had an impressive résumé and outstanding cooking skills, but she'd rubbed him the wrong way from the moment she'd opened her mouth, and Giovanni had to get rid of her before it was too late.

**Pamela Yaye** has a bachelor's degree in Christian education. Her love for African American fiction prompted her to pursue a career in writing romance. When she's not working on her latest novel, this busy wife, mother and teacher is watching basketball, cooking or planning her next vacation. Pamela lives in Alberta, Canada, with her gorgeous husband and adorable, but mischievous, son and daughter.

### Books by Pamela Yaye

### Harlequin Kimani Romance

*Mocha Pleasures*
*Seduced by the Bachelor*
*Secret Miami Nights*
*Seduced by the Tycoon at Christmas*
*Pleasure in His Kiss*
*Pleasure at Midnight*
*Pleasure in His Arms*
*Decadent Holiday Pleasures*

Visit the Author Profile page
at Harlequin.com for more titles.

# DECADENT
# HOLIDAY PLEASURES

Pamela Yaye

## Acknowledgments

I want to thank Kimani staff, past and present,
for your knowledge, professionalism and support
over the past twelve years.

Special thanks to the Yaye and Odidison families
for your love and encouragement.

Sha-Shana Crichton, you are the best agent an author
could have, and I'm grateful for everything you have
done for me since I signed on with your agency.

Last but not least, I want to thank Kimani readers
for buying, sharing and reviewing my novels.
I am humbled by your unwavering support
and I appreciate all of you.

Dear Reader,

I *love* Christmas (especially the delicious, decadent desserts) and so does executive chef Elise Jennings. The pain of losing her parents overwhelms her at times, but Elise knows she has a lot to be thankful for. She has fantastic friends, a great new job and a bright future in the culinary field. Elise only wished her boss, Giovanni Castillo, didn't look like *People*'s Sexiest Man Alive because every time their eyes meet her knees buckle, and Elise has to remind herself to breathe!

Giovanni hates Christmas, and wishes he could sleep until the New Year. Life sucks. His polo career imploded, his father is pressuring him to take over the family business and he can't stop fantasizing about Elise Jennings. Driven by lust, Giovanni kisses Elise in the restaurant kitchen, but one kiss isn't enough, and soon they're enjoying a secret Christmas fling. Elise and Giovanni's story is filled with tender, heartfelt moments, and I hope that it reminds you what matters most this holiday season.

All the best in life and love,

*Pamela Yaye*

# Chapter 1

Giovanni Castillo sat inside the award-winning restaurant at his family's polo club in the Hamptons on
Friday morning, bored out of his mind. Auditions for
the executive chef position at Vencedores had started
three hours earlier, but none of the candidates they'd
interviewed yet had impressed him. They were all stiff
and uptight, and their entrées had lacked originality,
flavor and presentation. Giovanni was an elite polo
player, not a New York food critic, but he knew what
exceptional cuisine tasted like, and the entrées had all
lacked the wow factor.

Giovanni wondered what his mother, Constanza,
would think of the tasting menus prepared. He was still
full from the elaborate Argentinian meal he'd had last

night at his parents' East Hampton estate, and none of
the candidates were in his mother's league.

Rosario was hopeful they'd find a suitable replace-
ment for Chef Cruz, but Giovanni didn't share his sister's optimism. And he didn't have to. He was the acting
CEO of the polo club while their father was recovering
from knee surgery, but Rosario was the chief operat-
ing officer, who ensured everything ran smoothly. The
polo club had hundreds of employees and Rosario knew
them all by name, even the cleaning crew. Dressed in
a floral-print suit, she looked youthful and pretty, but
she was a tenacious businesswoman and no one would
dare cross her. Giovanni had four younger sisters and
although Rosario was the smallest in stature, she was
the most feared.

Giovanni smoothed a hand over the base of his ponytail. He was due for a haircut and was looking forward to his trip to the barbershop tomorrow with his
best friend. He'd met Jonas Crawford, a successful entrepreneur born and bred in the Hamptons, at an international car show years earlier and they'd bonded
over their love of vintage automobiles, winter sports
and horror movies. Jonas was the brother he'd always
wanted, and even though they were polar opposites who
butted heads on a regular basis, he valued their friendship. Jonas was the twin brother of popular app developer Chase Crawford, and Giovanni enjoyed spending
time with the entire Crawford family.

For the second time in minutes, Giovanni glanced at
his diamond watch. If it were up to him, he'd be working out in his home gym with his personal trainer, not
sitting around with the restaurant staff interviewing

candidates for the executive chef position. He'd promised to help Rosario out during their dad's absence, and Giovanni wanted to be a man of his word—even though his dad thought he was irresponsible. They'd never been close, never had the father-son relationship he'd secretly longed for, but he wanted to make Vincente proud.

Sunlight poured through the floor-to-ceiling windows, blinding him, and Giovanni winced. Since his concussion, he'd become sensitive to light, and had migraines on a regular basis. Over the course of his polo career, he'd suffered several injuries and his neurologist, Dr. Kaddouri, was worried he'd done permanent damage to his health. Giovanni disagreed with him.

Crossing his legs at the ankles, he watched the waitstaff wipe the tables, set them with silverware and adjust the furniture. Sleek and stylish, with glitzy chandeliers, gold accents and designer seating, Vencedores was the trendiest restaurant in the Hamptons, and Rosario was the reason why. Energetic, hardworking and insightful, she was always on the lookout for the next big thing in pop culture and wasted no time implementing her ideas at the club.

Hearing his cell phone chime, Giovanni glanced down at the table. Reading the text message from Chef Cruz made him chuckle. A week ago, the head chef had collapsed while preparing breakfast and Giovanni had feared he'd die on the kitchen floor. After emergency surgery to repair a blocked artery, Chef Cruz, now on the road to recovery, had decided to retire. Finding an executive chef who was as talented and affable as Chef Cruz was a daunting task, but Rosario was excited about the last audition of the day and Giovanni hoped candidate number six lived up to the hype.

"Next up is Elise Jennings," Rosario announced, consulting the résumé she was holding in her hands. "Elise Jennings graduated from the top of her class at the International Culinary Center of New York, and spent five years working as a sous chef at By the Bay restaurant. Best of all? She's a seasoned traveler who's explored culinary delights all over the world and incorporated them into her scrumptious recipes and decadent desserts..."

*Thank God*, he thought, cracking his knuckles. *One more interview and I'm out of here.*

Rosario had insisted he attend the executive chef auditions and Giovanni didn't want to disappoint her. Though next week he planned to cut back his work hours at the club. If he wanted to be ready to hit the field for the start of polo season in January, he had to get back in game shape, and that meant increasing the duration, intensity and frequency of his daily workouts.

*Giovanni, you've done significant damage to your body. The next time you get a concussion, it could cause irreversible damage and severely affect your quality of life...*

To escape the voice playing in his mind, he pressed his eyes shut and gave his head a shake. Giovanni didn't care what Dr. Kaddouri said. Polo was his life and he wasn't giving up his career because his medical team was worried about the injuries he'd sustained last season. He had worked hard for everything he'd accomplished, for every championship and title he'd won, and he refused to let fear rule his life.

Warm memories filled his thoughts. He'd learned to play polo at twelve years old and had instantly fallen in love with it. Committed to being the best in the sport, he'd turned pro at nineteen and spent countless hours practicing, training and studying film. He'd won tournaments around the world, including in his native Argentina, and quickly become the face of the sport.

Two years ago, he'd been ranked the best polo player in the world, had several lucrative endorsement deals and a gorgeous wife, but everything had changed at the US Open Polo Championship. Thinking about one of the worst days of his life made his palms sweat. Anger infected his six-foot-four frame and a bitter taste filled his mouth.

A female voice speaking in Spanish seized Giovanni's attention and he surfaced from his thoughts. Straightening in his chair, he regarded the statuesque woman with the doe-shaped eyes, pecan-brown complexion and delicate features who entered the dining room, waving at the group. His gaze lingered on her crimson lips. They looked luscious and, when she smiled, he noticed there was a small gap between her two front teeth.

"You speak Spanish." Feeling like an imbecile for stating the obvious, he smiled in greeting. "Welcome to the Hamptons Polo Club, Ms. Jennings. Tell us about yourself."

Rosario kicked him under the table, but Giovanni ignored his sister. He'd hijacked the interview and for good reason. Elise Jennings was an exotic beauty with a warm disposition. Giovanni could tell by the way the restaurant manager and sous chef were gawking at Elise that they were smitten, and he didn't want them to embarrass him when they spoke. In addition, there was something about Elise Jennings that put him on edge, and since his instincts were rarely wrong about the opposite sex, he listened carefully to her response.

"It's an honor to be here," she gushed in an animated tone. "I know you've probably interviewed dozens of people for the executive chef position, but look no further. I'm the perfect person for the job. I'm an outstanding cook who's passionate about haute cuisine, and once you try my tasting menu you won't need to interview anyone else..."

A scowl curled his lips. *Someone has an inflated ego!* he thought, cocking an eyebrow. And more pride than the world's most decorated chefs combined.

Turned off by her speech, Giovanni leaned back in his chair and folded his arms across his chest. He didn't care if candidate number six was the female version of Wolfgang Puck. They couldn't hire her. He didn't want to bring anyone on board who'd create conflict or drama in the kitchen, and he suspected Elise would. Furthermore, in the seventy-year history of the polo club, the restaurant had never had a female executive chef, and his stubborn, old-fashioned father still thought European men were the best chefs. Yesterday, he'd advised them to find someone experienced, who knew about international cuisine, but Giovanni seriously doubted Elise Jennings was who their father'd had in mind.

"What do you want us to know about you?" Rosario asked, reaching for her water glass.

"I'm a hard worker who values and respects everyone in the kitchen, regardless of their position." Elise placed a hand on her chest. "Cooking is my life, and being named the executive chef at the Hamptons Polo Club would be a dream come true. Vencedores is the best restaurant in the Hamptons, and I want to be part of this incredible team."

Giovanni gave a polite nod. Elise spoke with a drawl, in a voice that was pleasing to his ears, and he guessed she'd been raised in the South. Out of the corner of his eye, he noticed Rosario was beaming and he hoped his sister hadn't been fooled by Elise's effusive speech. He sensed Elise was acting, feigning sincerity, and he wondered what she knew about his family. Had she googled them? Was she telling the truth or saying what she knew they wanted to hear? Or was she an opportunist looking out for number one? Giovanni studied her facial features for a long moment. Did Elise know their net worth?

*Of course she does*, chided his inner voice. *Everyone is blinded by your family's wealth, and Elise Jennings is no different! Like all the other staff, she'll say and do anything to gain your trust.*

Giovanni sniffed the air. Recognizing the spicy aroma tickling his nose, he straightened in his seat and peered into the kitchen. Two servers entered the dining room, pushing silver carts. Wearing a proud smile, Elise gestured to the spread with a wave of her hand. Seeing plates of barbecued meat with sautéed vegetables, stuffed tomatoes and *humita* made his mouth water.

"For the first course, I prepared favorites such as *pan de atún* in my creamy secret sauce, *sándwich de miga* and *la torre de panqueques*. I hope you enjoy every rich, flavorful bite."

"You created a traditional Argentinian meal for Christmas Day. Why?" Giovanni asked.

"Because the holidays are right around the corner..."

*Don't remind me*, he thought, stabbing an olive with his fork. "Thanksgiving is still weeks away," he pointed out. "Isn't it too early to be thinking about Christmas?"

"Not to me. The more time I have to think, plan and prepare, the better." Her eyes twinkled and a smile brightened her face. "I wanted my excitement for the holiday season to shine through in the menu I created, and I hope you'll agree that it does."

Giovanni tasted the beef. Savoring the spices, he was impressed with how succulent it was. He took a bite of the veal, then another, and cleaned his plate within seconds. *Wow*, Giovanni thought, nodding in appreciation. *Elise Jennings cooks as well as my mother!*

He wanted to ask for more food, but rested his utensils on his plate instead, then wiped his mouth with a napkin. Giovanni didn't think Elise was the right person for the executive chef position, but he was impressed with her cooking. Blown away by her tasting menu. Awed by her talent. Elise was the youngest person they'd interviewed, but the most creative. She'd added her own unique twist to each dish, creating a winning combination, and he'd loved every delicious bite.

Someone groaned and Giovanni cranked his head to the right. *Oh, brother*. The restaurant manager, Antoine Lecomte, was furiously licking his fork; the sous chef, Knox Bianchi, was snapping his fingers in the air;

and Rosario was dancing in her chair, oblivious to the wide-eyed expression on his face.

"I'm glad you enjoyed the first course, but I hope you're not full because there's more…"

Giovanni listened to Elise with rapt attention. His eyes strayed to her curves and his body failed him. Sweat clung to the back of his crisp white dress shirt and an erection stabbed the zipper of his pants. Her fitted uniform outlined her fine, feminine shape, and it took supreme effort to concentrate on what she was saying about the dessert menu. His intense physical attraction to Elise Jennings surprised him, and even though Giovanni was a single man, he felt guilty for ogling the Southern beauty.

As his tablemates sampled the items on the dessert tray, they moaned and groaned.

"I took the liberty of creating sample menus for the Holiday Cocktail Party, Breakfast with Santa and the Family Fun Buffet," Elise said, holding up a thin white booklet. "You'll see that I included decor ideas for each event, as well."

Cocking his head to the right, Giovanni shared a puzzled look with Rosario, then addressed the over-confident chef.

"I think you have us confused with another establishment, Ms. Jennings. We rarely host Christmas events at our club, and we don't have a seasonal menu, either."

"I know, but you should."

"Are you telling me how to run my club?" Giovanni asked, stunned by her gall.

"No, of course not. I'm simply giving you some free

advice. This is a gorgeous facility that's being under-utilized, and this is the perfect time to do something about it." Elise pulled out a chair at the table. Sitting, she took off her chef's hat, revealing lush honey-blond locks. "Host weekly Christmas events, and open the club to the public at a discounted rate—"

"This is a private club for a reason, Ms. Jennings. Not a community center."

"I understand that, Mr. Castillo, but it's the holidays—the season for giving—and if you open the Hamptons Polo Club to the community, you'll attract even more business and ultimately increase your bottom line."

"What an interesting perspective. One we've never considered, but definitely should." Rosario put down her fork, wiped her mouth with a napkin, then leaned forward in her chair, as if eager to hear more. "Elise, is there anything else on your mind?"

"Yes, as a matter of fact there is," she said, clasping her hands in front of her. "I'd like to know more about the role of the executive chef, the specific responsibilities and duties of the position, and the benefits and compensation you offer, because none of those aspects were covered in the online job posting."

Giovanni cocked an eyebrow. This was a first. They'd interviewed five other candidates, but none of them had been bold enough to inquire about the salary.

He listened as Rosario spoke, but his gaze strayed to Elise. It was hard not to imagine himself kissing her— Giovanni slammed the brakes on his thoughts.

Mad at himself for fantasizing about the know-it-all chef, he tore his eyes away from her. He didn't want to see Elise at the club every day. Not because he despised her, but because he was scared his desires would get the best of him one day, and he'd cross the line—or worse, jump over it and into her bed.

Worried Rosario would offer Elise the job on the spot, Giovanni realized he had to take control of the interview and plotted his next move. Elise had an impressive résumé and outstanding cooking skills, but she'd rubbed him the wrong way from the moment she'd opened her mouth—and Giovanni had to get rid of her before it was too late.

# Chapter 2

Giovanni stared Elise down, thinking she'd wither under his blistering glare, but she smiled brightly, showcasing every pearly white tooth, as if she didn't have a care in the world. He tried to remember what Rosario had shared about Elise's background but drew a blank. Curious about her story, Giovanni stared at the résumé on top of Rosario's iPad and skimmed the first page. His suspicions were right; Elise had graduated from a culinary school in North Carolina before relocating to New York, and had been a the sous chef at an upscale Hamptons restaurant known for its celebrity clientele.

A troubling thought passed through Giovanni's mind. Had Elise been fired? Had she left of her own volition or had management forced her out? If he asked her point-blank, would she tell him the truth? He opened his mouth, but Rosario interrupted him.

"Elise, what are your salary expectations?" Rosario asked, dusting crumbs off her lap.

"Based on my experience in this field, and my research on the current market, I'm expecting a six-figure salary and complete creative control in the kitchen," Elise explained, her tone matter-of-fact. "Is that something you're prepared to do? Or should I take my talents elsewhere? I don't mean to be blunt, but I want you to know exactly where I stand."

"I appreciate your transparency, Elise, and I want you to know the salary, the start date and the terms of employement are all negotiable..."

*They are? Since when?* Giovanni thought, astounded by his sister's words. He scowled—couldn't help it. Elise wanted ten thousand dollars more than they were offering, and that was reason enough to show her the door. It didn't matter that she had an impressive résumé; Elise was high-maintenence, a diva in an apron, and he wasn't going to give her his seal of approval.

Antoine and Knox questioned her about her leadership style, her weaknesses and strengths, and Elise responded with humility. Wearing identical smiles, they nodded as she spoke.

"Also," she said, raising a finger in the air, "we'll need to revamp the current menu."

"Why?" Worry lines creased Antoine's forehead. "We've had the same menu for years."

Elise wore a sympathetic smile. "Can I be frank?"

Giovanni grunted. *Why stop now? You're on a roll, Ms. Bossypants!*

"I checked out Vencedores' menu online while I was preparing for this interview, and the reviews were brutal. Diners' tastes and palates are constantly changing, and offering tired, boring dishes will turn people away. We need to be aware of food trends and shake things up from time to time, or customers will get their cravings fulfilled elsewhere and our business will suffer." She gestured to the empty restaurant with a wave of her hand.

Giovanni wanted to point out that Vencedores didn't open on Fridays until noon, hence the reason why there were no customers in the dining room, but Elise continued full steam ahead. He secretly hoped she'd talk herself into a hole and Rosario would dismiss her.

His cell phone buzzed and he glanced down at the table. The text was from Vincente, whom Giovanni suspected was anxious about the interviews. His father wanted to know if they'd hired someone, if the chef was from Europe, and the start date. The restaurant had been thrown into chaos with Chef Cruz's sudden departure and Vincente was worried that if they didn't hire someone immediately, the club's reputation would suffer and profits would slide. Deciding to text his dad once the interview ended, Giovanni returned to the conversation.

"If you hire me to be the executive chef, the first thing I'll do is revise the menu. And decorate for Christmas, of course. I love all things Christmas, so that's at the top of my list." Elise laughed then snapped her fingers. "I'd also have weekly staff meetings. I want to know what the restaurant employees are thinking and feeling, and ensure that their needs are being met."

Rosario picked up a white-chocolate truffle, inspected it for a moment, then took a bite. Her eyes fluttered closed and a moan rose from the back of her throat. "Oh, my, this is divine."

"I know. I had three!" Antoine chuckled. "Do you have any other thoughts you'd like to share with us, Ms. Jennings? As you can see, we're open to hearing your ideas."

"For me to do my best, I need to have a strong team behind me, so I want to be involved in hiring my staff when the need arises," she continued. "Is that something you would be open to? If so, I'd like that stipulation included in my contract."

*Contract? What contract? We're not hiring you!* Flabbergasted, Giovanni sank back in his chair. Who was interviewing whom? he wondered, scratching his head. In a matter of minutes, Elise had seized control and now she had his sister in the hot seat.

"That's certainly something I would be open to," Rosario said with a nod. "I admire your initiative, Elise, and your candor. It's refreshing, and you're just the kind of person we need at the Hamptons Polo Club..."

Giovanni almost choked on his tongue. *Refreshing? No, she's a sassy know-it-all with a huge ego.* He'd expected Rosario to put Elise in her place, but she stared at her in awe, as if the woman had just pulled a rabbit out of her hat. In the three months Giovanni had been acting CEO, he'd never seen his sister bend over backward to appease a potential employee. He wondered why Rosario was so desperate to hire Elise Jennings.

The interview forgotten, the women spent several minutes discussing their favorite Christmas dishes and traditions, and upcoming holiday events they were excited about.

"Every year, my husband and I attend the tree-lighting ceremony in the city square." Rosario had a faraway look in her eye, as if she was reliving a treasured memory. "It's always a special, magical night, and I love seeing the brilliant lights, the adorable, wide-eyed children and all of the elderly couples kissing and cuddling."

"You could have a similar event at the club and create your own Christmas traditions," Elise proposed. "I can see it now. The crackling fireplace, Santa and Ms. Claus posing for pictures with families, the mouth-watering aroma of apple cider and gingerbread cookies, and lively Christmas music playing in the background."

Interest sparked in Rosario's eyes. "I *love* the idea of cultivating our own traditions…"

Giovanni shot to his feet. He'd had enough. He didn't want to hear about creating new traditions or hosting holiday-themed events at the club, either. Not today, not ever. Christmas sucked. If he could sleep through the entire season, he would. The Hamptons Polo Club was one of the most expensive and exclusive polo clubs in the world, and he wasn't going to let Elise Jennings fill his sister's head with preposterous ideas.

And, contrary to what Elise thought, Christmas wasn't a time of goodwill and grand gestures of love and kindness. For him, it was the memory of broken promises, hurt and regret, and there was nothing to celebrate. His marriage was over, he had more aches and pains than a UFC champion, and his relationship with his father saddened him. He'd wanted to confide in his dad about his fears for the future, but Vincente hated talking about feelings, said it was a sign of weakness, and since childhood had advised Giovanni not to—so he hadn't.

"Thanks for coming, Ms. Jennings. It was a pleasure to meet you," he lied, leveling a hand over the front of his navy blue suit jacket. "We'll be in touch."

Rosario stabbed him in the arm with a long, manicured fingernail, and Giovanni winced. Staring down at her, he saw the pained expression on her face and wished he hadn't interrupted her. The conversation they'd had last night during dinner came to mind, and shame burned his cheeks. He'd undermined Rosario in front of the staff again, and it was wrong. He had no right to tell Rosario—who had an Executive MBA from Columbia University—how to run the club, or who to hire. He had no desire to manage the club, or any of the other family businesses, and hoped when his father was ready to retire he named Rosario as his successor. Giovanni was the only son, but his sister was the best person for the job, and she deserved to oversee the Castillo empire, even though Argentinian culture dictated otherwise.

Standing, Rosario raised her head high and pinned her shoulders back. "Is there anything else you'd care to discuss?"

"When will you make a final decision about the position?" Elise asked.

"As soon as we find a suitable candidate," Giovanni said, unable to bite his tongue.

"Look no further, Mr. Castillo. I'm right here!"

Rosario laughed loudly, as if it was the funniest thing she'd ever heard.

Giovanni groaned inwardly. *Here we go again*, he thought, noting his sister's giddy demeanor. Rosario was Miss Personality, a social butterfly who had more friends than a Kardashian-Jenner, and it was obvious she liked Elise Jennings immensely.

*So do you!* shouted his inner voice. *So much so, you can't take your eyes off of her!*

"It was wonderful meeting you all," Elise said with a wide smile. "Cooking has been in my family's DNA for decades, and it's all I've ever wanted to do, so I hope to hear from you soon about the executive chef position."

The group nodded, and Giovanni had to admit Elise was charming. Speaking Spanish, she bid them farewell, then shook hands with everyone at the table. She smelled sweet, of tropical fruits, and her light, airy fragrance tickled his nose.

The moment Elise touched him, a thousand bolts of electricity shot through Giovanni's body. Stunned by their immediate and undeniable connection, seconds passed before his thoughts cleared and his mouth worked. "Get home safe."

Giovanni winced. *Get home safe? What am I, a grandfather? What a bone-headed thing to say!* He'd never lost his cool before, but Elise was a knockout with a blinding smile and drool-worthy curves. Being in her presence made his senses short-circuit.

Relief and disappointment flooded his body. He'd never been so happy to see someone leave while part of him wanted her to stay. Elise was lively and entertaining, full of ideas and good humor, and even though Giovanni hated the suggestions she'd made for the club, he'd enjoyed listening to her talk about her travels and how they had influenced her culinary skills. Watching her on the sly, he marveled at how she moved through the dining area with poise and grace.

Giovanni swallowed hard. His mouth was wet and his heart was beating double-time, pounding violently in his ears. He tugged at the knot in his striped silk tie. In his peripheral vision, he saw Antoine mop his forehead with a napkin and Knox pluck at his shirt, and realized he wasn't the only one who was hot under the collar.

Everyone sat back down, but no one spoke. Elise Jennings was a whirlwind who'd taken them all for an exhilarating ride and it was obvious everyone needed a moment to catch their breath.

Giovanni wanted to try one of the chocolate desserts on the silver tray, but he remembered he was on a strict diet and reached for his glass of water instead.

Another text message popped up on his cell phone. Seeing the picture of his three other sisters posing with goofy expressions on their faces and chocolate ice-cream cones in their hands made him smile. He was traveling to Argentina next month to participate in a charity polo match for SOS Children's Villages, and he was looking forward to seeing the Troublesome Trio, as he affectionately called them. They all lived in Buenos Aires, and even though they called and texted each other regularly, Giovanni still missed them dearly. Beatriz was studying communications at the University of Buenos Aires, Josefa was a newlywed who had babies on the brain and Soledad was a set designer at an Art Deco theater in the heart of the city.

"I don't know what to say," Antoine said with a sheepish smile. "I'm speechless."

Knox nodded. "Me, too. Elise Jennings is a force who wowed me."

"That was the best audition we've had all day…" Rosario added.

*No it wasn't*, Giovanni thought, inwardly disagreeing with his sister.

"Elise isn't afraid to speak her mind, and she's an outstanding chef with a very unique approach to cooking." Rosario's voice was filled with awe. "I love her."

Giovani shook his head. "Well, I don't, so let's keep looking."

"Why not? Her presentation was brilliant, she's got a great head on her shoulders and she has a fearless personality. Those are all positives in my book, and if Elise's references check out, I'm going to hire her."

"No way," he argued, determined to change her mind. "She's arrogant, and she won't fit in well with the restaurant staff. Don't hire her. If you do, you'll be sorry."

"You're just salty because she disagreed with you."

"My gut feeling is that Elise Jennings is a diva, and I don't want her at the club."

Rosario's eyes widened. "Wow, she certainly rubbed you the wrong way."

"I don't like outsiders telling me what to do."

"Correction, you don't like *anyone* telling you what to do, including your friends, your family and even your doctors. Just admit it, Gio. You're stubborn and hardheaded, and you're not happy unless you're calling the shots."

"This isn't about me. It's about doing what's best for the restaurant," he countered, ignoring the dig. Rosario was two years younger than him, but she acted like his mother, and once he'd started working at the club, things had gotten worse.

Since they were kids growing up in their native Argentina, they'd always been exceptionally close. She'd been there for him through every failure, every disappointment, every setback, but he resented Rosario pointing out his shortcomings in front of their staff. Determined to stay the course, he buried his feelings and spoke in a calm voice. "Elise Jennings doesn't belong here. She's not the right fit for the restaurant—"

"Are you kidding me? Elise will be great for this place. She's charming, ridiculously talented and, best of all, drop-dead gorgeous. Hiring her is a no-brainer. We can't go wrong."

Giovanni frowned. "So you're hiring her because she's hot?"

"Damn right I am!" A smirk curled her lips. "Men are going to go crazy for her, especially the celebrities who frequent the club during the Christmas holidays. And once they taste Elise's exceptional cooking and spend a few minutes in her dazzling presence, I'll have them *right* where I want them."

Giovanni gulped down some water. For some strange reason, he didn't like the idea of Elise socializing with the club's wealthiest and most influential patrons.

*That's because you want her all to yourself!* argued his inner voice.

Giovanni dismissed the thought. If Rosario hired Elise, he'd have to change his daily routine, the schedule he'd had for months, and that bothered him. Every morning, he had breakfast at the club, but now that Chef Cruz was gone, he'd have no one to talk to. And he'd have to avoid the restaurant. He didn't recall seeing a wedding ring on Elise's left hand, but he hadn't looked. For all he knew, Elise was happily married with kids, but even if she wasn't, she was still off-limits. Mixing business with pleasure was a recipe for disaster. If he'd learned anything in the last five years, it was to keep female employees at arm's length, especially the ones he was insanely attracted to.

"You can't hire her," he repeated, unwilling to concede defeat. "We have interviews scheduled for Monday. Who's to say you won't find someone better?"

"I agree with Giovanni…" the restaurant manager interjected.

*Thank you! Finally! Someone on my side!* Giovanni thought, sighing in relief.

"Elise is a talented cook with an impressive résumé, but I was put off by her unreasonable demands," Antoine continued, nibbling on a bite-size brownie.

"I think she's terrific," Knox countered. "Elise has a strong sense of self and great ideas that are worth exploring. She's young, vibrant and creative, and I'm confident she'll hit it off with the rest of the staff."

Giovanni stood. "I have to go. I need to be in my office by ten o'clock—"

"Hot date?" Rosario teased, her grin tinged with mischief.

"No. I have a conference call with the president of the International Polo Federation about hosting a celebrity polo match at the club in March, so let's table this discussion until Monday, after the remaining interviews. That's only fair."

"I disagree. I think we need to hire Elise before we lose her to another restaurant."

*I hope we do!* Giovanni kissed Rosario on the top of her head. "Sis, we'll talk later."

"No," she corrected, folding her arms across her chest. "*I'll* talk, and *you'll* listen."

Ignoring the quip, he addressed Antoine and Knox, who were scarfing down the rest of the desserts. "Thanks for sitting in on the auditions this morning," he said, clapping each man on the back. "I know it makes your day longer, but Rosario and I appreciate you going the extra mile for the club. We wouldn't have survived Chef Cruz's sudden departure without you picking up the slack, day in and day out. You've gone above and beyond the job, and we're deeply grateful for you both."

"Finally! Something we agree on!" Rosario cheered.

Everyone laughed and the tension in the room receded, floating away like the snow flurries swirling in front of the windows.

Exiting the dining room, Giovanni responded to his dad's text message and checked his work email. The club was quiet except for the distant sound of a vacuum, and Giovanni knew the cleaning crew was hard at work. Set on four hundred acres, the club had five full-size polo fields, a state-of-the-art fitness center, an indoor arena and school, and heated barns that housed thoroughbred horses.

Marching through the lobby, nodding at employees

and guests in greeting, Giovanni spotted Elise outside the front entrance with Jonas.

Stopping abruptly, his gaze zeroed in on them. They were standing close, her shoulder to his best friend's chest, and he was holding her hand. They were acting familiar with each other, friendly and flirtatious, and Giovanni wondered if they were lovers. It wouldn't surprise him. Jonas knew everyone in the Hamptons and actively pursued young, successful women, but he didn't recall his best friend ever mentioning Elise Jennings. Not that it mattered. He wasn't interested in her, or anyone else, for that matter.

Forcing his legs to move, Giovanni tore his gaze away from the friendly couple and continued through the corridor. He'd touch base with Jonas later, after his conference call ended. Or tomorrow, when they met up at their favorite barbershop. Every morning, without fail, Jonas worked out in the fitness center. When Giovanni wasn't busy, he joined him. But not today. His schedule was jam-packed; he didn't have a second to spare.

His eyes found Elise again and his pace slowed. Clad in oversize sunglasses and a beige cashmere shawl, she looked stylish and sophisticated. As Giovanni admired her appearance, desire consumed him.

Entering his spacious corner office, he put Elise and his attraction to her out of his mind. He had bigger issues to deal with—like convincing his medical team that he was healthy enough to resume his polo career, and proving to Vincente that Rosario should be his successor, without losing his father's love and respect.

# Chapter 3

"How did your interview go yesterday?" Sariah Tiwari-Dhar asked, her breathy voice filling the phone line. "Did you wow them with your undeniable talent, charm and charisma?"

"You know it!" Elise shrieked, vigorously nodding though her best friend couldn't see her through her iPhone. "I had them eating out of the palm of my hand, *literally*! I don't mean to toot my own horn, but toot, toot, toot!"

The women laughed and Elise realized how much she missed joking around with her friend. She was a twenty-nine-year-old woman, but whenever she talked to Sariah, she giggled like a tween girl. They hadn't spoken in days. Even though Elise was busy looking for a parking space in front of the East Hampton cinema, she wanted to speak to her bestie for a few minutes.

Sariah, who worked full-time at her father's dental clinic and taught Zumba classes at an upscale fitness studio on the weekends, was one of the first people Elise had met when she'd relocated to the Hamptons.

"Tell me everything," Sariah persisted, her excitement evident in her tone. "I want details."

Finding an empty space across the street from the theater, Elise parked her Honda Civic then realized she had twenty minutes to kill before the movie started.

Settling back comfortably in her seat, Elise relived her audition in her mind's eye—and the exact moment her gaze had landed on Giovanni Castillo.

At the thought of him, her pulse raced. Giovanni was the sexiest man Elise had ever seen, and it had taken everything in her not to drool all over her chef's uniform. His skin was smooth, his goatee neatly trimmed, and his navy blue suit had complemented his chiseled physique. Every time their eyes had met, she'd lost her bearings. Elise had never had such an intense attraction to anyone, and hoped her feelings for him hadn't been evident to everyone in the dining room.

"Quit stalling. I want to know everything, so start talking, Madame Executive Chef."

Shaking her head to clear her mind, Elise told Sariah about the Hamptons Polo Club, the positive response to the food she'd made and the Castillo siblings. "Rosario's great, and we instantly hit it off, but Giovanni hates me."

"Wow, that's a strong statement. What makes you think that?"

"Because every time I spoke, he grimaced, as if he had a bad case of indigestion. When I asked about the salary and compensation package, he growled at me."

"Growled?" Sariah repeated. "Elise, he's a star polo player, not a pit bull."

"He's a polo player? Really? Are you sure?"

"Of course I'm sure. He's won every award there is, and he's a legend in his native Argentina," she explained. "From what I've read, Giovanni is the Tiger Woods of polo, and fans of the sport consider him one of the greatest players of all time."

"Wow, that's impressive. How do you know so much about him?"

"Duh. Google. *You* should try it sometime."

"Unlike you, I don't feel the need to google everyone I meet. Besides, I have cooking classes to teach at the nursing home, and I'm searching for a full-time job, as well. No time for surfing the internet."

"You should make time. Giovanni's going to be your future boss. You need to do your homework."

"I prepared extensively for my audition, but I had no clue Giovanni was the acting CEO of the polo club. Furthermore, I don't have the job yet, so you can't give me grief for not knowing who Giovanni is."

"He'll hire you. You're a phenomenal chef who's passionate about her craft, and soon everyone in the culinary world will know your name."

"Thanks for the vote of confidence," she said, touched by her bestie's words. Sariah and their mutual friend Paige Ward were the sisters Elise didn't have, and she couldn't imagine her life without them. Busy with their careers and families, the women didn't see each other as often as Elise would have liked, but she knew if she ever needed them, they'd be there for her in a heartbeat. "What's new and exciting with you? Did you and hubby have fun at the Apollo last night?"

"It was amazing! I don't think I've ever laughed so hard or danced so much."

Hearing a noise, Elise glanced out the windshield. Families strolled by wearing stylish winter jackets and boots. The wind whacked tree branches and snow flurries swirled in the air. Her car wasn't the ideal location to have a heart-to-heart conversation with her best friend, but she wanted to know how Sariah was doing. She was an overachiever who'd never failed at anything—except getting pregnant—and she was struggling to cope with her infertility problems. "How did your doctor's appointment go this morning? Did you and Aamir decide to give IVF another try, or are you going to take a break for a while?"

Silence infected the line. It lasted so long, Elise thought Sariah had hung up.

"Honestly, I'm ready to quit, but Aamir is adamant we see it through…"

Listening intently, Elise searched her heart for the right words to say. She could hear the strain in Sariah's voice, the frustration as she spoke about the side effects of the medication and the toll it was taking on her body and her nine-year marriage.

"Sometimes I think I can't get pregnant because God's punishing me for the horrible things I said and did to Ravi when we were younger."

Elise puzzled over her friend's words. Sariah's younger brother, Ravi, had an intellectual disability and still lived at home with their parents. Unable to speak, he spent much of his day watching cartoons, but once a week Elise went to the Tiwari residence to cook with Ravi, and it was obvious he loved being in the kitchen. In all the years Elise had known Sariah, she'd never seen her angry with Ravi, and wondered why she was beating herself up.

"Or maybe I'm just not meant to be a mom. Maybe I don't have what it takes…"

"Oh, sweetie, don't say things like that. It's not true. You'd be an incredible mother."

"I used to think that, too, but now I'm not sure. I feel like such a failure…"

"Stop it right now," she warned, speaking in a stern voice. "Or I'll drive over to your fancy estate and slap some sense into you."

Sariah laughed long and hard, and Elise did, too. All was right in the world again.

"You're ridiculous, you know that?" Sariah said.

"That's why you love me. I'm the gin in your juice!" Elise giggled. "Let's get together one day next week."

"For sure! We can meet at the Palm to celebrate your fantastic new job over cocktails."

"I love your optimism, and working at the polo club would be a dream come true, but—"

"But nothing," Sariah said firmly. "That position is perfect for you."

"I agree, and hopefully the hiring committee does, too, because I have great ideas."

"We'll meet up next Friday, and you can tell me all about it."

"It's a date. Love you, girl. Talk to you soon."

Ending the call, Elise exited her car and wrapped herself up in her cashmere shawl to brace herself against the bitter wind whipping her hair across her face. Worried she'd miss the start of the movie, Elise rushed into the theater, relieved to escape the cold. The air smelled of buttered popcorn and cinnamon pretzels. Her mouth watered at the tantalizing aroma tickling her nose.

Elise joined the slow-moving line. The theater was small, with comfortable seats and friendly staff. It showed both independent films and Hollywood blockbusters. An elderly black couple wearing identical Black Panther sweaters passed the box office, and Elise stared at them for a long moment.

Thoughts of her parents, Rhett and Coralee Jennings, filled her mind and sadness flowed through her body. It was her second year without them, but Elise still couldn't think about her mom and dad without tearing up. It had taken everything in her not to cry during her audition when Rosario had spoken about her favorite family traditions. Since she'd been a little girl, Elise and her parents had attended the Holiday Cocktail Party in Charlotte and she'd never forget all the laughs they'd shared at the event.

Her relatives wanted her to come home for Christmas, but Elise was scared history would repeat itself and she'd ruin the holidays for them again. Last year, she'd been a mess. Everything had made her cry. Hearing her mother's favorite Christmas song on the radio, seeing the framed photographs of her parents in the living room, watching old family videos and reminiscing with her relatives about her mom and dad.

"There's the culinary genius with the stunning smile," a male voice said.

Surfacing from her thoughts, Elise blinked and glanced over her shoulder. Her heart stopped. Jonas Crawford was standing directly behind her, wearing a toothy grin, and he wasn't alone. Giovanni Castillo was leaning against the wall, staring down at his cell phone.

Elise couldn't believe her luck. In all the years she'd lived in the Hamptons, she'd never seen Giovanni around town, but here he was at her favorite movie theater, looking devilishly handsome in his Argyle sweater, faded blue jeans and leather boots.

Heat flooded her cheeks. Drawn to him, Elise was suddenly hyperaware of everything about Giovanni— his rich, masculine cologne, his intense gaze, his mysterious aura. Elise struggled to keep her eyes on his face and off of his lean, chiseled physique. She'd always had a weakness for men with long hair, and she yearned to touch his thick, dark locks. Burying her hands in the back pockets of her denim jeggings, she smiled and nodded in greeting. "Hi, guys! What's up?"

"Nothing much." Unzipping his hoodie, Jonas pointed to the digital screen with a flick of his chin. "What movie are you here to see?"

"*In the Dark 3!* I loved the first two movies, and I heard this one is even better."

Jonas glanced around the concession area. His gray sweat suit and stark-white sneakers made him look fit and his Yankees baseball cap complemented his sporty outfit. "You're not here alone, are you?" he asked her.

"There's nothing wrong with going to the movies alone. I do it all the time—"

Jonas raised an eyebrow and Elise felt the need to defend herself.

"I enjoy my company immensely. In case you haven't noticed, I'm *fabulous*, and I bring the fun wherever I go!"

Jonas laughed, but Giovanni did not. Lines creased his forehead and a scowl pinched his lips.

*What a sourpuss!* Elise wondered what his problem was and wished he'd get off his stupid cell phone and talk to her. Who was he texting? Did he have a girlfriend? Several? And, most important, had he ever dated outside of his race?

Elise cleared her mind, dismissing every question that filled her thoughts. It didn't matter what Giovanni did in his personal life. She didn't know him and she planned to keep her distance. Though she was dying to know if the hiring committee had made a decision about the executive chef position. Maybe, when the movie ended, she'd pull him aside and inquire about the job.

"Next, please!" the male cashier hollered. "What movie?"

"Don't worry. I got this. You'll sit with us."

Before Elise could protest, Jonas slid in front of her, selected the movie and time on the mini-screen, and tapped his bank card on the debit machine. "Let's go to the concession stand. It's on me. Get whatever you want."

Elise didn't move. She'd met Jonas a few months earlier, when he'd had dinner with his brothers at By the Bay, and had sized him up in ten seconds flat. He was a player with a reputation that rivaled James Bond. Elise suspected every scandalous, salacious story circulating around the Hamptons about his sexual exploits was true. Add to that, she wanted nothing to do with the opposite sex. In the summer, a drunk had forced himself on her at a Fourth of July party, and even though she'd successfully fought him off, the ordeal had frightened her. So much so, Elise hadn't been on a date since.

"Your girlfriends won't mind you hanging out with another woman?" Elise asked. "The Hamptons is small, and I don't want people to talk."

"What girlfriends? We're single, and that's the way we like it, right, Gio?"

Giovanni didn't answer, just continued typing on his iPhone. Elise studied the polo player for several seconds. On the surface, he was every woman's dream man, but there was something profoundly sad about him, and Elise wondered why he rarely smiled. And when he did, it looked forced, as if it required every ounce of strength he had.

Her gaze strayed from his eyes to his mouth and her stomach muscles clenched. She wondered what his lips tasted like. Soft and moist, no doubt. Desire rippled across her skin and X-rated images bombarded her mind.

Elise thought hard, but she couldn't remember the last time she'd been intimate with someone. Sex without love was meaningless, something Elise had promised herself she'd never do, so why was she fantasizing about hooking up with Giovanni Castillo, a man she barely knew? He was the strong, silent type, and his quiet confidence appealed to her, but she would never act on her desires. If she was hired as the executive chef at the Hamptons Polo Club, Giovanni would be her boss, and Elise didn't want to do anything to jeopardize her dream job.

"Come on, crew, let's go see *In the Dark 3!*" Jonas said, tugging at his baseball cap.

Elise hesitated, considering returning to the box office to buy a single seat at the back of the theater, but when Giovanni joined them at the concession stand, she changed her mind. His cologne washed over her, and Elise was struck by a shocking realization.

Giovanni might dislike her, but there was nowhere else she'd rather be than by his side.

# Chapter 4

The theater was packed, filled with moviegoers of all ages, but it sounded as if a million teenage girls were in the auditorium, screaming at the top of their lungs. The noise was deafening and every shriek pierced Elise's eardrums, making her head throb in pain.

Taking a deep breath, Elise glanced around the darkened theater. Jonas was sitting beside her with his eyes closed, and Giovanni was eating barbecue potato chips. He looked relaxed, at ease, and Elise wondered if he liked the movie. She didn't. The plot was slow, the characters were bland, and even though Jonas had paid for her movie ticket, Elise wanted a full refund.

Swallowing hard, she picked up her water bottle and finished it. Elise knew if she didn't leave the theater, her headache would get worse, and she didn't want Jonas and Giovanni to know she wasn't feeling well. On the pretense of needing some air, she stood and exited the auditorium, desperate to escape the noise.

Elise used the ladies' room, washed her hands in the sink and then reapplied her lipstick. Not that she cared what Giovanni thought of her appearance, because she didn't. He didn't even know she was alive. He hadn't said a word to her all afternoon, and it was annoying. Yesterday, she'd noticed his tender interactions with his sister throughout the interview, but today he seemed sour. Elise wondered if he was upset because Jonas had invited her to join them.

While they'd waited for the movie to start, Jonas had shared some interesting facts with her about the star polo player. Giovanni was divorced. He loved fine cuisine and European sports cars. He had vacation homes in Maui, Ocho Rios and Santorini. And his greatest achievement was being named Athlete of the Decade by *Sports Illustrated*. Committing each anecdote to memory, she'd googled the magazine cover and openly gawked when the image of Giovanni astride a stallion had popped up on her cell phone. Hot and bothered in her cushy theater seat, she'd fanned her face. Elise didn't want to be attracted to him, was mad at herself for desiring a man who disliked her, and had wiped the image of the sexy cover from her thoughts.

*Right!* bellowed her inner voice. *Then why do you keep thinking about it, and all the wicked things you'd like to do to Giovanni in the darkened movie theater!*

Leaving the washroom, Elise dug her iPhone out of her purse and read her newest text messages from Paige. Giggling at her friend's jokes, she shook her head in amusement. Paige Ward was an adorable brunette with big hair, pale skin and an exotic dancer's body. She was the head stylist at one of the most popular salons in the Hamptons, and the last time Elise was at Beauty by Karma, they'd talked and laughed for hours.

"Are you okay? I saw you leave the auditorium and wanted to make sure you weren't upset."

Elise glanced up from her iPhone, searching for the owner of the deep, husky voice. Her gaze landed on Giovanni and her mouth dried up. He was leaning against the vending machine, a concerned expression on his face and his hands in his pockets.

"Why would I be upset?" she asked, puzzled over his words. "It's just a movie."

"I know, but it's a gruesome, violent film."

Elise inclined her head to the right, regarding him with interest. "Are *you* upset?"

"No, I'm starving!" Giovanni rubbed his stomach. "Those chips did nothing to satiate my hunger, and all I can think about is a juicy steak with yam fries and a Heineken."

"I'm not surprised. You're a growing boy with a healthy appetite, right?"

The sound of his loud, hearty chuckle made Elise feel proud, as if she'd finally done something right where he was concerned. *I made him laugh! Yahoo! Maybe he* doesn't *hate me, after all!* Wanting to know for sure, Elise decided to ask him about her interview. Why not? She'd never been one to beat around the bush, and she wanted him to give her a straight answer.

Second thoughts filled her mind. Would he think she was desperate? *I am*, she thought, deciding to take her chances with the gruff polo player and business-man. *I'll do anything to be the executive chef at the Hamptons Polo Club, and I'm not afraid to admit it!* Elise had nothing to lose. If having a frank conversation with Giovanni improved her chances of landing the executive chef position at his family's polo club, then being vulnerable was worth it.

"Why don't you like me?" she asked, approaching him.

Giovanni wore a blank expression on his face. "What makes you think I don't like you?"

"It was obvious. You scowled during my entire interview and glared at me when I suggested hosting more Christmas events at the club." On a roll, Elise spoke freely, without censoring her thoughts, even though his eyebrows were jammed together and his gaze was darker than night. "As I said yesterday at the interview, I would be honored to work at the Hamptons Polo Club and I'd give a hundred and ten percent to my coworkers, the managerial staff and the esteemed diners who frequent Vencedores."

"I appreciate your honesty, and I hope you don't mind me sharing my thoughts, as well."

"No, not at all. Please do. I'd love to hear what you thought of the meal and our discussion."

"You're a talented chef with a dynamic personality, but I was put off by your arrogance, your unreasonable demands and your know-it-all attitude..."

Elise heard someone gasp, realized the sound had shot out of her mouth and clamped her lips together. She felt weak, out of sorts, as she listened to Giovanni critique her interview, and couldn't think of anything to say in response.

"My sister likes you, but I don't think you're the right person for the position," he explained, an air of superiority in his tone. "And there is nothing you can say or do to change my mind. My instincts are rarely wrong, and I don't want to bring someone on board who's going to create conflict or drama in the restaurant kitchen."

"Excuse me?" Anger shot through her veins and her toes curled inside her suede booties. Who did Giovanni think he was? The Second Coming of Christ? He had no right to judge her. He didn't even know her! "You're way out of line."

"Am I? I don't think so, and since I'm the CEO of the polo club it's my job to do what's best for the restaurant, and that's what I'm going to do."

"I worked at By the Bay as a sous chef for five years and never *once* had a complaint brought against me. Not one," she pointed out, raising an index finger in the air. "I was a team player who got along well with my coworkers and managers—"

"Then why were you fired for poor performance and insubordination?"

Her stomach flipped. *What?* she shouted in her mind, blown away by his outrageous accusation. *Is that the lie my ex-boss told Giovanni? What* else *had Mr. Verbeck said?*

A million questions raced through her mind and, with each passing second, her dread grew. Elise wanted to know about Giovanni's conversation with her former boss, even though he wasn't one of the references listed in her CV, but the doors of the auditorium opened and she lost her opportunity. Elise was desperate to set him straight, but the crowded theater lobby wasn't the right place for their discussion.

Moviegoers flooded the corridor, chatting excitedly about the horror flick. "That movie was dope," Jonas said, walking up to them with a broad grin. "Best movie I've seen all year."

"Said the guy who dozed off during the previews and didn't wake up until the lights came on." Giovanni snickered. "Dude, you snored so loud you drowned out the sound system!"

"Bro, don't hate. You're just mad because Elise likes me more than you."

The smile faded from Giovanni's mouth and Jonas puffed out his chest, stood taller.

"Why do you look so surprised?" he jeered, clapping his friend on the shoulder. "I'm the total package, and I *always* get the girl."

Elise waited for the awkward moment to pass. She couldn't tell if Jonas was being serious or not, and hoped he wasn't romantically interested in her. Watching a Saturday matinee with him was fun, but Elise didn't want to date him, and she hoped he didn't do anything crazy like ask her out in front of Giovanni.

"Thanks for the movie and snacks, Jonas. Have a good night."

Waving with one hand, Elise reached into her purse with the other and pulled out her car keys. She moved through the lobby, hoping she could disappear in the crowd, but Jonas and Giovanni followed behind her, cracking jokes and sharing laughs.

"We're going to grab a bite to eat. Come with us." Jonas opened the door and stepped aside for Elise to exit the theater first. "I heard your stomach growling during the movie, so I know you're hungry. Girl, it was so loud, I couldn't hear myself think."

Elise stuck out her tongue, then swatted Jonas's shoulder. "Liar!"

"What are you in the mood for? Italian? French?" Jonas continued, glancing up and down the street at the various restaurants in the vicinity. "Elise, you're the expert. What do you recommend? Where do you want to go?"

"Home," she quipped, putting on her sunglasses. For some strange reason, the thought of breaking bread with Giovanni excited her, but she tempered her feelings. Remembered they weren't friends, just acquaintances. He'd insulted her and she was still smarting from his accusations. "It's been fun, fellas, but I have to run."

"But Giovanni's paying. We can eat and drink at the best restaurant in town for the rest of the night!"

Jonas chuckled and Elise realized she'd made a mistake. Why not go out for dinner with Jonas and Giovanni? Might as well. She was hungry, she had no other plans that evening and, most important, she wanted to talk to Giovanni. He'd pegged her all wrong, and she wanted him to know she worked well with others and respected authority. Contrary to what he'd heard from her former boss, she'd never been an insubordinate employee or created conflict at work.

"Giovanni's paying? Then count me in!" Elise beckoned to them with her hands. "Guys, follow me. I know just the place."

# Chapter 5

By the Bay, the five-star seaside restaurant in the Hamptons, was known for its sophisticated decor, outstanding wine list and spectacular views of the sunset. When Elise entered the establishment, she felt an overwhelming rush of emotion. The day she'd quit, she'd vowed never to step foot in the restaurant again, but there she was, in the place that used to be her second home, fighting back tears. It was arguably the best seafood spot in the city, and Elise had been proud to be the sous chef at a restaurant that A-list celebrities, socialites and international businessmen flocked to on a nightly basis.

Memories flooded her mind. Glancing around the dining room, she remembered the times she'd come to the restaurant early to help organize the kitchen, how she'd patiently trained new hires, the hours she'd spent creating seasonal menus and the fun she'd had working with the head chef and junior staff. They'd been a family, supportive and respectful of each other, and not a day went by that Elise didn't miss her former colleagues at By the Bay.

Emotionally distraught after her sexual attack, she'd struggled to function at work and her colleagues had rallied around her. Her girlfriends, too. Sariah and Paige had attended group therapy sessions with her, and her colleagues had dropped off meals when she was too depressed to cook. The love and support of her friends and coworkers had not only helped her heal, but also proved to her that she wasn't alone, that people cared deeply about her.

"Jonas! Welcome, how wonderful to see you again! How have you been, Handsome?"

Stepping past Elise as if she were invisible, the perky blue-eyed hostess approached Jonas with her hands outstretched. Elise tried not to take offense, but her rejection stung—just like the others. Since quitting, she'd texted her former coworkers several times, but none of them had responded to her messages, and she noticed they were dodging her gaze now. Mr. Verbeck was a control freak with an explosive temper. Elise wouldn't be surprised if he'd warned the employees not to speak to her—or else.

"I was hoping you'd be here tonight." Jonas kissed the hostess on each cheek and she giggled like a three-year-old on a swing. "As usual, you look sensational."

Toying with her bracelet-style watch, Elise considered her future. Her savings account was dwindling faster than the president's approval rating, and she was starting to lose hope of finding a new job. She'd applied at dozens of restaurants, for every kitchen position available, but four months after leaving By the Bay, she was still unemployed. That's why Elise had to prove to Giovanni that she was the best person for the job.

Someone cleared his throat and Elise surfaced from her thoughts. Mr. Verbeck was standing in front of the wooden podium, glaring at her. She didn't shrink under his darkened gaze; she stared back at him, projecting confidence rather than fear.

"What are you doing here?" he snapped, baring his coffee-stained teeth.

"My friends and I would like a table in the dining room, but first you need to tell Giovanni Castillo, the CEO of the Hamptons Polo Club, the truth about my departure."

Boisterous conversation filled the air, drawing Elise's gaze into the dining room. She wore a fond smile—couldn't help it. She used to love meeting customers and sharing a secret about her recipes. Even though she knew quitting her job had been the right decision, Elise missed the regulars, creating new dishes and goofing around with her coworkers after closing.

*Am I ever going to get another job? Have I been shunned from the Hamptons? Is that why I've only been called for one interview? Is my culinary career over?* Elise tried not to think the worst, tried to stay positive, but her fears persisted, tormenting her. It didn't matter that she had the knowledge and experience for the executive chef position at the polo club; Giovanni didn't like her and his opinion carried the most weight.

Mr. Verbeck glanced around the waiting area with a fake smile. "As you can see, the restaurant is packed and I don't have time to shoot the breeze."

"Why did you tell Mr. Castillo I was fired for poor performance and insubordination?"

A hush fell over the waiting area, and Elise knew they had the attention of everyone nearby. "Why did you lie to Mr. Castillo about my performance? Are you trying to ruin my reputation because I quit? Is that what this is about?"

"Get out," he snarled, pointing at the door with his chin, his wide, fleshy face quivering with rage. "You're not welcome here."

"Excuse me?" Jonas abruptly ended his conversation with the hostess and stepped forward, his arms folded across his chest. "Did you just ask Elise to leave? I hope not, because if she goes, I go, and I won't come back. Neither will my friends and family."

"I...I m-misspoke," he stammered, fiddling with his checkered tie. "*Everyone* is welcome at By the Bay, and it would be my honor to serve you and your friends, Mr. Crawford."

"Was I fired or did I quit?" Elise demanded, refusing to let him off the hook.

"You quit. Now please lower your voice. You're making a scene."

"Why did I quit?" She pressed on. "Why did I leave By the Bay in July?"

"Because you're an ungrateful, insubordinate *vaca* who doesn't know her place—"

*Did this jerk just call me a cow in Spanish?* Elise wanted to snatch Mr. Verbeck up by the collar of his gray dress shirt and shake the truth out of his mouth, but she exercised self-control. Didn't want to embarrass herself or her companions. She was a nobody, but Jonas and Giovanni came from esteemed families, and she didn't want to tarnish their reputations.

Her anger must have showed on her face because his voice faded and he tugged on his tie. Mr. Verbeck gave Jonas and Giovanni a pleading look, but they glared at him, too, as if he was their mortal enemy.

They stood on either side of her, shoulder-to-shoulder, and Elise felt supported, protected. On the drive to the restaurant in Giovanni's SUV, Jonas had surprised her by asking why she no longer worked at By the Bay. She'd vacillated over whether or not to tell the truth. She'd only been around Jonas a couple of times, but he'd made her feel comfortable, so she'd confided in him.

Elise told them everything—about how she'd worked tirelessly at the restaurant for five years, how she'd been passed up for three promotions, and the argument she'd had with her manager in July during her annual performance review. Jonas had listened to her with a sympathetic expression on his face, but Giovanni had frowned as if she were telling a tall tale. But Elise had told them the truth and she wanted Mr. Verbeck to do the same. Staring at him, she tried to remember the good times they'd had, but drew a blank. There weren't any.

"I'd hate to think that you called me under false pretense and lied about Ms. Jennings." Giovanni cocked an eyebrow. "Because if you did, I'll revoke your membership to the Hamptons Polo Club, and you and your sons will never step foot on the grounds again."

Mr. Verbeck mopped his forehead with the back

of his hand. "You quit abruptly, leaving me in a bind, and the restaurant took a huge financial hit during the summer…"

Elise cringed. She could smell whiskey on his breath, and wondered if he was still sneaking drinks in the back office when he was supposed to be doing paperwork.

"If anyone should apologize," he said, "it should be you. You screwed me over, but have the nerve to play the victim. How rich!"

Elise widened her eyes. She couldn't have been more shocked if Mr. Verbeck had snatched the toupee off his head and slapped her with it. For a moment, she couldn't think straight and didn't know what to say in response to his blistering insult.

"Now, if you'll excuse me, I have customers to tend to." Mr. Verbeck marched out of the waiting area, through the dining room and into the bright, open kitchen.

The next ten minutes were a blur. Jonas led Elise out of the restaurant and hustled her across the street to the sports pub with the signed football jerseys hanging in the front window. They sat at the bar and, within seconds of arriving at Ale & Billiards, Elise was sipping a raspberry cosmopolitan. The lounge had cozy couches, pool tables and arcade games, and the flat-screen TVs mounted on the walls showed various sporting events. All around the pub, fans whistled and cheered, but Elise didn't have the energy to join in the fun.

"By the Bay is nothing without you," Jonas said, squeezing her hand. "It's their loss."

His tone was sincere and his smile warm, but Elise

didn't believe him. Giovanni sat to her right and his piercing gaze made her mouth dry. Confronting Mr. Verbeck had been a mistake, and Elise wished she'd never gone to the restaurant.

For the second time in minutes, water filled her eyes. She'd given her all to By the Bay, thinking management would reward her for being a dedicated, hardworking employee. But over the years, she'd been passed over for numerous promotions and hadn't understood why— until the day of her yearly performance review.

She'd asked for a raise and Mr. Verbeck had lost it on her. He'd called her an emotional, hormonal *vaca*, and she'd realized that he was a sexist jerk who thought women were inferior to men. He'd hired an outsider— a male prep cook with a chip on his shoulder—for the head chef position instead of promoting her. When Elise found out, she'd quit on the spot. It was an impulsive decision, made in the heat of the moment, but it was the right choice.

"I've been to a lot of restaurants, and eaten a lot of spectacular meals in my life, but your grilled rib eye is one of the best things I've ever tasted." Closing his eyes, Jonas slowly licked his lips. "It's been months, but I'm *still* thinking about it!"

Elise laughed and the dark cloud hanging over her head lifted as she listened to Jonas praise her cooking. *It's too bad he's a player. He's great for my ego*, she thought, swirling her straw around her cocktail glass.

Giovanni hadn't said a word since they'd left By the Bay and Elise wondered what he was thinking. Not that it mattered. He had someone else in mind for the executive chef position, and she didn't stand a chance of working at his family's polo club.

"It was perfection," Jonas said, kissing his fingertips. "Like heaven in my mouth."

"Thanks, Jonas. You're right. It was!"

Giggling, Elise saw Giovanni crack a smile and wondered if he was warming up to her. Maybe all wasn't lost. She'd find another position, wow her new boss with her skill and professionalism, and fulfill her dream of being an executive chef. Last night, she'd applied for three more job postings, and Elise was hopeful one of them would result in a full-time position. She'd even apply for positions all across the state. Elise didn't want to leave the Hamptons, but she was tired of sitting at home fretting about her future, and was anxious to return to the kitchen. If that meant relocating to another city, so be it.

"I see someone in the lounge I need to get better acquainted with." Jonas stood, and downed the rest of his rum and coke. "Be back in a minute."

Curious who'd caught his eye, Elise peered over Jonas's shoulder and searched the lounge. A leggy brunette in a fitted New York Knicks jersey and skinny jeans was standing in front of a TV yelling in Spanish, and it was obvious Jonas was intrigued by the fiery beauty. "Have fun. Don't do anything I wouldn't do!"

"I most certainly will," he said with a wink and a grin, swaggering into the lounge.

A bartender arrived, cleared their empty glasses and wiped down the counter. Perusing the laminated menu, Elise decided on the bacon club burger with sweet potato fries and a strawberry milkshake. Giovanni ordered, then chatted with the bartender about the up-coming Spring Polo Cup tournament in Argentina. "So you're a polo player," Elise said. "Are you any good?"

"Is he any good?" the bartender repeated, his eyes bugging out of his head. "Giovanni's won every championship imaginable, was ranked number one longer than anyone else in the history of the sport and is arguably the greatest player of all time."

Elise smirked. "*Someone's* got a crush."

Blushing, the bartender moved down the bar, checking on his other customers.

"I think we got off on the wrong foot. Let's start over," she proposed, facing him. "I'm Elise. It's nice to meet you, Giovanni. Do you come here often?"

A grin crept across his lips. "You're funny."

*And you're dreamy*, she thought, admiring him.

"How did you learn to cook?" he asked, tossing a handful of peanuts into his open mouth.

"My parents taught me. They met while working at a hotel restaurant, and a year later I was born." Elise smiled. "My dad said it was love at first sight."

"So you were *literally* born to cook."

"I guess I was. We cooked together almost every night, and they taught me about Southern cuisine and decadent pastries," she explained as fond memories warmed her heart. "I grew up in a tough, working-class neighborhood, and watching my parents struggle to pay the bills and put food on the table made me resilient. I'm proud of who I am and where I come from, and I'm not going to apologize for being me."

"I'd never ask you to."

"Good, because I won't."

"And for the record, I believe you."

Relief flowed through her body. "You do?"

"It's obvious Mr. Verbeck hates you and wants to see you fail."

Sadness pierced her heart, making her feel low. Elise wished she'd left By the Bay on better terms, with the friendships with her coworkers intact, but Mr. Verbeck had poisoned their minds against her, and there was nothing she could do about it now. That chapter of her life was over and she was ready for bigger and better things.

"I want to apologize for the things I said earlier." Giovanni rested his elbows on the counter and clasped his hands in front of him. "I was out of line and I'm sorry. Mr. Verbeck lied to me, and I shouldn't have believed his version of events."

Hope surged through her veins. "Does that mean I'm still in the running for the executive chef position at your family's polo club?"

Giovanni coughed into his fist, then picked up his tumbler and gulped down his Scotch. His silence spoke volumes and the longer Elise stared at him, the harder it was to maintain her composure. Questions raced through her mind, angering her afresh. *What's Giovanni's issue with me? Does he know I'm attracted to him? Is* that *why he won't hire me?*

"I still think you were way out of line during your interview."

"Is that what this is about? You're mad at me because I came into the interview with ideas on how to increase business at the restaurant during the holiday season?"

Elise rolled her eyes to the ceiling. "Just because you hate Christmas doesn't mean everyone else should."

"And just because you think your ideas are golden doesn't mean they are."

"Mr. Verbeck made me believe I wasn't good enough to be the head chef at By the Bay because I was opinionated and outspoken, but I did everything in my power to help the restaurant succeed. If you hire me to be the executive chef at your family's polo club, I'll do the same."

"I'll take your comments into consideration, but I won't make any promises."

"Are you considering any other female candidates for the position?"

Giovanni scratched his cheek then rubbed his neck. "I'm not at liberty to say."

"Translation," she said, inclining her head to the right. "No, I'm not considering any female candidates for the executive chef position."

"I never said that."

"You didn't have to. The truth was written all over your face."

"I'm not sexiest. I have a strong, opinionated mother, and four younger sisters, as well."

"I never said you were, but I hope you hire the most qualified person for the job and not just the guy who looks the part. I've seen it happen countless times before, and it's wrong."

"Just because I don't want to hire you doesn't mean I have issues with women—"

"I know, just me, right?"

A chagrined expression covered his face. "You're putting words in my mouth. That's not fair."

Realization dawned and Elise slowly shook her head. Giovanni didn't like her because she was a proud, confident woman, but that was his problem, not hers. Life had been hard on her in recent years, and it was a miracle she'd survived her setbacks. She'd lost her parents, had overcome a frightening sexual attack and been forced to quit a job she'd loved. Four months later, she was still having nightmares about it. If not for therapy and the support of her girlfriends, Elise probably wouldn't be able to get out of bed.

"Be careful. Your food is hot, and I'd hate for you guys to burn yourselves." The bartender put their entrées on the counter and refilled their glasses with ice water.

"This was a bad idea." Standing, Elise slung her purse over her shoulder and retrieved her car keys from the side pocket. "Tell Jonas I said good-night."

"Wait! Where are you going?"

*Anywhere but here!* Elise backed away from the bar. She'd had enough of Giovanni's insults for one day and was anxious to go home. She had nothing more to say to him and would rather eat the leftover pasta in her fridge than spend another second in his presence.

Giovanni was ridiculously handsome and smelled divine, but he disliked her, and that was reason enough to stay away from him. She'd take a cab back to the movie theater to retrieve her car, and forget they'd ever met. "It's been a long day and I want to go home."

"Now?" He gestured to her entrée with a nod of his chin. "But your food just arrived."

Elise hit him with a look. "I lost my appetite."

Flinging her shawl over her shoulder, Elise marched out of the pub with her head high, wishing she'd never laid eyes on Giovanni Castillo.

Elise only hoped that when she went to sleep at night, the sinfully sexy polo player wouldn't be the star of her dreams again.

# Chapter 6

The polo pony tugged on the brown, leather reins, as if to protest leaving the comfort of his heated stall, but he was no match for Giovanni. Determined to complete his final chore of the morning, he pulled the horse out of the wooden box, latched the door behind him and led him into the open ring. "Come on, Trojan," he urged, rubbing his coat. "I know it's cold, but you're filthy and I need to give you a thorough washing."

Someone sneezed and Giovanni glanced over his shoulder, hoping none of the stable hands was watching him. Or worse, recording him on the sly. It had happened before, and Giovanni didn't want any secret videos of him posted online for the world to see. He didn't make it a habit to talk to the horses, especially when staff members were around, but he'd felt a special connection to Trojan from the first time he'd ridden him around the grounds eight years earlier, and treated the horse like a family member, not a pet.

Yawning, Giovanni stretched his neck from side to side, trying to alleviate the tension in his aching muscles. Having been up since dawn, he'd already worked out with his personal trainer in his home gym, had breakfast with a family friend and answered his emails. He planned to spend the next hour with Trojan, and hoped no one interrupted him.

Humming along to the Spanish song playing on the sound system, he tied the horse to the fence, grabbed the black currycomb from the bucket and patted the top of Trojan's head to remind him he was in good hands. He'd been around horses his entire life and loved grooming them. It was the perfect stress reliever. Twice a week, he groomed Trojan and looked forward to spending time with his beloved horse at the end of a long day. The horse whinnied then kicked his back hooves in the air, shooting mud at Giovanni, who shielded his face with his forearm.

"Good one," he said with a laugh, dusting the dirt off his hoodie. "But I'm still giving you a wash, so deal with it."

Gripping the comb, he moved his hands in a slow, circular motion to loosen the grime from Trojan's coat. In the distance, he heard a woman's voice and hoped Rosario hadn't come to the stables to talk. She'd called his cell twice that morning, but he'd let both calls go to voice mail. He didn't want to butt heads with her again. They'd done enough of that yesterday in her office.

The last round of interviews for the executive chef

position had been disastrous and afterward they'd argued about who to hire. Giovanni thought the silver-haired Dutchman with decades of experience in the culinary field would be a great addition to the club, but Rosario had refused to even consider him. He was the type of person their father had in mind for the position, and Giovanni didn't want to disappoint him—apparently, however, Rosario did.

Twenty-four hours later, he was still troubled by his argument with his sister. Tired of battling with her, he'd considered calling his dad for advice. Vincente should decide who to hire, not Rosario. It was their father's club, his legacy at stake, but Giovanni knew if he confided in his dad about the interviews, Rosario would feel he betrayed her trust, and he didn't want to do anything to ruin their close-knit relationship. Not after everything Rosario had done for him since his divorce. She'd been his confidante, his biggest supporter, even at times his chef and chauffeur, and he wouldn't have survived the dissolution of his marriage or his injury at the US Open Polo Championship without her.

Using the hose, he washed Trojan's face with warm water. He shampooed his coat then scrubbed his tail. A shovel scraped against the ground, drowning out the music on the radio, and the air smelled of manure, but there was nowhere else Giovanni would rather be. He loved being around horses and wished he could spend the entire day in the barn.

*Lies!* shouted his inner voice. *You'd ditch Trojan for Elise in a heartbeat and you know it.*

His thoughts returned to Saturday night and he reflected on his argument with Elise at the pub. After she'd stormed off, he'd grabbed Jonas from the lounge and told him what happened, but by the time they'd made it outside, Elise was gone.

Over the course of his polo career, he'd met people from all walks of life, but the Charlotte native perplexed him. Giovanni didn't know what to make of her. She was a mystery—a complicated, fascinating beauty who intrigued him, and he wanted to know more about her. Not just the bits and pieces of conversation he'd pieced together during her conversation in the car with Jonas as they were driving to By the Bay.

Giovanni shuddered at the memory of her argument with Mr. Verbeck. For a moment, he'd feared Elise was going to strangle her former boss for lying about her termination, but she'd pulled herself together. Rosario would have punched his lights out for calling her a cow, or worse. Giovanni was relieved that Elise had taken the high road even though Mr. Verbeck had insulted her.

Giovanni sighed. He didn't want to see Elise at the club every day. He'd never met a woman more comfortable in her skin, and her confidence was a turn-on, hence why he didn't want to hire her. Every time Elise was around, his desires raged out of control, threatened to consume him. In many ways, Elise reminded him of his ex-wife, which bothered him.

At the height of his career, he'd run with a crowd befitting a star athlete, but he'd secretly longed to find love. All he'd wanted was someone to share his life with, and he'd foolishly thought his personal assistant, Marisol Le Torre, was the woman of his dreams. He couldn't have been more wrong. These days, he hardly thought about his ex-wife, but when he did, his blood boiled. She'd screwed him over, made him the laughingstock of their friends, and he'd never forgive her for abandoning him when he needed her most.

"Oh, my, what a mess. Let me take Trojan from you, Mr. Castillo, so you can clean up."

Giovanni surfaced from his thoughts just in time to see one of the equine trainers take the hose from his hand and snuggle against Trojan. "Thanks, Alyssa. I'd better go. I lost track of time and if I don't hurry, I'm going to be late for my first meeting of the day."

"No problem, Giovanni. See you on Friday, same time and place, right?"

"Absolutely." He patted Trojan's head with one hand and retrieved his iPhone from his back pocket with the other. Scrolling through the day's new stories, he marched out of the barn, across the field and into the polo club. It wasn't open to the public yet, but it was a flurry of activity. Employees vacuumed, fluffed the pillows on the padded armchairs in the waiting area, polished every wooden surface and watered the plants and flowers in the lobby.

Giovanni glanced up from his phone and acknowledged everyone he passed with a nod and a smile. Deciding to shower in the men's changing room, he continued past the front desk to the fitness center, mentally reviewing his Tuesday schedule.

A text message popped up on the screen and Giovanni groaned. His dad wanted to see him, and Giovanni had a sinking feeling that Vincente wanted to talk to him about his future plans. *Oh, brother. Here we go again.*

Every time he saw his dad, he implored him to quit polo and take the reins of the family business once and for all. Castillo Enterprises owned hundreds of lucrative commercial properties from Argentina to New York, and if Vincente had his way, Giovanni would be the head man in charge.

Giovanni shuddered at the thought. It wasn't going to happen. He planned to play polo for many more years to come, and wouldn't let Vincente—or his medical team—talk him out of it. Polo was his life, what he was born to do, and he didn't want to do anything else. For years, his dad had begged him to join him in the family business, but he had stood his ground, hadn't lost sight of his goals. He'd refused to give up on his dream, and his hard work had paid off. He'd won every award in polo there was, but he wanted to shatter more records and cement his legacy in the sport he loved more than life itself.

"There you are! I've been looking everywhere for you."

Giovanni looked up just in time to see Elise rushing toward him waving her hands wildly in the air. Her voice was animated, full of excitement. Her smile was so bright, it lit up the lobby and, for a moment, all Giovanni could do was stare at her. Marveling at her natural beauty, he realized she glowed from within.

He was surprised to see her at the club, thought maybe she was a vision of his imagination, a breathtaking illusion. He hadn't thought they'd ever cross paths again and wondered what Elise was doing there two hours before the club was open to the public. Add to that, she was beaming, and he didn't understand why.

Three days ago she'd insulted him then stormed out of his favorite pub, and now Elise was staring at him with an awestruck expression on her face, as if he was the man of her dreams. The thought heartened him and warmed his six-foot-four frame.

Pocketing his cell, Giovanni stared at Elise with keen interest. He'd never seen a pantsuit look so good, and liked how the lightweight material skimmed her curves. Curls cascaded over her shoulders and Giovanni imagined himself running his hands through her long, silky hair. His hands itched to touch her, to caress her skin, but he'd never act on his impulses.

"Giovanni, thank you!" Elise gushed, throwing her arms around his neck. Hugging him tightly, she rocked him from side to side. "You've made me the happiest woman alive!"

Her words sounded garbled in his ears, didn't register in his brain. Instinctively he moved closer to her. She smelled of lavender and her light, floral fragrance aroused him. Holding her to his chest, he inhaled her fragrant scent. Elise felt even better than he imagined, and when she pulled out of his arms, disappointment flooded his body.

"Sorry about that," she said with a sheepish expression on her face. "I'm a hugger, but I didn't mean to smother you. I'm just really stoked and pumped and grateful to you right now."

Giovanni touched his chest. "Grateful to me? For what?"

"For putting your feelings aside and hiring me to be the new executive chef!"

Dread pooled in the pit of his stomach. *What!*

"I signed my contract in Rosario's office ten minutes ago, but I'm *still* shaking." Elise giggled, but she spoke in a serious voice. "I won't let you down, Giovanni. I promise. I'm going to be the best executive chef you've ever had."

His jaw dropped. It was the last thing he'd expected Elise to say and her words were a shock to his system. Anger welled up inside him, but he didn't take his frustrations out on Elise. It wasn't her fault Rosario had disregarded his wishes.

Conflicting emotions battled within him. On the one hand, he liked the idea of getting to know Elise better, but on the other hand he worried one day his desires would overwhelm him, and he'd act on his feelings—and that would be a disaster for the polo club.

"I better go," she said brightly, glancing at her wristwatch. "I have to meet Antoine in the kitchen in five minutes, and I don't want to be late."

Giovanni couldn't think straight, struggled to form a coherent sentence. Polo was a difficult sport to play, with technical skills such as horse riding, good posture and mental and physical toughness. Even a small mistake could result in fractured bones, paralysis and even death. But Giovanni had never been so stressed out in his life. Elise was all curves, temptation in a fitted suit and heels, and his temperature rose to dangerous heights when she touched him.

"See you later, Giovanni. Thanks again!" Elise waved, then dashed through the lobby and into the restaurant. Her perfume lingered in the air, tickling his nose and arousing his flesh.

Balling his hands into fists, he marched past the reception desk and down the sun-drenched corridor. In the management area, he heard telephones ringing and the distant sound of conversation. The sweet, heady aroma wafting out of the staff room roused his appetite, but Giovanni was too angry to think about eating, not when he had to settle a score with his sister.

Giovanni entered the corner office, decorated with round wall mirrors, fluffy carpet, modern furniture and pastel-pink colors, and slammed the door so hard the windows rattled. Rosario jumped in her seat then rested a hand on her chest. "Gio, don't do that," she scolded from behind her U-shaped glass desk. "You scared me half to death."

"Why did you hire Elise Jennings behind my back?" Giovanni realized he was shouting and lowered his voice, but there was nothing he could do about his erratic heartbeat. "We agreed to meet this afternoon to make a final decision, so why did you offer Elise a contract without discussing it with me first?"

"A decision had to be made immediately, and I did what I thought was best for the club."

"What was the emergency? Why couldn't you wait until our three o'clock meeting?"

"Because I was worried we'd lose Elise to another restaurant and end up back at square one," she explained in a somber tone. "Antoine is friends with the assistant manager at the Palm, and he let it slip that Elise was his top choice for their sous chef position. I couldn't risk him hiring her, so I beat him to it. Brilliant, right?"

No, it was impulsive and foolish, he thought, strangling a groan. *And I wish you'd talked to me first. After all, I* am *the CEO. I should have a say in who we hire.*

"Why didn't you let me know what you were thinking? Why didn't you give me a heads-up? You know I don't think Elise is the right person for the position, but you hired her anyway."

Rosario raised two fingers in the air. "I called you *twice* this morning and left you a voice mail, as well, so don't get mad at me because you were too busy sulking to return my call."

"Whatever." A thought popped into his mind. "Did you approve her salary demands and the Christmas events she discussed during her interview?"

Her face brightened. "I sure did! I love the idea of creating more holiday traditions at the club and fully utilizing the space. With Christmas around the corner, it's the perfect time to shake things up around here, and I want to attract more powerful, influential people to the club."

"Great," he grumbled, shaking his head. "You're letting her call the shots."

Confusion darkened her features and Rosario stared at him for a long moment. "Giovanni, I'm disappointed in you—"

"Why?" he challenged. "Because I have the guts to disagree with you?"

"No, because over the years I've shared with you how hard it is for me to be heard and respected as a female COO, even though I have an MBA from one of the best business schools in the country." Her gaze landed on her university diplomas proudly displayed on the wooden bookshelf. "You of all people know how hard it is for a woman to succeed in a male-dominated field. I was hoping you'd hire Elise because she's the best person for the executive chef position, period."

Her words were a painful blow, a fist to the gut, and for the first time in Giovanni's life he was speechless. Was Rosario right? Was he being stubborn and unfair? Was he putting his needs above what was best for the club? Giovanni dismissed the thought; refused to believe it. He wanted the club to succeed, wanted Rosario to be named Vincente's successor, and he was going to do everything in his power to help his sister's dreams come true. But that didn't mean he was going to agree with everything she said and did.

"It shouldn't matter that she's young, black and beautiful—"

"I never said that it did, but I know for a fact those things will matter to Dad." Giovanni took a deep breath and slowly counted to ten. They were supposed to be a team, and even though Rosario had hired Elise behind his back and then had the nerve to insult him, he was determined to keep the peace.

"Leave Dad to me." Rosario had a determined expression on her face and spoke with confidence. "I know what to do to get through to him."

"Sure you do. Just make sure you tell Dad that hiring Elise was your idea, not mine."

"Oh, I absolutely will, because there's no doubt in my mind that he's going to love her."

Giovanni considered her words, gave them some serious thought. Elise was delightful, full of energy, optimism and excitement, and it was hard not to like her, but Giovanni didn't think his dad would be swayed by

Elise's charm. Upon meeting her, he wouldn't be surprised if Vincente fired Elise on the spot and hired one of the male candidates who'd interviewed for the position instead. "What makes you so sure?"

"Elise is going to wow Dad with her talent, her creativity, her charisma and her adorable Southern drawl." Rosario put on her reading glasses. "And she'll impress you, too."

*She already has!* Giovanni thought with a heavy heart, raking a hand through his hair. *That's why I don't want Elise to work here! It's a recipe for disaster.*

"Now, if you'll excuse me, I have work to do, and *you* need a shower." Rosario wiggled her nose and waved a hand in front of her face. "You stink!"

"And you're impossible," he shot back.

Silence engulfed the office and the tension in the air was thicker than smoke.

Worried he'd lose his temper if they started trading jabs, Giovanni yanked open the door and left without another word.

He never should have gone to Rosario's office in the first place. It had been a waste of his time. She was as controlling as their father, and Giovanni had a better chance of winning *RuPaul's Drag Race* than getting through to his sister. It was her way or the highway, but as he relived their argument in his mind, his frustration waned and his anger abated. Why did he care who Rosario hired for the executive chef position? He wasn't staying in the Hamptons indefinitely. Once he convinced his doctors he was healthy, and his dad returned to the club full-time, Giovanni was buying a one-way ticket to Argentina, and no one was going to stop him.

Heartened by his thoughts, Giovanni entered the men's changing room at the fitness center, grabbed his toiletry bag from his locker and found an empty stall. He had nothing to worry about, was stressing out for no reason. In two months' time, he'd be back with his team, training hard, and Elise—and their sizzling attraction—would be a distant memory.

Giovanni turned the water on full blast. Closing his eyes, he allowed the steaming hot water to wash away the grime on his skin and his fears for the future. Soon he'd be back with his team, doing what he loved most. But until he left for Argentina, he'd stay far away from Elise and her delicious, decadent cooking.

## *Chapter 7*

Elise stood at the prepping station inside Vencedores' kitchen, mixing a bowl of walnut-cranberry muffin batter on the countertop, her thoughts a million miles away. Three days ago, she'd celebrated Thanksgiving with the Harris family, and she'd enjoyed the elaborate meal, the charming guests and the lively conversation. But her first week as the executive chef at the Hamptons Polo Club had been filled with one problem after another, and Elise was so stressed out she hadn't slept well since being hired.

Her gaze strayed across the room and pride flowed through her veins. A quiche, baked French toast, spicy Italian sausages and tropical fruit covered the counter, and pitchers of freshly squeezed orange juice were in the fridge. Peppermint tea was brewing and coffee was percolating, creating a tantalizing aroma in the restaurant kitchen. The staff meeting was in an hour and Elise wanted to make a healthy breakfast for her hard-working colleagues.

Elise admired her handiwork. Coming to the restaurant early had been the right decision. She wanted the restaurant staff to know how much she needed and appreciated them, especially Antoine. If not for his guidance, patience and support, she never would have survived her first week.

Elise considered the highs and lows of the past week. On Monday, she'd accidently cut her thumb with a steak knife. On Wednesday, she'd scolded a line cook for being twenty minutes late for her shift and the redhead had burst into tears. Yesterday, Elise had felt light-headed during the dinner rush and needed to take a break in the back office.

As the executive chef, Elise had a mind-blowing list of daily responsibilities, and even though she was overwhelmed, she was determined to make Giovanni and Rosario proud of her. They'd taken a chance on her, hired her when no one else would, and Elise felt indebted to the brother and sister management team. Rosario had welcomed her to the Hamptons Polo Club family with open arms, and stopped by the kitchen daily to touch base with her. Oddly enough, Elise hadn't seen Giovanni since she'd thanked him for hiring her, and she regretted hugging him in the lobby.

Wiping the frown from her face, Elise refused to let her thoughts wander. She told herself not to sweat it, to forget about the dashing CEO who gave her goose bumps, but she was curious about Giovanni and wondered how he was doing—or rather, who he was doing. He turned heads everywhere he went, and several of the female employees had a huge crush on him. According to Knox, the star polo player used to eat all of his meals at the restaurant and would visit with the employees after closing, often entertaining the group with stories about his illustrious polo career. But not anymore. And Elise couldn't help feeling responsible. She'd tried to hide her attraction to him, but failed, and now she suspected he was avoiding her.

Elise added a dash of nutmeg to the batter and a sprinkle of cinnamon. Inhaling the sweet aroma relaxed her. She smiled. Food wasn't just her passion, it was her life, and there was nothing better than connecting with people through meals.

Elise loved being in the kitchen at the first light of day. The fridge hummed, the floors gleamed and the pots glistened in the sunshine steaming through the windows. Prep lists hung from above each workstation, deliveries would soon arrive, and hungry employees would fill the restaurant within the hour. But for now, it was quiet, and Elise was in her element, at ease. The kitchen was her refuge, had been since she was a nine-year-old cooking with her parents, and it would always be her favorite place.

Memories warmed her heart. Soul music was playing on her iPhone, and hearing her mother's favorite song took Elise back to her childhood. Every time Aretha Franklin's voice came on the radio, she'd dance around the breakfast bar with her mom, singing and laughing hysterically. They'd always had a special relationship and Elise wished her mom were still alive so she could talk to her about what she was going through.

Yawning, her eyes teared up and her shoulders drooped. To avoid thinking about her parents, Elise kept herself busy 24/7 but her furious, nonstop schedule was sucking the life out of her. *Thank God for concealer or I'd scare small children*, she thought, staring at her tired reflection in the stainless-steel pots lined up above the stove.

Elise poured the batter into the metal muffin tins and put them inside the oven. She set the clock timer then washed her hands. Glad it was Friday, she mentally reviewed her plans for the weekend.

She'd planned to sleep in tomorrow and spend the afternoon doing chores, but Demi's baby shower was at one o'clock and during Thanksgiving dinner, the mother-to-be had threatened her with bodily harm if she didn't attend the party. Pregnant with twin girls, the YouTube sensation and first-time mom was more popular than ever, and Elise wished she had as much energy as the Philly native. She'd met Demi Harris at a networking event last year and they'd exchanged business cards. Once a month they met for cocktails at their favorite lounge, and Elise always looked forward to catching up with her bubbly, effervescent friend.

Swaying to the beat of the music, Elise washed the dirty dishes then cleaned the prepping station. She snapped her fingers and shimmed her shoulders. Grabbing a spatula from the utensils rack, Elise used it as a microphone and sang at the top of her lungs. She spun around the kitchen, her hair whipping across her face. Her muscles loosened with every twirl of her arms and shake of her hips. Every day, she did it all: checked the inventory, ordered the necessary items and ingredients, managed the budget and oversaw the kitchen staff. She deserved to have some fun, and gave herself permission to kick up her heels for a few minutes. Dancing around the kitchen was the ultimate stress reliever, and Elise suddenly felt light and free.

Elise swiped her iPhone off the counter and punched up the volume on the music. A reggae song came on and she shook her hips to the strong, pulsing beat. Elise whipped around, spotted Giovanni standing in the doorway and shrieked. Her knees buckled and she sank against the counter. Their eyes locked and her pulse soared. Attractive in a gray turtleneck, slim-fitted suit and dress shoes, he smelled of expensive aftershave and his gaze made her tingle from head to toe.

Elise snapped out of her haze and pulled herself together. Her hands were shaking, but she stopped the music and shoved her cell into the back pocket of her navy pants. Moistening her lips, she ripped off her apron and dropped it on the counter. Cold air flooded her skin and Elise frowned. Glancing down at her clothes, she noticed her navel was exposed and yanked down the bottom of her scoop-neck sweater.

"Giovanni, good morning," she said, trying to sound natural but failing miserably. "What brings you by?"

Giovanni vigorously clapped his hands, and Elise wished the floor would open up and swallow her. She couldn't remember ever being so embarrassed and wondered how long he'd been standing in the doorway watching her. A minute? Two? At the thought, heat burned her cheeks.

"Wow, Elise, you're got great moves." Mischief brightened his eyes and a grin curled his lips. "Ever consider taking your one-woman show on the road?"

"And leave all of this behind?" she said, spreading her arms out at her sides. "Never."

Giovanni chuckled. "I have two left feet, so I have great admiration for people who can dance well, and you're obviously a pro. How did you learn to move like that?"

"MTV, of course!" Elise laughed. "When I was a teenager, I used to spend hours in front of the TV, perfecting the latest dance moves and routines. I had dreams of being the next Rihanna, but it wasn't meant to be."

"What stopped you?" he asked, a thoughtful expression on his face.

"I was a tall, curvy teen with kinky hair, and my dance teacher said I didn't have the right look. Thankfully, I decided to become a chef and never looked back."

The timer buzzed and Elise grabbed her oven mitts off the stainless-steel stove, anxious to see how her mother's walnut-cranberry muffin recipe had turned out. "I'm sure you didn't come all this way to watch me dance around the kitchen or hear about my childhood aspirations, so what's up, Giovanni? What can I do for you?"

*You can do* me *right now.* Striking the thought from his mind, he coughed to clear his throat and buried his hands in the pockets of his tailored dress pants. Aroused by the sound of her Southern drawl and the twinkle in her eyes, Giovanni feared if he opened his mouth, a groan would fall out. He couldn't imagine anything worse than embarrassing himself in front of the sexiest woman he'd ever met.

His gaze strayed to the wall clock hanging above the storage room door and Giovanni realized his break was over. He had emails to read, phone calls to return and memos to write. He hadn't planned on coming into the restaurant, but he'd noticed lights on in the kitchen and assumed Antoine had come in early to prepare for the day. When he saw Elise dancing around, he'd smiled from ear to ear. Wouldn't have moved even if the fire alarm had sounded and the sprinklers had come on. Mesmerized, he'd stood in the doorway for several seconds, watching her intently. Elise was all curves and legs, and his temperature had climbed every time she'd whipped her hair and shaken her hips. Remembering why he'd come to the restaurant in the first place, he straightened his shoulders and leveled a hand over the front of his suit jacket.

"I have a meeting tomorrow at three o'clock, and I thought it would be a nice touch to have some drinks and appetizers on hand for my Venezuelan guests," he explained, forcing himself not to stare at her backside. "I know it's been crazy busy in here as of late, but is that something you think you can do, or will it be a burden for you and the staff?"

"Not at all. Consider it done." Elise took the metal muffin trays out of the oven, shut it with her hip and put them on the stove top. "We're prepping the appetizers for the Holiday Cocktail Party tomorrow afternoon, so it won't be a problem at all."

"The Holiday Cocktail Party?" he repeated. "That's still a go?"

"Yes, it's Sunday afternoon from three to six." Elise stared at him as though baffled by his question. "You didn't know about the event? But you're the CEO of the club. You're supposed to know everything that happens around here, especially the scandalous stuff!"

"That's Rosario's role, not mine." Eager to change the subject, Giovanni pulled back the sleeve of his jacket and glanced at his watch. "Why are you here so early?"

"I couldn't sleep, so I figured I'd come in early and make breakfast for the staff," she explained, smiling at him. "Have you eaten? Are you hungry?"

"I'm *always* hungry!" he said, patting his stomach.

"Good, then grab a plate and help yourself." Gesturing to the prepping station with a nod, she explained each dish. "There are cold drinks in the fridge, coffee and tea if you're interested, and fruit, as well."

Giovanni sniffed the air then licked his lips. His mouth was watering and his stomach was growling so loud he feared Elise could hear it from across the room.

"Go on," she urged. "Don't be shy. There's more than enough."

Giovanni shook his head. "I better not. The last time we grabbed a bite to eat, you bolted, and I don't want to do or say anything to upset you."

"I shouldn't have left the pub that night. I was wrong and I'm sorry." Elise wore an apologetic smile. "Please stay. I'd love the company, and I want to hear more about your polo career."

"Why?" he asked, raising an eyebrow. "Are you a budding polo player?"

"Absolutely not! I'm an adventurous girl, but polo is basically hockey on horseback, and I don't want to hurt myself. I like my feet on solid ground, thank you very much."

The air held an enticing aroma, and when Elise handed him a gold-rimmed plate, his resolve wavered. He hadn't seen her all week and he liked the idea of sharing a meal with her.

"Breakfast time," she quipped, pouring herself a cup of coffee. "Let's eat!"

"You don't have to tell me twice!" Chuckling, he filled his plate, pulled a stool up to the counter and sat. "Thanks, Elise. Everything looks and smells incredible, and I'm starving."

"Me, too," she confessed, sitting across from him. "I'm glad you dropped by. Meals taste better when you have someone to share them with, and we have a lot to discuss."

Giovanni glanced up from his plate. "We do? Like what?"

"For starters, I'd love to discuss ways to boost staff morale and recognize employees who go above and beyond the job." Elise cut her sausage into small pieces and then forked one into her mouth and chewed slowly. "I know I haven't been here long, but since I've been given complete creative control of the restaurant, I want to shake things up around here."

"Do as you see fit. You're the captain of this ship, and Rosario and I trust your judgment." Giovanni tasted his French toast and nodded in appreciation. It was moist and melted in his mouth. "How have things been overall? I hope Antoine has been answering your questions and showing you the ropes as you settle into your new position."

"Everyone's been incredibly helpful, and it feels like home."

Surprised by her confession, he stared at Elise with keen interest. He wanted to hear more about her first week at the club, so he asked her to elaborate. Talking with her about the staff and her short-term goals, Giovanni saw Elise in a different light. At her interview, she'd come across as being pushy, but now it was obvious she wanted the restaurant and the employees to succeed.

Conversation flowed smoothly while they ate, and his admiration for Elise grew as she talked about her formative years in Charlotte and her large Southern family. She spoke about her parents, Rhett and Coralee, with deep reverence, and her love and respect for them was evident in her smile.

Giovanni enjoyed her outrageous stories about culinary school, and her bubbly laugh warmed him all over. Even though Giovanni had just met Elise, he recognized she was a woman any man would be thrilled to have on his arm. Thoughts of kissing her bombarded his mind, but Giovanni vowed to control himself during breakfast.

"Would you like some more?" Elise asked, reaching for her coffee mug.

Licking his lips, Giovanni eyed the food on the counter. He wanted more sausages and French toast, but he remembered he was supposed to be eating smaller portions, and dropped his napkin on his empty plate. "No thanks, I've had more than enough."

Hip-hop music filled the air. Elise took her iPhone out of her pocket. Beaming, she tapped the screen and then put her cell to her ear. "Hi, Antoine! How are you? I hope you slept well because we have a *long* day ahead of us…"

Giovanni frowned, watching Elise on the sly. *Her voice is higher*, he thought, dissecting her body language. And she licked her lips—twice. She was sitting taller on her stool, straighter, and there was a twinkle in her eye. Was Elise dating Antoine? Were they lovers? Giovanni gave his head a shake. It was none of his buisness what his employees did in their personal lives. Even if he discovered Elise and Antoine were an item, there was nothing he could do about it. More important, he couldn't sit around in the kitchen for the rest of the day playing detective. He had work to do and needed to return to his office.

Giovanni finished his coffee and wiped his mouth with a napkin. Feeing full and satisfied, he picked up his plate, put it in the sink and washed it. He'd had his fun, but now it was time to leave. He wanted to thank Elise for the delicious meal, but he didn't want to wait around for her to end her phone call.

"Okay, no worries, I'll go check." Elise surged to her feet, plucked a pen out of a drawer and grabbed the clipboard dangling from the wall. She strode through the kitchen, into the storage room, and flicked on the light. "I'll call you back."

Glad Elise was off the phone so he could say good-bye, Giovanni joined her in the storage room and in-

spected the wide, bright space. Built-in shelves lined
the walls, colored containers filled with fruits, vegetables and dry goods covered the metal racks, and
the refrigerator was positioned beside the freezer. The
door had a chalkboard attached to the inside and several notes were scrawled on it for Elise.

Frowning, he folded his arms across his chest.
Giovanni recognized Antoine's handwriting, and
peered intently at the board. Reading the messages
confirmed his suspicions and, for some strange reason, his spirits sank.

"Sorry about that. It was Antoine. He wants me to
double-check the food order."

*I bet that's not* all *he wants*, Giovanni thought, his
mind returning to the day of Elise's audition. Antoine
had stolen glances at her ass when he'd thought no one
was looking. The restaurant manager definitely had
feelings for Elise and Giovanni wondered if their colleagues knew about their illicit affair.

"You're an incredible talent… Your truffles give me
life!… After-work drinks at my place!" Giovanni read
out loud, gesturing at the chalkboard with an index
finger. What Elise did on her days off was none of his
business, but his curiosity got the best of him and he
asked her point-blank about her love life. "Are you dating Antoine?"

Elise stared at him with wide eyes, as if he'd just
sprouted a horn in the middle of his forehead. Leaning against a produce rack, he tried to appear casual,
even though sweat drenched his shirt. Giovanni wanted
to know the truth and he wasn't leaving the restaurant
until he got to the bottom of things.

"No, of course not. We're colleagues." Checking the labels on the fronts of the containers, Elise tapped her pen absently on the clipboard. "Besides, Antonie's dating an adorable masseuse named Trinity, and I'd never do anything to break up their happy home."

"And that's the truth?"

"Absolutely," she insisted, placing the clipboard on the nearest shelf. "I have no reason to lie. But why are you asking me about my relationship with Antoine? Did someone say something to you? Is that why you're here?"

Giovanni raked a hand through his hair, wishing he could go back in time. Feeling guilty for upsetting Elise, he searched for the right words to say to put her fears to rest. He shouldn't have asked her about her personal life. He was her boss, not her man, and he'd overstepped. "I saw the notes on the chalkboard and thought maybe you and Antoine were an item," he explained. "Elise, I'm sorry. I didn't mean to upset you or to create distrust in your mind about your colleagues. Everyone thinks you're great. And so do I."

Giovanni didn't know what had come over him. One minute he was apologizing to Elise and the next he was devouring her lips.

And once he started kissing her, he couldn't stop.

# *Chapter 8*

Alarm bells rang in Giovanni's mind and a stern male voice that sounded like his father told him to leave the kitchen—or else. Instead of heeding the warning, he tightened his hold around her waist and inclined his head toward her, deepening the kiss.

Elise must have been in shock because she remained perfectly still with her hands hanging rigidly at her sides. Tasting a hint of maple syrup on her lips, he licked them slowly, savoring the sweet flavor on her tongue. Aroused by her scent and the warmth of her mouth, he struggled to control his emotions, and imagined them making love. Wanted her in his bed, tonight. Elise was a stand-out beauty who'd seized his attention the moment he'd first laid eyes on her, and Giovanni was smitten with her. He liked the idea of having a fling with the feisty chef with the charming drawl, and hoped Elise shared his feelings.

Elise moaned. The sound was music to his ears, a turn-on. Her arms closed around his neck and her hands played in his hair, fingering his ponytail. Knowing that she was enjoying the kiss and she wanted him, too, bolstered his confidence and assuaged his guilt. His instincts were right, bang on. Elise was attracted to him and their chemistry was undeniable, unlike anything he'd ever experienced before. And his body yearned for more.

Giovanni backed her up against the door, slamming it shut with his right hand. Perfect. Now he didn't have to worry about anyone interrupting them, ruining the moment. He hadn't kissed anyone in months, hadn't wanted to until he'd first locked eyes with Elise, and he didn't want their spontaneous make-out session to end. Not until he had his fill of her.

Heavy breathing filled the air, mingled with their desperate moans, and groans. Giovanni knew what he was doing was wrong, but he couldn't tear himself away from her. Didn't want to. He wanted to continue kissing and caressing her. He cupped her bottom in his hands and rubbed himself against her, wishing he could fulfill his desires right then and there.

His cell phone rang from inside his back pocket, but Giovanni ignored it, wouldn't have answered it if his life depended on it. Nothing mattered more to him than kissing Elise, than pleasing her with his mouth and hands. He caressed her shoulders, her neck, played in her hair. Giovanni didn't know why he'd thought he could stay away from Elise. He couldn't. He thought about her every day, even though they'd only known each other for a couple of weeks, and was tired of avoiding her at the club.

Kissing her was like a birthday present, more exhilarating than test-driving an Italian sports car, and now that Giovanni had experienced the pleasure of her lips, he could never go back to just being her boss, even if he wanted to. Ten days ago, he'd reamed Rosario out for hiring Elise, and now he was kissing her with everything he had. What his sister didn't know couldn't hurt her, and as long as they were discreet, no one would ever know they were lovers. At the thought of being intimate with her, shivers rocked his spine and an erection stabbed the zipper of his Armani dress pants.

Giovanni cupped her face in his hands, stroking her cheeks as he tenderly kissed her. He was done—wasn't going to fight his feelings for her anymore. Why should he? His marriage had imploded, but that didn't mean he was a failure, a lost cause when it came to relationships. Unlike most of his friends, he'd rather have one special woman in his life than a dozen, and had no desire to play the field. He wanted to know more about Elise and liked the idea of wining and dining her after dark.

"Elise? Elise? Hello? Are you here?"

His eyes flew open and his heart stopped. At the sound of his sister's voice, panic ballooned in his chest, making it hard to breathe. The color drained from Elise's face. Giovanni pressed a finger to his lips. Backing away from him, she straightened her crooked clothes then fanned her cheeks. Thinking fast, Giovanni turned off the lights. He couldn't think of anything worse than Rosario finding them in the storage room, and hoped they weren't discovered.

Questions troubled his mind. What was Rosario doing in the kitchen? Shouldn't she be in her office returning emails, answering phone calls and closing deals? Another thought came to mind, chilling him to the bone. Had Rosario spotted him entering the restaurant? Had she rang his cell earlier? Was she standing in the kitchen, waiting for them to surface from the storage room? Fearing the worst, Giovanni reached into his back pocket, took out his cell phone and lowered the volume.

Damn. His suspicions were right. Rosario had called twice while he was in the storage room with Elise. He'd been dazed, so caught up in the moment, he'd forgotten about his position and his responsibilities as CEO of his family's polo club. Guilt tormented his conscience. He'd lost his control, his composure, had allowed his flesh to get the best of him. He'd never want to do anything to embarrass his family or the polo club, and hoped his actions didn't come back to haunt him.

Footsteps echoed in the kitchen and the tension in the storage room thickened. Giovanni couldn't see Elise, but he sensed her unease, her growing fear as the footsteps got closer to their hiding spot. They were too old to be playing hide-and-seek, and Giovanni felt foolish for putting them in such a precarious position, but he didn't have any other options. It was either hide or run, because if Rosario caught him in the storage room with Elise, she'd kill him with her bare hands—then rat him out to their father.

The footsteps faded and Giovanni released the

breath he was holding. *There really* is *a God!* Turning on the light, he wore an apologetic smile. He hoped he looked sincere, because he was.

"Giovanni, please leave. I have things to do."

*I wish you'd do* me *instead!* Intent on being heard, he leaned against the door and met her gaze. Elise touched the silver chain at her neck, fiddling with the heart-shaped tag pendants. Giovanni had mixed feelings about their encounter. He felt guilty for kissing Elise without asking her permission first, but their spontaneous make-out session had given him an adrenaline rush. If it were up to him, they'd still be pleasing each other.

"This is why I didn't want to hire you," he confessed, his voice so husky he didn't recognize it. "I was afraid my emotions would get the best of me and one day I'd act on my desires. What I did was reckless and impulsive, and I'm sorry. I wasn't thinking."

Her face softened. Her shoulders visibly relaxed, and she exhaled a deep breath. Giovanni did, too. Turned out he was worried for nothing. Elise wasn't mad at him; she understood him.

"It happens, even to the best of us. Don't beat yourself up about it."

"Phew," he said, plucking at his dress shirt for effect. "I thought you were pissed at me."

"I'm not, but I will be if you don't get out of here and let me get back to work." Glancing at her wristwatch, she gasped. "Oh, no! The staff meeting starts in ten minutes and I haven't finished writing the agenda yet!"

Giovanni scratched his head. *We were in here for half*

*an hour? Too bad it wasn't an hour,* he thought, stroking his jaw. *Imagine what we could do with more time.*

"I have to go. See you around."

Elise reached for the door handle but Giovanni captured her hand in his own and pulled her to his chest. Hungry for her, his gaze dropped from her eyes to her mouth, but this time he didn't act on his impulses. "Not so fast, Dancing Queen."

A giggle fell from her lips and the sound warmed his heart. Elise was full of fun and excitement, and her sultry smile was dangerous. Deadly sexy. Gave him goose bumps. If she didn't have a meeting to prepare for, he would pick up where they'd left off. Or scoop her up in his arms and make a beeline for his office.

The thought shocked him. He was acting out of character, as if he'd never been in the presence of a beautiful woman before. But he was weak for Elise and suddenly couldn't control his feelings.

"We need to talk about that kiss and what it means for us—"

"No, we don't," she insisted in a firm tone. "It's no big deal. It meant nothing. In a week, I'll be a distant memory, and you'll be on to the next girl. Now, if you'll excuse me, I have a staff meeting to prepare for."

On a mission, Elise picked the clipboard up off the storage shelf, yanked open the door and marched into the kitchen. All Giovanni could do was stare at her. He wanted to go after her, but stayed put. He didn't want Elise to think he was desperate. Or worse—think less of him.

Giovanni didn't chase women down, but he wanted to pursue her, longed to kiss her again. He'd monopolized enough of her time, though, and worried what would happen if he was still in the restaurant when the kitchen staff arrived. No doubt Antoine would get suspicious, and Giovanni didn't want the nosy restaurant manager to start asking him questions about everyone's favorite chef.

"Thanks again for breakfast. It was incredible, and I enjoyed your company immensely."

Glancing from the clipboard to her tablet, she nodded absently, a confused expression on her face. To capture her attention, he cupped her chin in his hand, forcing her to look at him. Lowering his face to hers, he brushed his mouth against her lips, relishing the feel of her. Giovanni wanted to spend the rest of the day kissing, but he had to get back to his office. Reluctantly ending the kiss, he straightened to his full height then strode out of the kitchen.

Damn. He'd done it again. Crossed the line. But it was worth it—Elise was worth it—and he wouldn't let her downplay their connection. Not after what had happened in the storage room.

Marching through the lobby, Giovanni wondered if he'd blown it with Elise. There was no telling what would happen the next time they were alone, and even though he didn't want to tempt the hand of fate, he decided he'd return to the restaurant at the end of the day, once he was sure Rosario was gone for the night. Better yet, he'd call the restaurant, order his favorite entrée for dinner and request that Elise deliver it to his office.

A grin claimed his mouth as a plan took shape in his mind. Elise was wrong. Their first kiss *was* a big deal. It had meant something to him and he wasn't going to deny himself the pleasure of her sweet, delectable mouth. Giovanni wanted Elise, and he was going to have her, even if it meant breaking the rules. He only hoped his family didn't find out he was pursuing Elise and ream him out for sneaking around with her. He'd made the mistake of dating an employee once before, but this time he'd be smart, wouldn't do anything stupid like fall in love or propose. They'd have a holiday fling and, when their relationship had run its course, he'd move on.

Entering his office, he couldn't help but grin at the thought of the feisty chef—and all the fun they could have after dark in the restaurant kitchen.

# Chapter 9

"There you are! I *knew* I'd find you in here with the catering staff instead of socializing with the other guests." Lifestyle and beauty expert Demi Harris waddled into the stone-accentuated kitchen of her fiancée's estate with a scowl on her lips, and Elise knew she was in trouble with her friend. Elise adored Demi and didn't want to upset her, so she wore an apologetic smile.

"What kind of friend would I be if I didn't help cook at your baby shower?"

"Elise, you're a guest, not a member of the catering staff, so take off your apron, back away from the stove and get out of the kitchen," Demi instructed, blowing her bangs out of her face.

A laugh tickled Elise's throat. It was hard to take Demi seriously when she was huffing and puffing her words like the Big Bad Wolf. The social media darling and tech entrepreneur Chase Crawford were polar opposites who'd met in Ibiza and instantly hit it off. Now, they were happily engaged and expecting twins. Demi and Chase were a strong, committed couple, and every time Elise was around them, they renewed her faith in true love.

"I'm eight months pregnant with twins. You shouldn't be stressing me out." Looking adorable in a diamond tiara, a printed trapeze dress and jeweled ballet flats, Demi cocked her head and hitched a hand to her hip. "Now, go into the great room and mingle with all of the fabulous people at my star-studded baby shower, or else."

Elise gave the mom-to-be a hug then tenderly rubbed her stomach. She'd been one of the first guests to arrive at Chase's Southampton estate, and her mouth had dropped open when she'd entered the ten-bedroom mansion. Stunned by the opulent decor, Elise, having never seen so much gold, crystal and marble in one place, was scared to touch anything. "I can't leave now. I'm about to make shrimp cocktails."

"You've done more than enough." Demi untied Elise's frilly pink apron, ripped it off and tossed it on the granite countertop. "Let's go. I want to introduce you to Chase's extended family and my girlfriends who drove up from Philly, as well."

"But I'm having fun in here," she said, gesturing to the tray of perfectly shaped bacon cheese bites she'd helped prepare minutes earlier. After grabbing a mocktail and posing for pictures with Demi, she'd slipped into the kitchen to help make appetizers for the well-heeled guests. There was no shortage of star power at Demi's Saturday-afternoon baby shower. Everywhere Elise looked, there was an A-list celebrity posing for pictures. "I'll finish up in here then rejoin the party."

"No, you'll rejoin the party *now*," Demi said in a firm voice, flipping her lush auburn curls over her shoulders. "The Crawford family loves throwing brunches, formal dinners and cocktail parties during the holidays, and I want them to meet my beautiful, talented friend, whose cooking is to die for, so she can cater all of their upcoming events."

"I like the way you think, Demi. Thanks for the vote of confidence."

"The way I see it, it's a win-win for everyone. You'll wow my future mother-in-law with your decadent holiday recipes, she'll feel indebted to me for introducing you to her, and our relationship will finally blossom." A mischievous expression crossed her face, and a smirk curled her plump lips. "And if that doesn't work, I'm relocating with my man and our babies to Papua New Guinea!"

Giggling, Demi led Elise through the kitchen, down the hallway and into the great room.

Giant pink and purple balloons were swathed around columns, heart-shaped paper lanterns hung from the ceiling, a diaper cake towered above the glass bookshelf, and lavish flower arrangements with long-stemmed roses perfumed the air. Round tables, fashioned with tutu-style skirts, were covered with an assortment of appetizers, desserts and candy, and baby bottles with nonalcoholic drinks.

A gold metallic banner that read *Welcome to Demi's*

*Baby Shower* stretched from one wall to the next, and pacifier wreaths were positioned along the fireplace mantel. Over the years, Elise had been to many family celebrations, but she'd never attended such a glamorous baby shower, and it was obvious the Crawford family had spared no expense for the first-time mom's party.

"Demi, how are things? Starting to get excited about the big day?" Elise asked, raising her voice to be heard above the music and chatter.

"Friend, you have no idea. I can't complain, because overall I've had a really good pregnancy, but these days I feel tired and heavy and irritable. I can't wait for January fourth to arrive so I can see my beautiful twin girls, *and* my feet again!"

Elise touched her stomach. She wondered what it would be like to be pregnant. Demi often joked about her symptoms—the itchy skin, the lower back pain, the mood swings—but Elise still envied her friend and wished she had a family of her own. Demi had a life most women dreamed of, and Elise hoped one day she'd meet her soul mate, too. Someone thoughtful, romantic and attentive, who'd put her needs above his own. For years, Elise had been so busy chasing her culinary dreams she'd had no time for the opposite sex, and she didn't know the first thing about having a successful relationship.

*Maybe if you'd dated more, you wouldn't have thrown yourself at Giovanni yesterday,* quipped her inner voice in a righteous, matter-of-fact tone. *You were all over him! How will you ever live that down?*

Swallowing hard, Elise finger-combed her hair behind her ears then adjusted her burgundy keyhole dress.

To assuage her guilt, she'd convinced herself that Giovanni had been the aggressor, that she'd been an innocent victim who hadn't known what to do when he crushed his lips to her mouth. But last night in bed she'd replayed their encounter repeatedly in her mind and forced herself to face the truth: they'd kissed *each other* and it had been one of the most exhilarating moments of her life. No one had ever kissed her with such passion before, with such hunger and intensity, and Giovanni's exquisite technique had left her speechless.

The spontaneity of the kiss and the risk of being caught in the storage room had added to the thrill of their wild, frenzied encounter. Twenty-four hours later, Elise was still walking on air and her debonair boss with the juicy lips was the reason why. Giovanni had dominated her thoughts all night, and she'd woken that morning thinking about him—and the kiss that had taken her breath away.

Touching her fingertips to her lips, she mentally reviewed the exact moment Giovanni had crushed his mouth to hers, sending shock waves through her body. Elise liked being close to Giovanni and had never desired a man more, but hooking up with him was out of the question. A high-stakes gamble Elise was unwilling to take. Career suicide, no matter how she looked at it.

After everything she'd been through at By the Bay, she couldn't afford to squander the opportunity she'd been given. Proud to be the executive chef at the Hamptons Polo Club, Elise wanted to keep the position, and also keep her reputation for being a consummate professional intact. As long as she remembered what was at stake, she wouldn't lose her composure again.

"Welcome to Demi's baby shower!" Jennifer "Geneviève" Harris appeared beside Demi, blew a glittered noisemaker and draped an arm around her sister's shoulder. The former child star and award-winning singer was one of the greatest voices of the twenty-first century and had six platinum-selling albums to her credit. The total package, Geneviève had an angelic voice and a fun-loving personality people couldn't get enough of. Elise had met the pop star before, but every time she saw Geneviève, she was sporting a different look. Today, it was a honey-blond bob with bangs, a striped sweater dress and the largest diamond ring Elise had ever seen up close.

"I'm thrilled that each and every one of you are here to help us celebrate the impending arrival of my precious nieces," Geneviève gushed, her voice filled with excitement. "Demi is an amazing daughter, sister, fiancée and friend, and she's going to be an outstanding mother, too…"

Demi wiped at her eyes with the sleeve of her designer dress. Standing beside the Harris sisters, watching them hug, Elise felt a rush of emotion—a knot in her chest and a heavy heart. Thirsty, she helped herself to one of the cocktail glasses on the granite bar and tasted her virgin margarita.

Listening to Geneviève's speech, Elise nodded as the pop star spoke. Moved by her poignant words, she willed herself not to cry. Demi had a loving, supportive family, and moments like this made Elise wish she had siblings, too, especially now that her parents were gone. Feeling all alone in the world, she longed for a family of her own, but feared her career would eclipse her dreams and she'd never find true love.

"Demi's kind, lovable and beautiful, and I'm not just saying that because we look alike," Geneviève quipped, with an innocent smile. "I'm just calling it like I see it."

Laughter filled the air and the pop song playing on the stereo system added to the festive mood inside the estate. Elise's gaze darted around the room, searching for Sariah and Paige. These days, pregnancy announcements, baby showers and kids' birthday parties were hard for Sariah, and Elise wanted to make sure her friend was okay. She didn't see her anywhere, so she texted her.

"There's no doubt in my mind that you're going to *slay* motherhood," Geneviève said, brushing a lock of hair away from her sister's face. "And look damn good doing it, too!"

The guests cheered, whooped and hollered for several seconds, and Demi giggled.

Elise licked her lips. The sweet aroma wafting out of the kitchen made her mouth water. Sniffing the air, she had to stop herself from drooling. Her gaze strayed across the room to the Instagram-worthy appetizers on the round tables. Wanting something to eat, Elise crossed the room and picked up a gold-rimmed plate.

"Everyone, please, mingle, dance and help yourself to refreshments," Geneviève continued. "But don't stray too far because we're going to play some fun baby shower games and I want everyone to have a chance to win one of the amazing prizes."

Gathering around Demi, guests snapped pictures of the mom-to-be with their cell phones.

Elise sent another group text to Sariah and Paige, then tasted the food on her plate. The appetizers were seasoned with unique spices and she made a mental note to return to the kitchen to tell the catering staff everything tasted delicious.

Elise sipped her mocktail. Taking Geneviève's advice, she moved around the great room, introducing herself to everyone in attendance. She'd never seen so many celebrities, trophy wives, socialites and social media personalities in one place before, and enjoyed meeting the most dynamic women in the Hamptons.

In good spirits, Elise chatted excitedly about her new executive chef position and invited Demi's friends and family to the upcoming holiday events at the polo club. Exchanging numbers with Geneviève's bandmates, Divalicious, Elise promised the all-female group VIP treatment whenever they visited the club, and hoped they kept their promise to attend the Holiday Cocktail Party with the beloved pop star.

"You're here! How wonderful to see you, Elise," a high-pitched voice said.

Someone touched her forearm and Elise spun around. Her tongue swelled inside her mouth. Frozen stiff, Elise couldn't move. Rosario was standing directly behind her, wearing a broad smile and a money-green pantsuit that complemented her skin tone.

Worried Rosario would take one look at her and see the truth on her face, Elise stared down at her cocktail glass. She'd kissed Rosario's brother, not her husband, so why did she feel like crap? Why was she consumed with guilt? Why couldn't she meet Rosario's gaze?

Elise forced her lips to move but nothing came out. With each passing second, her panic grew.

"Small world, huh?" Rosario took a bite of the stuffed pepper on her plate then wiped the sauce off her mouth with a napkin. "You never told me you knew Demi and her family."

"Come on," Elise quipped, cracking a joke. "*Every-one* knows Demi. She's the unofficial ambassador of the Hamptons!"

Rosario laughed, and Elise smiled in relief.

"How is everything going at the restaurant? Are you starting to get the hang of things?"

Nodding, Elise slowly sipped her drink.

"I'm glad to hear that," Rosario said with a sigh of relief. "I came by yesterday, hoping to finalize the menu for the Holiday Cocktail Party, but you were no-where to be found…"

*That's because I was busy kissing your brother in the storage room!*

"Do you have a few minutes to spare right now? I'd love to pick your brain about the tentative plans I've made for the Breakfast with Santa and Family Brunch."

Her food forgotten, Rosario chatted about the holiday-themed events. Her excitement was palpable, contagious, and soon the women were bouncing ideas off of each other. Rosario was determined to make the polo club an even greater success, and Elise admired her ambition.

"I'm *so* glad we ran into each other," Rosario told her, flipping her dark brown hair over her shoulders. "I know you've got your hands full right now, but let's make time on Monday to finalize all of the necessary details. Does 9:00 a.m. work for you?"

"I'll make it work." Elise unlocked her phone and added the meeting to her calendar.

"Awesome! I'm going to schmooze with the Real Housewives. Talk to you later."

A text message from Sariah popped up on Elise's phone and her heart dropped. Exiting the room, she strode down the hallway and up the winding staircase. Hearing voices, she realized Demi was giving some of the guests a tour of the house, and followed the group into the nursery.

Bright and spacious, with ivory furniture decorated with printed cushions, it had butterflies painted on the walls, a decorative toy box filled with books, puzzles and stuffed animals, and a vibrant alphabet-themed rug. Elise took one look at Sariah, who was standing beside the window, tugging at the sleeve of her belted teal jumpsuit, and feared her friend was on the verge of an emotional breakdown. Tears glistened in her eyes and she was biting her bottom lip. Thinking fast, Elise took Sariah by the arm and led her out of the room.

"Finally," Paige trilled, appearing in the hallway, holding two cocktail glasses. "I thought you'd never show up. Where have you been?"

"Not now, Paige. We'll talk later. Sariah needs some space."

"Nonsense," she argued, rolling her eyes to the ceiling. "Demi invited us to check out the nursery and I'm dying to see what it looks like. I bet it's bigger than my apartment."

Wanting privacy, Elise ushered Sariah inside the

bathroom and turned on the lights. The air smelled of potpourri, water gushed out of a miniature bronze fountain, creating a soothing ambience. Impressed with the stone and marble accents throughout the space, Elise felt as if she'd entered a luxurious spa and hoped the tranquil mood helped her bestie calm down.

Paige asked a million questions as she followed them inside, wanting to know what was wrong and why Sariah was upset. She put the glasses on the marble sink, then slammed the door. "Is someone going to tell me what's going on, or do I have to ask Demi?"

"No!" Sariah shouted, her voice ricocheting off the alabaster walls. "Please don't."

"Sweetie, what's going on?" Elise asked.

Sariah dropped down on the oversize velvet stool and stared at the wooden sculpture displayed on the side table.

Anxious to get to the bottom of things, Elise crouched down beside Sariah and spoke in a sympathetic tone. "Sariah, talk to us. What is it?"

"I adore Demi, and I'm thrilled that she's going to be a mom, but I wish *I* was the one expecting twins," she confessed. "I wish *I* was giving birth next month."

Paige nodded. "I understand—"

"Do you?" Sariah challenged. "I doubt it. You have no idea what it's like trying to conceive month after month, with no success."

Elise grabbed a tissue from the decorative gold box on the counter and wiped the tears spilling down Sariah's cheeks. It broke her heart to see her best friend cry, and she wanted to help her. Sariah had been her rock during her parents' memorial service, and Elise would never forget the times her bestie had supported her on her darkest days.

"I'm tired of seeing everyone around me get pregnant, especially couples who aren't even trying to conceive," she complained, a bitter edge in her voice. "And if one more person tells me I'll get pregnant in God's time, I'm going to scream."

Paige smirked. "It'll happen in God's time."

Sariah stuck out her tongue then giggled.

Elise did, too. She could always count on Paige for a laugh, and she gave her friend a high five for lightening the mood. Sariah's face brightened and Elise hoped she'd be able to rejoin the baby shower, even though she was frustrated about her fertility problems. "And if it doesn't, you can buy a pig and start a farm."

"Yuck!" Sariah rolled her eyes to the ceiling. "I swear, sometimes you guys suck at being friends. I'd be better off calling the Psychic Network for advice."

"We love you, too," Elise said with a cheeky smile on her lips. "And when you bring little piglet home from the animal society, we promise to help you train him."

The women cracked up, laughing long and hard, and Elise gave Sariah a one-armed hug.

"Please don't tell Demi I was crying," she begged. "I don't want her to think I'm jealous. I'm not. I just really want a baby and thinking about my fertility struggles makes me sad sometimes."

Paige picked up her glass and took a sip of her cocktail. "Don't worry, no one will ever know what happened in here. It'll be our little secret."

"Thanks. I knew I could count on you guys." Sariah stood, went over to the sink and peered at the oval mirror. Sighing, she fluffed her short black hair. "This is definitely *not* my day. I'm hormonal, and I feel like crap—"

"Join the club. Giovanni kissed me yesterday and my conscience is still tormenting me."

Elise didn't realize the words had left her mouth until Sariah gasped and Paige gripped her shoulders. Her eyes were wild, and she was talking so fast, Elise didn't understand what she was saying.

"You kissed Giovanni Castillo! No way! Where? When? What happened? Is he a good kisser?" Giggling, she slapped her forehead with her palm. "What am I saying? *Of course* he's a good kisser! He's dreamy and he reeks of raw, potent masculinity."

*Raw, potent masculinity?*

Paige was shouting, and Elise feared one of Demi's family members would hear the racket and come running. She smelled alcohol on Paige's breath, and guessed her best friend had added tequila to her virgin margarita when no one was looking. "It was a harmless five-second kiss," she lied, hoping to downplay the encounter, even though she'd fantasized about Giovanni all night. "It didn't mean anything, and we both agreed it wouldn't happen again."

"Yeah, right, and Sariah's *actually* going to adopt a pig!"

A laugh exploded out of Elise's mouth and Paige wore a proud smile.

"You haven't been on a date since Obama was president, but you expect us to believe you didn't enjoy kissing Giovanni and that you're not *dying* to do it again?

Girl, please. You're lying, and if you don't come clean, I'll contact that fine-ass polo player myself."

Elise glanced at the door, her pulse thundering in her ears. "Keep it down. Someone might hear you and tell Rosario, and I'll be fired. Is that what you want?"

"No, of course not, but I want you to tell the truth."

"Yeah," Sariah agreed. "It was hard, but I told you guys how I was feeling about Demi's pregnancy. We're girls, and that's what we do. We confide in each other."

Checking her watch, Elise frowned and shook her head. "We should get back to the party. We've been in here for twenty minutes, and Demi's going to wonder where we are."

"Oh, please," Sariah said sarcastically. "Demi's too busy posting and tweeting to come find us. Now, quit stalling and tell us what's going on at work."

"I don't know where to start." Elise shrugged. "Everything happened so fast."

"And we want to hear every juicy detail, so spill it." Paige hopped up on the counter, crossed her legs and clasped her hands around her knees. "Where did he kiss you?"

*On the lips, but I wished he'd kissed me everywhere!*
Her throat was dry as images of Giovanni flashed in her mind, but Elise parted her lips and pushed the truth out of her mouth. Her friends' opinions mattered to her, and she wanted their advice about how to deal with her attraction to Giovanni.

Opening up to her girlfriends was cathartic, better than a session with her therapist, and by the time Elise was finished telling Sariah and Paige what had happened with Giovanni in the storage room yesterday, she felt a hundred times better.

"I'm *so* happy for you!" Sariah draped her arms around Elise's neck and squeezed tight. "This is the best news I've heard in months. Imagine, my best friend dating one of the most famous athletes in the world. Wait until I tell Aamir. He's going to flip."

"Get it, girl!" Leaping off the counter, Paige danced around the soaker tub with glee, wiggling her hips and snapping her fingers. "Giovanni doesn't go around kissing people, so he must like you a lot. How exciting!"

Elise started to speak but someone banged on the door and she trailed off. Was Rosario in the hallway? Was she listening in on their private conversation? Her heart thumped. Did Rosario recognize her voice and figure out Elise had a crush on her brother? Before Elise could decide what to do, Sariah opened the door.

"Back downstairs, ladies," quipped a petite silver-haired woman in a peach dress. "It's time for party games, and Geneviève wants everyone to return to the great room."

Tucking her clutch purse under her forearm, Elise followed her girlfriends out of the bathroom, eager to return to the party. But when her cell phone rang and Giovanni's name and number popped up on the screen, she froze. There had to be a good reason for why Giovanni was calling on her day off, though Elise couldn't think of one. Curiosity burned inside her. She was dying to know what he wanted, but she couldn't risk someone at the party overhearing their conversation.

Her phone stopped ringing and Elise sighed in relief. She'd call him when she got home. *No*, Elise decided, fervently shaking her head. She'd delete Giovanni's number from her phone, put all thoughts of him out of her mind once and for all, and pretend he'd never called—or kissed her passionately in the storage room.

# Chapter 10

Giovanni marched into the polo club on Sunday afternoon, noticed the lobby was filled with celebrities, political figures, wealthy and influential members and their equally esteemed guests, and stopped dead in his tracks. Christmas decorations were swathed around the columns, dangling from the ceiling and around the windows, and he suspected Elise was to blame for the over-the-top decor. From what he'd seen, she was a chef, an event planner and a restaurant manager all rolled into one, and even though he wanted to dump the decorations into the closest garbage bin, Giovanni was impressed by her talent and creativity.

Surveying the scene, Giovanni took off his sunglasses and unbuttoned his double-breasted wool coat. *I have to look at these decorations for the next three weeks?* he thought, strangling a groan. *You've got to be kidding me! I know Elise loves Christmas, but this is torture!*

The lobby had been transformed into a winter wonderland and everywhere Giovanni looked, he saw garlands, tinsel, mistletoe and poinsettias. Stars had been stuck to the ivory walls, fake snow covered the hardwood floors and round tables were laden with appetizers. A soaring evergreen, decorated in layers of twinkling lights and glass ornaments, commandeered the corner of the lobby, and was surrounded by dozens of presents. Worse still, Christmas music was playing on the sound system and guests were singing along.

Giovanni shook his head in disbelief. *Wow, what a star-studded turnout.* He'd never expected hundreds of people to attend the Holiday Cocktail Party, let alone an Oscar winner and a former US president, but what shocked him most of all was Elise's red, eye-catching outfit. His gaze trailed her around the room, watched her every move.

She was wearing a velvet Santa hat, a belted dress that skimmed her knees and stilettos. Her sexy, fitted outfit made his mouth water. She was comfortable in her skin, and it showed. All of the servers were wearing velvet hats and Christmas-themed outfits, but Elise was the only one who took his breath away.

Images of their first kiss played in his mind and his temperature rose about a hundred degrees. He remembered the softness of her lips, the delicious taste of her mouth, the smell of her floral fragrance and how she'd tenderly stroked his neck, her touch arousing him. For the past forty-eight hours, he'd thought of

Elise and nothing else. But Giovanni was determined to put their kiss out of his head—at least during the Holiday Cocktail Party.

The hostess appeared, took his coat from his hands and disappeared into the crowd. The men were in designer suits, the women were in formal attire and several couples of Asian descent were wearing traditional clothing. Guests kissed under the mistletoe, danced cheek-to-cheek and snapped selfies in front of the towering Christmas tree.

Making his way through the lobby, Giovanni smiled at guests, shook hands and posed for pictures with friends and associates, all the while keeping a watchful eye on Elise. She sashayed around the lobby with a smile on her lips, a silver tray in her hands and a bounce in her step. He noticed several Hollywood actors checking out the curvy executive chef. And Giovanni didn't blame them. Energetic, gregarious and lively, Elise was the life of the party. When she breezed by him, humming along with the upbeat Christmas song playing on the sound system, he felt the overwhelming urge to kiss her again, even though he knew Rosario would kill him on the spot. Elise had an attention-grabbing presence, and it took every ounce of self-control he had not to pull her into his arms.

A loud, hearty laugh drowned out the music, drawing Giovanni's eyes across the room. Fashionably dressed in a velvet burgundy suit, Jonas swaggered around the lobby, flirting with socialites and Instagram models. Wanting to know more about his favorite chef, Giovanni made a mental note to pull Jonas aside to ask him about Elise's personal life.

Last night in bed, he'd checked out her social media pages. Her online profiles were filled with her favorite recipes, pictures of the entrées and desserts she'd recently made, and photographs of her parents. For several seconds, he'd peered at the screen. Elise was the same height and complexion as her father, but she was the spitting image of her mother. Questions had crowded his mind. Had Elise ever dated outside her race? Would her parents like him, or think he was a conceited athlete who didn't deserve their daughter?

Giovanni shook his head to clear his thoughts. Glancing around the lobby, he realized his mother was standing in front of the Christmas tree with several family friends, and cringed. He was so busy ogling Elise, he hadn't even noticed his mother was at the party, and felt guilty for overlooking her. Crossing the room, he licked his lips. The scent of spiced wine and dark chocolate sweetened the air; if Giovanni wasn't following a strict healthy diet, he would have sampled every item at the food table.

"I was hoping you'd be here." Flashing a smile, he hugged his mom and kissed her on each cheek. "Mom, you look incredible, and your haircut really suits you."

"I know," Constanza Castillo cooed, fervently nodding. "Everyone says my new hairstyle makes me look like the Argentine version of Marilyn Monroe, and I agree!"

Giovanni tried to restrain his laughter, but a chuckle shot out of his mouth like a blast from a gun. His mom was a petite, overweight housewife with a thick Spanish accent. The only thing she had in common with the iconic actress was her gender.

"Where's Dad?" he asked, searching the lobby for Vincente.

"At home taking a nap. He'd planned to come, but once he had lunch and took his pain medication, he was out like a light. I didn't have the heart to wake him up."

His surprise must have showed on his face, because his mom wagged a finger at him.

"Your dad needs his rest," she scolded, a note of frustration in her voice. "Vincente isn't a young man anymore and he just doesn't have the energy to keep on top of things like he used to. Contrary to what everyone thinks, he's *not* Superman…"

A lump formed in his throat. He turned her words over in his mind, listening quietly to what his mother had to say. These days, all his family wanted to talk about was his father's health, the ongoing struggles of Castillo Enterprises, and Giovanni's responsibilities as the eldest child and only son. No one asked him what he wanted, and he didn't feel comfortable confiding in his mother about his inner turmoil. Next Friday, he had another appointment with his neurologist and, if everything went according to plan, he'd be one step closer to leaving for Argentina and resuming his career.

"I know you love traveling the world playing polo, but it's time you step up and take your rightful place in the business," she continued with a nod. "Son, we're counting on you."

*But I'm not the heart and soul of the company! Rosario is, and* she *should be named CEO, not me.* Getting through to his mom was an uphill battle Giovanni didn't have the energy to fight. There'd be plenty of time to discuss his future plans, and what should be done to help his dad with the day-to-day operations of Castillo Enterprises, when Vincente decided to retire. Swallowing a yawn, he rubbed his eyes and stretched his neck. Anxious about his upcoming doctor's appointment, he hadn't slept well all week.

"Son, what's wrong? And don't tell me you're fine, because it's obvious you're not." Frowning, Constanza cupped his chin in her hand and studied him, as if he were a specimen under a microscope. "Tell Mama what's wrong. I'm listening."

"Mom, it's nothing." A server approached and Giovanni inspected the items on his silver tray. Forgetting his diet, he took a glass of wine and a plate topped with appetizers. "I've been binge-watching *La Casa de Papel*. That's why I'm so tired."

"Alone?" she prodded, raising an eyebrow. "Or with one of your many female fans?"

Pretending he didn't hear the question, Giovanni tasted a garlic-Parmesan beignet. It melted in his mouth and he groaned in appreciation. Seasoned with bold spices that his taste buds enjoyed immensely, it whet his appetite and he finished everything on his plate in seconds. Helping himself to more, Giovanni marveled at the delicious pistachio cheeseballs. They were soft and succulent, and he wanted more. Elise wasn't afraid to try new things or to experiment in the kitchen, and all of the appetizers he'd sampled were exceptional. He wanted to tell Elise how much he'd enjoyed her cooking, but she was deep in conversation with a music mogul and Giovanni didn't want to interrupt them.

"Rosario introduced me to the new executive chef, Elise Jennings. Interesting choice, son."

"Don't look at me. I had nothing to do with it. Your daughter hired her, not me."

"If you say so, but remember, this is a place of business and not your bachelor pad."

Giovanni drank his wine. He was annoyed by his mom's comment but didn't respond. For the second time in minutes, his gaze strayed to his favorite chef. Elise garnered more attention than a presidential motorcade, and he couldn't take his eyes off of her. He'd hemmed and hawed about attending the Holiday Cocktail Party, but Giovanni was glad he'd showed up. Watching Elise in action, socializing, mingling and serving the club's guests, was the highlight of his day. Elise needed her own reality TV show, and he wouldn't be surprised if one of the network executives at the party offered her a deal on the spot.

"I believe in looking forward, and God knows I'm not one to dwell on the past, but need I remind you about how you met Marisol, and how your ill-fated union embarrassed our family?"

*No, I'm well aware of what a screw-up I am in your eyes.* He gestured to a server, put his empty glass and plate on her tray, then wiped his mouth with a napkin. Hanging his head, his thoughts drifted back to three years earlier.

He'd hooked up with his personal assistant, Marisol, and even though his friends and family thought the former beauty queen was the wrong woman for him, he'd pursued her relentlessly. Dating her had been a mistake, but not because she was his employee. She'd fooled him into believing she was a homebody who loved to cook, sew and garden, but after they eloped and moved into his villa in Buenos Aires, he'd seen another side to her—an ugly, vindictive side that he disliked.

His mom jabbed him in the arm with her elbow and Giovanni snapped to attention.

"Son, you're older and wiser now, so I expect a lot more from you when it comes to how you interact with your female employees. You have to think with your brain and not your—"

"Mom, I have to go," he said, interrupting her. "Since Dad's not here, I have to ensure I socialize with our guests and explain what services and opportunities we offer here at the club."

Constanza beamed. "That's my boy! But remember what I said. Elise Jennings is an employee, not your office plaything, so treat her with respect or you'll have *me* to answer to."

Giovanni dodged his mother's gaze. Shame burned his skin and the weight of his guilt felt heavier than an anchor around his neck. He had a terrible habit of living in the moment, of doing whatever he pleased, but if he wanted to make his parents proud—and avoid his mother's wrath—he'd have to ignore his feelings for Elise. She'd caught his eye without even trying and, although he desired her more than anything, he was determined not to act on his impulses again.

But as he watched Elise waltz with a silver-haired oil tycoon, Giovanni realized it was going to be impossible to resist the Southern beauty with the dazzling smile.

"We need more Swedish meatballs and coconut shrimp, *pronto*!" Elise yelled, entering the sweltering kitchen. "Come on, people. Let's make it happen. We have a roomful of guests who paid *big* bucks to attend this cocktail party, and we can't disappoint them."

Working fast, Elise transferred the lemon-flavored biscotti from the metal baking sheets to the wooden cutting board, and chopped them into squares. She drizzled glazed sugar on top, along with a dash of cinnamon. Sweating profusely in her velvet outfit, Elise longed for an ice-cold drink, but there was no time for a break. She couldn't think of anything worse than running out of food during the party, so she yanked open the fridge, grabbed the items she needed and whipped up another batch of bacon-wrapped apricot bites.

Hearing the distant sound of music and boisterous laughter brought a smile to Elise's mouth as she worked. By all accounts, the event was a success. While serving the mayor and his wife drinks, he'd said the party was one of the best events he'd ever attended at the Hamptons Polo Club. Elise was so moved by his words, tears of joy had filled her eyes. From the time the party had started, her staff had been professional, polite and attentive to guests, and when the night was over, she planned to commend them on a job well done.

Grabbing silver trays off the counter, Elise filled them with peppermint fudge, tree-shaped brownies and chocolate-cranberry mini cakes. Instructing servers to grab a dessert tray and return to the party, she remembered there was peanut brittle cooling on top of the oven, and marched toward the stove. Retrieving the large baking sheets, Elise broke the candy into pieces, filled the decorative Christmas containers to the brim and asked a server to put them on the food tables.

"The meatballs are ready to serve!" Antoine called, mopping his brow with his palm.

"Thanks, Antoine! You're a lifesaver!" Elise grabbed the tray off the stove and headed through the kitchen, pleased that her staff was working hard. For the past two hours, they'd been running back and forth, serving Christmas-themed drinks, appetizers and desserts, and Elise was thrilled about the compliments she'd received from the guests.

"Hurry back," Antoine said, gesturing to the stove with a flick of his head. "The coconut shrimp and sausage-stuffed jalapeños will be finished in ten minutes, so don't get carried away socializing. Remember, you're the executive chef, not a waitress."

Without breaking her stride, she continued into the lobby. Antoine was mad at her because she'd defied his orders, but Elise didn't care. Wanting to make her presence known at the club, she'd offered to help the waitstaff serve guests during the cocktail party, but Antoine had refused, insisted her place was in the kitchen. Thankfully, Rosario had disagreed with him. All afternoon, she'd introduced her to members and celebrities, and Elise had enjoyed meeting the city's wealthiest, most revered citizens—and watching Giovanni on the sly.

At the thought of him, Elise sucked in a breath. Forty-eight hours later, she was still reeling from their kiss and yearning for more. He'd arrived at the party fashionably late, and the moment she'd seen him, she'd lost her train of thought. It was hard to keep up her end of the conversation with the cast of the hit reality TV show *Dating in the City* and watch Giovanni at the same time. His designer ensemble made him look like a boss, like the kind of man used to calling the shots and having his way.

*Giovanni can have his way with me* any *day of the week!* quipped her inner voice.

Entering the lobby, Elise was swarmed by guests who hungrily licked their lips as she served them appetizers. She saw Sariah and Paige approach Giovanni, and narrowed her gaze. Why were her girlfriends talking to Giovanni? Deciding to find out, Elise adjusted her Santa hat and smoothed a hand over her wavy hair, hoping it didn't look as lifeless as it felt.

Someone poked Elise's shoulder and she turned around, wearing a bright smile.

"The mocha-chocolate cupcakes are everything," the brunette gushed, licking the icing off the dessert in her bejeweled hand. "They're scrumptious and oh-so-divine!"

Elise enjoyed watching guests eat her cooking, got a kick out of seeing their eyes light up and the blissful expression on their faces as they savored each delicious morsel. "I'm glad you like them. It was my mother's recipe and they're one of my favorite desserts, too."

"Do you cater? Name your price and I'll pay." Devouring the cupcake, the brunette grabbed another one from a waiter passing by with a tray of desserts and admired the candy decorations on top of it. "I'm hosting my sister's bachelorette party at my East Hampton estate on February ninth, and I want you to prepare the food."

"I have a better idea. Book one of the club's private rooms and customize the menu." Leaning forward, Elise shielded her mouth with her hands and spoke in a quiet voice. "I hate to brag, but my steak short ribs are out of this world, and have made grown men weep tears of joy!"

"*Everything* Elise makes is incredible, and I should know. She's my favorite chef."

Demi and Chase appeared, wearing broad smiles, and Elise hugged them.

"Girl, you look sensational," Elise praised, admiring her friend's stylish maternity dress. "Your skin is radiant and you're positively glowing."

"Thanks, Elise. Everyone says pregnancy agrees with me, but I beg to differ. My back hurts, my sides ache and, for some strange reason, my skin is itchy."

Chase kissed her forehead. "Hang in there, baby. Only one more month to go."

"That's easy for you to say. You're not the one with swollen feet and nonstop heartburn." Rubbing her baby bump, Demi sighed as if she had the weight of the world on her shoulders. "I swear, after our daughters are born and I get my push gift from Lamborghini, I'm closing up shop!"

Laughing, Elise discreetly checked her watch, realized it was time to return to the kitchen and excused herself from the conversation. But before she could leave, Rosario grabbed her arm and led her over to the Christmas tree.

Elise hated being put on the spot, and feared that Rosario was going to ask her to address the crowd. The kitchen was her refuge, her favorite place in the club, and Elise wished she could escape there now, before her nerves got the best of her and she tripped over her tongue. To make matters worse, Giovanni strode over, rested a hand on the small of her back and stared at her in admiration. Goose bumps pricked her skin and her legs wobbled, but Elise returned his smile. She didn't know what had gotten into him, but she liked it, and hoped he saw her as an ally now rather than a liability.

*Oh, please*, argued her inner voice. *All you care about is seeing him naked!*

"This has been an incredible evening, and I want to thank you all for attending The Hamptons Polo Club's first annual Holiday Cocktail Party," Rosario said, raising her voice to be heard over the chatter in the lobby.

"And," Giovanni added, emphasizing the word, "we'd like to recognize and give special thanks to Ms. Elise Jennings, our dynamic new executive chef, and her talented team."

Guests whistled and cheered as if they were watching a World Series game at Yankee Stadium, and Giovanni led the charge. Bowing her head in gratitude, Elise smiled at the crowd. Her gaze fell across Antoine, and her body tensed. His mouth was a hard line, and his arms were folded. No doubt, he was angry at her for not returning to the kitchen as instructed, and Elise owed him an apology.

"We want you to eat and drink and dance the night away," Rosario announced. "This is *your* club, your home away from home, and we want you to party like there's no tomorrow!"

Elise spotted a familiar face in the lobby and froze. *It can't be him*, she thought, peering into the crowd to get a better look at the gentleman in the black pin-striped suit. Elise told herself she was being paranoid, that the stranger wasn't the person who'd attacked her on the Fourth of July, but her fears intensified with each passing second. Resting a hand on her chest to calm her erratic heartbeat, Elise hightailed it out of the lobby as fast as her red-heeled stilettos could take her and dashed into the kitchen.

# *Chapter 11*

Loosening the knot on his charcoal-gray tie, Giovanni staggered into his office, slammed the door shut and dropped onto the leather couch. He pressed his eyes shut. Swallowing hard to alleviate the lump in his throat, Giovanni wished the voices in his head would stop tormenting him. *This isn't real*, he thought, fervently shaking his head. *Haven't I done enough? Lost enough? What more do I need to do to get my life back?*

His thoughts returned to that afternoon. He'd arrived at Dr. Kaddouri's posh East Hampton medical clinic at four o'clock for the results of the yearly physical he'd had weeks earlier, hopeful his doctor would declare him physically fit to play polo.

Since his concussion, he'd worked hard to strengthen his body. He'd avoided alcohol, increased the intensity of his workouts, made sure he got adequate sleep each night and successfully managed his stress. To ensure he was on the right track, he'd done his due diligence. He'd researched concussions, visited several sports medicine physicians and spoken to experts and former polo players who'd also been injured during their career.

He'd wanted to make a sound decision about his mental and physical health, and realized he wasn't ready yet to throw in the towel. Giovanni felt as sharp as he'd ever been, and was anxious to resume playing the sport he loved. At thirty-two, he was in the best shape of his life, and his test results would prove it.

He'd been ushered into a conference room by a nurse and the moment Dr. Kaddouri opened the door, Giovanni felt a painful knot in his chest. Listening to his neurologist speak, he'd struggled to understand what Dr. Kaddouri was saying but couldn't make sense of his words. It was the worst possible news. A living nightmare.

"I know this isn't the news you wanted to hear, but I wouldn't be doing my job if I didn't tell you the truth," Dr. Kaddouri had said, adjusting his eyeglasses. "There's a harrowing physical cost to playing any professional sport, but polo carries a significantly higher risk, and although you look fit and strong on the outside, your CAT scan and other test results tell a different story…"

Giovanni had gawked at Dr. Kaddouri. He couldn't believe it. Didn't know what to say, couldn't think let alone speak. For several minutes, he'd sat with his eyes wide and his mouth agape.

According to his neurologist, his career was over.

The door was sealed, nailed shut, and the realization that he'd never play in another polo tournament or championship game had shaken Giovanni to the core. It wasn't the first time his doctor had expressed concerns about him returning to polo, but it was the first time Dr. Kaddouri had refused to sign off on his medical clearance form. Even worse? He'd contacted Giovanni's longtime physician in Buenos Aires to discuss his concerns, and faxed a copy of his test results to ensure his medical team knew the truth about his health.

Sitting in his padded chair, clutching the armrest so hard his hands throbbed, he'd had an out-of-body experience. Hovering above the room like a ghost, Giovanni saw himself seated at the round table with his head down, but he couldn't hear what his doctor was saying. Troubling thoughts had come to mind, ones he'd tried to ignore but couldn't. He wanted to do what was best for his health, wanted to make a smart, informed decision, but he didn't want to stop playing polo. It wasn't just his livelihood; it was his life, and he couldn't live without it. When Dr. Kaddouri used the *R* word, tears had pierced Giovanni's eyes. He couldn't retire. He was in his prime, a force to be reckoned with on the polo field, and desperate to win more championships. But how, when Dr. Kaddouri was standing in his way?

Giovanni didn't remember leaving the conference room or exiting the clinic, or the fifteen-minute drive to the polo club. Surprisingly enough, the first person he'd thought of calling after he'd parked his SUV was Elise. He'd only known her for a few weeks, but since the morning they'd kissed in the storage room, he'd seen her every day. Sometimes he'd go to the restaurant and have an early-morning breakfast alone with her; other times they'd have coffee at the end of the day, or end up in the lobby together, chatting while they waited for their cars to warm up in the parking lot.

Giovanni looked forward to seeing Elise at the club, and although they hadn't kissed again, their bond was growing—their attraction, too. Bubbling with personality, Elise was insightful and smart, and Giovanni enjoyed hearing her opinions about popular news stories, controversial issues and viral videos making the rounds on the internet.

His cell phone buzzed inside the pocket of his suit jacket, cuing him that he'd received new text messages. He decided to check them later. He thought of going to Rosario's office, to confide in her about his appointment with Dr. Kaddouri that afternoon, but he remembered she'd left the club at noon to catch a flight to Dallas to attend her husband's speaking engagement. If he'd been thinking straight when he'd left the clinic, he would have gone home instead of driving to the club. Standing, his legs felt weak, but he wandered over to the window and stared outside. Snowflakes were falling from the sky and the wind was howling.

In all his life, he couldn't recall ever feeling so low or hopeless, and the more Giovanni thought about his meeting with Dr. Kaddouri, the harder it was for him to find the silver lining.

Elise stood in the narrow, dimly lit hallway of the management wing of the polo club, unsure of what to do. Five minutes earlier, the front desk clerk had told her that Giovanni was in his office, but she'd knocked on the door several times with no luck. It didn't make any sense. Why would the clerk say Giovanni was in his office if he wasn't? Had he been toying with her? Did he know she had a crush on the dreamy polo player?

Over the last week, they'd seen each other daily, sometimes two or three times, and their conversations were often the highlight of her day. His quiet confidence drew her in, appealed to her in every way, but Elise wouldn't let history repeat itself. She loved talking with Giovanni, joking around and even flirting with him, but that was the extent of it. Elise didn't care how gorgeous he was, there'd be no more kissing or making out at the club. Cognizant of their attraction, she avoided touching him or going into the storage room whenever they were alone in the kitchen. It was hard to keep her eyes off of him, but Elise was determined to maintain her composure. Her future was at stake, and even though Giovanni was her type, she had to keep him at arm's length.

Yawning, Elise rubbed at her eyes then at the dull ache in the back of her neck. Officially off the clock and anxious to go home, she decided to send an email to the senior management team regarding her concerns about the upcoming Christmas events instead of waiting around for Giovanni to show up. She'd been at the club for fourteen hours, rushing from one end of the restaurant to the next preparing meals, supervising the staff and visiting with dinner guests. All she wanted now was a hot bath and a glass of wine. But Elise didn't move. She hadn't seen Giovanni all day or received one of his hilarious text messages and she didn't want to leave the club until they talked.

Leaning forward, Elise grabbed the gold knob, pressed her ear to the door and listened intently, blocking out the noises of the surrounding offices. She couldn't hear any sounds from inside the dark corner office, and wondered if Giovanni had fallen asleep at his desk. It wouldn't surprise her. He exercised in the fitness center before work, often during lunchtime and at the end of the day. And when he wasn't sprinting on the treadmill or lifting weights in his free time, he was in the barn, helping the staff care for the horses.

Elise turned the knob and the door opened. Peering inside the room, she smelled the faint scent of cologne and coffee. Bathed in darkness except for the twinkling city lights visible through the window, the office was cold and empty. Elise frowned. Or was it? Entering the room, she spotted a figure, back to her, sitting at the desk. She took her cell phone out of her back pocket, pressed the flashlight app and used it to light her way.

"Hi, Giovanni. Sorry to bother you, but Rosario's gone for the day and I need you to approve the menu for the Breakfast with Santa next Saturday so I can order the necessary supplies," she explained as she crossed the room.

The coral rug, modern furniture, potted bamboo plants and watercolor paintings on the ivory walls created a soothing space, but with each step, her trepidation grew.

A cell phone rang, filling the office with classical music, but Giovanni didn't answer it or respond to her question.

"Hello? Giovanni?" she said in a quiet voice. "It's me. Elise. Are you okay?"

Her question was met with silence. She called his name a second time, in a stronger, louder voice, but he didn't respond or acknowledge her presence.

Concerned, Elise turned on the floor lamp beside the bookshelf, came around the desk and rested a hand on his shoulder.

Studying his face, she noticed his empty gaze and lifeless disposition. He looked broken, crushed, and Elise suspected he was grieving the loss of a friend or family member.

She hated seeing him in pain and wanted to help, would do anything to make him smile again. "Giovanni, what is it? What's wrong?" she asked. "Talk to me."

He wiped at his eyes with the back of his hand then cleared his throat.

"You wouldn't understand," he grumbled, his voice gruff. "Just go."

"I've been told I'm a great listener who gives smart advice, so talk to me. Maybe I can help."

"You can't…no one can…my life is over…"

His words knocked the wind out of her. Was Giovanni sick? Had he been diagnosed with an incurable disease? Did he only have a few months to live? Refusing to think the worst, Elise wiped every troubling thought from her mind and rested a hand on his back. Hoping he'd confide in her, she leaned forward and inclined her head toward him.

The silence stretched on, but Elise remained close to his side, gently rubbing his shoulder. For a split second, she considered calling Rosario to tell her what was going on, but Rosario was out of town for the weekend, and Elise didn't want to worry her. It didn't matter how long it took, she'd convince Giovanni to open up to her. And if that didn't work, she'd contact his parents. Elise didn't want him to be alone, not in the state of mind he was in, and she wondered if she should reach out to Jonas, as well. The men were great friends. If anyone could cheer Giovanni up, it would be the loud, boisterous New Yorker who loved to crack jokes.

"I can't play polo anymore…"

His voice was so low Elise had to strain to hear what he was saying, but she listened closely.

"My doctor says it's too risky, that another concussion could cause irreversible damage and would significantly lower my quality of life," he explained, tugging at the knot in his tie.

Elise reached out and squeezed his hand. Giovanni was being forced to give up his career and her heart broke for him. At times, Elise still couldn't believe she'd landed the executive chef position at Vencedores, and couldn't imagine what she'd do if for some reason she was told she could never cook again.

"Giovanni, I'm so sorry to hear that. I know how much you enjoy playing polo, and how desperate you were to resume your career."

"What am I going to do now? Polo is everything to me. It's my life, my passion, my reason for living, and I'm nothing without it." His voice cracked, broke under the weight of his despair. "If I don't have my career, I have nothing."

"That's not true," Elise argued. "You're more than

just a polo player. You're a successful athlete and businessman, with an incredible wealth of knowledge, intelligence and insight, and you can do anything you set your mind to."

"I don't want to oversee the family business. I want to play polo."

"But that's no longer an option, so you could mentor up-and-coming players, develop new, intensive programs for the club, teach at camps or give private lessons."

Facing her, his gaze was dark and his lips were a thin line. "You make it sound so easy."

"Giovanni, I never said it was, and I'm not trying to minimize your feelings—"

"Good, because you have no idea what it's like to lose what you love most."

"You're wrong. I do…" Trailing off, Elise contemplated whether or not to share her personal story with Giovanni. Maybe if she told him about her loss and how she'd survived the worst time of her life, he wouldn't feel so hopeless or stare at her with disdain.

Feeling compelled to open up to him, Elise cleared her throat and wiped her damp palms along the sides of her gray dress pants. "My parents died in a train crash two years ago and I was devastated—inconsolable. Completely and utterly lost. For weeks, I couldn't get out of bed and, when I did, I got violently sick. I was a mess."

Giovanni's expression was sympathetic.

Elise dropped her gaze to her hands. Overcome with emotion, her throat closed up and her limbs trembled. She needed a moment to gather herself, to right her thoughts, and feared if she didn't, she'd crumble in front of Giovanni. Elise wanted to comfort him and she couldn't do that if she broke down in tears.

Unlike most people, he didn't pry or ask questions about the accident, and Elise was grateful. "I'm living proof that you can overcome life-changing setbacks and come through on the other side—strong, healthy and whole. Not a day goes by that I don't miss my parents and wish that they were alive, but instead of allowing my sadness to swallow me up, I make a conscious decision to face the day, come what may. It's what my parents would want me to do and, most important, it's what I want for myself."

He cringed, as if he'd just heard a spine-tingling scream. "You must think I'm a spoiled, self-absorbed athlete. I'm lamenting the loss of my career, complaining about how cruel and unfair life is, but that's nothing compared to what you've experienced. Elise, you have my deepest condolences."

Giovanni held her hand tight. He caressed her skin with his thumb, and tingles rippled across her flesh. Butterflies swarmed her stomach and Elise gulped. She had to be careful around him. Couldn't let her guard down, not even for a second. Not because she thought he'd take advantage of her, but because she feared she'd lose her composure again and kiss him passionately.

*Who is consoling whom?* Elise wondered, relishing the feel of his warm, soft touch. *I could stay here with you forever!*

"Elise, I'm in awe of you. You're the strongest and most resilient woman I know."

"We both are. If I can survive losing my parents, you can survive losing your career."

"You're right. I can."

"It doesn't matter how bad things get or how low you feel, because you'll always have your memories and they're more valuable than gold. They're treasured moments that will remain in your heart and mind forever." Elise smirked. "*And* on the internet, of course. I've watched some of your matches online and you should, too. They're incredible."

"And so are you."

At a loss for words, Elise didn't know what to say. They shared a long, meaningful look, and heat coursed through her body. He stared deeply into her eyes, as if he was searching her soul.

Scared her emotions would get the best of her and she'd pounce on him, Elise tore her gaze away from his mouth and stepped back. She couldn't risk embarrassing herself or losing her composure. Giovanni was exactly her type, and that was the problem. She liked his look, his confidence and how he carried himself, but she wanted someone to share her life with—not a Christmas fling—and she refused to settle for less than she deserved.

"Elise, I'm glad you stopped by," he confessed with a sad smile. "Your honesty was refreshing and just what I needed to hear, so thank you. I really appreciate it."

"Do you have plans tonight? Are you meeting up with Jonas later?"

"No, I'm heading home. I have a lot on my mind and I want to be alone."

"I'm free, too. We should hang out..." Elise tried to

sound casual, as if her invitation was no big deal, but her voice quavered and she let the words trail off. She didn't like the idea of Giovanni being alone, not after the devastating news he'd received from his doctor that afternoon, and decided to take him to one of her favorite spots in the Hamptons. "You need something to take your mind off your troubles. I know somewhere we can go that you'll love."

"Maybe another time. I feel like crap right now and I wouldn't be good company."

"I'm not asking you, Giovanni. I'm telling you. You're going and that's final."

He quirked an eyebrow. "Is that right?"

"It sure is!" Elise clasped his hand, dragged him to his feet and gestured to the door with a flick of her head. "Let's go. We've both had a long, stressful day, and I know the perfect place we can go to blow off steam for a couple hours."

Hope brightened his eyes and a devilish grin curled his lips. "Your condo?"

"You wish!" she quipped, patting his cheek good-naturedly. "Bring a change of clothes, because your tailored designer suit is all wrong for the activity we're doing. And hurry up! The clock's ticking."

"Yes, ma'am," he joked, saluting her with his right hand. "Anything else, Your Highness?"

"Meet me in the parking lot in ten minutes, or I'll come find you, and it *won't* be pretty."

Throwing his head back, Giovanni released a loud, hearty laugh.

Pride spread through her veins and a smile tickled her lips. Spinning around on her high heels, Elise marched through the office with a pep in her step, hoping her desire for Giovanni wouldn't get her into trouble—or cost her the best job she'd ever had.

# *Chapter 12*

Extreme Sports Dome was located along a deserted gravel road on the outskirts of the city, but the brown brick building was packed with so many thrill-seekers, college students and couples, Elise couldn't move without someone bumping into her. The venue was clean, the staff attentive, and the hip-hop music blaring on the sound system added to the lively atmosphere.

Elise watched Giovanni for a moment, marveling at his inner strength. Two hours ago, he was sitting in his darkened office agonizing about his future, and now he was cracking jokes with their instructor. Giovanni was in his element, enjoying himself immensely at the indoor activity center, and chatting with the polo fans who recognized him seemed to bolster his spirits. Arriving at the sports dome, they'd decided to play Black-

Ops laser tag, and the assistant manager had taken a selfie with them in their helmets, camouflage vests and matching headbands.

Black-Ops laser tag was the perfect activity for Giovanni. Fun and realistic, it had felt like they were in an actual battle. The game was so competitive and intense, Elise had been forced to take cover behind Giovanni several times to avoid enemy fire.

"Hold your ax at a ninety-degree angle, but make sure you have a firm, solid grip on it," instructed the assistant manager, demonstrating the correct technique.

Elise blinked, realized the instructor was staring at her expectantly, and moved to the solid white line. It was her turn to go and she was ready to kick butt. To score, she had to stick the ax in the wooden target and, even though Elise hadn't played Axes & Arrows in years, she was confident she'd win. Giovanni had beaten her at darts, Ping-Pong and billiards, and Elise wanted to give him a taste of his own medicine.

"You shouldn't even bother playing," Giovanni said, an amused expression on his face. "I've won every game tonight, and I'm going to win this one, too."

"Sticks and stones, Pretty Boy. Sticks and stones."

The men chuckled. Giovanni had an easygoing nature and a great sense of humor. From the moment they'd entered Extreme Sports Dome, he'd been making her laugh.

Elise picked up the ax. The instructor corrected her stance and gave her some helpful pointers. Narrowing her gaze, she envisioned herself hitting the bull's-eye square in the middle, and hurled the ax toward the target. It missed the board completely and Elise yelped.

"Say *one* word and I'm out of here," Elise warned, jabbing Giovanni in the shoulder with her index finger. "I'm serious, Giovanni. Not one word."

Raising his hands in the air, a devilish grin on his face, he shook his head vigorously. "I wouldn't dream of it. It's all love out here tonight. I'm cheering for you, Elise, not against you."

"Yeah, right, just like you lobbied for me to get the executive chef position at the club!"

His expression sobered. "You have to forgive me. Obviously, I wasn't thinking straight, because anyone who spends five minutes in your presence can see that you're a dynamic young woman who's as talented as she is beautiful."

"You can say *that* again!" she quipped, flipping her hair over her shoulders. "I'm *all* that!"

They shared a laugh. What surprised Elise most was how comfortable they were with each other. They'd talked about their backgrounds, their dreams and even their past relationships, though Elise didn't have much to say on the subject. Over the years, she'd been on numerous dates, but no one had ever swept her off her feet or captured her heart.

"This is key. Bring the ax over your head as if you're rebounding a basketball, then throw the ax with your arms extended forward," the instructor said. "Try again. You can do it."

Taking his advice, she took a deep breath, focused on her target and released the ax. It hit the bull's-eye and Elise screamed for joy. She gave the instructor a high five, winked at Giovanni, then grabbed another ax off the table. Her next three throws were kill shots and, by the time the game ended, she'd beat Giovanni by double digits.

"You won fair and square, so drinks are on me." Giovanni wrapped an arm around Elise's waist, pulled her close to his side and dropped his mouth to her ear. "Thanks for dragging me out of my office tonight. This is the most fun I've had in months, and you're the reason why."

"If this is the most fun you've had in months, then you need to get out more!"

Glancing at her cell phone, Elise was surprised to see it was nine o'clock. They'd been at the facility for three hours, but Elise wasn't ready to go home yet. She liked the idea of spending more time with Giovanni. They bought drinks and popcorn from the concession stand, then wandered around the complex, checking out the games and activities on the second floor.

Finding an empty bench at the entrance to the arcade, they sat to eat their snack. Men and women alike were gawking at Giovanni, and Elise didn't blame them. The polo star was a force, sexier than any cover model, and his voice was deep and husky.

Elise loved hearing Giovanni's stories about growing up in Argentina, the greatest moments of his decades-long polo career and his favorite vacation spots. Well versed in every subject, Giovanni was a man of deep feeling, who challenged her way of thinking. Time flew by as they chatted in the arcade. But what stood out most about Giovanni wasn't his dashing good looks, his dreamy voice or even his remarkable intelligence. It was how much he loved his family and wanted to please his parents. Elise had never met a man of his caliber before, and she was enamored with the charismatic polo star with the brilliant mind.

A shadow fell across Giovanni's face and he heaved a deep sigh.

Elise studied his profile, his furrowed eyebrows and clenched jaw, and suspected he was thinking about his doctor's appointment that afternoon. Giovanni was going through a rough time and Elise wanted to be there for him. "Giovanni, I know you're hurting right now, but you have to believe that things will get better and that your life will have meaning and purpose again."

Giovanni nodded but his frown deepened. "I wish that was true."

"It is. I'm living proof," she said firmly. "You will get through this. Have hope."

They sat in silence for a moment. She reached out to touch his shoulder then remembered what had happened the last time they'd touched. She hugged her arms to her chest instead. It didn't matter that she was weak for him, he was her boss, the heir to the Castillo empire, and she had to be smart around him, no matter what.

The sound of his low, solemn voice interrupted her thoughts.

"I've had numerous injuries during my career, but I never thought in a million years that my health would prevent me from playing the sport I love." He dragged a hand down his face then rubbed his neck. "And the timing couldn't be worse. I'm supposed to fly to Buenos Aires on December twenty-third to participate in a charity polo match for an organization I'm the official sponsor of. But after my conversation with my neurologist, I feel like canceling the trip."

"Why?" she asked, raising an eyebrow. "Are you afraid of getting hurt?"

"No. Of course not. It's a friendly match, and I've participated in the event for years."

"Then go, have fun and be careful." Elise winked. "And remember to bring me back a souvenir. FYI, I love malbec wine and gourmet chocolate."

Giovanni inclined his head to the side and stroked his chin. "You've definitely given me something to think about."

"You should go. You're the pride of Argentina, the Golden Boy, and I'd hate for you to disappoint your loyal, die-hard fans."

His stare was bold and his smile was broad. "Come with me."

"Sure! Sounds fun! When do we leave?" she asked, her voice dripping with sarcasm.

"Elise, you don't know what you're missing. Buenos Aires is one of my favorite cities in the world, and I'm not just saying that because I was born and raised there." His face brightened and his tone was full of excitement. "The architecture is striking, the neighborhoods are colorful and unique, the people are charming, the nightlife is stellar, and the food is second to none."

"Buenos Aires sounds like my kind of place, but you and I both know I can't go. I have to work. And, even if I didn't, I couldn't risk someone finding out about our trip and blabbing to Rosario about it."

"I understand, but start saving your vacation time. My birthday is in March, and I always travel home to celebrate with my friends and family. I'd love for you to come."

Elise inclined her head. Was he for real? Did he actually want to take her to Argentina in the spring? Or was he pulling her leg? She opened her mouth, realized she didn't know what to say in response, and slammed it shut. Her mind drifted back to the storage room, to the exact moment they'd kissed, and Elise wondered what would happen if they spent the weekend together in one of the most romantic cities in the world.

Conversation turned from the charity tournament to the club, and as Giovanni spoke about the dedicated staff, esteemed clientele and Rosario's ideas for the restaurant in the new year, Elise found herself agreeing with every word that came out of his mouth.

"All this talk about the restaurant is making me hungry. Let's go downtown and get something to eat." Giovanni hung his head and shielded his face with his left hand. "Damn, I hope she doesn't see me, or we'll never get out of here."

Elise glanced around the second floor, spotted a large bridal party exiting the Escape Room and wondered which of the young, attractive females Giovanni was hiding from. "Which one's your ex and why are you dodging her?"

"None of them, but I know one of the bridesmaids. Years ago, a friend set me up with Hannah Lacroix and, even though she has a sweet girl-next-door vibe, she turned out to be one of the craziest people I know."

A laugh exploded out of Elise's mouth, drawing the attention of everyone walking by, and she swallowed her giggles.

Giovanni folded his arms across his chest, as if he was pissed with her, but amusement gleamed in his eyes and the corners of his lips twitched. "Don't laugh at my pain, because I'm not the only one who's been on a disastrous blind date, so spill it. What's the worst date you've ever been on?"

"It wasn't a date." Elise shuddered at the memory of the terrifying encounter. "I went to a Fourth of July party with my girlfriends, and I met a charming Spanish guy with the most amazing sense of humor. We had drinks, danced and laughed all night."

"It sounds like you guys made an instant connection."

"I thought so, too, but he forced himself on me when we were alone in the media room."

Giovanni leaned forward in his seat. "That must have been terrifying for you."

"No," she said firmly. "It was terrifying for *him*."

Lines creased his forehead. "I don't understand."

"When I was a kid, my dad taught me how to defend myself against bullies, so when that drunken creep tried to kiss me, I kneed him so hard in the groin he dropped to the floor like a sack of potatoes."

His eyes were the size of golf balls. "You're kidding."

"No. He started it, but *I* finished it."

Giovanni whistled. "Remind me never to piss *you* off. You're a beast!"

"And as long as you're a perfect gentleman, we won't have any problems."

"Do you remember the guy's name? I want to talk to him, man to man."

"Unfortunately I don't, but that's a good thing because my bestie would have tracked him down and beaten him within an inch of his life. You think I'm tough? Well, Sariah is fierce."

"I'm glad you fought back and got away from him," he said, touching her hand with his own, his fingertips tenderly caressing her skin. "What you did took incredible strength and courage. Way to go, Elise."

Her breath caught in her throat. They were sitting so close on the bench their shoulders and legs were touching, and Elise liked feeling his body against hers. His cologne washed over her, weakening her resolve, and she moved closer to him on the bench. *Damn, his lips are sexy*, she thought, fixing her gaze on his mouth. *And they taste delicious.*

Elise wished she could turn back the hands of time. If she hadn't kissed Giovanni in the storage room, she wouldn't be craving his lips now. Mad at herself for wanting him, she struggled with conflicting emotions. One minute she was keeping Giovanni at arm's length and the next she was fantasizing about kissing him again—and more. She had to stop sending him mixed messages. Elise didn't want Giovanni to think she was a tease, or worse, toying with his feelings. She wasn't. Her mind and body were at odds, both battling to have their own way, and it was stressful.

"I've always been an honest, forthcoming person, and I'm not going to change who I am now." Giovanni squeezed her hand. "I promised myself I wouldn't pursue you, but I'm fighting a losing battle because the more I try to resist you, the stronger my desires are."

Elise stared at him with wide eyes.

"Can I kiss you?" he whispered, stroking her cheek with his thumb. "Please?"

Her inner voice shouted no, but she closed her eyes and pressed her lips to his mouth. Lust spiraled through her body, giving her an adrenaline rush. Elise was shocked by her boldness, couldn't believe she'd kissed him again after vowing not to.

*This is* so *wrong, but it feels* so *right!* Caught up in the moment, Elise ignored her doubts and enjoyed the pleasure of his kiss. Forgetting they were in a public place and could be spotted by someone they knew, Elise draped her arms around Giovanni's neck, pulling him even closer to her. She wouldn't be surprised if people were watching them, but she didn't care. *Is this actually happening? Are we actually making out in the arcade?*

"I can't help myself," he confessed in a low, throaty voice, his hands stroking her neck and shoulders. "One look is all it takes. One kiss and I'm a goner, Elise, unable to stop…"

Elise opened her eyes, her head so fuzzy she couldn't think straight or focus on what Giovanni was saying. All she knew was that she wanted to kiss him again. Taking a deep breath, she willed her thoughts to clear. She didn't know what to make of his confession, but sensed he was being honest with her, speaking from the heart.

Elise couldn't remember ever feeling this excited about someone and was tempted to throw caution to the wind and live out her fantasies with the devilishly handsome polo star. Hooking up with Giovanni could end up being the worst mistake of her life, or a thrilling adventure. She suspected it would be the latter.

"Your lips are my undoing, and your mouth is my new guilty pleasure."

"How do you know that for sure when you haven't tasted the rest of me?" The moment the quip left her mouth, Elise realized she'd verbalized her inner thoughts aloud and dodged his gaze.

"Let's get out of here before we really give the locals something to talk about," Giovanni said, brushing his chin against her cheek. "Come on. I'm taking you home."

# Chapter 13

"Watch your step." Giovanni led Elise into the dimly lit foyer of his sprawling bachelor pad, down the hallway and into the great room. It was surrounded by a wall of glass windows that offered breathtaking views of the city. Stars shone in the night sky, filling the space with an ambient glow, and colored lights twinkled in the distance. "Welcome to my humble abode."

Inhaling the fragrant scent in the air, Elise took in her luxe surroundings. The estate had a stone fireplace, ornate stone carvings, contemporary furniture and vaulted ceilings. But Elise was most impressed by the chef's kitchen. It had top-of-the-line appliances, a breakfast bar with cobalt-blue stools and gleaming dark wood. "Humble abode? No, you mean your fancy oceanfront mansion dripping in marble and gold that deserves a spread in *House Beautiful* magazine."

A broad grin fell across his mouth. "So you like it? I'm glad. I decorated it myself."

"*Like* is an understatement!" Elise enthused, spreading her hands out at her sides. "This is the house of my dreams, and when I grow up I'm going to get one just like it."

Giovanni chuckled. "If you think this place is nice, wait until you see my villa in Buenos Aires. It has a heated pool, a home theater, a state-of-the-art gym and a steam room."

"Show-off!" Elise quipped. "And I thought you were a sweet, humble guy."

"I am," he conceded. "And to prove it, I'm making you dinner tonight."

"Or you could give me a tour of this stunning estate and tell me more about your work for SOS Children's Villages and your upcoming charity match in Buenos Aires," Elise proposed.

"As you wish." Giovanni strode over to the granite bar, selected a bottle from the top shelf and filled two flutes with the dark, sweet-smelling liquid. Smiling, he crossed the room and offered one of the glasses to Elise. "Try this. It's my favorite Argentinian wine."

Taking a sip, she nodded in appreciation. "It's fruity and rich," she said, savoring the refreshing taste. "It's got a kick to it, and I like the spicy flavor."

"Now that we have our drinks, let the tour begin!"

Elise followed Giovanni through the main floor, listening closely as he disclosed personal details about his estate. She'd expected to see pictures of his polo matches, his trophies and championships prominently displayed throughout the mansion, but the souvenirs from his world travels were front and center, not his awards. The estate, decorated with designer furnishings, mercury-glass lamps and South American–themed art, had a tranquil ambience.

Upstairs in the media room was the largest TV Elise had ever seen, along with a foosball table. The walls were covered from top to bottom with framed portraits. Standing on her tiptoes, Elise peered at the picture of a young, bright-eyed boy on a raised stage. He was clutching a trophy in his hands. "You won a spelling bee?" Elise tapped the black-and-white photograph with an index finger. "Wow, I never would have guessed it."

"Why? Because athletes are all brawn and no brains?"

"No, because you're a sports fanatic whose game room is filled with autographed jerseys and World Cup–themed soccer balls, not Oxford dictionaries." Elise studied his face. "What word did you have to spell to win the competition?"

"Discombobulated." He grinned. "And that's how I feel every time you look at me."

Smirking, Elise patted his shoulder. "I feel for you, man. Stay strong!"

They laughed together. Her cell phone rang but she decided to leave it inside her back pocket. She didn't want anyone to infringe on her time with Giovanni, and made a mental note to check her messages later.

Admiring the other images on the wall, Elise asked about the people in the photographs, when they were taken and the unique, exotic locations.

Giovanni spoke about his parents and sisters in a jovial tone, but his gaze fell across pictures taken at a family reunion years earlier and his face darkened. From the outside looking in, Giovanni seemed to have it all, but he confessed that relatives had betrayed him in the past, fracturing their relationship. He acted as if it were no big deal, said it was one of the downsides of being rich, but Elise disagreed with him. It didn't matter that he was a star athlete with millions of dollars in the bank; he deserved to be treated with respect, not like a human ATM.

They exited the media room, but Giovanni's confession weighed heavily on Elise's mind as they entered the master suite. It had plush drapes and bedding, a bronze console table and bench, velvet club chairs and a platform bed dressed with monogrammed cushions and pillows. A mini-fridge was beside the entertainment unit, and the air smelled of amaretto liquor. "So *this* is party central," Elise teased, smirking. "You must entertain in here a lot."

"My bedroom is my sanctuary, my private escape from the world, and very few people have seen these four walls."

Her cheeks burned with fire. "Giovanni, I'm sorry. I was kidding. I wasn't trying to imply that you're a player with a revolving bedroom door."

"Contrary to what you think, my world is quite small," he confessed with a sad smile.

Giovanni gestured to the ivory sofa in front of the window and they sat.

"For decades, people have tried using me for financial gain, which makes it hard for me to trust," he explained. "Every woman I meet always seems to have an agenda—"

"I don't." Elise felt compelled to defend herself and wanted Giovanni to know he'd never have to worry about her using him or asking for favors. "You looked like you could use a friend tonight, and now that I've gotten to know you better, I can see that you're a great guy."

"Maybe we're not destined to be friends. Maybe we're destined to be lovers."

Her heart stalled. Elise was flattered by his attention, but nothing mattered more to her than being the executive chef at the Hamptons Polo Club; she wasn't going to risk her future for a Christmas fling. "We've discussed this several times, and my perspective hasn't changed."

"It should," he said in a smooth voice. "I don't know if you've noticed, but I'm dreamy."

Elise refused to be distracted by his dimpled grin. "I can't lose my job. I know I've only been at the club for a few weeks, but I love being the executive chef of Vencedores, and I don't want to do anything to jeopardize my position."

"I'll talk to Rosario. Don't worry. You won't be fired. She thinks you're incredible."

"No. Don't! Please don't say anything to her about us," Elise begged, clutching his forearm. "I don't want Rosario to know I like you."

A frown curled his lips. "Why? What's wrong with me?"

"You mean besides the fact that you're a spoiled, entitled athlete who's utterly ridiculous?" she teased, flashing an innocent smile.

"Yeah, besides that." Blinking uncontrollably, Giovanni pointed a finger at his face. "It's my lazy eye, isn't it? I knew it. I *really* should get that fixed before we hook up."

Tossing her head back, Elise cracked up.

"You have the best laugh," he praised in an awe-filled voice. "It's full and rich and loud, and one of the happiest sounds I've ever heard."

"Are we going to spend the rest of the night discussing my many admirable traits, or make out on this gorgeous designer couch?" Elise asked, playfully batting her eyelashes.

"I love the way you think."

"And I love the way you taste, so shut up and kiss me."

"With pleasure."

Inclining her head, her eyes fluttered closed as she waited impatiently for his kiss. Giovanni pressed his lips to her mouth and Elise inched closer to him on the couch. Resting a hand on his chest, her thoughts scattered and a moan rose in her throat.

"No one has to know we're lovers. It'll be our little secret," he whispered against her lips between kisses. "We'll take it one day at a time. No pressure."

Elise remained quiet. It was a challenge, but she restrained herself from devouring his mouth and ripping his clothes off.

"I've wanted you from the moment you walked into the restaurant looking like a beautiful ray of sunshine. So please don't deny me the pleasure of making love to you tonight."

The silence was profound. For several seconds, Elise

mulled over her options. Doubts flooded her mind and her confidence waned. *Will Giovanni like my body? Will I please him? How will I measure up to the other women he's hooked up with?* It was hard to concentrate, impossible to think clearly when Giovanni was kissing and caressing her skin. The truth was, she didn't want to deny her feelings for him anymore. Maybe he was right. Maybe they could have a Christmas fling and no one would ever have to know.

"My career is everything to me, Giovanni, and I don't want to lose the best job I've ever had. Promise me you won't tell anyone about us. No one at all. Not even your friends."

"You have my word." He cupped her face in his hands and spoke in a firm tone. "You can trust me, Elise. I won't betray your trust."

His words were sweet music to her ears. Desire consumed her, temporarily blinding her judgment, and Elise kissed him with a ferocity she didn't even know she had. Making out with Giovanni gave her a high she'd never experienced before. Their clothes were a barrier, a nuisance Elise wanted gone, and she envisioned herself stripping him naked. At the thought, her mouth dried. Worried she'd scare him off by being too aggressive, she cautioned herself to relax.

Sucking the tip of his tongue into her mouth, she caressed his chest through his shirt. The moment they'd left Extreme Sports Dome and climbed into Giovanni's SUV, she knew they'd end up making love—even though she'd been in denial—but Elise had never dreamed it would be like this. She was desperate for him. Ravenous. Consumed with desire. Out of control—and each passionate French kiss intensified her need.

They rose from the couch and stumbled through the suite, the glow of the crescent moon lighting the path to the bed. They shed their clothes then stretched out on the silk sheets. Elise licked his lips and sucked the tip of his tongue as she caressed the length of his face. She took out the elastic band in his ponytail and his thick hair fell around his shoulders, tickling her skin.

Giovanni blew in her ear, and Elise shrieked with laughter. She was high. Giddy. In a playful and goofy mood. From the day they'd met, she'd been fighting her feelings for him, but not tonight. Giovanni was a catch, the kind of man women dreamed about meeting, and Elise was crazy about him. There was no denying the truth: she desired him more than anything and she didn't have the power to resist him anymore.

"You're gorgeous," he praised, tenderly caressing her hips with his hands.

"I know, right?" Giggling, she touched his chest. His muscles had muscles and his strong, toned body was a masterpiece—one she wanted to enjoy for the rest of the night. "You're the one with the *Sports Illustrated* cover body, not me."

Giovanni stared deep into her eyes and the intensity of his gaze took her breath away.

"Pleasing you is all that matters to me, so don't be afraid to tell me what you need…"

*Oh, wow*, she thought, stunned by his words and the vulnerability in his voice. *He really is a dream come true!* Giovanni acted as if she was a bombshell, the most desirable woman in the world, and his compliments gave her a mind-blowing rush.

Giovanni yanked open the top drawer on the side table, grabbed a gold packet and ripped it open. Kissing her passionately, his tongue stimulated her mouth and aroused her flesh. Elise moaned. Her skin was on fire, tingling uncontrollably. Locking eyes with him, she felt her body come alive as he positioned his erection between her legs. They'd reached the point of no return, but doubts still crowded her mind. *Stop stressing*, she thought, giving herself a much-needed pep talk. *You're beautiful and sexy and vivacious, so get out of your head and go with the flow!*

"Open up wide," he whispered against her ear, his voice a throaty growl.

Eager to please, Elise spread the lips between her legs with one hand, and used the other to guide his erection inside her. His kiss pleased her and his slow grind thrilled her flesh. In the past, she'd never had a great appetite for sex, had often joked that she could live without it, but hooking up with Giovanni had proved otherwise. She was desperate for him, didn't want their lovemaking to ever end, and his penetration was so deep, Elise saw the sun, the moon and the stars. *It's true what they say*, Elise thought, clamping her legs possessively around his toned waist. *A hard man is good to find!*

Their lovemaking was passionate and playful, everything Elise wanted and more. They were in sync, connected by mind, body and soul. They took their time pleasing each other, savored every moment. Giovanni was confident in the bedroom, knew exactly what she wanted and needed, and Elise couldn't have asked for a more thoughtful lover. She felt as if she was walking on water, floating in the sky, and hoped her feet never touched the ground.

Wanting Giovanni to know how much she desired him, Elise rolled on top of him, gripped his shoulders and lowered herself onto his erection. A moan fell from her mouth as his length filled her sex. Goose bumps tickled her skin, flooded her spine. Her body was shaking, but there was nothing Elise could do to stop it.

On top, she had the freedom to do whatever she wanted, and she did—she played with his hair, tweaked his nipples, sucked his earlobes. Rocking her hips back and forth, Elise grabbed his hands and used them to cup her breasts, then pushed her nipples into his open mouth. Her hair was glued to her face and neck, but Elise had never been happier.

"Harder. Faster. Yeah, that's it," he growled, clutching her hips.

Elise increased her pace, vigorously pumping her legs. She loved being on top, relished being in control, but her excitement was short-lived. An orgasm seized her body and her climax was so powerful Elise collapsed onto his chest, her mind reeling.

"That was incredible," he acclaimed in an awe-filled voice, stroking her hair.

Elise took a moment to catch her breath. Their lovemaking had exceeded her wildest dreams, and even though her legs were sore, she was ready for round two.

She raised her head, met his gaze, then kissed his lips. "Of course it was. You're Giovanni Castillo, the sexiest polo player alive, and you aim to please!"

"Now I *really* want you to come with me to Argentina for my birthday. Imagine all the fun we'll have in my beautiful hometown. *And* at my secluded villa."

"What makes you think we'll still be lovers in March?" she asked, turning his words over in her mind. "That's three months away. Anything can happen between now and then."

Giovanni cupped her chin, forcing her to look at him. "We will be. There's no doubt in my mind. I have a feeling I'll never have my fill of you, and that suits me just fine..."

*Me, too! I could stay with you like this forever!*

He kissed her forehead, her cheeks and the tip of her nose, making her feel cherished and adored. It was a surreal moment. She'd fantasized about making love to him since they'd kissed in the storage room, and Elise was shocked that it had actually happened—still couldn't believe she was lying in his arms.

Sighing in contentment, she closed her eyes and nestled her head against his chest, hoping their sizzling secret fling survived the Christmas holidays.

# Chapter 14

Elise rolled onto her side, pulled the quilted duvet cover over her head and sniffed the air. Her stomach growled, and if Elise wasn't naked, she would have ventured downstairs to the kitchen for something to eat. Opening her eyes, she squinted at the blinding light inside the master suite. The open drapes allowed sunshine to stream into the room through the windows, and the scenic view made Elise feel relaxed.

Elise buried her nose in the thick, fluffy blanket. She heard the wind howling, the unmistakable buzz of a snowblower, and wondered how many inches of snow had been dumped on the city overnight. It was another cold winter day. If Elise didn't have to teach her weekly cooking class at the East Hampton Senior Center at four o'clock, she wouldn't leave the comfort of the bed. Just the thought of venturing outside made her teeth chatter. At Giovanni's instance last night, she'd left her Honda at the polo club so they could drive together to Extreme Sports Dome in his SUV and she hoped no one had noticed her vehicle parked at the property overnight and grown suspicious.

"Shoot! I forgot the maple syrup and the napkins..."

Hearing Giovanni's voice, Elise inclined her head and frowned in confusion. *He's here? But earlier, after we made love for the second time, he told me he was going to the polo club to check on the horses but said he'd be back by lunchtime.*

Peeking out from the underneath the blanket, she glanced over her shoulder and spotted Giovanni standing in the middle of the room, typing on his phone. Her heart fluttered at the sight of him. Stylishly dressed in a black crew-neck T-shirt, athletic pants and suede slippers, Giovanni oozed masculinity and the stubble on his jaw gave him a rugged bad-boy vibe.

Her eyes widened. The round wooden table was set with crisp linens; the decorative glass vase was filled with pink roses; and her favorite breakfast foods were laid out. None of the men Elise had dated in the past had ever cooked for her before, and she was floored by Giovanni's thoughtful romantic gesture.

Elise listened to his every move. She heard Giovanni exit the bedroom then jog down the staircase, and she sprang into action. Tossing the blanket aside, Elise surged to her feet and dashed into the bathroom. Flicking on the light, she noticed a pink Post-it note on the mirror and ripped it off the glass. Elise read the note and the smile in her heart exploded across her mouth.

*I hope you slept well. Everything you need is in the wicker basket.*

Overcome with emotion, Elise held the note to her chest. Giovanni's aftershave lingered in the air and she inhaled the refreshing scent. Curious to see what he'd left for her, she peeked into the oversize basket on the limestone countertop. Elise gasped then cupped a hand over her mouth. He'd thought of everything—toiletries, perfume, a change of clothes, undergarments and even a pair of slippers—and she was pleased by the contents in the basket.

A troubling thought came to mind, stealing her happiness. Where had Giovanni gotten the items from? Did they belong to his ex-wife? A lump wedged in her throat. Questions crowded her thoughts. Elise wanted to know what had gone wrong in Giovanni's marriage, but he was still reeling from the results of his doctor's appointment yesterday and she didn't want to add to his stress by pressuring him to talk about one of the worst times in his life.

Elise gave her head a shake. She'd had an incredible night with Giovanni, and she didn't want to ruin the mood by acting jealous and insecure. R&B music was playing in the bedroom and hearing the popular Bruno Mars song brightened her mood.

Brushing her teeth, she glanced around the spa-inspired bathroom and admired the decor. Clean, modern and awash with sunlight, it had metallic wallpaper, a stone shower stall, a Persian carpet, and the bronze horse sculptures gave the space a touch of class.

Anxious to see Giovanni, she took a quick shower, got dressed and pulled her damp hair up into a bun.

Elise opened the door just in time to see Giovanni do the Cupid Shuffle across the bedroom floor. Amused, she whistled and cheered. "You're handsome, you're charming *and* you dance? Wow, you weren't kidding. You really *are* the total package."

"Told you," he said with a nod and a proud smile. "But you wouldn't believe me."

Approaching him, Elise batted her lashes. "Do you blame me? I'm an innocent Southern girl who's never met a famous athlete before, and I was starstruck."

"Innocent my ass. You wore me out last night!" Chuckling, Giovanni pulled her into his arms and caressed her shoulders. "How did you sleep?"

"Wonderfully. I had the most delicious dream."

A grin dimpled his cheeks. "Is that right? I didn't realize dreams could be delicious."

"They are when I dream about you."

Lowering his face to hers, Giovanni kissed her lips. He took his time ravishing her mouth, acted as if it was his greatest joy. Her heart sighed. She was a twenty-nine-year-old woman who'd traveled all over the world, experiencing thrilling adventures in exotic countries, but there was nothing better than being with Giovanni. His kiss gave her a dizzying rush. Standing in the middle of the bedroom, flirting and kissing, Elise realized one night with the polo star wasn't going to be enough. He made her laugh out loud; they had similar hobbies and interests; and his kisses left her weak. Last night had been one of the happiest moments of her life and she'd never forget how special Giovanni had made her feel as they'd made love.

A hunger pang stabbed her stomach. Elise was starving, but she didn't want to leave the comfort of Giovanni's arms. She wanted to spend the rest of the day with him, chatting and hanging out at his gorgeous estate, but she didn't want to cancel her cooking class at the nursing home. She looked forward to seeing the participants every month and was confident the seniors would have fun making and decorating sugar cookies that afternoon. "What an elaborate spread," she said, peering over his shoulder at the round table. "What did you make?"

"Brunch for my beautiful, sexy houseguest."

"Brunch?" Elise repeated. "How late is it?"

Giovanni reached into the pocket of his pants, retrieved his phone and raised it in the air.

Her eyes flew open and her jaw dropped. She hadn't checked her cell phone since they'd left Extreme Sports Dome last night, didn't even remember where it was, but if she didn't text her girlfriends soon, they'd panic, and Elise didn't want to worry them. "I can't believe it's eleven forty-five! I should have been up hours ago. Why did you let me sleep so late?"

"Because you work seventy hours a week and it was obvious you needed your rest."

"Where did you get these clothes from?" she blurted out. "Did they belong to your ex?"

"No, of course not." Giovanni tightened his hold around her waist. "I had to run to the grocery store to grab some things for our brunch, and since Impulse

Boutique is nearby, I decided to go in and look around. Do you like the jumpsuit?"

Elise released the breath she was holding. "Yes. Thanks, Giovanni. I love it."

They sat on the couch. Sipping her orange juice, Elise was reminded of how they'd fooled around on the love seat the night before and smiled at the memory of their frisky make-out session.

Elise ate two bowls of fruit, then filled her plate. Beside her, Giovanni discussed his early-morning trip to the polo club and the stormy weather.

Elise tasted a garlic-cheese biscuit and chewed slowly. It was moist and flavorful, and familiar somehow. Staring down at it, she furrowed her eyebrows. Giovanni must have seen her confused expression because he leaned in close and draped an arm around her shoulder.

"What's wrong?" he asked in a concerned tone. "You don't like it?"

A smirk curled her lips. "Of course I do. It's my recipe."

He dodged her gaze, but he had the nerve to wear a boyish smile on his lips. "Elise, what are you talking about? I made everything from scratch this morning."

"Liar," she quipped, poking him in the shoulder with an index finger. "You didn't make this. These biscuits came from By the Bay. And don't try to deny it, because I worked there for five years and these garlic-cheese biscuits are one of *my* recipes."

Elise tasted everything on her plate, realized Giovanni had tricked her and rolled her eyes. "You ordered this food from By the Bay, put it on fancy plates and tried to pass it off as your own, but you're not fooling anyone, Giovanni. I'm on to you."

He picked up a piece of sausage, broke it in two and popped it into his mouth.

"Are you purposely trying to deceive me?" she asked, propping her hands on her hips.

"Absolutely! I want you to think I'm an amazing guy, which I am, so I bought brunch from your favorite restaurant and tried to pass the food off as my own. Brilliant, right?"

Swallowing a laugh, Elise shook her head. "No, but you get an A for effort."

While they ate, they talked about the upcoming holiday events at the polo club, their favorite Christmas memories and their plans for the rest of the weekend. His cell phone rang, then chimed repeatedly, but Giovanni didn't answer it. He asked about her formative years in Charlotte and what she missed most about her hometown. Opening up to him about her background, Elise felt as if she could tell Giovanni anything, and didn't feel compelled to sugarcoat her past, even though they'd only known each other for a few weeks. In turn, he told her about his past relationships, how he'd met his ex-wife, Marisol, and why they'd eloped to Niagara Falls on her thirtieth birthday.

Her food forgotten, Elise put down her fork, and moved closer to him on the couch. His confession about his marriage stunned her. Marisol had been his personal assistant and although their family and friends had been against them dating, Giovanni had pursued her anyway. Elise let him talk without interruption, even though she was burning to ask him questions about his ex.

"I'd never dated one of my employees before, but Marisol seemed to have my best interests at heart and I trusted her implicitly..."

Elise couldn't relate but she nodded in understanding. She'd never been madly in love, or met someone she could be her true, authentic self with. Giovanni was the first person she'd confided in besides her girlfriends about her disastrous dating history. And the more she admired his handsome profile, the more Giovanni looked like the man of her dreams.

"Marisol never loved me," he said, staring down at his hands, his jaw clenched tight. "It was all an act. All she ever really cared about was being Mrs. Giovanni Castillo, meeting A-list celebrities and spending my money faster than I could earn it."

"What makes you think that? Was it something she did, or just a feeling?"

"All of the above." His face was sour and bitterness seeped into his voice. "I collided with another player during the US Open Polo Championships in Miami last summer, and suffered a vestibular concussion that landed me in the hospital for nine days."

"That sounds like a frightening ordeal."

"It was. I was in excruciating pain and, for weeks, I felt as if I were in a fog." Closing his eyes as if to block out the bitter memories, he dragged a hand down the length of his face. "I've never been so sick in my life, and if my mom and sisters hadn't traveled to South Beach and nursed me back to health, I might not be here today."

Elise didn't want to reopen old wounds, but she burned with curiosity and asked the questions at the forefront of her mind. "Where was Marisol? She was your wife, the one you'd committed your life to. Why wasn't she there for you in your time of need?"

Giovanni grabbed the remote off the table and lowered the volume on the stereo system. "Marisol claimed she had to work, that her movie-star client needed her on the set of her film in Hong Kong, but it was obvious she didn't want to be around me while I was sick, and that hurt."

"Is that why your marriage ended? Because your ex-wife chose her career over you?"

"Among other things, such as her selfishness and her inability to acknowledge her mistakes. I wasn't a perfect husband, but our marriage was my top priority. It wasn't for Marisol."

*If you were my man, I'd put you first, no matter what, and you'd never have to worry about playing second fiddle to my career or anything else.*

Silence descended on the suite, amplifying the noises outside. Elise could hear tires screeching, dogs barking and the chug of a snowplow, and wished she'd driven her car to Giovanni's estate last night instead of leaving it at the polo club. It was probably buried under ten feet of wet, heavy snow, and just the thought of digging it out made Elise groan inwardly.

"In the Argentinian culture, divorce is still frowned upon, so I did everything in my power to make my marriage work. I suggested counseling, and even a three-week couples retreat in Vermont where we could fix our problems, but Marisol refused."

Elise fixed a blank expression on her face but her mind was blown. Spinning faster than a ceiling fan. Some women have it all and don't even realize it, she thought, shaking her head in disbelief. Giovanni's confession made her think hard about her future and what she desired most, and it wasn't having a fat bank account. She'd never been madly and desperately in love, but wanted to be. *Marriage is forever, a lifelong commitment, and if I'm ever lucky enough to find my soul mate and walk down the aisle, I'll cherish my husband all the days of his life.*

"Three days before Christmas, Marisol rented a U-Haul, packed up her things and moved out." His eyes were sad and his shoulders were bent. "I was shocked and confused and begged her to stay, but Marisol said she didn't love me anymore and wanted a fresh start."

To comfort him, Elise touched his hair and stroked his neck. He spoke and the anguish in his voice took her by surprise.

"How do you fall out of love with someone after only three years of marriage?" He heaved a sigh. "Sometimes I just can't catch a break. I lost my health, my wife and now my career, and it's the worst feeling in the world."

Choosing her words carefully, she took a deep breath then spoke from the heart.

"I'm sorry about your recent setbacks, but you have to put the past behind you and move on," she said, hoping he'd give her advice some serious thought. "Sometimes life isn't fair, but you're strong enough and brave enough to not only weather the storms, but overcome them."

A pensive expression filled his face and he slowly nodded.

"Giovanni, no minute or breath or moment is promised, so make the most of each day. Cherish the people you love, do what brings you joy and embrace every adventure."

"Thanks for the reminder. I needed to hear that."

"No worries. I'll send you my bill in the mail."

They shared a laugh and the color returned to his cheeks, brightening his skin tone.

"Elise, you're as beautiful as you are wise, and I think the world of you."

He took her hand in his, lowered his head and kissed her palm. Tingles rocked her spine.

"And you're the sexiest houseguest I've ever had..."

His cell phone buzzed on the table and Elise glanced down at the screen. Narrowing her gaze, she stared at the clock, shocked to see that it was already two thirty. They'd been eating and chatting for hours, and she was enjoying his company, but Elise had to leave. She wanted to be at the nursing home on time for her cooking class and worried that, if she didn't leave Giovanni's estate within the hour, she'd be late and would disappoint her students.

Working fast, Elise piled the silverware onto the wooden tray, picked it up and rose to her feet. "You made brunch, so it's only fair I clean up," she said, a smile on her face. "I'll meet you in the kitchen."

Standing, a devilish grin lit up his eyes. "I'd rather meet you in bed."

An explicit image popped into Elise's mind. She pictured Giovanni naked, handcuffed to the headboard, and struggled to breathe. And when he crushed his mouth to hers, the room spun around her. He tasted sweet, of syrup and strawberries, and Elise enjoyed kissing his lips. Remembering her schedule, she reluctantly ended the kiss and backed away from the couch. "Come on, Loverboy." Elise beckoned him to follow her with a toss of her head. "If we work together, we can have the kitchen cleaned faster than you can say malbec!"

Carrying the wooden tray, Elise exited the bedroom and walked downstairs and into the kitchen. Giovanni joined her at the sink and helped load the stainless-steel dishwasher. While they worked, he entertained her with stories about his family members and the most embarrassing moments of his polo career, and Elise laughed hysterically.

Being with Giovanni was easy, effortless, the most natural thing in the world. Her personal life had never been as successful as her professional life, but Elise was hopeful about her relationship with Giovanni. She believed him when he said they were a perfect match, and she boldly flirted with him as they cleaned the kitchen. Spending the night at his estate had not only strengthened their bond, but also enhanced their sexual chemistry. Elise couldn't look at him without thinking about making love—on the marble counter, against the fridge, in the pantry—and wondered if Giovanni had sex on the brain, too.

Elise noticed her purse at the foot of the leather armchair and sighed in relief. Eager to retrieve it so she could check her phone for missed calls and messages, she marched through the kitchen, but Giovanni caught her arm and pulled her to his chest.

"Where are you rushing off to?"

"I know it's freezing outside," she said, relishing the feel of his touch against her skin. "But I need you to drop me off at the polo club to retrieve my car."

"Why? I thought we were spending the rest of the day together."

"I told you I'm teaching a cooking class at the Hamptons nursing home at four o'clock this afternoon."

Giovanni shook his head. "No, you didn't."

"Yes, I did," Elise countered. "I mentioned it last night at Extreme Sports Dome—"

"That was *before* we made love."

"Why does it matter?"

"Because now we're one."

"You're corny," she teased, though his words touched her heart.

"Yeah, corny for you."

"And to think, a month ago you couldn't stand me."

Giovanni shook his head. "That's not true. I liked you a lot. That was the problem."

Picking her up off the ground, he put her down on the breakfast bar and draped his arms around her waist. In a playful mood, she clamped her legs around his, pulling him toward her.

"You can't leave. I have a romantic date planned for us that you don't want to miss. We're going ice-skating at Southampton Ice Rink. Afterward, we'll have dinner at the Palm, then cap off the night with drinks at my favorite lounge. The drinks are fantastic, the service is top-notch and the live jazz band is outstanding."

"It sounds amazing, Giovanni. Can I take a rain check?"

He shook his head. "No. Sorry. It's a one-night-only offer."

Trying hard not to laugh, Elise rested her hands on his shoulders and met his gaze. "Fine, come to my cooking class, and we'll go skating when it's finished."

A grin brightened his face. "Sounds like a plan. I'm in."

"Seriously?" she asked, bewildered by his enthusiasm. "You'll come to the nursing home?"

"Of course. I love seniors and they love me!"

Cracking up, Elise watched as he admired his profile in the stainless-steel microwave.

"Paige and Sariah both said I should model professionally, and I think they might be onto something," he continued. "I don't know if you've noticed, but I'm sexy as hell."

His comment jogged her memory and Elise snapped her fingers. Her girlfriends had been mum when she'd asked them about their lengthy conversation with Giovanni at the Holiday Cocktail Party, and bribing them with peppermint-candy-cane brownies hadn't helped Elise uncover the truth. "I saw you chatting with them at the cocktail party. What did you guys talk about?"

Shrugging a shoulder, he scratched at his cheek. "You know, this and that."

"No, I don't know. That's why I'm asking you for answers," she said, dying to know what the trio had discussed at the event. "Did they mention me? Did they ask you tons of personal questions? Did they tell you that I have an enormous crush on you?"

He wore an innocent expression on his face. "I'll never tell."

"Oh, really? We'll see about that." Feeling bold, she slid her hands under his shirt and stroked his chest. She craved him, desired every inch of him, and loved the idea of having her way with Giovanni in his swanky kitchen. The thought shocked her. Twenty-four hours ago, she'd been dead-set against hooking up with him, and now it was all Elise could think about. All she wanted.

She absolutely adored him. He was a man of incredible strength and vulnerability, but his playfulness was one of his greatest traits. Pressing her mouth against his ear, she tweaked his nipples with her fingertips. "I have a feeling after I have my way with you on this breakfast bar, you'll be singing a *very* different tune."

"I sure hope so." Giovanni took off his shirt, tossed it to the floor then dived on top of her. "There's only one way to find out, so let the games begin!"

# Chapter 15

The pastries at Espresso & Confections were so beautifully displayed in decorative cases in the front window that Elise didn't want to touch them, let alone eat them. It was known as the coolest bakery in the Hamptons, and locals flocked to the establishment in droves to satisfy their chocolate cravings. Every morning, people lined up down the street and around the block for a seat in the small, quaint bakery, and Elise noticed several famous faces signing autographs as Giovanni led her into the shop on Sunday evening. For weeks they'd been inseparable, and Elise was proud to be on his arm. A savory aroma wafted through the air from the kitchen, and although Elise had finished a scrumptious seven-course meal at a nearby French restaurant minutes earlier, her mouth watered for dessert.

Entering the private room, Elise was impressed by the upscale decor. The silk-draped ceiling, vibrant murals painted on the cobalt walls, dainty glass tables and oversize flower arrangements added to the charm. Classical music played, candlelight flickered and the sultry ambience created a sensual mood.

"Where do you want to sit?" Giovanni asked, glancing at her. "Do you have a preference?"

"I want to be as close to Johanna as possible, so let's grab a table at the front of the room."

He wiggled his eyebrows. "*Someone* has a crush."

"Sure do!" Giggling, she nodded fervently. "Johanna Schumacher is the Beyoncé of the baking world, and I just hope I don't faint when I meet her!"

"Don't worry. If you do, I'll catch you."

Giovanni pulled out a chair at table one and when Elise sat, he rubbed her shoulders. Her limbs relaxed and her heart smiled. Giovanni was the most attentive and affectionate man she'd ever dated. He gave her hugs and kisses when she least expected it, and loved to hold hands. These days, Elise was less concerned about her colleagues finding out she was dating Giovanni and more concerned about pleasing him.

The past two weeks had been a whirlwind, filled with nonstop action, but Elise had never been happier. Not only did she have breakfast with Giovanni every morning at the restaurant, he took her on a date every evening after work.

Elise never knew what to expect. One night they'd go to a musical or a Broadway show; another day they'd go for drinks and a long scenic drive, or play squash at one of the indoor gyms. Yesterday, they'd attended a live taping of *The Rachael Ray Show* and meeting the celebrity chef had been the highlight of Elise's week.

Each date was an adventure, something new, different and exciting, and her appreciation for Giovanni had grown since their first kiss. He brought out the best in her, made her smile and laugh out loud, and Elise cherished every moment they spent together. A great listener, he always seemed interested in what she had to say, which made her feel comfortable with him.

It was hard to believe there was a time when they'd disliked each other, because these days they were inseparable. When they weren't hanging out, they were texting, and his messages about their lovemaking always put Elise in an amorous mood—like right now. Giovanni was caressing her shoulders, but she wished he was caressing her breasts instead.

"Welcome to Espresso & Confections." A server appeared and placed two champagne flutes on the table. "The chocolate tasting with Ms. Schumacher will begin at seven o'clock sharp, so please enjoy a complimentary glass of Bollinger while you wait."

"You don't have to tell me twice," Giovanni joked with a grin. "Keep them coming."

Elise felt like royalty, sitting on the plush velvet chair laced in gold, sipping from a crystal glass, and she resisted the urge to pinch herself. Life was wonderful, better than it had been in years. She had Giovanni, supportive friends, good health and the best job in the world. The hours were long, the pressure was high, but Elise enjoyed working at Vencedores and wanted to be the executive chef of the award-winning restaurant for many years to come.

"This time next week, you'll be in Buenos Aires with your family for Christmas," she pointed out, crossing her legs under the table. "Are you excited?"

"Yeah. I'm looking forward to seeing my sisters and getting some sun, because I'm sick of the cold." Giovanni tasted his champagne. "What have you decided? Are you going to Charlotte for the holidays or staying here?"

"I'm not sure what I'm doing yet, but I still have a few days to decide."

"Come with me to Argentina for Christmas and celebrate the holiday in style."

"You know I can't. During dinner, you mentioned that your parents, Rosario and her husband, and several other relatives are traveling with you to Buenos Aires on the Castillo private plane on Friday, and I don't want to be the odd one out," she said, toying with the gemstone pendant on her silver chain.

"Elise, you won't be, and my family would be thrilled if you spent Christmas Day with us, especially Rosario. I don't know if you've noticed, but my sister adores you. She thinks you're the best thing that's ever happened to the polo club."

"Smart woman! I *knew* there was a reason I liked her." Leaning into him, Elise snuggled against his shoulder and entwined her fingers with his. "You've planned a lot of incredible dates for us, but this chocolate tasting event is my favorite so far."

"How do you know that for sure? It hasn't even started yet."

"I know, but I'm a huge Johanna Schumacher fan and I'm so excited I could scream!"

"Please don't. It's a serious-looking crowd in here, and I don't want us to get kicked out."

"Really? I'm surprised. I figured you'd rather go home to bed."

"Damn right I would, because there's nothing better than making love to you." Giovanni kissed her forehead and affectionately squeezed her hands. "I love that you know me so well."

*And I love your smile, your humility, your thoughtfulness and your tender caress.*

"We've been so busy today, I forgot to tell you that I got tickets to John Legend's '*A Legendary Christmas* at Madison Square Garden' on New Year's Eve."

Elise squealed. Realizing everyone in the room was staring at her, she clamped her lips together to trap the noise inside her mouth. Beaming with joy, she threw her arms around his neck and held him tight. Before Elise could stop herself, she was kissing him. Passionately. Giovanni made her feel special, and his thoughtfulness never ceased to amaze her. She had an insatiable appetite for him, and even though they were in a popular bakery, she couldn't keep her hands off of him.

Electricity crackled in the air and the scent of their desire filled the room. Elise couldn't believe she was French-kissing Giovanni in public, but she couldn't stop, desperately wanted to convey everything that was in her heart through her kiss. He made her want to dance around the room, and if she wasn't afraid of someone capturing the moment with their cell phone and posting it online, Elise would have burst into song.

"I take it you're pleased," he said with a boyish grin.

"*Very* pleased. I wanted to see the concert last year, but Sariah couldn't get us tickets."

"The concert starts at eight o'clock, but let's leave the Hamptons by four so we can grab dinner before the show starts. There are lots of restaurants near the arena to choose from."

Elise wore an apologetic smile. "I cook with Sariah's brother on Wednesdays, remember? We're usually done by five, but I'll try to finish earlier so we're not late for the concert."

The sound of boisterous laughter drew her gaze to the table behind them. The young, fashionably dressed females were making eyes at Giovanni, but he didn't seem to notice them.

"Elise, you work too much."

"Tell me something I *don't* know," she said with a shrug and a laugh.

His frown deepened. "Baby, I'm serious. When you're not at the restaurant, you're teaching cooking classes, testing out new recipes at home or baking care packages for friends. You're pushing yourself too hard and I'm worried about your jam-packed schedule."

A searing pain gripped her heart. Dropping her gaze to her lap, she swallowed hard to alleviate the lump in her throat, and wrung her hands. Elise loved the hustle and bustle of the holiday season, welcomed the chaos. If she filled every minute of the day with work and activities, she wouldn't have to think about her loss, the sadness that consumed her every time she remembered her amazing parents. "What?" she argued, feeling the need to defend herself. "I like to keep busy.

Why is that a problem? Everyone has their vice, and mine is cooking."

"Have you ever heard the expression all work and no play makes Elise a dull girl?"

A smirk curled her lips. "No, because you just made it up!"

They laughed. Elise tried to change the subject by asking him about his upcoming trip to Argentina, but Giovanni interrupted her.

"A wise, insightful woman from Charlotte recently reminded me that no minute or breath is promised, and to make the most of each day. She admonished me to cherish the people I love, to do what brings me joy and to embrace every adventure."

Hearing Giovanni repeat her mother's favorite quote made her heart smile and, for a split second, she wondered if he could be "the one." It was an outrageous thought, considering they'd only known each other for a few weeks, but she couldn't fight her feelings.

In many ways, Giovanni reminded her of her dad, and she'd always wanted to marry someone with integrity, morals and an unwavering commitment to their family. In all the years her parents had been married, she'd never seen her father lose his cool, or heard him yell at her mom, and she wanted a loving, respectful relationship like the one her parents had had.

"Elise, you mean the world to me, and I want a future with you," Giovanni whispered against her lips, cupping her chin in his hand. "But I can't cherish you if you run yourself ragged, so promise me you'll slow down in the new year."

His confession took her by surprise. It was one of

the nicest things anyone had ever said to her, and his words brought tears to her eyes. His opinion mattered to her, and she didn't want to ever disappoint him, but Elise didn't want to change her schedule. She was afraid of having too much time on her hands and worried about being alone with her thoughts. Struggling to free the truth from her mouth, she wiped at her eyes with an index finger.

Taking a moment to collect her thoughts, she finished her champagne. Someone in the room cackled, a cell phone played country music and a server dropped her empty tray.

"I work a lot so I won't think about my parents," she confessed, willing herself not to cry. "Because when I do, I fall apart."

"Elise, you lost your parents, and you have every right to mourn their loss. Do whatever you need to do to feel better, and whenever you need a shoulder to cry on, call me and I'll be there."

Elise had no words, and when Giovanni kissed her lips, she smiled through her tears.


"I'm the founder of Espresso & Confections and head chocolatier, Johanna Schumacher, and I promise you this will be a memorable event. Before we start, let's discuss the ground rules…"

Giovanni glanced at Elise, realized she was taking notes on her Christmas-themed napkin and draped an arm around the back of her chair. Blocking out the noises in the room, he listened intently to the frizzy-haired brunette. She spoke with a thick German accent, and he wished there were subtitles on the projector because he struggled to understand her. It didn't matter; Elise was his focus, not learning about where chocolate was grown, produced and processed. Elise had been a great support system for him since his last doctor's appointment, and when he'd learned about the chocolate tasting session at Espresso & Confections, he'd immediately signed them up. Giovanni wanted Elise to know how much he appreciated her, and he'd do anything to please her, including sitting through a ninety-minute class about chocolate.

Squinting, Giovanni crossed his legs at the ankles. He guessed Ms. Schumacher was in her fifties, but she had the fashion sense of Nicki Minaj, and even though she was wearing a crisp white smock over her printed sweater dress, the color of her outfit hurt his eyes.

"Sampling high-quality chocolate is an experience like no other, so I highly recommend you put away your phones, clear your mind of every stress and focus on this unique, wonderful moment," she continued, her eyes bright with excitement. "To start, my staff are bringing you a serving tray with three of our most popular flavors at Espresso & Confections, a bowl of apple wedges and a cup of water to cleanse your palate."

Giovanni choked down a laugh. The chocolatier spoke in a theatrical voice that made him think of his high school drama teacher, and she gestured wildly with her hands, as if fending off a swarm of killer bees.

"Now, let's begin." Ms. Schumacher raised an index finger in the air. "First, you must look at the chocolate. Is it smooth? Does it have a radiant sheen? Next, you must smell the chocolate. What is the aroma? Does it engage the senses? Are you aroused?"

*I'm always aroused when I'm with Elise!*

Giovanni's gaze strayed to Elise and a grin claimed his mouth. He'd never met a more vivacious, energetic woman. It didn't matter how tired or how busy Elise was, she always found time to brighten someone else's day. She didn't know anything about horses, but she helped him with his chores in the barn every week, and every morning she left pastries and hot apple cider in the staff room for employees to enjoy.

"This is the most important step," Johanna announced. "Place the chocolate carefully on your tongue, close your eyes and wait for that rich, scrumptious morsel to melt."

Giovanni leaned forward in his seat. He watched Elise smell a piece of thin, dark chocolate, then put it in her mouth. His erection throbbed inside his pants. He had an insatiable appetite for Elise; he wanted her every second of every day and was addicted to her moist, lush lips. When they were apart, he thought of ways to please her, and enjoyed planning dates that encompassed all of her favorite things.

Though he was having doubts about their trip to the mountains. Maybe they should stay home and rest. Elise needed a break, and he liked the idea of pampering her for seventy-two hours. Since the night they'd made love at his estate, they'd seen each other every night, which was a challenge with her extreme workload. Besides his father, he'd never met anyone who worked as hard as Elise did, and Giovanni worried she was pushing herself beyond her limits.

She was an all-out go-getter, with a fierce drive to succeed, and he was awed by her ambition. Elise was feminine and sexy, but she wasn't afraid to kick butt if she had to, and often did. Giovanni wanted to protect her and take care of her, even though he knew she could handle herself. He'd shared his concerns with Elise about her full schedule, and she'd promised to cut back, but Giovanni had to see it to believe it.

"Remember to cleanse your palate with an apple wedge and water," Ms. Schumacher instructed through her headset, circling the room. "Take the time to savor and enjoy every bite, because there's nothing better than gourmet chocolate."

Glancing around the room, Giovanni spotted his neurologist at one of the tables to his right and waved. "Dr. Kaddouri, what are you doing here? Shouldn't you be at home reading medical reports?" he joked with a grin.

Dr. Kaddouri gestured to the rail-thin woman beside him. "I wish, but my wife, Reyna, loves this bakery, and threatened me with bodily harm if I didn't bring her to this chocolate tasting class. What's your excuse?"

"I wanted to impress my girlfriend, and I think it worked."

"I was right. You are a smart young man who makes good choices."

Ms. Schumacher returned to her post, clapped her hands and called for quiet.

"Happy holidays, son, and all the best in the new year," Dr. Kaddouri said.

"Likewise, Dr. Kaddouri. Enjoy the rest of the class."

Giovanni turned his attention back to Elise. *She's my girlfriend, my everything, and I'm tired of sneak-*

*ing around with her. I want the world to know she's my lady.*

He hated keeping secrets from his family, especially Rosario. Yesterday, during their executive lunch meeting, he'd almost told her about his relationship with Elise, but he'd stopped himself from blurting out the truth. They'd agreed to keep their relationship under wraps until they knew what they wanted, but Giovanni didn't need more time to figure things out. He wanted Elise and only Elise, and he wanted the world to know that they were a committed couple.

A text from Esteban popped up on Giovanni's phone. He held his cell phone under the table to read his cousin's message. Esteban wanted to have dinner at the polo club tomorrow night, but Giovanni had a special surprise for Elise after she finished her shift at the restaurant and he didn't want to cancel their plans.

"Oh, my, this sea-salt-flavored chocolate is everything," she gushed, resting a hand on her chest, as if overcome with emotion. "You have to try it. It's a bite of heaven."

Elise waved a square under his nose and then pushed it past his lips. Chewing slowly, he inclined his head then nodded. "It's good, but I'd rather *lick you*."

His gaze closed in on her mouth and she anticipated his next move because she braced her hands against his chest and spoke in a stern no-nonsense voice.

"And you will, *after* the tasting class, so slow your roll, baby."

His erection stabbed his zipper, as if begging to be released, and desire singed his skin. Giovanni understood why they couldn't sneak away for a quickie, but her words didn't cool the fire burning within him, they intensified it.

When they returned to his SUV at the end of the night, Giovanni pulled Elise inside and made love to her until he was spent.

# Chapter 16

The fancy light fixtures in the women's washroom at the Hamptons Polo Club were harsh and unforgiving, and as Elise washed her hands in the sink, she gawked at her reflection in the mirror. Stunned by her appearance, she noticed the dark circles under her eyes and her weary disposition. She'd been at Vencedores for twelve hours—preparing meals, training the new staff, doing purchase orders and socializing with patrons—and fatigue showed on her face.

*That's what I get for staying up late with Giovanni,* she thought, remembering their romantic date twenty-four hours earlier. *I'm exhausted now, but it was totally worth it!*

Last night, she'd invited him over for dinner and after their delicious Mexican meal and flavored rum, they'd stretched out on the living room couch to relax. But instead of watching their favorite telenovela on TV, they'd made love then cuddled in each other's arms. They'd talked about the Christmas holidays, his upcoming trip to Argentina and their future as a couple. His honesty had taken her by surprise. He'd confessed that he was tired of them sneaking around and wanted to tell his family they were dating.

Panic had seized her heart, filling her with dread. Elise was afraid of what Rosario's reaction would be to the news, and had asked Giovanni to wait until the new year. His body had tensed and silence had descended upon the room. Elise must have dozed off, because when she woke up, sunshine was streaming through the windows and she had twenty minutes to get to the polo club for her shift. A quick shower, a kiss for Giovanni, and she was out the front door of her condo, dashing down the snow-covered steps.

Peering at her reflection in the mirror, Elise considered her future. Until meeting Giovanni, she'd never considered settling down in the Hamptons permanently. Her plan had always been to work for a few years, gain experience, then return to Charlotte and open a Creole restaurant. But now that her parents were gone, her desire to return to her hometown had waned. Giovanni was the most romantic man on the face of the planet— an old-school gentleman who put her on a pedestal— and Elise adored him. She'd never expected to find love at the Hamptons Polo Club, but she'd fallen hard for Giovanni and couldn't imagine her life without him.

On more than one occasion, while they were making love, she'd been overwhelmed by her emotions and the words *I love you* had consumed her mind. Each time, she'd buried the truth in her heart. Elise didn't know how she'd feel if she bared her soul to Giovanni and he rejected her. More important, she didn't want to spook him. Elise wanted their relationship to flourish, not fizzle out.

Wanting to look great for their date that evening, Elise unzipped her chain-link purse, opened her over-size makeup case and searched for her gold compact powder. They were going to Bay Street Theater & Sag Harbor Center for the Arts to see a Christmas musical, and Elise wanted to look great on Giovanni's arm.

Her cell phone rang, filling the washroom with the unmistakable sound of Adele's powerhouse voice. Excited to speak to Paige, Elise retrieved her phone from the pocket of her black polka-dot dress and greeted her friend. "Hey, girl, what's up?" she said, cradling her cell between her ear and shoulder. "Sorry I didn't text you back earlier, but the restaurant's been crazy-busy all day and I never had a moment to myself. We had a private brunch this morning, the cast of *Dating in the City* dropped in for lunch, and we had a catered business meeting, as well."

"I know you're probably exhausted, so I won't keep you. I just wanted to know if I can bring a date to your ugly Christmas sweater party next Friday," she said in an animated tone. "Last week at the salon, I met a gorgeous Austrian stuntman who practically worships the ground my Jimmy Choos walk on, and I want the gang to meet him."

"Sorry, Paige, no guys allowed." Elise dabbed the powder puff into the loose powder, then rubbed it across her face. Every year, she hosted a party at her condo, and she couldn't wait for her friends to see the surprises she had in store for them next Friday. "It's girls' night, remember? Absolutely no men, no babies and no dates."

"That's not fair," she whined, sounding like a nine-year-old girl. "Giovanni will be there."

"No, he won't. He's leaving with his family for Argentina the day after tomorrow and, even if he was in town, I wouldn't invite him to my party. It's all about spoiling my girls."

Paige scoffed. "Yeah, right. You're all talk. These days you and Giovanni are practically joined at the hip. So much so, it feels like I haven't seen you in months."

"The ugly sweater party is in less than a week," she pointed out, adding a second coat of mascara to her eyelashes. "We'll catch up then. I promise."

"Or you could have lunch with me and Konstantin at East Hampton Grill tomorrow at noon," she proposed. "I *really* want you to meet him, and tell me what you think of us as a couple. Please say you'll come. It'll be my treat."

Elise heaved a deep sigh, drumming her fingernails on the counter. She wanted to be a supportive friend whom Paige could count on, but she'd promised Giovanni she'd start taking better care of herself instead of trying to be everything to everyone, and had planned to rest at home tomorrow.

Since the chocolate tasting session two weeks earlier, she'd stopped working overtime at the restaurant, reduced the cooking classes she taught at the nursing home and had attended Sariah's yoga class, as well.

And whenever grief overwhelmed her, she'd talk to Giovanni or journal about her feelings. Yesterday, she'd bought a first-class plane ticket to Charlotte, and although Elise was nervous about returning to her childhood home for the holidays, she was excited to see her relatives. Her parents were gone, but she loved her city, and baking pastries for her old friends and neighbors was a great way to spread holiday cheer—and honor her parents' legacy.

"Paige, I can't," she said, hoping her friend didn't get mad at her. "Maybe the three of us can get together in the new year."

"You have big plans with your polo star tomorrow, don't you?"

"Nope. I have big plans with myself!" Elise said with a laugh. "I've been going nonstop for weeks, and if I don't slow down and make time to recharge my batteries, I'm worried I won't make it to Christmas in one piece."

Elise reapplied her red matte lipstick and then sprayed Dior J'Adore perfume on her neck.

"I understand, and I'm proud of you for putting yourself first for once. You deserve some R&R, *and* that smokin' hot Argentinian, too. So, girl, do him until it hurts."

Unable to contain her laughter, Elise shrieked and giggled at her friend's joke.

The bathroom door opened and a mother of two hustled her daughters into the accessible stall and locked it. Elise pulled her phone away from her ear to check the time and gasped. Not wanting to be late to meet Giovanni, she tossed her makeup case back into her purse and then brushed the knots out of her hair. Pleased with her appearance, Elise beamed at her reflection. Just the thought of seeing Giovanni excited her.

"I was thinking about your party..." Paige continued. "We should do something wild to spice things up..."

The smile slid off Elise's face. Turned off by her girlfriend's outrageous suggestions, she fervently shook her head. "Paige, forget it. I don't want exotic dancers at my party."

"You're no fun."

"And you're out of control," Elise shot back.

"Leave everything to me. It'll be my Christmas gift to you!" Her shrill laugh was loud enough to shatter a window. "I need to make some calls. Talk to you later!"

"Paige, I'm serious. Do not hire strippers for my holiday party." Exiting the bathroom, Elise hustled down the corridor, admonishing her mischievous best friend in a firm voice. "My coworkers will be there, and I don't want them to think less of me."

Her comment was met with silence and Elise realized her soon-to-be-*ex* best friend had hung up on her. Stopping abruptly, she took a deep breath and counted to ten. It didn't help. Wanting to set her bestie straight, Elise punched in Paige's cell number and waited impatiently for her to answer. The call went straight to voice mail. Even though Elise was fuming, she spoke in a calm voice and reiterated her wishes in her message. Hanging up, she unzipped her purse and dropped her phone inside.

"Damn, ma, you got a nice rack and a fat, juicy ass, too..."

Elise wrinkled her nose. Disgusted by the stranger's words, she glanced to her right and regarded the short, stocky jerk in the black sunglasses. "Excuse me?"

"No, gorgeous, excuse *me*," he said, winking.

He reeked of whiskey and Cuban cigars, and his rancid odor made her stomach churn.

"I'm drooling like a dog, but don't hold it against me. Your curves are everything, ma."

The word *ma* echoed in her thoughts, tickling her memory. There was something familiar about him, leading her to believe she'd met him before, but Elise couldn't remember where. Was he a friend of a friend? Had they been introduced to each other at the restaurant?

"I'm Esteban." He took off his sunglasses, stuck an arm in the front of his button-down shirt and slowly licked his lips. "We should hook up sometime, so slide me your number, ma."

Esteban looked straight into her eyes and something in her mind clicked. It was him. The guy who'd attacked her at the Fourth of July party. A lump formed in the back of her throat. Struggling to breathe, she cautioned herself to stay strong, willed herself not to fall apart in front of the man she loathed.

A cold chill flooded the corridor. It felt as if the walls were closing in on her; the knot in her chest was suffocating. She wanted to yell at him, to tell him how his actions had changed her forever, but the words didn't come. Forcing her legs to move, she backed away from him.

"Wait! Where are you rushing off to? You didn't give me your number, gorgeous."

Esteban seized her hand and flashbacks of the Fourth of July party popped into her mind, chilling her to the bone. Before Elise could stop herself, she slapped him so hard in the face a sharp pain stabbed her wrist. Eyes wide, he touched his cheek with his palm.

"What's the matter with you? Are you insane?" he roared.

Elise gathered herself, projecting confidence, not fear, even though she was shaking. Esteban had been no match for her five months ago and he was no match for her today. He looked dazed and confused, as if he were seeing stars, and stared at her in bewilderment. They stood in silence, glaring at each other for what felt like an eternity. Her thoughts grew dark and dangerous. *I* wish *looks could kill, because you'd be toast!*

"You're lucky I'm a gentleman," he snarled.

"And you're lucky I forgot my stun gun in my other purse."

Esteban stepped forward, his gaze dark with anger. Elise raised a fist in the air. "Touch me again and it will be the last thing you *ever* do—"

"Elise? Esteban? What's going on?"

Hearing a familiar voice, Elise dropped her hands to her sides and peered over Esteban's hunched shoulders. Her heart stalled. Rosario wasn't alone. Giovanni was standing behind her, his arms folded across his chest. The anguished expression on his face pierced her heart. How much had he heard? What had he seen? Was he mad at her for losing her temper with a guest? Panic seized her. Would Rosario fire her for her unprofessional behavior at the club?

"She's loco," Esteban said, raising an index finger to his temple and making circles.

"And you're a sexual predator!"

"Elise! Stop it right now. That's enough." Adjusting his silk pin-striped tie, Giovanni glanced around the corridor, nodding and smiling at everyone who passed them in the hallway.

A biracial woman in a frilly party dress openly stared at them. Had she overheard their conversation? Did she recognize Giovanni? Was she going to tweet about what she'd heard?

"Everyone, follow me. We're resolving this issue right now."

Leading the way, Giovanni escorted Elise through the corridor, past the front desk and into his office.

Elise wanted to crash through the emergency exit, but her parents had raised her to be brave, not a coward, and she wanted to tell Giovanni and Rosario her side of the story. Her gut feeling was that they'd believe her. Comforted by her thoughts, she entered Giovanni's office and stopped beside the leather couch—the one they'd made love on three days earlier. He'd used his teeth to take off her panties, had pleasured her with his tongue, lips and hands, and the moment their bodies had come together as one, fireworks had exploded behind her eyes.

"Why are you threatening my cousin?" Giovanni asked, fine lines wrinkling his forehead.

"The chick did more than just threaten me. She slapped me, too," Esteban confessed.

"Elise, you can't go around hitting people for no reason." There was a note of anger in Rosario's voice and her posture was stiff. "This is a place of business, not a wrestling ring, and I won't let you tarnish this club's outstanding reputation."

Inhaling sharply, Elise rested a hand on her chest to slow her erratic pulse. *Cousin?* she repeated in her mind, her gaze darting between the two men. *You guys are related? How is that possible? You're smart, sophisticated and urbane, and Esteban's a snake.*

Elise swallowed hard. It felt as if someone were holding her head underwater. She couldn't get enough oxygen into her lungs, and feared she'd pass out on the plush beige carpet. Taking several deep breaths, her mind cleared, her shoulders relaxed and her confidence returned.

"Your *cousin* forced himself on me five months ago, and he tried to do it again tonight," she explained. "I apologize for losing my temper, but I wasn't going to let him disrespect me."

Esteban sneered like the villain in a horror movie, but Elise didn't flinch, held her ground.

"You lying trick. I wasn't even in the Hamptons last summer. I was in the Cyclades islands."

"I met you at a Fourth of July party in South Hampton," Elise continued, trying to recall everything he'd said that fateful night. "You told me you were an entrepreneur whose family owned a winery in Mendoza, and you bragged about partying on Diddy's yacht days earlier."

A cell phone rang, shattering the silence, but no one moved. For a long moment Elise inwardly pleaded with Giovanni to look at her, but he stared at his cousin instead. She wondered what he was thinking. "You attacked me—"

"That never happened. I never laid eyes on you before tonight," he argued, interrupting her midsentence. "You have me confused with someone else, so check your facts, ma."

Elise narrowed her gaze. She couldn't remember her attacker's name, but she remembered the sound of his voice, the stench of alcohol and nicotine on his breath, and Elise was a hundred percent sure that it was Esteban. "I don't need to check my facts. You tried to force yourself on me, but I fought back and won."

"I'm out of here." Esteban marched over to the door, yanked it open and fled the office.

Giovanni and Rosario shared a look and Elise didn't know what to make of it. She opened her mouth to defend herself, but Rosario interrupted her and Elise swallowed her words.

"I want to meet with you in the restaurant first thing tomorrow morning." Rosario pinned her shoulders back and tugged at the bottom of her navy blazer. "In the meantime, please don't discuss what happened tonight with the other staff. It would be unprofessional and also detrimental to your position here as executive chef. It's a private matter and, regardless of how you feel about my cousin, you must continue to uphold the integrity of the club."

Too choked up to speak, Elise simply nodded in response. Rosario left, and it took everything in her not to run into Giovanni's arms and bury her face in his chest. Her mind was in turmoil, filled with a hundred conflicting thoughts, and she wanted him to comfort her. But he didn't. He couldn't meet her gaze and suddenly seemed incredibly interested in the canvas paintings hanging above the couch. Until that moment, Elise thought she knew who Giovanni was. He'd always made her feel safe, special, as if she meant the world to him—but if he cared about her, he would have supported her, not bailed on her when she needed him most.

"It's late," he announced in a solemn tone. "I'll walk you to your car."

Her spirits plunged to her feet. "We're not going to the theater to see the Christmas musical tonight?"

"In light of what just happened, I don't think it's wise. You should go home."

Elise read the look in his eyes and what she saw made anger course through her veins.

"You don't believe me. You think I'm lying. You're mad at me."

"I don't know what to think, because none of this makes sense. Esteban would never do the things you're accusing him of. He's just not that guy." Hanging his head, Giovanni rubbed at his eyes with his fingertips. "You have the wrong person, Elise. My cousin didn't attack you."

"Yes. He. Did. But I'm not going to argue with you about the most traumatic experience of my life, because *you* weren't there." Elise stepped past him and headed for the door. Remembering all the good times they'd shared, she stopped in the doorway and glanced over her shoulder. "Have a safe trip to Argentina and a great Christmas with your family."

"I'll call you on Christmas Day—"

"Please don't," she said in a firm voice. "It was foolish of us to embark on a romantic relationship and, going forward, I think it's best if we don't talk or see each other outside of work."

"Are you sure that's what you want?"

*No. I want you to fight for me. For us. I want you to believe me!* Her mind flashed back to the first time they'd kissed, and her heart shattered into a million pieces, but she didn't crumble in despair.

Elise thought hard before she answered his question, didn't want her emotions to get the best of her when she spoke. Just the thought of being without Giovanni made her tear up, but she wasn't going to let him hurt her again. "Yes, it is. I'm already in trouble with Rosario for slapping Esteban, and if she finds out we're lovers, she'll fire me."

"Do you care about anything besides work or is that all that matters to you?"

"Giovanni, that's not fair," she shot back, whipping around to face him. "You were born with every advantage in life, with the best of everything money could buy, but I wasn't."

He started to argue, to refute her claim, but she raised a hand in the air to silence him.

"For as long as I can remember, I've worked tirelessly to prove myself to teachers, administrators, then to my instructors in culinary school," Elise continued.

A sympathetic expression covered his face, but she finished her thought.

"I've had to contend with sexist bosses and racist colleagues who despised me just because of my skin color, so forgive me for putting my career first. I've dreamed of being an executive chef since I was sweeping floors at my aunt Lucinda's restaurant at ten years old, and I won't lose the best job I've ever had."

Marching out of the office with Giovanni hot on her heels, Elise willed herself to maintain her composure. In the lobby she heard animated voices, laughter and conversation, and forced a smile as she breezed past a well-known Italian businessman.

Elise increased her pace. Spotting Demi and Chase posing for a picture in front of the Christmas tree, she hoped the parents-to-be didn't see her, and shielded her face with her hands. They were a shining example of what a healthy relationship should look like. Seeing them together only made Elise feel worse about her argument with Giovanni.

"Text me when you get home so I know you arrived safely," Giovanni said.

"Don't hold your breath," she grumbled, exiting the club through the sliding-glass doors. Flinging her shawl over her shoulders, Elise braced herself against the bitter wind as she dashed through the parking lot.

Inside the safety of her car, Elise collapsed into the driver's seat, dropped her face into her cold, chilled hands and let the tears fall.

# Chapter 17

"Only two more minutes left in regulation," said the sports commentator from his seat along the sidelines at the Buenos Aires Polo Association. "Do Giovanni Castillo and his team, the Four Kings, have what it takes to win a fifth straight title, or is their spectacular winning streak about to come to an end?"

*Over my dead body!* Giovanni decided, shooting across the field on his horse. The charity polo match for SOS Children's Village didn't have a monetary prize, but it was a sold-out event, attended by the Who's Who of Argentinian royalty, and he was determined to win the silver trophy for his team. The club had been closed to the public for the exclusive event, and the thrilling atmosphere, glasses of sparkling champagne and A-list guests added to the glamorous ambience.

Sweat dripped into his eyes. Roasting in his helmet, jersey, riding pants and boots, Giovanni wiped at his forehead with his sleeve. He steered the horse around the other competitors, struck the small, hard ball with his wooden mallet and then chased it down. Out of the corner of his eye, he spotted Beatriz, Josefa and Soledad near the goalposts, waving wildly, and couldn't help but smile at his kid sisters. He didn't see his parents or Rosario on the grounds, but he guessed they were eating, drinking and socializing inside one of the white VIP tents.

He focused his gaze on the ball, zeroing in on it. He'd scored five of his team's seven goals, but it wasn't enough. The game was tied, and if he wanted the Four Kings to be crowned the champs, he had to dig deep, push himself harder than he ever had before. It was the sixth and final period and time was running out. As team captain, he was expected to do it all—score, defend, strategize and dominate—and he had, but Giovanni had to find a way to do more.

A bell sounded, cuing the players that there were only thirty seconds left in the game. Giovanni shifted into high gear. Leaning forward, he tugged on the horse's reins and vigorously pumped his legs. Desperate to win the match, he blocked a defender's shot and stole the ball. He struck it with all his strength. It soared in the sky, through the goalpost, and dropped onto the grass. Giovanni pumped his fist in the air and the crowd went wild.

Galloping the length of the field, he celebrated the win with his teammates. He reveled in the victory, taking a moment to soak it all in. After the charity tournament ended, he'd treat them to dinner in the VIP lounge and share his retirement news. Every year, he gave Joaquin, Pedro and Emanuel a hefty Christmas bonus, and Giovanni hoped the check would soothe any hard feelings. Still, he worried about how his teammates would receive the news. Would they understand? Would they be supportive? Or would they curse him out? Giovanni cringed at the thought. He couldn't handle anyone else being mad at him, and wanted his final polo tournament to end on a positive note.

The sky was radiant and a warm breeze blew across the field as Giovanni climbed down from his horse. He took off his helmet and tucked it under his forearm, petted the pony's coat and kissed the top of its head. Then, taking the towel out of his back pocket, he cleaned his face and neck.

Guests sipped champagne and nibbled on Beluga caviar and mini sandwiches, and the aroma wafting in the air made his mouth water. He wanted to find his family and celebrate his win Castillo style, but event organizers escorted the Four Kings to the middle of the field for the ceremony. The trophy was presented by a famous girls' group known for their catchy songs and skintight costumes, and when the quartet gathered around Giovanni and showered his face with kisses, he froze. The only woman he wanted in his arms was Elise; he had no desire to flirt with the young, brazen pop stars from Mar del Plata. Scared his emotions would get the best of him, he took a deep breath and shook his head to clear his mind.

Giovanni swallowed a yawn. He posed for so many pictures his jaw ached and his legs fell asleep, but he didn't complain. He didn't want his teammates, his fans or the event organizers to think he was a spoiled, ungrateful athlete, so he suffered in silence. Millions of dollars had been raised for a worthy, life-changing organization for which he was proud to be the celebrity ambassador.

"Oh, my goodness, Gio, you were amazing!"

Recognizing Beatriz's voice, he excused himself from the group then hugged his sisters. He led them across the field and into one of the VIP tents. His gaze searched the crowd. He'd expected to see Esteban at his final polo match, but his cousin hadn't yet put in an appearance. He'd called and texted him for days, but he hadn't heard back.

Giovanni hated to think Esteban was ignoring him, especially after he'd vehemently defended his name to Elise, but his gut feeling was that his cousin was avoiding him and Giovanni was disappointed in his behavior.

Guests approached him, requesting selfies, autographs and hugs, and Giovanni granted every request. He'd had a career most athletes only dreamed of, and he appreciated his fans.

"You were a beast out there," Josefa declared, taking the seat beside him. "Yay, Gio!"

Soledad fanned her face with a napkin. "Did you hear me cheering out there? I screamed so loud, I gave myself a headache!"

Giovanni chuckled. "Not bad for an old, washed-up athlete, huh?"

"Oh, stop," Rosario drawled, joining her siblings at the round table. "Just because you can't play polo professionally anymore doesn't mean you're washed up.

You're embarking on an exciting new chapter of your life, and it's a thrilling, wonderful time."

He smoothed a hand over the top of his ponytail. "You sound like Elise."

"You're fortunate to have such a smart, insightful girlfriend," Rosario said.

Giovani nearly choked on his tongue. His sisters all spoke at once, wanting to know who his new mystery lady was, and Rosario had the nerve to wink at him.

"Gio has a BAE? No way! What does she look like? Is she Spanish?" Beatriz asked.

Josefa glanced up from her phone. "Let's check out her online profile. What's her name?"

"Elise Jennings," Rosario said, leaning forward in her seat. "She's the new executive chef I was telling you guys about. They've been secretly dating for weeks, and Gio's *totally* into her."

Waiters descended on the table, covering it with champagne flutes, appetizers and desserts. Rosario grabbed two glasses and pushed one into Giovanni's hand.

He finished the champagne in three quick gulps. He didn't want to discuss his personal life with his family at the charity tournament, but his sisters badgered him about Elise and, as he answered their questions, an incredible thing happened. His mood lightened and a grin overwhelmed his mouth. But he wanted to know who'd told Rosario he was dating Elise. When he asked her for details, she laughed in his face.

"Oh, you're serious." Sobering, she reached out and patted his cheek. "You're so cute. *Everyone* knows you're a couple."

"You're not mad at me for dating an employee?" Giovanni asked in a quiet voice.

"Not at all. How could I be mad at you for following your heart? Elise is a dynamic woman with a beautiful spirit, and I knew you were interested in her from day one."

Giovanni hid a grin. *So much for keeping my feelings under wraps!*

"In fact, there's an office pool going on about how long it will take you to propose." Smirking, Rosario flipped her curls over her shoulders. "Most of the staff think you'll pop the question by the summer, but I disagree. It won't take you that long. Three months tops."

For the second time in minutes, Giovanni was speechless. Needing a moment to collect his thoughts, he blocked out the noises in the VIP tent and considered what Rosario had said. Giovanni was relieved that he didn't have to hide his feelings for Elise anymore, but he was embarrassed that the staff at the polo club knew he was crazy about her.

And he was. Elise stood out from the other women he'd dated in the past for three reasons: She wasn't impressed with his wealth or celebrity status. She genuinely cared about him. And she often did kind, thoughtful things to brighten his day. Best of all, since meeting Elise, his life had drastically improved. He ate healthier, slept soundly, laughed more and smiled constantly. He missed her terribly and, even though Giovanni enjoyed spending quality time with his sisters, he couldn't stop thinking about Elise.

He'd had a great game and the only thing that would have made the day better was having his girlfriend by his side. Torn between following his heart and being loyal to his cousin, Giovanni deliberated over what to do. He considered asking his parents for advice, but he feared Constanza would give him a tongue-lashing for dating an employee and he didn't want to get on her bad side during the Christmas holidays.

"Oh, wow, Elise is stunning," Beatriz gushed, an awestruck expression on her face. Raising her phone in the air, she showed everyone the pictures she'd found online of the talented chef at the polo club's holiday party. "I love her unique look."

Pride flowed through his veins as he listened to his sister praise the woman he loved.

"What are we going to do about the incident at the club on Friday night?" Rosario asked.

Josefa finished her crab cake and dusted the crumbs from her hands. "What incident?"

Rosario told their sisters about Elise and Esteban's heated encounter at the club, the accusations Elise had made and their conversation in her office yesterday. Listening to Rosario reminded Giovanni of the anguished expression on Elise's face when he'd found her in the corridor on Friday night. The confusion, the suffocating tension in the air and Esteban's fervent denials had fuddled his brain, and he'd lashed out at Elise in anger. In the heat of the moment, he'd yelled at her, and seventy-two hours later guilt still tormented his conscience.

Conflicted emotions battled within him. Why would Elise lie? What did she have to gain by accusing Esteban of sexual assault? But why wouldn't she even consider Giovanni's argument that she may have blamed the wrong man? His cousin couldn't have done the things Elise was accusing him of. Not Esteban. He was a stand-up guy who was generous with his time and money, and when his mother, Annabelle, had been diagnosed with ovarian cancer, he'd practically nursed her back to health.

"I love Esteban, and he's always been my favorite cousin, but he can be a jerk when he's had too many drinks, and he's been partying *hard* lately," Soledad said.

Josefa nodded. "You could say that again. Every time I see him, he's drunk, and it's embarrassing. He needs to go to rehab before it's too late."

"Esteban lied to you. He was definitely in the Hamptons in July." Beatriz tapped an index finger on her phone. "His social media pages are filled with selfies of him around the city."

Giovanni ripped the device out of Beatriz's hand, flipped it over and stared at the screen. His sister was right. According to Esteban's online posts, he'd attended not one but three Fourth of July parties in the Hamptons.

Giovanni gripped the phone so hard his knuckles cracked. Esteban had lied? Why? What was he trying to hide? Giovanni didn't know what to think, how to feel, and the pain spreading through his chest burned like fire.

"*There's* the greatest polo player alive!" Esteban shouted, clapping Giovanni on the back and vigorously rubbing his shoulders. "Grab the Cristal! A toast to the GOAT!"

"You're here," Giovanni said, noticing his cousin's bloodshot eyes. "I didn't think you'd make it."

"And miss your charity Christmas match? No way. You couldn't pay me to stay away."

Esteban reached for Rosario's champagne flute and she slapped his hand away.

"Don't even think about it," she warned, grabbing him by the collar of his white-linen shirt. "Better yet, quit drinking altogether or you could lose your freedom."

"Relax, cuz, it's not that serious. I'll get my own bubbly—"

"You lied to me about being in the Cyclades islands in July. You were in the Hamptons." Rosario shoved Beatriz's phone in Esteban's face and forced him to look at the screen. "Look! I have the evidence right here."

"Sis, calm down. I don't want you to lose your temper and cause a scene."

"Soledad, stay out of this," she snapped, her anger evident in her ice-cold tone.

"Fine, but don't blame me when someone records you losing it and the video goes viral."

Glancing around the VIP tent, Rosario smiled at the guests seated nearby as she released Esteban's shirt. "If witnesses can confirm you were at that Fourth of July party, and corroborate Elise's version of events, you could be charged with sexual assault," Rosario said, nodding fervently. "Is that what you want? For all your friends and associates to think you assault and abuse women?"

"I swear I didn't do it. I don't even remember the party, or meeting that sexy chef chick."

"Therein lies the problem, Esteban." Giovanni released a deep sigh. "You drink so much and party so hard that you don't even know what you've done."

Rosario spoke in a whisper. "Esteban, you need to get your drinking under control, and we're going to help you get treatment."

"Rehab is for suckers, and I don't need it. I'll quit drinking when I'm good and ready."

His sisters stared at Giovanni and Rosario elbowed him in his side underneath the table. He had to do something. But what?

Giovanni prided himself on being an honest, trustworthy person, but he had to lie to save Esteban from himself, and spoke in a grave tone. "The way I see it, you have two choices. Either go to rehab and clean yourself up, or turn yourself in to the NYPD, because once Elise files a police report, you'll lose your freedom."

"Imagine how your parents would feel," Rosario added. "It would break their hearts, and tarnish their reputations in the community."

Esteban shot to his feet, knocking his wooden chair over, and stormed out of the tent.

"That went well," Soledad said, wearing a grim expression.

"He'll come around. Give him time. He'll think it through and make the right choice."

Giovanni wasn't convinced, but hoped Josefa's prediction came true for Esteban's sake. He wanted to go after him and find out what he was thinking, but he decided to give him space. They were both frustrated and angry, and Giovanni needed a moment to catch his breath, too.

"I believe Elise," Rosario said. "And we can't afford to lose her. Her love and passion for fine cuisine are unparalleled, and since we hired her, the restaurant profits have doubled. I can't go anywhere in town without someone telling me how much they love the new and improved menu. And our beautiful, sensational chef."

"I'm not surprised." Images of Elise flashed in Giovanni's mind, warming his heart. "Her recipes don't just look good, they *are* good, and she's my favorite chef."

Someone coughed loudly, seizing Giovanni's attention, and he glanced over his shoulder. He groaned inwardly. His parents were standing behind him, wearing identical frowns. Dressed in designer attire, their arms intertwined, they carried themselves as if they were royalty.

"I'm sorry, I missed that. *Who* did you say is your favorite cook?" Constanza asked, cupping a hand behind her right ear. "Choose your answer carefully, or you'll never taste my corn empanadas with chimichurri sauce again!"

Everyone at the table laughed. Giovanni stood, hugged his parents and kissed them both on the cheek. His dad had lost weight since his October knee surgery, and his goatee was dotted with gray hair, but he still looked younger than his seventy years.

"Son, you were amazing tonight," Vincente said with a proud smile. "Just incredible."

Constanza agreed. "I was on the edge of my seat the

entire match, and when you scored the winning goal, I screamed for joy."

Sitting at the table, his parents tasted the appetizers and sipped champagne.

Peering at the entrance of the tent, Giovanni noticed Esteban pacing the field and decided to touch base with his cousin before he left the grounds. The party was winding down, but Giovanni wanted to talk and laugh with his family for hours more.

"Now that you've officially ended your polo career, let's discuss my burning desire for you to take the helm of Castillo Enterprises when I retire…"

Giovanni coughed into his fist. He knew this day was coming, that his dad would waste no time making plans for his future once he ended his polo career, but he was calling the shots, not Vincente. Reaching out, he clasped Rosario's hand, raised it to his chest and held it tight. Rosario had a leadership quality that their staff respected and responded enthusiastically to, and the polo club was nothing without her. They were a formidable duo who helped each other learn, grow and thrive in their respective positions, and Giovanni felt fortunate to have Rosario by his side.

"Dad, I'm willing to work full-time at Castillo Enterprises and take complete control of the company when you retire in the new year—on one condition."

Vincente bolted upright in his chair. Excitement twinkled in his eyes and brightened his wrinkled face. "Anything, son. What is it?"

"To succeed, I need someone in my corner I can trust, so Rosario has to be named CEO, too. We'll be joint CEOs and run Castillo Enterprises together."

Rosario gasped and rested a hand to her chest. "You want us to work as a team?"

"Yeah, sis, I do. We'll be based in the Hamptons, but travel to Argentina when needed."

Sniffling, she tilted her head back and fanned her face. "I'm so happy I could cry!"

"You *are* crying," Josefa teased, wiping her sister's tears with her fingertips. "Now, cut it out or I'll start bawling, too, and stain my cute Valentino party dress, and I paid big bucks for it!"

The women laughed and Giovanni studied Vincente.

"Dad, what do you say? Do we have a deal, or do I need to look for another job?"

Everyone at the table stared at Vincente. Lines creased his forehead and his lips curled into a scowl.

Giovanni worried his dad was going to reject his business proposition, but Vincente slowly nodded, as if he was warming up to the idea.

"I've read about several Fortune 500 companies that have two or three CEOs, and if anyone can do it successfully, it's *my* kids. Ingenuity, tenacity and killer instincts are in your DNA, so get out there and make your old man proud."

"Outstanding!" Beaming, Constanza cupped Vincente's face in her hands and kissed his cheek. "That's the smartest decision you've ever made, besides marrying me, of course."

Everyone laughed and Giovanni glanced around the table, smiling at his family members.

"A toast," Vincente proposed, raising his flute high in the air. "To the dynamic new CEOs of Castillo Enterprises, and to my retirement, effective immediately."

"Effective immediately?" Giovanni repeated, confused by his dad's words. "Last month, you told me you were returning to the club in the new year."

A pensive expression covered his face. "I changed my mind. Now that Castillo Enterprises is in good hands, your mother and I can return to Buenos Aires to do all the things we love."

Giovanni sat in his chair, drinking his second glass of champagne, but his mind was on Elise. He couldn't think of anything but her. He had to see her again, had to apologize for hurting her feelings and lashing out at her in anger. In his heart, Elise was "the one" and he didn't want to spend the rest of his life wondering what could have been. The biggest obstacle between them had been his fear of getting hurt again, but she'd gained his trust by being honest, sincere and transparent, and he wanted to be with her more than anything. Elise was his soul mate, the best thing that had ever happened to him, and Giovanni didn't want to lose her.

Taking a moment to consider his options, he leaned back in his chair and stroked the length of his jaw. Giovanni was tired of feeling sorry for himself and was ready to do something about it. A thought came to mind, one so brazen it could explode in his face, but he was willing to take the risk. If he didn't, he could lose Elise forever, and he couldn't imagine a worse fate than living the rest of his life without the woman he loved.

After dinner, he'd tell his family he was leaving, drive to the airport and catch the red-eye to New York. He knew he'd hurt Elise, but Giovanni hoped she'd give him the best Christmas gift ever—her forgiveness.

# Chapter 18

"Girl, you *really* outdid yourself," Paige proclaimed, popping a coconut-rum ball into her open mouth. "I've eaten so many appetizers and desserts, the button on my skinny jeans popped off!"

Laughing, Elise rubbed her girlfriend's shoulder, then gestured to the elaborate spread on the breakfast bar with a nod. "Don't sweat it, Paige. What's the point of attending an ugly sweater Christmas party if you can't indulge a little bit?"

"You mean indulge *a lot!*" Paige picked a chocolate-peppermint cupcake up off the glass tray and took a bite. "It's no biggie. I'll work off the calories later with Konstantin."

*Spare me the details*, Elise thought with a heavy sigh. She returned to the stove, stirred the pot of mulled wine with a metal spoon, then added a cup of brandy to the recipe.

"Konstantin is such a passionate, attentive lover. I think he might be the one..."

*I know what that's like. I felt the same way about Giovanni, after our first night together, too.*

Overwhelmed by a wave of sadness, Elise choked back tears. She hadn't seen or spoken to Giovanni since they'd argued at the polo club on Friday night, but he'd dominated her thoughts for the past five days. Elise wished she could go back in time. She should have walked away when Esteban grabbed her instead of slapping him. In the heat of the moment, she'd lost her temper, embarrassing herself and the club, and she felt horrible about it.

Elise opened the cupboard, grabbed the bottle of cinnamon and poured some into the pot. Images of Giovanni popped into her head, but she dismissed them. All week, she'd struggled to focus. To keep her mind off of him, she'd baked Christmas gifts, cleaned and decorated her town house, and packed for her trip to Charlotte. During the day it was easy to keep herself busy, between working at the club and teaching cooking classes, but at night she couldn't escape her thoughts and replayed her argument with Giovanni countless times.

Her thoughts returned to that afternoon. She'd found pictures online of the polo charity match with the Argentine Polo Association, and seeing Giovanni surrounded by a famous female pop band had made her jealous. Had Giovanni replaced her already? Had he found someone else to keep him warm at night? Was he romantically interested in one of the singers?

Giving her head a shake to clear her mind, Elise glanced around the main floor of her cozy three-bedroom condo. Guests were nibbling on appetizers, admiring the resplendent white Christmas tree she'd decorated weeks earlier, snapping selfies in front of the ornament-covered wreath and dancing to the music on the stereo system. They'd played holiday-themed party games, crowned Paige's elf hoodie the winner of the ugly sweater contest and exchanged Secret Santa gifts. Hanging out with her girlfriends was the perfect stress reliever, and even though hosting a party on Christmas Eve was an enormous amount of work, Elise was glad her closest, dearest friends were at her condo.

Turning off the stove, Elise listened to Paige gush about her new boyfriend and their red-hot relationship. She thought of asking her for advice about Giovanni, but decided against it and filled the mini ceramic cups to the brim. She'd made the recipe for Giovanni weeks earlier, and he'd finished the entire pot of mulled wine during their romantic seafood dinner.

Deep down, Elise knew she had no business dating him, and not just because he was her boss. His polo career was up in the air, he was at odds with his dad about the family business, and his ex-wife had soured his views on marriage. Elise missed Giovanni and hated being without him, but she didn't want to date him long-term only to realize marriage wasn't in the cards for them. Still, she longed to be back in his arms. For years, she'd been focused on her dreams of becoming an executive chef—and nothing else—but meeting

Giovanni had changed her mind-set. She didn't have to choose between her career and her personal life; she could have it all, and one day she would.

An idea popped into Elise's mind and she gave considerable thought to it. When Giovanni returned from Argentina, she'd call him and ask if they could meet. Just because they weren't a couple anymore didn't mean they had to be enemies. Elise loved Giovanni, and wanted the best for him, and she didn't want them to end up hating each other one day.

*Giovanni could never hate you*, insisted her inner voice. *He respected you, spoiled you, and gave you foot rubs and massages at the end of a long day. If that isn't love, I don't know what is!*

"Gather around, ladies. The mulled wine is ready," Elise shouted, beckoning to her guests with her hands. "And there's still tons of food left, so eat up. 'Tis the season to be merry!"

Her friends swarmed the breakfast bar, grabbing mugs and desserts. Sariah gave Elise a hug, and her spirits soared. She didn't have Giovanni in her life anymore, but she still had her girlfriends, and they meant the world to her. The night she'd ended things with Giovanni, she'd found solace and understanding in their arms, and Elise appreciated their support.

"I need to ask you guys something," Sariah said, clasping Paige's right hand. She led her friends over to the front window then released a deep breath. "Aamir and I have officially started the adoption process, and we wanted to know if you'd be our character references for the application."

"I'd love to." Elise lowered her voice to a whisper. "Are you sure you guys are done with IVF?"

"Yes, but just because I can't physically give birth doesn't mean I can't be a mother."

"I couldn't agree more." Beaming, Paige nodded as she rubbed Sariah's shoulders. "And I'm going to be the best auntie ever. Just watch me!"

The women hugged and laughed for so long, Elise momentarily forgot her problems. In the morning, she was catching a flight to Charlotte, and her friends wanted to know if she was worried about returning to her hometown. She was, but Elise refused to dwell on her fears. Losing her parents had changed her forever, and she wanted to honor them by being the strong, fearless woman they had raised her to be. "I'm nervous about the trip, but I'm going to make the most of the holiday season and support my family members the best I can."

"And you will," Sariah insisted. "But if you need me, just call and I'll be there."

The doorbell chimed, drawing Elise's gaze to the foyer, and she frowned. Everyone she'd invited to her party was inside her town house except the Harris sisters, and she wasn't expecting them to put in an appearance at midnight. Demi had given birth to her twin daughters yesterday, and she was still in the hospital recuperating from her emergency caesarean section.

"Finally!" Paige trilled, clapping her hands. "The entertainment is here. Let's *do* this!"

Squealing, she tore out of the living room and down the hallway before Elise could stop her. She loved Paige and couldn't imagine her life without her, but she was the most hardheaded person Elise had ever met, and she didn't appreciate Paige disregarding her wishes. Fuming, but not wanting to make a scene, she returned to the kitchen, poured herself cup of mulled wine and tasted the warm, sweet-smelling drink.

"You have to give me the recipe for your brownies. They're scrumptious."

Elise smiled at Sariah's cousin Mishka, then nodded. "I'll email it to you."

"Guess who I found on your doorstep? A gorgeous polo star who wants to apologize."

At the sound of Paige's voice, Elise glanced up from her cup and stared at her best friend. A gasp shot out of her mouth. The earth shook under her feet and her knees buckled. Elise couldn't believe what she was seeing. Giovanni was standing in the hallway, wearing a slim-fitted black suit, and an earnest expression on his face. His cologne wafted through the air and smelling his fragrance instantly calmed her nerves.

A hush fell over the room as someone turned off the music. The lump in her throat was the size of a baseball and when Elise tried to speak, her voice failed.

"Elise, I apologize for barging into your party like this, but I had to talk to you tonight and it couldn't wait." Stepping forward, Giovanni smiled as he smoothed a hand over the front of his suit jacket. "Can we go somewhere private?"

Her friends shouted no in unison and Elise swallowed a laugh. She put down her empty cup and came around the breakfast bar, hoping her legs didn't give away her nerves. "Giovanni, what are you doing here?

You're supposed to be in Argentina celebrating the holidays with your family."

"The only place I want to be is right here with you."

"Save it," she said, rolling her eyes to the ceiling. "Five days ago you called me a liar, so forgive me for not jumping into your arms. I thought you cared about me, that you trusted me, but if you did, you would have believed me, not picked apart my story about one of the worst moments of my life."

"Elise, I'm sorry. I didn't mean to disrespect you. I was in shock, and I didn't know what to think. My gut reaction was to defend my cousin, but I know now that that was a big mistake."

Holding her breath, she wanted to hear more. What was Giovanni saying? Did he believe her account of what happened on the Fourth of July? Had Esteban finally admitted the truth?

"I spoke to Esteban yesterday, and although he doesn't remember meeting you on the Fourth of July, he admitted he was out of line on Friday night at the club. He agreed to get treatment for his alcohol addiction, and I think it's a step in the right direction."

Unsure of what to say in response, Elise wore a blank expression on her face. She hoped Esteban got the help he needed, but the next time she saw the flashy businessman at the polo club, she was avoiding him at all costs.

"It's a good thing your cousin didn't grab me," Paige said, shaking a fist in the air. "I would have poked his eyes out, stomped on his feet, then kicked him where the sun don't shine, *twice!*"

Snickers and giggles filled the room, lightening the tense mood in the town house.

"Giovanni, why are you here?" Elise asked, wringing her hands like a damp washcloth.

"To tell you I love you and miss you and can't live without you."

Guests cheered, and Sariah shrieked.

"You love her?" Sariah repeated in a high-pitched tone, happiness shimmering in her eyes. "I *knew* it! How wonderful! See, Elise, Giovanni loves you, too!"

Elise inclined her head and crossed her arms. "Actions speak louder than words."

"I agree. That's why I'm here. I believe in being open and transparent, so let me prove to you, right here, right now, how much you mean to me so there's never any doubt in your mind."

Giovanni unbuttoned his suit jacket, reached inside the inner pocket and retrieved a velvet ring box. Lowering himself to one knee, he cleared his throat and adjusted his tie.

Gasps and chatter filled the air, and Elise couldn't think straight. She suddenly felt dizzy and out of sorts. The room was hotter than a campfire, and her pulse was pounding in her ears like a steel drum. The miniature gold bells on her red, fuzzy sweater jingled every time she moved, and her legs were shaking so hard Elise feared they'd give way and she'd drop to the floor.

"Giovanni, what are you doing?" she asked, her voice quavering. "Please stand up."

"Not until you accept my proposal."

Someone pushed her forward, directly in front of

him, and Giovanni took her left hand in his. He squeezed it, and his touch alleviated the tension in her body.

*This can't be happening... This can't be real... God, I hope I don't cry, or worse, faint!*

"I never thought in a million years I'd find love again, but I did in you, and I'm deeply grateful to have you in my life," he began. "You're smart, talented, thoughtful and beautiful, and your cooking is outstanding—"

"Let the church say amen!" Paige quipped, snapping her fingers in the air.

"Elise, I know I've made mistakes, but I'm deeply sorry and, going forward, I promise to always put you first, no matter what."

"We can't get married," she blurted out, doubts streaming from her mouth. "Your family will never accept me... I'm not Argentinian... They won't think I'm good enough..."

"You're wrong. They just want me to be happy, and since I'm the best version of myself when I'm with you, I know they'll support our relationship wholeheartedly."

Sniffling, Elise stared at Giovanni in disbelief, willing the tears in her eyes not to fall. She loved him deeply, madly, with everything she had, and regretted arguing with him on that Friday night. There was nothing sexier than a sensitive, vulnerable man who spoke from the heart, and his words touched her soul.

"I adore you, Elise, and I couldn't have asked for a better girlfriend. When I fall asleep at night, I see your beautiful face staring back at me, and it's the greatest feeling in the world."

Elise beamed. In her peripheral vision, she saw her guests dabbing at their eyes, fanning their faces and snapping pictures with their cell phones. Sariah smiled at her, Paige gave her a thumbs-up and Mishka waved her hands wildly in the air.

"I want you in my life for the rest of my life, and I vow to love and honor you always."

Angling her body toward him, Elise met his gaze.

"I want to travel the world with you, exploring exotic lands and fine cuisine, and enjoying thrilling adventures," he continued. "I also want to beat you at ax throwing, because I think you cheated the last time we played at Extreme Sports Dome. You're sneaky like that."

Elise giggled. "Any time you want a rematch, just say the word."

"I also want to visit your hometown with you. I want to see where you were born, where you grew up and all the places you went with your parents, so I can have a greater understanding of who you are as a woman and love you the way you deserve."

"Giovanni, I leave for Charlotte in a few hours. I'm spending Christmas with my family."

"Can I come?" he asked quietly. "I'd love to be your plus-one."

Elise reached out and cupped his chin. "I love you."

"I was hoping you'd say that, because I feel the same way. You're my everything, Elise."

"As I should be." A saucy smile curled her lips. "I'm fabulous!"

"Does that mean you'll marry me? That you'll become Mrs. Giovanni Castillo?"

"Do rich people like Dom Pérignon?" Elise quipped, with a laugh. "Yes, I'll marry you. You're the man of my dreams, my one true love and the greatest Christmas gift ever!"

Giovanni took the ring out of the box, clasped her left hand and slid the stunning three-carat diamond onto her fourth finger. Elise stared at the pear-shaped jewel for a long moment, admiring the unique design. It was a gorgeous ring and she loved the flawless diamond almost as much as she loved her new fiancé.

Guests gathered around them, offering hugs and well wishes. The outpouring of love and support from her girlfriends moved Elise, and she burst into tears. It was the most wonderful and romantic moment of her life, and she'd remember Giovanni's surprise proposal for the rest of her life.

Cupping his face in her hands, Elise pressed her body flat against his and kissed his lips. She cherished the moment, reveling in his love and his commitment to her. Their relationship was new and fresh and exciting, and Elise was confident their future would be bright. Snuggling against him, she wrapped her arms around his waist and kissed his chin. "You know this is crazy, right? No one gets engaged after a couple months of dating."

Giovanni rubbed his nose against hers. "Of course they do. My grandparents did, and they've been married for over fifty years. If they can do it, so can we. I'm a catch, remember?"

"I love you, Giovanni, and I always will, but don't push your luck!"

"I love you more, Elise, and don't worry, I won't."

He smiled in a way she'd never seen before and hope surged through her heart. "Baby, you mean the world to me and I can't wait for us to tie the knot."

"Prove it." Giovanni flashed a flirtatious grin then whispered against her ear. "Kick everyone out so we can be alone. It's officially Christmas Day, and I want to unwrap my gift!"

Tossing her head back, Elise shrieked with laughter. They hugged and kissed, and slow danced to the music playing in their hearts. There was no doubt in her mind that they'd have a long and prosperous relationship. They had all the ingredients for a successful marriage—trust, honesty and mutual respect—and Elise vowed to put Giovanni first, always, no matter what.

And she would, all the days of their lives.

* * * * *

We hope you enjoyed these soulful,
sensual reads.

Kimani Romance is coming to an end, but
there are still ways to satisfy your craving
for juicy drama and passion.

Starting December 2019, find great new reads
from some of your favorite authors in:

**Drama. Scandal. Passionate romance.**

**New titles available every month,
wherever books are sold!**

Harlequin.com

"That's it, Peterson Higgins, no more. You've had three servings already," Myra said, laughing, as she guarded the pan of peach cobbler on the counter.

He stood in front of her, grinning from ear to ear. "You should not have baked it so well. It was delicious."

"Thanks, but flattery won't get you any more peach cobbler tonight. You've had your limit."

He crossed his arms over his chest. "I could have you arrested, you know."

Crossing her arms over her own chest, she tilted her chin and couldn't stop grinning. "On what charge?"

The charge that immediately came to Pete's mind was that she was so darn beautiful. Irresistible. But he figured that was something he could not say.

She snapped her fingers in front of his face to reclaim his attention. "If you have to think that hard about a charge, then that means there isn't one."

"Oh, you'll be surprised what all I can do, Myra."

She tilted her head to the side as if to look at him better. "Do tell, Pete."

Her words—those three little words—made a full-blown attack on his senses. He drew in a shaky breath, then touched her chin. She blinked, as if startled by his touch. "How about 'do show,' Myra?"

Pete watched the way the lump formed in her throat and detected her shift in breathing. He could even hear the pounding of her heart. Damn, she smelled good, and she looked good, too. Always did.

"I'm not sure what 'do show' means," she said in a voice that was as shaky as his had been.

He tilted her chin up to gaze into her eyes, as well as to study the shape of her exquisite lips. "Then let me demonstrate, Ms. Hollister," he said, lowering his mouth to hers.

The moment he swept his tongue inside her mouth and tasted her, he was a goner. It took every ounce of strength he had to keep the kiss gentle when he wanted to devour her mouth with a hunger he felt all the way in his bones. A part of him wanted to take the kiss deeper, but then another part wanted to savor her taste. Honestly, either worked for him as long as she felt the passion between them.

He had wanted her from the moment he'd set eyes on her, but he'd fought the desire. He could no longer do that. He was a man known to forego his own needs and desires, but tonight he couldn't.

Whispering close to her ear, he said, "Peach cobbler isn't the only thing I could become addicted to, Myra."

*Will their first kiss distract him from his duty?*

*Find out in*
Duty or Desire
*by* New York Times *bestselling author Brenda Jackson.*

*Available December 2019 wherever*
*Harlequin® Desire books and ebooks are sold.*

Harlequin.com

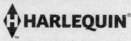

SPECIAL EXCERPT FROM

(H) HARLEQUIN

*Presents*.

*Lottie Dawson is stunned to see her daughter's father on
television. She'd lost hope of finding the irresistible stranger
after their incredible night of passion. Having never known
her own father, Lottie wants things to be different for her
child, even if that means facing Ragnar Stone again!*

Read on for a sneak preview of
Louise Fuller's next story for Harlequin Presents
Proof of Their One-Night Passion

The coffee shop was still busy enough that they had to queue for their
drinks, but they managed to find a table.

"Thank you." He gestured toward his espresso.

His wallet had been in his hand, but she had sidestepped neatly in front
of him, her soft brown eyes defying him to argue with her. Now, though,
those same brown eyes were busily avoiding his, and for the first time since
she'd called out his name, he wondered why she had tracked him down.

He drank his coffee, relishing the heat and the way the caffeine started
to block the tension in his back.

"So, I'm all yours," he said quietly.

She stiffened. "Hardly."

He sighed. "Is that what this is about? Me giving you the wrong name."

Her eyes narrowed. "No, of course not. I'm not—" She stopped,
frowning. "Actually, I wasn't just passing, and I'm not here for myself."
She took a breath. "I'm here for Sóley."

Her face softened into a smile and he felt a sudden urge to reach out and
caress the curve of her lip, to trigger such a smile for himself.

"It's a pretty name."

She nodded, her smile freezing.

It was a pretty name—one he'd always liked. One you didn't hear much
outside of Iceland. Only what had it got to do with him?

Watching her fingers tremble against her cup, he felt his ribs tighten.
"Who's Sóley?"

She was quiet for less than a minute, only it felt much longer—long
enough for his brain to click through all the possible answers to the
impossible one. The one he already knew.

He watched her posture change from defensive to resolute.

"She's your daughter. Our daughter."

He stared at her in silence, but a cacophony of questions was ricocheting inside his head.

Not the how or the when or the where, but the why. Why had he not been more careful? Why had he allowed the heat of their encounter to blot out his normally ice-cold logic?

But the answers to those questions would have to wait.

"Okay…"

Shifting in her seat, she frowned. "'Okay'?" she repeated. "Do you understand what I just said?"

"Yes." He nodded. "You're saying I got you pregnant."

"You don't seem surprised," she said slowly.

He shrugged. "These things happen."

To his siblings and half siblings, even to his mother. But not to him. Never to him.

Until now.

"And you believe me?" She seemed confused, disappointed?

Tilting his head, he held her gaze. "Honest answer?"

He was going to ask her what she would gain by lying. But before he could open his mouth, her lip curled.

"On past performance, I'm not sure I can expect that. I mean, you lied about your name. And the hotel you were staying at. And you lied about wanting to spend the day with me."

"I didn't plan on lying to you," he said quietly.

Her mouth thinned. "No, I'm sure it comes very naturally to you."

"You're twisting my words."

She shook her head. "You mean like saying Steinn instead of Stone?"

Pressing his spine into the wall behind him, he felt a tick of anger begin to pulse beneath his skin.

"Okay, I was wrong to lie to you—but if you care about the truth so much, then why have you waited so long to tell me that I have a daughter? I mean, she must be what…?" He did a quick mental calculation. "Ten, eleven months?"

*Don't miss*
Proof of Their One-Night Passion
*available December 2019 wherever*
*Harlequin Presents® books and ebooks are sold.*

www.Harlequin.com